SECOND CHANCES IN TUPPENNY BRIDGE

SHARON BOOTH

Storm

To request permissions, contact the publisher at rights@stormpublishing.co

Ebook ISBN: 978-1-80508-105-0
Paperback ISBN: 978-1-80508-157-9

Cover design: Debbie Clement
Cover images: Shutterstock

Published by Storm Publishing.
For further information, visit:
www.stormpublishing.co

ALSO BY SHARON BOOTH

Christmas at Cuckoo Nest Cottage

The Moorland Heroes Series

Resisting Mr Rochester

Saving Mr Scrooge

The Witches of Castle Clair Series

Belle, Book and Candle

My Favourite Witch

To Catch a Witch

Will of the Witch

His Lawful Wedded Witch

The Other Half Series

How the Other Half Lives

How the Other Half Lies

How the Other Half Loses

How the Other Half Loves

For Shirley, Mandy, Kathryn, Carolyn, Daina, and Anne,
who each walked a little way with me along the path of life.

ONE

Kat Pennyfeather sailed across the kitchen and landed with a painful thud on the tiled floor. After taking a moment to catch her breath, she looked around and saw one of her baby daughter's toys lying on its side, thanks to their collision.

She wasn't sure how she hadn't noticed it, though she suspected she would have avoided it if she hadn't been stumbling around in the dim morning light, with the blinds still closed and her half asleep.

She gingerly got to her feet, grateful that nothing seemed to be badly damaged, although she'd have a bruise on her hip tomorrow where she'd landed as she fell. It wouldn't be the first one.

'Hell's bells!' She was about to kick the baby's activity table which had so wickedly tripped her up, but remembered just in time that she was in her bare feet and didn't want to add a broken toe to her woes.

Sighing, she rubbed her hip, then rinsed out the kettle, filling it with fresh water before flicking it on to boil. There should be enough in there to make Hattie's first bottle and a cup of tea for herself.

How much easier it had been, she thought wistfully, when she'd breast fed her baby girl. Although, it hadn't been as easy as Kat had expected, and there'd been long, harrowing weeks when Hattie screamed in frustration and hunger. It had devastated Kat to give up, but even her health visitor had run out of helpful suggestions so, with huge reluctance, she'd switched to formula milk. She couldn't deny Hattie had thrived on it, but it didn't stop her feeling like a big, fat failure.

Kettle boiled, she quickly made herself a cup of tea and left the rest of the water cooling while she sat at the little table in her kitchen and looked around, wondering where she was going to stuff the activity table so it wouldn't trip her up again.

The trouble was, there was nowhere to put it. When she'd been pregnant, she'd assumed everything for the baby would go in the baby's room. Well, that hadn't worked out too well, had it? Hattie was now in a proper cot, which seemed to take up half the space. Then there was her changing table, her little wardrobe with its drawers underneath, the toy chest, the little cupboard for nappies, wipes and creams, and everything else that this tiny person seemed to need.

The living room had become increasingly crowded, thanks to more toys from well-meaning people, and the buggy that had to be folded and propped against the wall every night because it was too bulky to leave on the narrow landing.

The bathroom was cluttered with bath toys, lotions, and baby shampoo. Kat thought it was probably a good thing that she'd forgotten how to put make-up on, and never bothered straightening her hair or doing her nails any longer. She didn't have any room for her personal belongings. Even her own bedroom was taken up by Hattie's things rather than her own.

There was no getting away from it. She'd been naïve. She remembered people warning her that the flat was too small for a baby, but she'd laughed at the suggestion. After all, babies were tiny, and how much stuff could they possibly need? She'd learned the hard way that babies grew fast, and they needed a *lot* of stuff.

She glanced at the clock. Ten past seven. Hattie would hopefully sleep until about half past. That was when she usually woke up these days. She'd got into a decent routine; Kat couldn't complain about that.

The awful soul-destroying days when she'd woken up multiple times through the night were over, thank goodness—for now at any rate. Kat still wasn't sure how she'd got through it all. She wondered how *any* mother got through them, although she supposed most mothers had help of sorts, if not a spouse or partner, maybe a mother of their own. Kat had none of those people in her life and everything had fallen on her shoulders.

Not, she reminded herself sharply, that she had any regrets. She'd desperately wanted her baby and thanked the universe for her every day. It was just sometimes, she wondered how they were going to cope as Hattie grew, and the flat became increasingly unsuitable for their needs...

Well, she'd have to do something about it. She needed to save up and find herself a bigger flat. Maybe even a house with a garden and—

She laughed to herself as she realised what an impossible dream that was. For a start, most flats and houses in Tuppenny Bridge that weren't passed down through generations of families ended up being sold off as holiday lets.

This pretty market town in the Yorkshire Dales drew many visitors, and there was a good deal of money to be made from letting out properties to holidaymakers. It caused a fair bit of resentment and a lot of grumbling among the residents of the town.

Conversely, it provided many of them with a good living. It was the visitors who vastly swelled the number of people touring the museum and the brewery, browsing the market, visiting the art gallery, drinking in the pubs, eating in the restaurants and cafés, and paying the frankly extortionate prices charged in some of the gift shops.

As annoying as it sometimes was to find the riverbank packed with picnickers when all you wanted to do was go for a peaceful stroll, finding yourself jostling for a seat in the pub, or queueing at a market stall, Kat couldn't deny the tourists were the town's life blood. It did, though, mean that for people like her, finding somewhere suitable to live was almost impossible.

Maybe, she thought, she'd have to look a bit further afield. But then, her job and her friends were in Tuppenny Bridge— not to mention the only relatives she had left in the world. Well, in Yorkshire, which was practically the same thing. She smiled fondly as she thought of Birdie and Rita, her great aunts. They were eccentric, to say the least, but they'd been nothing but kind to her, and she didn't know where she'd be without them.

It was their wool shop she worked in—at least, when she wasn't on maternity leave—and they allowed her to live in the flat above the shop, paying a ridiculously low rent.

Cradling the cup of tea between her hands, she realised she was incredibly lucky really. Okay, life had dealt her a few harsh blows, but it could have been worse. A lot worse.

The aunties had made so many things possible for her. Not least having Hattie.

She wondered if she should cut her maternity leave short and go back to work earlier than planned. It would mean she could put a bit extra aside to save up for a deposit on a bigger place. She might have to look in one of the villages, one with regular public transport because she didn't drive. There must be something out there that she could afford.

She wrinkled her nose as Hattie's wail echoed around the flat. She was a bit early, and the bottle wasn't ready yet, but hopefully she'd wait patiently while Kat prepared her breakfast. Hattie had taken a liking to porridge lately, so there was that to make too.

And after breakfast, when they were both fed and dressed, she was meeting her best friend, Sally Kingston, at the Market Café for a coffee and a pastry. Sally had offered to come round to the flat, but Kat had been glad of an excuse to get out. These four walls were driving her crazy, and she fancied sitting somewhere where she could see real people living real lives, instead of getting her only fix of society through a television screen.

Maybe, she thought, getting to her feet as Hattie wailed again, she'd even put a bit of mascara and lippy on. If she could remember where she'd left them.

* * *

'I don't like porridge.'

Tommy's statement was enough to make Jonah stand stock still in dread. He closed his eyes briefly then spun round to face the six-year-old, who was sitting at the table looking impossibly angelic with his round face, big brown eyes, and mop of dark curls.

'Since when?'

Tommy shrugged. 'Ages. Can I have toast and peanut butter?'

'No, you can't.'

'But I love peanut butter!'

'I know you do. That's why you've got peanut butter sandwiches in your packed lunch, and you can't have practically the same thing for breakfast. Besides, I haven't got *time*...'

His voice trailed off as he wondered how many times a day he uttered that phrase. Time. The most precious and, it seemed to him, rare commodity of them all.

'Well, I don't want porridge,' Tommy said flatly, pushing the bowl away from him and staring at Jonah with a challenging look on his face.

'Fine.' Jonah didn't have the energy to argue.

He ran a hand through his hair, gazing at the mess on the worktop in front of him: the knife smeared in butter which had fallen off the dish and landed amongst a pile of crumbs on the counter; the dollop of peanut butter which had inexplicably fallen next to it; the roll of sandwich bags that seemed more buttery than the sandwiches he'd just made. It occurred to him that he also had butter on his fingers and that he'd just run them through his hair. Bloody hell!

He opened a cupboard door and grabbed two bags of crisps, throwing one to Tommy.

'Here, eat this,' he said, pushing aside the feeling of guilt as Tommy gleefully grabbed the bag and ripped it open.

Well, he'd tried, hadn't he? He'd made Tommy porridge—nice, healthy, tasty porridge that was full of fibre and vitamins and all-round goodness. He couldn't be blamed if Tommy refused to eat it. Could he?

Muttering a curse under his breath, he stuffed the bag of peanut butter sandwiches, the other bag of crisps, a carton of apple juice, and a banana in Tommy's Superman packed lunch box. It would have to do. He'd try to get to Maister's supermarket today at some point. Stock up.

It was his own fault. It wasn't as if he hadn't known the first day of term was creeping round. He had it marked on his calendar, for goodness' sake. A big, red ring around Monday 4th September, and *Back to School* written in big, joyful letters, with three exclamation marks after it.

So he should have known. Should have been prepared. He'd meant to go to Maister's on Saturday for Tommy's packed lunch, but realised he needed to iron his son's uniform, which had been scrunched up in a carrier bag for weeks, ever since he'd bought it at the beginning of the school holidays, determined to be ahead of the game for once.

And then, of course, he realised that he'd forgotten to buy Tommy new shoes, and his old ones didn't fit properly, so he'd had to dash to Lingham-on-Skimmer, where the only decent shoe shop was, and get some new ones for him, uttering a prayer of thanks that they had suitable ones in his size.

And yesterday it had been Sunday lunch at his sister's. He'd been so tired when he got home, he'd completely forgotten about the packed lunch, and Tommy refused point blank to have school dinners so...

He glanced at the calendar, grimacing as he scanned the other word written on today's square. Dentist. As if he didn't have enough to do, he also had that pleasure to look forward to. He wished he could cancel it, but getting a dental appointment was so hard these days he wouldn't risk it.

His eyes flicked along the row to Friday's square, and his stomach lurched with dread. What the hell had he been thinking? Wasn't life terrifying enough without inflicting more torture on himself?

A date. Worse than that. A blind date. Why had he agreed when his sister had begged him to meet up with one of her work colleagues?

'You'll love her,' she'd promised. 'She's smart, funny, and really attractive.'

'Sounds perfect,' he'd said. 'How come she's still single then?'

Tawnie had rolled her eyes. 'How come *you're* still single? Oh come on, Jonah. Take a chance for once! Just one date, that's all I'm asking. If it doesn't work out—well, what have you lost?'

Now that he was thinking about it, he realised he might have a lot to lose. His pride, for one thing. His dignity. His self-respect. His peace of mind. He'd learned, long ago, that his judgement in these matters was dodgy, to say the least.

This Jodie woman might be lovely. On the other hand, she might be an out-and-out liar, with ulterior motives. How would he know? He hadn't before and look where that had got him.

'Dad, can I have another bag of crisps?'

Jonah blinked and turned to face Tommy, who was gazing up at him with a plea in those dark eyes.

Struggling to resist such an appeal, he smiled. 'No, but you can have a banana if you like?'

Tommy pulled a face. 'I don't like bananas.'

'You do like bananas! There's one in your lunch box anyway, so if you don't eat it you'll go hungry.'

Tommy considered. 'I'll have a banana sandwich.'

'But I haven't got time!' Jonah took a deep breath. 'Fine, I'll do you a banana sandwich, but you'll have to eat it really quickly.' He glanced at the clock. '*Really* quickly. Is everything else done?'

Tommy nodded and Jonah thought, just maybe, they might be on time for school after all. He made the banana sandwich and handed it over, then packed the lunch box into Tommy's school bag.

Zipping it up, he wondered what to do about Friday. He really couldn't face it. How had Tawnie persuaded him? The more he thought about it, the sicker he felt, and he realised he absolutely, one hundred per cent, did not want to go on this date.

Tawnie would kill him for this, but for his own sanity he had to cancel. He couldn't face it. Women were never what they seemed to be, and anyway, didn't he have enough to do with looking after Tommy?

He had a couple of minutes to spare while Tommy ate his sandwich, and this couldn't wait or it would hang over him all morning.

'Hurry up and eat that,' he instructed his son as he strode into the living room, closing the door behind him so he could make the call to Jodie in private. His heart thudded as he waited for her to pick up, wondering what on earth he was going to say to her. He didn't want to hurt her feelings. She hadn't done anything wrong, and he didn't want to appear rude.

'Hello?' She sounded brittle, distracted.

'Oh, hi. Is that Jodie?'

'Yeah, hang on.' There was a pause and Jonah frowned. He heard her mutter, 'Thanks for nothing, you moron! Oh no, you're welcome. Not like I'm in a hurry or anything.'

Was she talking to him? 'I'm sorry?'

'Huh? Oh, not you. I'm in traffic and this complete idiot just—'

'You're driving? I'll call you back later.'

'No worries, I've got Bluetooth. Jonah, right?'

He swallowed. 'Er, yes. That's right. I'm Tawnie's brother.'

'Well obviously. I don't know any other Jonahs.'

He rolled his eyes, realising he was making a complete fool of himself. 'Sorry, can we start again?'

'Yeah, but can you be quick? I'm running late for work as it is and traffic's horrendous. Bloody kids are back at school today and all the yummy mummies in their Chelsea tractors are out in force. That's all I need, isn't it? What can I do for you?' She laughed. 'Don't tell me. You're cancelling our date.'

Jonah swallowed.

There was silence for a moment, then she said coldly, 'You are, aren't you?'

'I'm really sorry. I don't know what Tawnie's told you, but I'm not ready to get back out there just yet. I've got—'

'You jerk!'

He blinked. 'Well, I understand it's a bit of a disappointment but—'

'Huh? Oh no, not you. I was talking to this halfwit in front of me. Doesn't know what indicators are for obviously. Sorry, you were saying? Oh, yeah. Cancelling our date. Is that cancelling as in permanently cancelling, or are you just postponing it for a bit?'

She didn't sound as if she cared one way or the other.

'I think, probably, it's permanent.'

'Well, it's saved me another boring night with a loser, I guess. At least you let me know early. Last one gave me half an hour's notice and wasted my entire evening.'

'So there's no—'

The phone went dead, and Jonah stared at the screen in shock. '—Hard feelings,' he finished and shook his head.

'Lucky escape there,' he muttered to himself, stuffing the phone in his jeans pocket. He went back into the kitchen where Tommy was finishing his banana sandwich.

'All done? Great. Go upstairs and clean your teeth and then we'll get off,' he said.

'All right, Daddy.' Tommy slid off his chair and gave him a beaming smile. Jonah's heart melted.

Why did he need a woman in his life anyway? Tommy was all he cared about and giving him the life he deserved after such a rocky start meant everything to him. He'd tried to explain that to Tawnie so many times, but she seemed incapable of believing he was happier single.

Next time she tried to set him up, he'd remember the conversation he'd just had with the less-than-charming Jodie. Nothing would persuade him to say yes ever again.

TWO

Kat knew she was early, but it had seemed a good idea at the time. Having somewhere to go, and someone to talk to, was such an exciting prospect that she'd perhaps not considered the possible flaw in her plan. Arriving at Market Café half an hour before she was due to meet Sally would mean an extra thirty minutes of entertaining Hattie to keep her quiet in public.

She'd hoped her daughter would fall asleep in the buggy as they made their way across the market square, but no such luck. Hattie was wide awake and extremely cross at being strapped in her buggy, when she'd clearly rather be on the floor at home, playing with some of her vast collection of toys.

As Hattie began to scream in protest, Kat hurriedly unstrapped her. Sat on Kat's knee, Hattie quietened down immediately and began to look around in interest. Well, this was something new. She hadn't been in here before—or any café for that matter.

Kat thought that, as cafés went, it probably wasn't the most inspiring one to introduce Hattie to. No wonder few of the locals bothered with it. She eyed the dull, green walls dubiously, and thought at the very least the owners could have given it a lick of paint.

This café, though, never did well. The Lavender Ladies— her great aunts and their friend, Miss Eugenie Lavender— insisted that the place was cursed. Something to do with a previous owner back in the days of the Second World War. Kat couldn't remember the story, but whatever it was, the Ladies were convinced that no one would ever make a living from this café. The fact that it had had five owners in the previous thirteen years tended to give credence to their theory.

She'd ordered a coffee as soon as she arrived, mindful of the fact that most café owners took a dim view of people sitting in their premises without buying anything, even if they intended to buy later.

The woman who brought the mug of coffee over looked worn out and fed up. Briefly, Kat wondered if she was a single parent too, although possibly her children had grown up now. She had an exhausted look about her that Kat recognised all too well. Maybe it never left. Maybe, once you looked this ravaged, your face never recovered.

'Aw, she's a little cutie, isn't she?'

Having put the coffee on the table, the woman gently ruffled Hattie's dark hair. Hattie's big blue eyes widened as she tried to decide whether this was a friendly gesture or a threat.

Kat hastily smoothed her baby's hair and planted a reassuring kiss on her forehead.

'How old is she?' the woman asked.

'Seven months. Just,' Kat told her.

'You must be knackered. I remember them days,' the woman said with a sigh. 'Never again. Thank God all that's behind me. Who does she look like then? You or her dad?'

Kat forced a smile. 'Probably me.'

'Gonna be a little stunner, aren't you, lovey?' The woman ruffled Hattie's hair again and Kat held her breath as her baby thrust her lower lip forward, something which usually signalled she was about to start crying.

'Would you like anything to eat?'

Desperately trying to distract Hattie, Kat didn't even look up. 'Er no, not yet. I'm meeting a friend. We'll order food then.'

'Fair enough.' The woman winced as Hattie began to cry. 'Does *she* want anything to eat? Keep her quiet, like?'

'No, it's all right,' Kat assured her, hoping she wasn't going to get any complaints about the noise coming from her table. Then again, there weren't many customers in here. Just a couple of middle-aged women, too engrossed in gossip to pay attention, and an elderly man reading a newspaper. 'I'll quieten her down, don't worry.'

'Hmm. I do have my other customers to think of you see.' The woman frowned and headed back behind the counter. With an attitude like that, Kat thought, she wouldn't mind if the Market Café soon got its sixth owner in thirteen years.

She reached into the buggy and grabbed Hattie's precious teddy bear, jigging it up and down in front of her and putting on a funny voice, pretending it was talking to her.

Hattie's face crumpled and she grabbed the teddy, throwing it with surprising force across the café.

At that moment, the bell above the café door jingled as a new customer entered. It was Jonah Brewster, the local farrier, who had a mobile phone clamped to his ear and was clearly in the middle of a heated conversation.

'I can't believe she complained to you! Honestly, I was perfectly polite.' The door swung shut behind him and he stepped forward. 'No, I'm not calling her a liar! Well, okay, maybe I am. If she said what you say she said then yes, I can't think of any other word—'

He leapt back, clearly alarmed, as something emitted what sounded suspiciously like a giggle beneath his foot.

'Sorry,' Kat said with an apologetic smile. 'That's Hattie's favourite toy you've just stepped on.'

'Oh, hell!' Jonah bent down and picked up the teddy. 'I'll call you back later. Bye.'

He shoved the phone in his pocket and handed the toy to Kat.

'Is it okay? Have I broken it?'

Kat examined it carefully then squeezed its tummy. As it emitted another giggle, she put it back on the table and said, 'Seems okay to me. It wouldn't have been your fault anyway. It was madam here, throwing a tantrum *and* the bear. She's not happy here.'

Jonah looked around and gave her a wry smile. 'Well, you can hardly blame her, can you?'

She smiled back. 'Not really, no. Oh, Hattie, please stop!'

Hattie was blubbing again, and Kat gave the woman behind the counter a wary look. They'd be thrown out of the café before Sally even got here at this rate.

Jonah wiggled the bear's arms in Hattie's face and greeted her in a funny voice.

Hattie stopped crying and stared at the teddy in amazement, and Kat wondered how it was that her own funny voices never fooled her child for an instant.

Jonah sat down opposite her at the table and handed the bear to Hattie, who clutched it to her and smiled at Jonah as if he was the best person she'd ever seen in her admittedly short life.

'You're a superstar,' Kat said. 'Can I hire you?'

He grinned. 'That bad?'

'Oh, you know.'

He nodded. 'I do indeed, although Tommy was already a year old before I met him, so I wasn't around at this stage.'

'Yeah. Missed all the good bits, didn't you? Not.' Kat raised an eyebrow. 'What are you doing lurking in a café at this time on a Monday morning anyway? Shouldn't you be out somewhere, banging nails into horses' feet or something?'

'What a charming description of my job.'

'You should put it on your dating profile,' she told him. 'Who knows who you'd attract?'

'That I'm good at banging?'

She spluttered with laughter as two pink spots appeared on his cheekbones and he said, 'Sorry, I don't know where that came from.'

'Well, I wouldn't put modesty down as one of your attributes.'

He pulled a face. 'Don't worry about that. Hell will freeze over before I go on a dating app. Do you mind if I grab a coffee and sit here for five minutes? Do you need a top-up? Something for Hattie?'

'Go ahead, and we're both fine thanks.' If nothing else, she thought, it would be good to have him on hand if Hattie decided her lungs needed a workout again. She sipped her own coffee as he stood and headed over to the counter.

Jonah was a nice man, she thought, eyeing him with compassion. He'd had a rough year—well, a rough few years actually. A divorce that had clearly knocked his confidence, being apart from Tommy, then the shock news of his ex-wife's sudden death, followed by the unexpected discovery that he was now Tommy's sole guardian. It couldn't have been easy for him. At least she'd had nine months to prepare for single parenthood. He'd had less than twenty-four hours.

She watched as he ordered a coffee from the woman behind the counter. He was wearing smart jeans and a pale blue sweatshirt, with a black leather biker jacket. Not his work clothes obviously.

He turned and, seeing her watching him, gave her a warm smile before turning back to the woman. He had a nice smile,

Kat thought, and lovely thick, dark hair too. She'd bet he smelled lovely.

He picked up the mug of coffee from the counter and headed back to her table. Hattie waved her arms in glee as he sat down opposite them, and Kat wondered if the sudden waft of cologne she'd just caught as he passed her had pleased her daughter as much as it had her.

Bloody hell, what was up with her? Had her hormones chosen today, of all days, to wake up from hibernation? For the first couple of months after she'd had Hattie they'd gone haywire, but after that she was convinced they'd fallen asleep. Not surprising really, given that she'd turned into a robot, carrying out all the necessary day-to-day tasks as if she'd been programmed, with no time or energy to think or feel about anything other than making sure her child's needs were met.

Now, as she gazed across the table at Jonah and he met her gaze steadily through blue-grey eyes, fringed with dark lashes, she felt a weird sensation that—if she didn't know better—she'd have sworn was lust.

But this was Jonah! She'd known him forever and had never, not once, looked at him in that way. There must be some-thing wrong with her.

Blushing fiercely, she took another sip of her rapidly cooling coffee and said, 'So, you never did tell me what you were doing here.'

'Oh yeah.' He rolled his eyes. 'What a morning I've had, Kat. You'd never believe it.'

Why was her stomach fizzing just because he'd used her name? She wondered if the woman behind the counter had put something in her coffee.

'So tell me,' she said, not looking at him but gazing steadily at Hattie, just in case he could tell what she was thinking if he saw her face properly.

Briefly, he told her about the rigmarole of getting Tommy

ready for school, and how he'd rushed to the primary school, arriving just in time for the bell, only to realise that he'd forgotten to pick up the Superman school bag, and after all that messing about packing it too. So of course he'd had to rush back home to get it and then drop it at the school office, before dashing to the dental surgery on Station Road for his check-up, only to discover his appointment had been cancelled.

'They insisted they texted me,' he said, shaking his head in denial. 'Absolutely swore it, in fact, but I didn't get any text message. I'd have remembered if I had, wouldn't I?'

'To be honest,' Kat said, 'if you're anything like me you might well have missed it. I seem to be oblivious to everything these days unless it involves feeding a baby, changing a baby's nappy, or basically any other activity with the word baby in it.' She sighed. 'And I'm guessing it's much the same for you with Tommy.'

'Hmm. Well, possibly.' He considered the matter then shook his head. 'No, I really don't see it. I'm organised. I have to be with my job. I'm self-employed. I run my own business and that takes organisational skills and attention to detail. I'm not so scatty that I'd miss a text message from my dentist, or acciden-tally delete it.'

'You don't sound very organised,' she pointed out, smiling. 'What with forgetting Tommy's school bag this morning.'

He blew out his cheeks, looking fed up. 'I don't know what's wrong with me. I've always been so good at time management. Since Tommy arrived everything seems like a struggle, and a million times harder to deal with than it did before.'

She saw the trace of anxiety in his eyes and felt a pang of sympathy for him.

'Sorry,' he said, picking up his mug of coffee. 'Here I am moaning about my life and I'm sure you've got it much worse than I have. Babies must be harder to deal with than six-year-olds. How are you managing?'

Kat stiffened, on alert as she always was when someone questioned her ability to cope with Hattie alone.

'It's not that bad,' she said. 'We make it work, don't we, sweetheart?'

Hattie was sucking on one of her teddy bear's ears and took no notice.

Jonah smiled, and Kat noticed how perfect his teeth were. They didn't look in urgent need of a dentist anyway.

'So what are you going to do about your dental appointment?' she asked, to distract herself from the inconvenient way her mind was dwelling on his stunning smile.

'What? Oh, they made me another one. Got to wait a week but there you go. At least I'll get to see him, and my teeth aren't giving me any problems so it's okay.'

'It wasn't the dentist you were having a go at on the phone then?' she asked lightly, then blushed. 'Sorry. I wasn't eavesdropping. I didn't hear everything you said, just the tone of your voice as you said it.'

'It's okay. I wasn't exactly discreet.' He glanced round the café then leaned closer to her, and she tried not to react as she got another direct hit of his cologne, which was subtle but delicious. 'Truth is, that was my sister.'

'Tawnie?' Kat vaguely knew Jonah's sister. She was four or five years older than him, she guessed, remembering how she'd been a cool sixth former when Kat had first gone up to high school. Tawnie had got married and moved to a village a few miles away about—heck, it must be around fifteen or sixteen years ago now. 'What's she done?'

'Nothing really.' He sighed. 'She set me up on a blind date for this Friday.'

Kat tried to ignore the disappointment she was feeling at this news. 'And you're not impressed?'

'Far from it. I cancelled this morning, and Tawnie's not happy with me. Worst thing is, the woman told her I was rude to her on the phone, and I wasn't. If anything, she was rude to me. But hey, what does it matter? The main thing is, I've averted the crisis. Hell!' He visibly shuddered. 'Can you imagine anything worse than a blind date?'

'Sounds horrendous,' she agreed.

'Bacon sandwich!'

They both looked round as the woman at the counter waved a paper bag in Jonah's direction. Jonah quickly collected it from her with thanks.

'Are you hungry?' Kat asked, smiling as he returned to the table, the bag clutched in his hand.

'I didn't have time for any breakfast,' he admitted. 'And even if I did, there was nothing in the cupboard except for crisps. I'll go home and change my clothes and eat this—' he nodded at the bag, 'then it's off to work I go. I must remember to go to Maister's this evening for a shop. Honestly, you're right, you know, my brain seems to be turning to mush.'

He gently tapped Hattie on her nose, and she immediately held out her arms to him. Kat's eyes widened in surprise.

'Wow, you're honoured. She wants a hug.'

'Really?' Jonah sounded touchingly thrilled about it. 'Aw, that's so sweet.' He pushed the sandwich and the half-empty mug of coffee away and took Hattie from Kat's knee. 'Well then, a quick cuddle and then I'll have to go because I've got a lot of horses to shoe today.'

Hattie gurgled and Jonah hugged her, patting her gently on the back.

There was a funny noise and Kat stared in dismay as Jonah held her daughter away from him. She saw all too clearly that he'd paid the price for patting her back. Hattie had thrown up all over his expensive jacket.

'I'm so sorry!' She leapt to her feet and grabbed some serviettes from the counter, then began dabbing at his jacket.

'It's okay, it's all right, don't worry.'

Jonah laughed and Kat looked at him in amazement.

'But your jacket...'

'Oh.' He shrugged. 'This old thing?'

Who was he kidding? Kat knew it wasn't some cheap old jacket he'd bought off the market. She also knew it was his favourite jacket because he'd certainly worn it enough times over the last couple of years. Ever since his divorce in fact. Then she wondered how she knew that.

Hattie grabbed Jonah's hair and pulled, and he tried his best to untangle her fingers while Kat frantically wiped away baby vomit, which was in danger of running onto his sweatshirt if she wasn't quick.

She looked up and Jonah met her gaze. They stared at each other for a moment.

'I think that's got the worst of it off,' she said weakly.

'Great. Thanks.' Jonah blinked. 'Er, you'd better have your baby back before I forget and take her to work with me.'

'Well, you can take her if you like,' Kat said in a feeble attempt at a joke to distract herself after that weird moment.

'Sorry. I've got enough on with Tommy, thanks.' He smiled again but handed Hattie back. She couldn't blame him. Her daughter had thoroughly disgraced them both.

He picked up the sandwich bag and said, 'Right, well, nice to see you again, Kat. You too, Hattie. Look after that teddy bear, miss. Next time someone stands on it he might well lose his giggle for good.'

'And that would never do. See you, Jonah.'

Kat busied herself strapping Hattie back into the buggy before gathering up all the soggy serviettes. She heard the bell above the door jingle and realised Jonah had left, so she sat back in her chair and let out a long breath.

That was the weirdest experience ever. Why had she got so bloody ridiculous over Jonah? Jonah of all people! She fixed Hattie with a stern look.

'This is all your fault, you know. You've messed up my hormones and now I don't know what I'm doing. Did I make a complete fool of myself?'

Hattie laughed and Kat broke into a smile.

'Little monkey,' she said, taking her daughter's hand and feeling the usual warmth and delight as Hattie's fingers curled around her own. 'Well, you were worth every moment of embarrassment, sweetheart. I wouldn't have it any other way.'

* * *

Kat was relieved when the door pushed open, distracting Hattie with its jingling bell, and Sally hurried in, an apologetic smile on her face.

'Sorry I'm late, love. Have you been waiting long?'

Kat pulled a face. 'Only forty minutes.'

'You're kidding!' Sally looked horrified. 'Did I get the time wrong? I thought—'

'I got here early,' Kat reassured her. 'Anyway, you're here now and that's all that matters.'

'Oh well, shall we have something to eat? What do you fancy? My treat.'

Kat felt the familiar twist of anxiety at her words. Did Sally think she couldn't afford to buy her own food from a café? Then she saw the open smile on her friend's face and pushed away her worries. Of course Sally didn't mean anything by it. They'd bought each other food many times before now. Sally would never judge her anyway.

They perused the admittedly uninspiring menu and ended up choosing two coffees and two pecan and maple pastries.

'Barbara's looking fed up,' Sally observed, sitting down at their table after placing their order.

'Barbara? Is that her name?'

'Yes. Didn't you know? Mind you, I only found out after

Mam interrogated her last Christmas,' Sally admitted. 'You should have heard her insulting this place. It's a wonder Barbara agreed to serve me really.'

Kat grinned, all too aware of how tactless Sally's mum, Mona, could be. She thought there were probably quite a few residents of Tuppenny Bridge who gave thanks that Mona lived in East Yorkshire and had only visited Sally twice in the past year.

'And how's this little cutie?' Sally asked, smiling down at Hattie, who was cuddling her teddy bear and looking distinctly sleepy.

Hattie immediately kicked her legs and waved the bear frantically.

'Oops, did I say something?'

'Nope.' Kat shook her head. 'That's her latest trick. Every time she thinks she's falling asleep she wakes herself up by jigging around or kicking out. She's like that in her cot. I lay her down for a nap or for bedtime and she does everything she can to stay awake. Sometimes it's so funny it makes me laugh.' She sighed. 'Other times, when I'm really tired, I could cry.'

'Bless you.' Sally covered Kat's hand with her own. 'I remember that feeling with Summer. Billie wasn't so bad at getting herself off to sleep but Summer always wanted to be awake. Frightened she was missing something, my mam used to say. It passes though, love. Trust me.' She laughed. 'There'll come a point, when she's a teenager, when you'll be hard pressed to get her out of bed at all.'

Kat nodded, determined not to show any sign of weakness to her friend. 'Oh, I know that. And like I said, usually I just laugh at her.' She shrugged. 'Anyway, how are things with you? Keeping busy?'

Sally, who along with her husband Rafferty ran The White Hart Inn in Market Place, leaned back in her chair. 'As full on as ever. We've been making the most of it, though, because now the kids are back at school it won't be quite as busy. We were so lucky with the weather this summer, and there were loads of day trippers and holiday makers, so the pub's been packed all month.'

'You've hardly had time to enjoy married life,' Kat observed.

'I know! Can you believe it's been a month since the wedding already? Three weeks ago we were just about ready to leave Paris behind.' She gave a sigh of pleasure. 'That was some honeymoon.'

Kat grinned. 'All right, Sal. Don't go on about it. Some of us haven't had the pleasure for quite some time.'

'Sorry! When was the last time you went on holiday?'

'I wasn't talking about the holiday,' Kat said wistfully.

'Oh!' Sally's face reddened. 'Oh yes, I see. It must have been, what...' Sally did a quick mental calculation, 'sixteen months since Hattie was conceived. Assuming you haven't since—'

'No!' Kat lowered her voice. 'No I haven't.'

She knew Sally wouldn't ask and sure enough she didn't, moving on to another subject and leaving Kat grateful that she had a friend who didn't ask questions she knew Kat wouldn't want to answer.

'How come you were in here so early then?'

'I wanted to get out of that flat,' Kat confessed. 'It's doing my head in, Sal. I hate to admit it, but your mum was right. It's too small now that Hattie's arrived, and it sometimes feels like the walls are closing in on me, you know?'

'Oh heck.' Sally nodded. 'I can imagine. It's amazing how much stuff one baby accumulates. What are you going to do about it?'

'Look for somewhere else? Although how I'm going to find anywhere round here I have no idea. So many places go for holiday lets these days, and anyway, the deposits are huge, not to mention the rent. My job doesn't exactly pay top dollar, so I don't know.'

'What about house sharing?' Sally suggested. 'Do you know anyone who might be looking for a lodger?'

'What, with a baby in tow?' Kat gave her a doubtful look. 'I can't imagine anyone wanting that, can you? Even if I knew someone who was looking, which I don't.'

'You could ask Joseph at Whispering Willows,' Sally teased. 'He's got that big old house and just him living there. Or there's Clive at Stepping Stones. I'm sure he's got room.'

'Very funny.' Kat rolled her eyes. 'I don't think so, somehow. Do you?'

Joseph Wilkinson's house was certainly big enough, but it was drab and needed work doing, since all Joseph's money seemed to go on running the horse sanctuary rather than repairing his own living quarters.

As for Stepping Stones, that was a lovely house, but it also served as a veterinary surgery, and somehow Kat didn't think she or a baby would be Clive's idea of the perfect housemate.

As a thought crossed her mind she couldn't resist saying, 'Jonah was in earlier.'

'Jonah? Oh thanks, love.' Sally gave Barbara a grateful smile as she brought over a tray carrying their coffees and pastries. As Barbara returned to the kitchen with the used coffee cups she said, 'How is he?'

'He's fine. Well, he was until madam here was sick all over him,' Kat confessed, glancing at her daughter, and giving an inward sigh of relief that she was finally asleep.

'She never was! How did he take that?'

'He was brilliant about it,' Kat said wistfully. 'Just laughed it off. Didn't even get annoyed when Hattie practically yanked his hair out while I was wiping him down.'

Sally raised an eyebrow. 'Wiping him down?'

Kat's face burned. 'I couldn't just let the baby vomit trickle onto his sweatshirt, could I? Besides, he had that jacket on. You know.'

Sally frowned. 'What jacket?'

'*The* jacket. That expensive-looking black biker jacket. He's worn it for a couple of years, ever since Sofia cleared off in fact. I think it was his divorce present to himself.'

She broke a piece off her pastry and popped it in her mouth, then the burning sensation in her cheeks deepened as she saw Sally's expression.

'What?'

'Oh, nothing. Just—well, fancy you noticing something like that. I never have.'

'You weren't living here when they got divorced,' Kat pointed out.

'No, but I've never noticed the jacket either. Can't say I've ever taken any notice of what he wears. Mind you,' she added, taking a sip of coffee and watching Kat steadily, 'I always knew exactly what Rafferty was wearing on any given day of the week.'

'You're barking up the wrong tree,' Kat assured her hastily. 'This is Jonah we're talking about.'

'And what's wrong with Jonah?' Sally demanded. 'Nice looking fella, good job, own house, *and*,' she added meaningfully, 'very good with kids.'

Sorry. I've got enough on with Tommy, thanks. That's what Jonah had said when she'd joked about him taking Hattie. Yes, it had been said with humour, but he had a point. Jonah's world was Tommy. He had no room for a woman in his life, let alone one with a baby. Besides...

'It's just Jonah!'

Sally frowned. 'I still don't get your point.'

Kat hesitated. 'We hung out back in the day. Years ago. When—when Leon was around.'

'Oh.'

Sally had never asked her about her relationship with Leon Callaghan, who'd been killed in a car accident fourteen years ago. In fact, she realised, fourteen years ago next month. Kat supposed she could have mentioned it. Sally was, after all, her best friend. But somehow the subject had never come up, and besides there was still a lot of baggage from that time—baggage that Kat wasn't sure she was ready to unpack, even now.

'There were five of us. Me, Leon, Jonah, Noah Lavender, and Isobel. Isobel Finch as she was then.'

'You hung out with Isobel?' Sally's nose wrinkled in disbelief, and Kat couldn't blame her. Isobel had been a spiky, rather bitchy person back in the day, and if anything she'd only got worse over the years. Despite being married to Noah, who was now the headmaster of the local primary school, having a lovely home overlooking the green, and owning her own flower shop, Petalicious, nothing seemed to satisfy Isobel Lavender.

'Yeah, because of Noah. They both went to that posh private school that Jamie's at now—St Egbert's. To be honest, I didn't much care for her even then, but obviously Noah was besotted with her, so she got to hang out with us. And then Noah went off to university for four years, so we got stuck with her.' She couldn't help smiling at the memory. 'Jonah was always nice to her. Leon and me—well if we could have shaken her off we would have, but she wasn't the sort to take a hint.'

'So there were the five of you in this little gang,' Sally said thoughtfully. 'And Jonah was one of you.'

'Yeah, him and Leon, and to some extent Noah, they were like brothers. Ben and Jamie might have been Leon's real brothers, but they were a lot younger than Leon—something like seven years between Leon and Ben. Ben hung out with Ross Lavender at the time, so Jonah and Leon were probably closer. And of course, Jamie was just a baby himself.'

She chewed her pastry thoughtfully, saying nothing for a few moments.

'You know, I never realised before how much it must have hurt Jonah when Leon was killed. I was so much in my own head that it never occurred to me—'

She broke off and took a gulp of coffee, desperate to swallow down the tears that were suddenly threatening.

'Are you okay, love?' Sally asked sympathetically.

'Fine. I'm fine.' Kat forced a smile. 'Wow, isn't it weird how things can affect you, so long after the event?'

'You're not wrong. Look at Ben. Bless him, he's been carrying the guilt of Leon's accident around with him all these years, and no one realised it. Thank goodness he's finally coming to terms with it.'

'It wasn't Ben's fault,' Kat said heavily. 'Any of it.'

'Well, we know that, love, and hopefully he realises it now too. But it's as you say, things like that affect you for years, even when deep down you know you're not to blame. Don't they call it survivor's guilt?'

Kat nodded, not speaking. She broke off another piece of pastry and chewed it, though it tasted like sawdust in her mouth.

Jonah. Of all the people in Tuppenny Bridge, he was the last person she should develop feelings for.

If she hadn't been certain of that before, she was now.

THREE

Wednesday morning was gloriously sunny, with blue skies that made the idea of staying indoors unthinkable.

Kat had already decided that a meander around the market was called for, even though she didn't need anything and couldn't afford anything anyway. Gazing out of the window she watched the stallholders laying out their wares and could hear the general buzz from the market place from up here in her flat.

Maybe, she thought, it really was time to rejoin the land of the living. She could stay off work for another few months if she chose, but the more she thought about it the less appealing that seemed.

She was more than ready to go back to work. Get some kind of normality back in her life. She missed the shop, which she'd always enjoyed working in. Although it wasn't as busy as it had been when she'd first started working there, she loved being surrounded by the balls of wool, the knitting patterns, the crochet kits, and sewing supplies.

It was a comforting, nostalgic world that reminded her of her mum, who'd been a keen knitter and had taught Kat to knit when she was a little girl—something that had come in useful while she'd been off work all these months. She'd made lots of baby clothes for Hattie but there were only so many cardigans and hats and mittens a little girl needed. It was time to get back behind that counter.

Hattie, she thought, would be fine if she could set up some sort of play/sleep area in the large back room of the shop. At the moment, the Lavender Ladies used it as a meeting room; they told everyone they used it to crochet but no one who knew them believed that for a second.

Everyone knew that the aunties and Miss Lavender spent all their time gossiping about what was going on in Tuppenny Bridge. Eugenie Lavender liked to pretend that she felt responsible for the town, since her ancestor, the famous Georgian artist Josiah Lavender, was Tuppenny Bridge's most famous son and had put the place on the map.

She certainly interfered enough, and was quite vocal on the town council, as well as supplying the Christmas tree and lights for the town in exchange, naturally, for being asked to switch on the illuminations every year at the beginning of December.

She and the aunties communicated via walkie-talkie when they weren't physically together and had a lucrative sideline taking bets on various events in Tuppenny Bridge. They'd recently, for instance, made a small fortune on the relationship status of Summer Fletcher, Sally's daughter, and Ben Callaghan the local vet. Previously they'd earned a good few quid on Sally's own relationship with Rafferty.

Then there was the unofficial book they were currently running on when Market Café would pass into new hands, not to mention the wagers that were still being placed—as far as she was aware—on the identity of Hattie's father.

Despite that, Kat was very fond of all three women, and thought that she had a good chance of persuading them to meet elsewhere so she could keep Hattie in the back room, enabling her to keep a close eye on her while she worked in the shop. It was, she thought, the only way she could afford to work. Child-care would cancel out anything she earned, so permission to use the room was a must.

They could even meet in her flat if they wanted. She smiled to herself. Give them a chance to poke around looking for clues about who'd got her pregnant. Yeah, good luck with that, ladies!

She tied her long, light brown hair up in a ponytail, then dressed Hattie in a pretty summer dress and put a bonnet on her head, although how long that would remain in place she wasn't sure. She also smothered herself and her daughter in sun cream, then headed downstairs, her baby in one arm, having already carried the buggy down earlier.

Having strapped Hattie in, she wheeled the buggy into the shop, rather than going through the back door and into Little Market Place, and greeted her aunts who were, as always, delighted to see her. They fussed over Hattie, making faces and cooing over her while she watched them in amazement, as if wondering what on earth she was witnessing.

Kat couldn't blame her. As usual, her aunts were dressed in their multi-coloured crocheted waistcoats. Birdie teamed hers with orange Crimplene trousers that must have been made in the nineteen-seventies, along with a yellow blouse whose large, flapping collar indicated it had been made at around the same time.

Rita, meanwhile, wore a floor-length green and yellow dress, and had a pink paper rose clipped in her dyed red hair.

No one could ever accuse them of dressing down.

'Are you going to the market?' Birdie asked.

'Yeah. I thought I'd get a bit of sunshine and see some life for a change. I'm going stir-crazy up there,' Kat told her.

'I don't blame you. It's not good for you, being stuck up there all day every day. And Hattie needs to start socialising, don't you, poppet?' Rita tickled Hattie's chin.

'Er, that's actually what I was going to talk to you about,'

Kat said. 'I know I've got a few months left of maternity leave, but how would you feel about me coming back to work early?' She smiled at them both. 'I expect you're both fed up working here full time, and it will be good for you to have your days back to yourselves, right?'

Her smile faded as she saw them exchange nervous looks.

'What's up?'

'Oh, nothing. Nothing at all, lovey. What could possibly be up?'

'It sounds—er—like a good idea.' Birdie cleared her throat.

Kat eyed them suspiciously. 'Is there something I should know?'

'Of course not! When were you thinking of coming back to work?' Rita asked.

'Well, there's nothing to hang on for. How about I start back on Monday?' Kat suggested.

Rita and Birdie frowned.

'But what about Hattie? Who's going to look after her?'

'I was thinking she could stay in that back room,' Kat said, nodding at the door to the Lavender Ladies' inner sanctum. 'I can put her travel cot and some toys and things in there and have my baby monitor on. It's not like she'll be alone much because I'll be in there when there aren't any customers.' She laughed. 'And let's face it, there's a lot of time without customers. So—'

'Oh, I don't think that would work,' Birdie said anxiously.

'No, Eugenie wouldn't like that,' Rita agreed. 'That's our room. Our meeting room. Where we—er—crochet.'

'You can *crochet* upstairs in my flat,' Kat offered immediately. 'Honestly, I wouldn't mind.'

'I think it seems a bit cruel leaving Hattie in there alone all day,' Birdie said thoughtfully. 'Aren't there laws about that sort of thing?'

'But it's like I said, she wouldn't be alone. I'd be in there most of the day. I'd have a playpen for her for when I'm in the shop, but she'd be napping in the afternoon anyway. And obviously I'll take her out for some fresh air in my lunch break and—'

'I still think it sounds cruel,' Rita said.

'And whether it does or it doesn't, Eugenie won't want to be traipsing upstairs to your flat,' Birdie added. 'She's very attached to that room. I think you should hold off for now, lovey. Think again.'

'But I need to get back to work!' Kat realised she'd perhaps spoken louder than she'd intended, but really, this was ridiculous. Hattie would be perfectly safe and happy. The room was easily big enough, and Kat would have the door open so she could see her baby and Hattie could see her. It wasn't like she was putting her in a dog cage or anything.

Besides, she really needed the income. If she was ever going to save up enough to pay for a deposit on a bigger place the sooner she started earning again the better.

'I'll tell you what,' Rita said soothingly, 'why don't you come round to ours for Sunday dinner?'

'Ooh yes, good idea,' Birdie said, nodding vigorously. 'We'd love that, and we can talk it all through then, can't we?'

'Talk what through?' Kat asked, perplexed. She gave them suspicious looks. 'You haven't hired someone else to take my job, have you?'

Rita and Birdie gasped.

'As if we'd do that!' Birdie said indignantly.

'Of course we haven't. What do you take us for? We're only thinking of you,' Rita added. 'And Hattie, of course.'

'Okay. Sorry.' Kat shrugged. 'Well, okay, Sunday dinner sounds great. About one?'

'That would be perfect,' her aunts assured her.

'Now,' Rita said, 'you go off and enjoy yourself at the

market. It's a lovely sunny day, so don't worry about anything else.'

Still unsure, Kat pushed the buggy out of the shop and into the busy market place. She gazed around her, wondering if the baby stall was here this week. Hattie didn't really need anything, but it was always nice to browse.

She glanced back at the shop and frowned. Something was up with the aunties; she would swear to it. Whatever they said about there being nothing wrong she knew them too well to believe it. They were up to something. And when the aunties were up to something the whole of Tuppenny Bridge should be worried.

Somehow, Kat had a feeling that she was going to get more than a hot dinner at their cottage on Sunday.

* * *

The best thing about being self-employed, Jonah realised, was that he could set his own hours. And even though it meant his income had dropped, he never worked past three o'clock these days, so he could pick Tommy up from school.

He had to admit he loved Fridays. There was a general feeling of relief as he walked Tommy home from All Hallows' Church of England school on Chestnut Lane and they arrived back at Forge Cottage, knowing that tomorrow they'd be able to relax into the day, rather than chasing around dealing with some last-minute crisis which, despite his best efforts, always seemed to occur at breakfast time.

This evening, he planned to get Tommy's school uniform in the wash so there was no eleventh-hour panic on Sunday night. Tomorrow the two of them would go to Maister's and do a big shop. He'd make sure he got enough food for Tommy's packed lunches and something for them to have for tea every night.

This weekend would be the start of their new organised,

healthy regime. This evening, however, would be burgers and a night in front of the television. Maybe he'd even have a glass of beer after Tommy had gone to bed.

He groaned inwardly as they approached Forge Cottage. Tawnie was leaning against the garden wall waiting for them.

'What are you doing here?'

'Nice to see you too, brother dear.' Tawnie rolled her eyes and opened the gate for them. 'Honestly, I drive all the way here out of the goodness of my heart and that's the greeting I get.' She ruffled Tommy's hair. 'What's your daddy like, eh?'

Tommy grinned at her, and Jonah unlocked the front door.

'Sorry. I didn't mean it like that. Just, aren't you supposed to be at work?'

'I left early. I had an appointment at the doctor's.'

'Oh?' Jonah ushered Tommy indoors and raised an eyebrow at his sister. 'Nothing serious I hope.'

'Smear.'

He winced and she laughed. 'You asked. Anyway, thought I'd take the opportunity to see how my favourite brother's doing.'

'Your only brother,' he reminded her, as she headed past him into the cottage. He closed the door behind them and led her through to the kitchen, where Tommy had already removed his coat and thrown it on the small sofa in the dining area.

'You know where your coat goes and it doesn't go there,' Jonah reminded him sternly.

Tommy sighed and handed it to him. Jonah took Tawnie's jacket and hung them both up in the hallway, along with his own.

'So,' he said, returning to the kitchen, 'I expect after that ordeal at the doctor's you're ready for a cup of tea?'

'Coffee please, if it's not too much trouble.'

'Tommy, go upstairs and get changed and I'll put your uniform on to wash, okay?'

Tommy nodded and went up to his bedroom and Tawnie turned to him, clearly impressed.

'Washing his uniform on a Friday afternoon? Well done! It's usually Sunday afternoon before I remember. Although,' she added, 'Iris is old enough to wash her own uniform these days, and she's been quite good about washing Lilly's too.'

'One of the benefits of having daughters I suppose,' Jonah said, filling the kettle.

'Sexist pig!' she retorted.

He laughed. 'You're the one who won't let Keith do any housework.'

'Because he works hard!'

'So do you.'

She folded her arms. 'Okay, point taken. To be honest, it's more about him making such a mess of everything that it's easier and quicker for me to do it myself.'

'And that's exactly what he wants you to think,' Jonah said. He spooned coffee into two mugs and shook his head. 'It's shameful that someone as smart as you still falls for the oldest trick in the book.'

'Oh, shut up.' She stuck her tongue out at him and sat down on one of the stools at the kitchen island, tucking her dark hair behind her ears. 'So.'

He sighed inwardly, knowing she'd been building up to this moment ever since she got here. She'd probably been building up to it since Monday.

'So?' he asked, playing dumb as he finished making their drinks and placed the mugs on the island.

'Jodie.'

'Jodie?' He pretended he'd forgotten the woman's name, which in retrospect probably wasn't the best move to get her onside. 'Oh, of course. Jodie.'

He turned his back on her while he poured Tommy a glass

of milk and rummaged in the cupboard for some biscuits that would keep his son going until teatime.

'Don't play the innocent with me. You knew who Jodie was. What I don't get is why you cancelled the date. Look, I've got a photo of her on my phone. See for yourself. She's quite attractive.'

'I really don't care if she looks like—' Jonah rummaged around in his mind for any famous woman he considered beautiful, flummoxed to discover he couldn't summon a single name. Realising it had been so long since he'd given the matter any thought he gave up and sighed. 'Well, whoever.'

He gave Tommy a bright smile as the little boy entered the kitchen, carrying his folded-up school uniform. 'Good lad. Just dump it on the floor by the washing machine. Here, have some milk and biscuits. Why don't you go in the living room and watch a bit of television for an hour?'

Tommy's face brightened. 'Can I watch *Paddington*?'

'Sure. You know how to find it.'

He certainly did. Despite being only six years old Tommy was quicker at navigating the television remote than Jonah. It never ceased to amaze him how quickly his son could flick between Netflix, Disney Plus, and multiple terrestrial channels with ease. Anyone would think they were being taught how to do it at school.

'Does he watch a lot of television?' Tawnie asked.

Jonah gave her a look and she held up her hands. 'Just asking. No judgement, honestly. I remember what it was like with kids that age in the house. I'm just bloody grateful mine are old enough to entertain themselves these days.'

Her daughters, Iris and Lilly, were fourteen and eleven and both at high school now. In fact, he recalled guiltily, Lilly must have started there this week.

'How did Lilly get on at school?' he asked.

She widened her grey eyes. 'Well remembered! Not too

bad. It was a bit overwhelming obviously, but she had her friends from primary school with her, so they stuck together and helped each other out. Anyway, she's discovered the library and she's in heaven. You know Lilly and books.'

He smiled, knowing his niece's passion for reading, and glad that she'd settled in okay.

'Even so,' Tawnie said, 'that doesn't get you off the hook. About Jodie—'

He groaned. 'Honestly, Tawnie, give it up. I'm not interested and that's final.'

'In Jodie? But—'

'In any woman! Can't you see you're wasting your time? Don't you think I have enough to worry about, taking care of Tommy?'

'But that's my point,' she said gently. 'All you do is work and look after Tommy, and you need something more in your life than that. You'd make someone a good husband you know.'

'Husband? Bloody hell, Tawnie, slow down. You were talking about a blind date a minute ago. Look, I've been there, done that, remember? I *was* a husband, and quite clearly I fell way short of the mark.'

'Oh, she doesn't count!' Tawnie waved her hand dismissively. 'No bloke could have pleased Sofia. You had no chance. We all know what she wanted from you, and she got it in the end, didn't she? Not,' she added hastily, 'that I'd have wished that on her. No way. Even so.'

Jonah didn't know what to say to that, so he didn't say anything. He sat down next to her at the island and cradled his mug of tea, trying not to dwell on Sofia.

'Look, I get that it was a horrible experience, okay?' Tawnie persisted. 'But no one should be alone. I'm worried about you, Jonah. You know what they say about all work and no play.'

'All work? Chance would be a fine thing!' He shook his

head. 'I've had to cut back on my work hours so much lately, to fit around Tommy, that it's a wonder I've any clients left.'

She eyed him worriedly. 'But isn't that affecting your income?'

'Naturally.'

'Well, that's no good then! I wish I could help you more, but it's so tricky to fit in babysitting with my job, and then there's the kids and their seemingly endless list of after school activities.'

'I don't expect you to help any more than you already have,' he assured her. 'You, Keith and Iris saved my bacon over the holidays. I wouldn't have been able to work at all if you hadn't pitched in to babysit. And I know you've got your hands full as it is. We'll work something out eventually. And Tommy won't be a little boy forever. Before I know it he'll be at high school too.'

'But by then you might not have a business left.' Gloomily she sipped her coffee and Jonah decided it was time to change the subject.

'Have you seen Mum? How is she?'

Tawnie lowered her mug and gave him one of her looks. 'Moaning about not seeing you. You need to visit her, Jonah. I don't know why you spend so little time with her.'

'You know why,' he said grimly.

'She might have got over all that now. Anyway, just ignore her. That's what Keith and I do. You know Mum. You know what she's like.'

'Yes, I do. But don't you think there comes a point when we have to stop making excuses for her? All this, *oh but you know what Mum's like* stuff. That's just giving her a get-out—a licence to be rude and obnoxious. Maybe it's time one of us pulled her up about it.'

'Good luck with that. Do you want to go first?' She grinned at him, and he smiled back, despite his annoyance.

'Anyway,' she continued, 'you can't avoid her forever.'

'Watch me try.'

'Aw, Jonah, please. Look, she's not getting any younger. Why don't you come over to us for Sunday dinner? Mum's coming so you'd get to see her, but you'd have me and Keith for backup.'

When he didn't respond, she said, 'I know she hasn't always been the perfect mum, but she does care about you, deep down.'

'Funny way of showing it.'

'I know. But in her head somehow it all makes sense. Come on, Jonah. One last try, eh? For me? It's the least you can do since you cancelled your date and showed me up in front of Jodie.'

He gasped. 'How did I show you up? And by the way,' he added, as the thought occurred to him, 'I wasn't rude to her. She was rude to me, and it sounds like she was rude to every other driver on the road that day too. I was talking to her while she was driving and the stuff she was saying! I can't believe she told you that.'

'If you say so I'll believe you,' Tawnie said comfortably. 'See? That's what brothers and sisters do for each other. They back each other up. Take each other's side. They're there for each other.'

'Okay, I get it,' he said, realising she had another agenda. 'You want me to be there on Sunday to back you up with Mum. What bombshell are you going to drop on her?'

She wrinkled her nose. 'That obvious?'

'Yes.'

'Hmm. Well, if you must know, we won't be able to invite her round to ours for Christmas this year because we're going away. We've booked a holiday in Lanzarote instead. Warmth and sunshine but also Christmas markets and parades. The girls will love it. Ooh, and dinner in a hotel instead of slaving away in the kitchen all Christmas morning. But as you can imagine...'

'Mum will be fuming.' He could imagine it now. She'd play the abandoned mother all too well, even though poor Tawnie had hosted her every year since Iris was born. 'As long as she doesn't expect me to invite her here,' he added firmly. 'Although I don't suppose she'll want to spend Christmas here, anyway, given the circumstances.'

The circumstances, he thought wretchedly, being Tommy. Why his mother couldn't just accept him and love him was beyond him.

'Okay,' he said reluctantly. 'I'll be there on Sunday. But I'm not putting up with any of her crap, okay? Not this time.'

He would give her one last chance, but after that he was done. She might be his mother, but Tommy was his son, and if she couldn't accept that, well, he didn't see what else they had to say to each other.

FOUR

Kat couldn't help feeling nervous as she pushed Hattie's buggy down the front path of Whistlestop Cottage early that Sunday afternoon. There was something in the air, she could feel it and wondered exactly what Birdie and Rita were up to.

The aunties lived towards the bottom of Forge Lane—or the top, depending on which way you approached it from—just before it reached Chestnut Lane and the railway line.

Whistlestop Cottage had, like most of the warm, sandstone cottages down that particular road, been built about two hundred years ago. Birdie and Rita had lived there all their lives. They'd been born in that house, along with Kat's grandad, their older brother.

Although his sisters stayed resolutely single, Robert Pennyfeather had married quite young, and he and his wife had also had a son—Kat's dad, Stephen.

Robert had owned The Black Swan on Bankside, facing the river. It had been, and still was, a popular pub, and Stephen had also worked there, taking it over when Robert retired and moved to the coast.

Kat had been born in their flat above The Black Swan, and

had grown up there, having a happy and contented childhood, surrounded by family and friends.

Things had changed drastically for her when she was just fifteen years old; her mum had died unexpectedly of a heart attack. Within six months of her death, her grieving dad had decided to put the past behind him and sell The Black Swan to go into partnership with two friends of his, who ran a hotel in Dorset.

There'd been a suggestion that Kat should go with him, but that was never an option as far as Kat was concerned. Luckily for her, the aunties had stepped in and offered her a home with them at Whistlestop Cottage, and her dad had raised few objections, probably realising that he'd be more welcome in Dorset without Kat in tow.

To be fair to him, he'd been in no fit state to care for a teenage daughter and had no real idea how to deal with her grief on top of his own. She and her dad kept in touch, albeit by texts in the main, since he'd moved from Dorset to Majorca several years ago when he'd remarried. He'd been there for her at a crisis point in her life, though, and she'd always be grateful to him for that.

Kat had been given a job in Pennyfeather's Wool Shop when she left school, and then, in her early twenties, she'd been allowed to move into the flat above it, paying a nominal rent from her wages.

Needless to say, she felt she owed her aunts everything, but despite their kindness towards her and their obvious love for her, she was still suspicious about their recent behaviour.

If she'd had any doubt, it was immediately dispelled when she saw Birdie's face as she opened the front door. Guilt was written all over it, and Kat's heart sank as she saw her aunt quickly look away, as if she couldn't face her.

Just what was going on? Surely they hadn't really taken someone else on in her place? They wouldn't, would they?

She'd half expected them to take on temporary staff months ago, having assumed they wouldn't want to cover her hours in the shop while she was on maternity leave. She'd been quite surprised when they hadn't, but they'd assured her they were enjoying themselves.

'It's like a trip down Memory Lane,' Rita had said brightly. 'We spent years working in this shop, didn't we, Birdie? Ever since we were little girls helping Mother out when we weren't at school. It's fun getting back to it.'

So if they'd taken someone new on now it really made no sense.

'We're doing lamb,' Birdie told her, taking Hattie's changing bag from her while Kat unstrapped the baby from the buggy. 'It's a special occasion after all, and we're sick of chicken, aren't we, Rita?'

Rita agreed. 'We thought we'd have a treat since you're here. Come in, Katherine. Make yourself at home.'

Katherine! No one called her by her Sunday name unless things were very serious. Kat's stomach lurched with anxiety, but she pushed her worries aside as the aunties did their best to make her and Hattie feel at home.

She settled into the sofa and glanced around the chaotic, cluttered living room of Whistlestop Cottage. Her own living room above the shop might be cluttered too, but it didn't look anything like this.

The aunties owned furniture that had belonged to their own parents and took great pride in the fact that people had built things to last back in those days. They may have done, but the ancient dark brown leather suite was hardly built for comfort, and even the crocheted antimacassars and armrest covers, lovingly made by the aunties themselves, couldn't disguise how ugly it was.

There was a beige tiled fireplace that had been there since the nineteen-thirties, and a brown carpet with orange swirls that had been laid in the nineteen-seventies. The walls were covered in a cheap woodchip, although that hardly mattered since you could barely see an inch of it between the vast number of decorative plates on the walls, depicting scenes of rural and animal life, and displayed on plastic racks.

Net curtains hung at the windows, along with gold satin curtains complete with fussy tasselled pelmets. The mantel-piece was full of porcelain ornaments, picked up from charity and second-hand shops and probably not worth a tenner between them, and there was a red rug in front of the fireplace that only drew attention to the cracked and broken titles on the hearth.

It was a minimalist's nightmare, and enough to induce a migraine in anyone with even a modicum of good taste.

She couldn't deny, though, that something smelt good. Rita and Birdie might be at the bottom of the ladder when it came to home decorating or fashion, but they were pretty near the top rung when it came to good, old-fashioned home cooking.

Soon they were sitting round the hideous mahogany table in the dining room, its scratched and battered top hidden under a red and white wipe-clean tablecloth. Hattie was in the high-chair that Birdie and Rita had kindly bought and kept at their cottage for when the two of them visited, even though they rarely stayed to eat.

Kat's eyes widened as she saw the huge pile of food on her plate.

'Crikey, you've really gone to town today,' she gasped, staring at the mountain of food on her plate, all smothered in a rich gravy.

'Oh, it's nothing special,' Birdie assured her. 'Tuck in, lovey.'

Hattie had a little bit of everything, all cut up into tiny pieces for her to try. Kat tried to feed her with a spoon, but

Hattie preferred to pick her food up and stuff it in her mouth herself, leaving Kat free to eat some of her own meal.

After that, Hattie downed her bottle of milk, while Kat and the aunties had sherry trifle—home-made by Birdie.

Kat took a mouthful and gave her aunt a wan smile. 'Er, lovely. I think you may have gone a teensy bit overboard with the sherry, though.'

'Don't be daft, Kat,' Rita said, waving a hand dismissively. 'You can never go overboard with the sherry.'

Finally pushing away their empty bowls they sat back in their chairs, barely able to breathe. Kat wasn't sure if she was just full or slightly intoxicated. She felt it only proper, though, that she offer to wash up.

'Certainly not,' Rita said immediately. 'You just settle yourself on the sofa and we'll do it. As if we'd expect you to wash up for us!'

'You don't usually mind,' Kat said suspiciously. 'What's so different today?'

'Oh, away with you,' Birdie said, laughing.

Ten minutes later Rita brought her a good, strong cup of tea and she sipped it thoughtfully while the aunties finished in the kitchen and Hattie slept peacefully, lying on the armchair.

'Okay,' she said at last, as Rita and Birdie finally stopped faffing about and sat down in the living room, 'what's going on?'

They looked at each other then back at her. To be fair, they'd done a good job of trying to look innocent, but not quite good enough.

'We don't know what you mean, Katherine,' Rita said indignantly. 'Nothing's going on. We just wanted to cook you a nice dinner and look after you for a change. We can imagine how hard you work looking after Hattie.'

'A full-time job I should think,' Birdie mused. 'I don't know how you do it. I know I couldn't.' She hesitated. 'Especially if I was working in a shop too. Far too much to expect.'

Kat's eyes narrowed. 'This is about the job, isn't it? What have you done? Please,' she said, holding up her hand as the aunties started to protest, 'don't even pretend that you don't know what I'm talking about. You've clearly brought me round here to tell me something, so why don't you just get on and tell me? You're making me fear the worst.'

Her aunts looked deeply worried, and Kat felt a moment's pity for them. They obviously didn't want to break the news to her, whatever it was.

Rita hung her head, and Birdie wrung her hands as she said, 'I'm so sorry, Katherine.'

'Who? Who have you given my job to?' Kat demanded, annoyed to find tears pricking her eyes. How was she going to manage now?

'We haven't, honestly we haven't,' Rita protested. 'We'd never do that!'

Kat felt a moment's relief, but it quickly disappeared as she realised that, if that wasn't the problem, something else was. And whatever it was, it was huge.

'So what?' she asked flatly.

Rita and Birdie exchanged glances, and Rita nodded.

Birdie twisted her string of artificial pearls between her fingers and sighed.

'The fact is, we do have some news to tell you, and I know you'll be upset. I just want you to know that if we could have avoided it we would, but as it stands...' She sighed. 'Oh dear.'

Rita tutted. 'The thing is, Kat,' she said kindly, 'we're putting the shop up for sale.'

Kat stared at her incredulously. 'Pennyfeather's? You're putting the wool shop up for sale?'

She couldn't believe it. That shop had been started by their own mother, and the aunties were very proud of that fact. It had stayed in the family throughout the hardest of times, including the Second World War. Great-Granny Pennyfeather had continued to work there right up until the early nineteen-sixties, when her daughters had taken the reins. Kat simply couldn't imagine it not being in her family.

In fact, when she thought about it, it made her quite upset to think of it being sold to outsiders. Why would the aunties do that?

'I don't understand,' she said, feeling dazed. 'What possible reason—'

'If we didn't have to we wouldn't,' Rita said bleakly. 'Believe me, my lovely, we've tried every which way to get out of it. The shop's not making enough money and that's the truth of it. We can't keep it going and that's that. I'm sorry.'

Sorry? What good was sorry going to do when she had no job? As a thought occurred to her, she stared at them in horror.

'The flat? Are you including that in the sale?'

'The whole building will be sold,' Birdie confirmed.

'We thought about just selling the shop premises, but that estate agent, Mr Rustill, said we'd get far more interest if we sold it all.'

'So I'll be jobless *and* homeless?' Kat gasped.

'Oh no, dear, of course not! We'd never let that happen,' Rita assured her. 'Your old room is ready and waiting for you, and you and Hattie will be welcome to stay here as long as you need to. We're going to clear out the little box room for Hattie too, so she'll have her own little bedroom. It will be like the old days, Kat, but with the added bonus of a baby here too. It will be fun, won't it, Birdie?'

Birdie nodded. 'It will keep us young. We can't wait.'

Kat gazed around the living room and her stomach contracted with dread. She loved the aunties, she really did, but the thought of moving back here...

Hell's bells! As if her flat wasn't cluttered enough! She imagined the state of this place with Hattie's toys and parapher-

nalia on top of all Rita's and Birdie's mess, and her heart sank
into her boots.

'I know it's come as a shock to you,' Birdie said, dabbing at
her eyes. 'It was a horrible shock to us too, once we realised
what we'd have to do.'

'We tried everything to avoid it,' Rita said tearfully. 'The
fact is, we have no other choice. What Mother would say about
it I dread to think.'

Kat swallowed, remembering how much the shop meant to
them, and feeling ashamed that she'd put her own feelings
ahead of her aunts, who'd done so much for her.

'What about Miss Lavender?' she asked hopefully.
'Wouldn't she consider investing in the shop?'

'She offered,' Birdie said, pursing her lips at the thought.

Rita nodded. 'We said no. We love Eugenie dearly, but with
the best will in the world she wouldn't be able to stop herself
from changing everything. It would kill us to work with her. As
awful as it sounds, we'd rather hand the shop on than let her
turn Pennyfeather's into something it should never be.'

Kat could understand their feelings on that score, knowing
how overbearing Miss Lavender could be in her opinions. 'I'm
sorry,' she said. 'I can imagine what a difficult decision this has
been for you.'

'Oh, Kat my lovely, thank you so much for understanding,'
Birdie said. 'We were so worried about telling you, weren't we,
Rita?'

'We were, but Eugenie said you were old enough to face it
head on. I suppose we forget that you're all grown up now.
After all, you're a mother. You're perfectly capable of taking all
this in your stride, aren't you? And it's not as if you won't have a
home to go to. You and Hattie.'

Kat smiled, but her heart was sinking. Yes, she was a
mother, and it was her responsibility to provide for her daugh-

ter. She'd had such high hopes and had been stupidly certain that she could make a good life for herself and her baby.

To add insult to injury she was going to have to bring Hattie up in Whistlestop Cottage, with all its mess and disorder, and the aunties interfering in everything. They were good-hearted and kind, but they couldn't help themselves. She and Hattie wouldn't have a minute's peace.

And without a job, how was she ever going to save up enough to get out of here?

Life, she thought glumly, had just got a whole lot more complicated.

* * *

'That roast beef was a bit too rare for my taste, Tawnie. You know I don't like it pink. Makes me feel proper queasy just thinking about it.'

Mrs Brewster shuddered as if to emphasise the fact, and Jonah gave his sister a sympathetic look as she rolled her eyes behind their mother's back and murmured something under her breath.

'It was medium rare, Mum. Just how you like it,' Tawnie assured her.

'Hmm. Not my idea of medium rare,' Mrs Brewster said, pushing her chair under the table as her daughter scraped plates. 'Ten minutes less in the oven and it would have been mooing at us. No wonder our Iris barely touched a thing. And next time, can you make sure you mash the potatoes properly? I remember the other Sunday when there were lumps and I did tell you about it then. I'll do it myself in future if you like, just to make sure.'

'Duly noted, Mum,' Tawnie said, her jaw tight as she fought to stay polite. 'Just go through to the living room and relax, and don't worry about a thing. I'll load the dishwasher then I'll make us all a nice cup of tea.'

She flashed her eyes at Jonah, who knew he was being instructed to talk to their mother and distract her from Tawnie's failings. He attempted to tell his sister with his own eyes that he'd tried. Evidently, Mrs Brewster wasn't much in the mood to talk to him.

So much for her missing him.

Conversation between them at the dinner table had been stilted, to say the least. Other than a few barbed comments, she'd more or less ignored him. Then again, matters hadn't been helped when Tawnie had dropped the bombshell on their mother that they were spending Christmas in Lanzarote, so for the first time in years their mother wouldn't be staying with them from Christmas Eve until Boxing Day after all.

There'd been a shocked silence at first, which Jonah considered a result. His mother, however, soon recovered. He'd known they wouldn't be that lucky.

'Christmas abroad? I've never heard such a ridiculous idea,' she'd blustered, clearly thrown by Tawnie's announcement. 'You definitely haven't thought this through, my girl.'

'I can assure you we have,' Tawnie said, a slight crack in her voice revealing she was more nervous than she was letting on. 'We didn't rush into this. We've been thinking about it for a couple of years actually.'

'Have you indeed?' Mrs Brewster's tone was icy. 'Nice of you to finally let me in on your secret then.'

'It's hardly a secret, Mum,' Tawnie protested. 'There was no point in telling you until we'd decided.'

'And now you have. Very kind of you, I'm sure, making a decision without even consulting me.'

'I wasn't aware we had to consult you, Maureen,' Keith said evenly.

A fair-haired, stocky man with an easy-going nature, Keith

seldom got involved in any sort of confrontation, so his contribution was unexpected. Mrs Brewster's head whipped round, and she glared at him, sensing an easy target.

'Oh, weren't you? So it didn't occur to you that this will ruin all my plans for Christmas? You didn't spare a thought for how this will affect me? Or don't my feelings count?'

'Well, now you come to mention it—' Keith began, but Tawnie laid a hand on his arm as she gave her mother an appealing look.

'It's not that, Mum. Of course we understand that you'd expect to come to us again this year. That's why we're giving you a few months' notice. It's not like you won't have time to make other arrangements.'

'Don't worry about me,' her mother said bitterly. 'I'm quite sure I'm the least of your problems. It's you I feel sorry for. It will be a nightmare. You know that, don't you? Nine times out of ten these foreign holidays get cancelled because of strikes at the airport. Everyone knows that. And travelling abroad's only got worse in recent years. I just hope you've got insurance.'

'Of course we have,' Tawnie said with a sigh, as Jonah gave her a sympathetic look. 'Lots of people go abroad for Christmas, Mum. I'm sure we'll be fine.'

'Don't say I didn't warn you,' her mother said, shaking her head. 'Sunstroke, food poisoning, cockroaches in the hotel kitchens, mouldy rooms, pickpockets... I've seen it all on the television, you know. I watch the documentaries. Why you'd want to inflict all that on your poor children I have no idea, but don't listen to me. I'm sure you can cope with anything that happens to you. And I'll be all right on my own. At least I'll be able to drink the water, which is more than you'll be able to do.'

'Good grief,' Keith said, rolling his eyes. 'I've heard it all now.'

Jonah couldn't help but smile, which was a big mistake. His mother's gaze locked on him immediately.

'And what do you think about this, eh? Or was it your bright idea? It wouldn't surprise me. Anything to spite me.'

Jonah decided not to take the bait. He merely shrugged and said, 'It's none of my business. Up to them what they do for Christmas.'

'Oh, you would say that,' she snapped.

'Jonah didn't know anything about it until Friday,' Tawnie said immediately. 'You can't blame him.'

'Even if he had known, he wouldn't have tried to talk you out of it,' their mother said bitterly. 'God forbid that Jonah should have an opinion on anything. It's all about going with the flow in his world. We all know that.'

At that point, Keith had loudly asked everyone if they were finished, and suggested to Lilly and Iris that they take Tommy into the garden and let him play on the old swing for a while which, thankfully, Jonah's nieces had agreed to do.

Mrs Brewster got to her feet and headed into the living room, and Keith and Tawnie gave Jonah an apologetic look.

'I'll sort the dishwasher and make the tea,' Keith said firmly. 'You two go through to placate the dragon.'

'Must we?' Tawnie groaned.

'You were the one who told me to give her another chance,' Jonah reminded her. 'Changed your mind now?'

'Sometimes I forget how horrible she can be,' Tawnie admitted, plucking the buttons of her cream blouse, a wistful expression on her face. 'Although, I have to say, she's worse when you're here. I don't know why. It's like she shows off in front of you, making sarcastic comments to me for your benefit. She's much nicer to me when we're on our own.'

'Lucky you,' Jonah said. 'Come on then. Safety in numbers, as they say.'

He grinned at the dismay on her face and nudged her in the direction of the hallway. Entering the living room, they found Mrs Brewster sitting in an armchair by the window, watching a programme on the television. Her bony arms were folded in obvious disapproval, and her lips, now missing the coral lipstick she'd worn before eating and drinking, were pursed tightly. Her heavily lacquered, silver-streaked dark hair was as stiff and unyielding as she was.

She didn't look up but remarked, 'Finished talking about me?'

Jonah exchanged rueful looks with Tawnie.

'What makes you think we were talking about you, Mum?'

'You must think I'm daft. I can imagine what you were saying. "Oh, isn't Mum horrible?" "Isn't she mean to us?" "Doesn't she say awful things?"'

'Well,' Tawnie said slowly, 'now you mention it...'

The television screen turned black as Mrs Brewster pressed the off button on the remote and glared at them.

'It's only because I care about you both! Why can't you see that?'

'Maybe because you hide it bloody well,' Jonah said bluntly. 'All we ever get from you is criticism. Try being nice for once. It might work wonders.'

'Well pardon me for trying to help you,' she said bitterly. 'If your father was alive he wouldn't let you speak to me like that.'

No, Jonah thought. He'd have been hiding in the kitchen with his son-in-law, or more likely, he'd have dragged Jonah and Keith off to the pub, unable to stand any more bitching from his wife. She was kidding herself if she thought Dad would have been on her side.

'I don't see why you think I need helping,' Tawnie said, sitting down on the settee and tapping the cushion next to her for Jonah.

He sat down too, and they faced their mother, who was looking very hard done by, even though she'd been the one pouring out nasty comments while everyone else had been polite and soothing.

'Christmas in Lanzarote! It's not right, Tawnie,' her mother said. 'It's not right for those kiddies either. Memories are made at Christmas that last a lifetime, and to take the girls away from their family and home at such a special time of year! And for what? Foreign food and sunshine instead of—'

'A glorified Sunday dinner and the *Eastenders* Christmas special?' Tawnie raised an eyebrow. 'It's hardly child cruelty, Mum. It will do them good to experience something new and different. I think we're doing them a service.'

Her mother folded her arms. 'And just what am I supposed to do with myself while you're away? Oh well, I suppose I'll be okay on my own. I'll have beans on toast and a yoghurt, and I'll watch the carol service on television and remember what it was like when you were little, when I devoted my entire Christmas to making sure you two had a day to remember.'

Tawnie puffed out her cheeks as she exhaled.

Jonah shrugged. 'Sounds like a plan.'

His mother's eyes swivelled in his direction, and he braced himself for her to suggest that she join him for Christmas dinner. After all, Forge Cottage had been her marital home, so he supposed she still felt she had every right to be there, even though the place had passed to him when his dad retired from being a farrier and Jonah took over the business.

The plan had been that his parents would live in a swanky new retirement village while renting out the cottage to Jonah, but neither his mum or dad had settled in their new home.

Jonah had been paying a good rent for Forge Cottage which had enabled his dad to buy a small place called Silverbank, just five miles from Tuppenny Bridge. Dad had signed the cottage and forge over to him as a gift some years ago, which was lucky as it meant death duties were avoided when Dad died. The mortgage on Silverbank had been automatically paid off, thanks to insurance, and left to Tawnie, on the understanding that their mum be allowed to remain there rent-free for the rest of her days.

His mother often complained bitterly that she was nothing more than a glorified squatter, and that her children had done very well out of their parents, and it was a pity they didn't show the same consideration in return.

Any moment now, Jonah fully expected her to remind him that he wouldn't be the owner of Forge Cottage if it hadn't been for his dad, and that it was his duty to invite her over. He thought, sadly, that if she'd only been nicer to him she wouldn't have needed to ask. As it was, he couldn't imagine anything worse than Christmas with his mother.

Jonah's mother was terrible with money and always had been, spending cash she didn't have, running up credit cards and taking out loans without telling him.

His dad had been a mild sort of man, happy to let her have her way in most things, but he was also wise. When he realised just how out of control her spending was, and that she'd been wasting most of her money on scratch cards and multiple lottery tickets, he'd taken professional advice and tied up their financial affairs in such a way that she couldn't inflict any more damage on them.

If his mother felt she was nothing more than a glorified squatter, that was her own fault, and nothing to do with either Tawnie or himself.

Instead of mentioning Christmas however, Mrs Brewster delivered a killer blow.

'Any word from that boy's father yet?'

Jonah inhaled sharply and Tawnie squeezed his hand.

'Jonah *is* Tommy's father, Mum,' she said firmly. 'You know that as well as I do.'

'Except he's not, is he?' His mother gazed steadily at Jonah. 'Well, am I wrong?'

'That,' Jonah said coldly, 'depends on your definition of father.'

She waved her hand at him, dismissing his words as if they meant nothing. 'You know perfectly well what I mean. Same as everyone else means. His biological dad. That's not you, and even you're not daft enough to say it is. Which reminds me, why does he insist on calling you daddy? You're not his daddy, and I sincerely hope you're not lying to him about it.'

'I've never lied to him,' Jonah said coldly. 'Tommy met his real father. He knows the truth. Like me, he doesn't care. As far as we're concerned I'm his daddy and that's that.'

'Hmm. So he met him, did he? More than I ever did, which is a pity, as I'd have a few home truths to tell that useless oxygen thief. So has he been in touch yet, or is he still letting you deal with his mess?'

Jonah glared at her as Tawnie gasped. 'Mum!'

'Tommy's not a mess,' Jonah managed, with some difficulty. 'Whatever you think or say, he's my son, and that's the end of it.'

'Oh for God's sake, Jonah,' she snapped. 'Grow up! You've been used long enough, don't you think?'

Despite his sister's hand on his arm, he leaned forward, his heart thudding with anger. 'Tommy is my boy! I officially adopted him years ago, and you know it. I'm his dad and that's all there is to it.'

'Oh yes, you adopted him, and whose bright idea was that, eh? She saw you coming. And now look at you, saddled with someone else's kid, having to turn down work to look after him, running yourself ragged for him while his real father gets to do what he pleases. You've got mug written across your forehead. You've always been the same.'

'You told her I've cut my hours?' Jonah asked Tawnie, hurt.

'I'm sorry,' she murmured. 'I never thought...'

'You never thought? Have you forgotten that she saves up every snippet of information about us to fashion into weapons?'

The door opened and Keith entered, carrying a tray of cups, teaspoons, a jug of milk, and a bowl of sugar.

'Tea,' he said brightly, then glanced round at them all and sighed. 'Help yourselves.'

'What a thing to say to me!' Mrs Brewster cried at Jonah, as if Keith had never interrupted them. 'Anyone would think I said things out of cruelty. All I ever do is try to help you, to make you see what's really going on. It makes me sick to see how you've been used and hurt, and I only want you to wake up and see it too.'

'When are you going to get it into your head—' Jonah broke off and leaned back in the sofa, his pulse racing as Tommy entered the room, followed by Lilly and Iris.

His heart melted as his little boy ran over to him and put his arms around Jonah's neck for a hug before clambering next to him on the settee.

'I went really high on the swing,' he announced, his eyes shining. 'Lilly pushed me proper hard, and I wasn't scared.'

'Weren't you? Good boy.' Jonah put his arm around his son and gave his mother a defiant stare.

She eyed Tommy coldly then turned to Lilly, smiling at the eleven-year-old who, with her fair hair and amiable expression, was the double of her father.

'Aren't you a good girl? Tell me, how are you getting on at your new school? Here—' she patted the arm of her chair. 'Come and sit with me and tell me all about it.'

Jonah felt sick, and Tawnie clearly knew it, as she quickly passed him his tea and said, 'Drink this.'

'Are you okay, Iris?' Keith asked, eyeing his eldest daughter doubtfully. She didn't look her usual lively self, that was true, and Jonah realised his mother had been right about one thing at least; Iris had hardly touched her dinner.

'Yeah, fine,' Iris said. 'Would you mind if I went upstairs to get on with my homework?'

Tawnie frowned. 'I thought you'd already done it?' As Iris shook her head she said, 'Oh, well of course, if you need to.'

'Such a good girl,' her mother said approvingly. 'All her homework to do and she still went outside to keep the boy occupied. Bless you, darling.'

Jonah stared at his mother so hard it was a wonder his eyes didn't explode. *The boy!* Who the hell did she think she was, talking about Tommy in those terms? And the difference in her attitude towards him and her treatment of Iris and Lilly was so obvious he wanted to scream.

As Iris headed out of the room, Jonah turned to Tawnie.

'Thanks a lot for the dinner but I think Tommy and I will be going home now.'

'So soon?' Keith asked, but Tawnie gave her husband a slight shake of the head, which he evidently interpreted correctly, as he said nothing more but merely sipped his tea, a resigned look on his face.

'Okay, Jonah. Thanks for coming.'

Jonah got to his feet and held out his hand to Tommy.

'Say thank you to Tawnie for the nice dinner, Tommy.'

'Thanks, Tawnie,' Tommy said, smiling at his aunt, who ruffled his hair and assured him he was very welcome. 'Bye, Keith. Bye, Lilly. Bye, Grandma.'

Jonah stiffened, seeing his mother look pointedly away from his son without acknowledging that he'd spoken to her. Not even trusting himself to speak, he gave Lilly a quick hug and called a goodbye to Iris, then headed towards the front door, his hand gripping Tommy's.

Tawnie was right behind him, and as he stepped outside she stood on the doorstep, her expression troubled.

'I'm so sorry you had to go through that again. She never learns, does she?'

'It's me who never learns. Did you see the way she ignored him?' he whispered, as Tommy peered through the bars of the gate and looked out on the lane with interest. 'I can't stand it, Tawnie. It makes me feel sick to my stomach. How can anyone be like that with a little boy who's done no harm to anyone? And to talk about his real father...'

'I know,' she murmured. 'I do know, honestly. But you're his real dad, Jonah, whatever she says. You're the only dad he's ever known. Ignore her. I'm sorry I made you come here, but I promise I won't again. You gave her one last chance and she blew it. That's on her, not you.'

He sighed. 'It's not your fault. You were only trying to put things right, but they never will be. If she can't accept Tommy as her grandson then I can't see any way forward for us. All this stuff about her only being this way because she cares about me is bullshit. She's a horrible woman, Tawnie. Dad knew it too. You know he did.'

'I know.' Tawnie managed a smile. 'Well, look on the bright side. At least you won't have to invite her round for Christmas dinner.'

'Yeah, there is that.' He smiled back. 'Take care, okay?'

'I will.' She kissed him lightly on the cheek. 'Just remember, we all accept Tommy as yours, and whatever his birth certificate says, that's what Tommy will always feel, too.'

He nodded and took Tommy's hand, then lifted him into his booster seat in the van and strapped him in. Giving Tawnie a final wave he climbed into the driving seat and headed away from his sister's house back towards Tuppenny Bridge.

As Tommy chatted happily beside him about how much he liked Lilly, and how much fun the swing had been, and could they have a swing in the garden, Jonah thought grimly about his mother's awful attitude.

He couldn't see why she wouldn't accept the situation. He loved Tommy, and none of what had happened was his son's fault. If anything, Jonah felt he owed Tommy a huge apology for the way he'd abandoned him—even if he had tried to put that right. Tommy had gone through a lot in his short life, and all Jonah wanted was to make it up to him and see that beautiful boy smiling.

He would do anything to make him happy. Tommy was all that mattered. Nothing and no one else would ever come close.

FIVE

Kat was sitting on a bench in the market place eating an apple. Hattie was fast asleep in her buggy, which wasn't surprising as Kat had taken her for a long walk around the town, going from the river all the way up to the railway station and back again. It was a bright, sunny day, but there was enough of a breeze to ensure Kat kept her jacket on, and periodically check that Hattie was warm enough.

Since it was Tuesday, the market wasn't on, and there was a peaceful atmosphere in Market Place today. With the children back at school and most of the holidaymakers having left, it was a convenient place to sit and think.

Unlike almost everyone she knew, she never liked sitting in the churchyard. So many people raved about the place and told her how they did their best thinking sitting on one of the benches there, but Kat didn't see the attraction.

It was full of graves. Who wanted to go and sit by those?

Churchyards, she thought, were for the dead, and she was staying as far away from them as possible. She was glad her mum had been cremated and her ashes scattered, so she didn't have to tend to any grave. Kat liked to surround herself with the living, and even though it was a quiet day in the town today, there were still enough signs of life to keep her spirits from spiralling downwards—something she badly needed.

Yesterday had been a low point. She'd struggled to see a way out of her dilemma and had done a fair bit of panicking, even a little bit of crying, which was something she rarely gave in to.

It was hard to stay positive, knowing that her only option appeared to be moving back to Whistlestop Cottage with her aunts, and as if it hadn't been difficult enough last time, she would now have Hattie with her, making things even more complicated and messy.

Maybe, she thought glumly, she should just buy a tent and camp out somewhere. Perhaps Eugenie Lavender would let her pitch up in the grounds of Lavender House? Or Joseph might let her camp in one of his paddocks in exchange for a little light work.

The way things were going it might be her only other option.

'Oh wow, you look happy.'

Kat glanced up and her stomach did an annoying and completely uncalled-for jig. Honestly, even abject misery didn't seem to have stifled her hormones. Funny how they only seemed to wake up around Jonah.

'I was being sarky by the way.' He grinned at her, and she forced herself to give him a casual smile back.

'Yeah, I gathered.'

He pointed to the space on the bench next to her. 'Do you mind?'

'Go ahead.' Oh heck, he was wearing *the jacket* again. In black jeans, and a moss green shirt he looked so hunky and attractive and downright *sexy*... She blinked, reining in her ridiculous thoughts while she still could. 'Are you not at work again?' she said, sounding grumpier than she'd intended in her attempt to prove to herself that she wasn't interested in him in *that* way.

'Don't you remember? Dental appointment.' He nudged her. 'Wow, not only do you look miserable, but you sound seriously fed up, too. What's up?'

'Believe me,' she said, 'you don't want to know.'

He shrugged and opened a paper bag, removing a sandwich from it.

'Hungry again?' she asked.

'Starving. I'm at a racing stable this afternoon and I'll have a lot of horses to see to, so I'll need plenty of energy, and I didn't have time to get breakfast this morning. I had an early call for work, and a few jobs to fit in before I broke off for the appointment, and Tommy was playing up this morning, refusing to eat breakfast and being very whingey. I just didn't have the patience for it, today of all days. Anyway, I ended up doing without something to eat and I'm pretty sure the dentist heard my stomach rumbling all the way through the examination.'

'Did you pass?' she asked, smiling in spite of herself.

'A plus. Come back in nine months' time. Do you remember the good old days when it was six months and dentists weren't harder to find than—erm, what's hard to find? I can't think of anything. Starvation's addled my brain.'

'A decent place to live in Tuppenny Bridge?' She hadn't meant to say that and wished she hadn't when he peered at her over his sandwich.

'You've got one of those, haven't you? Above Pennyfeather's?'

'Ah well, therein lies a tale.' Kat sighed heavily and took another bite of her apple.

Jonah watched her curiously as he chewed his cheese sandwich. He finally swallowed and said, 'Okay, you win. I'm intrigued. What's going on in that head of yours?'

'You really want to know?'

'I wouldn't ask if I didn't, would I?' he said reasonably. 'Besides, I've started eating my dinner now when I had every intention of taking it home and eating it there before I got changed and went back to work. You've thrown me off my schedule so the least you owe me is an explanation. What's wrong, Kat?'

There it was again—that funny, wobbly sensation in her tummy when he said her name. She mentally rolled her eyes at herself. Anyone would think she was fourteen.

'Nothing much,' she said, determined not to let him see how upset she really was. 'Just that the aunties are selling the wool shop, so I'll be out of a job. And since they're selling the entire building I'll also be out of a home.'

'They're making you homeless?' he asked incredulously.

'Not strictly speaking,' she said hastily. 'They've said I can go and live with them at Whistlestop Cottage, but honestly, can you imagine it?' She shook her head in despair. 'Me and Hattie crammed into that little place with all their clutter and tat. Oh!'

She threw her apple core in the nearest bin in disgust. 'Listen to me moaning. They've been nothing but kindness itself to me and here I am whining on about having to move in with them again, when they're about to lose their business.'

Jonah leaned back on the bench. 'I must admit, I'm amazed. I never thought those two would give up the wool shop. Besides, it's part of Tuppenny Bridge. It wouldn't be the same without Pennyfeather's.'

'It's not making much money apparently,' Kat said sadly. 'And to be honest, Jonah, I'm not surprised. Sometimes I wondered what they were paying me for, because I could be on my own in that shop for hours without a single customer. Even when the market place is heaving with tourists, few people bother coming into a wool shop. The only person doing any knitting around here seems to be me. I got loads done when I was waiting for customers.'

'So they really don't have a choice?'

'Not really.' She sighed. 'I can't blame them for selling up. I'm just being selfish, that's all. Worrying about how it affects me as if I'm all that matters.'

'Except,' he said gently, 'it affects Hattie too, and I'm sure you're much more worried about her than you are about yourself.'

Her eyes filled with tears; partly at the thought of Hattie growing up in Whistlestop Cottage, and partly because he'd *got* it, and she wasn't sure how many people would.

If it had just been her she'd have gritted her teeth and got on with it, but this was about Hattie. What kind of start was she giving her, crammed into a box room in the aunties' cottage, a place that looked more like a junk yard than a home?

'I need to earn money fast,' she said brokenly. 'I have to raise a deposit for my own place as soon as I can. But the thing is, how can I save up without a job? And,' she added before he could speak, 'where am I going to find somewhere to live anyway? Have you seen any decent-sized rental properties around here lately?'

'Only holiday lets,' he admitted, folding the empty sandwich bag and dropping it in the litter bin. He sat back down and stuck his hands in his jacket pockets. 'I see your dilemma. It's rough. I'm sorry, Kat.'

'Thank you.' Even though he hadn't offered any solutions, he'd been of some comfort. Just having someone to pour it all out to was something, and the way he'd said he was sorry, with that look in his eyes that told her he genuinely meant it... It was almost worth being miserable to see that expression in those blue-grey depths. Almost.

'There's always something, isn't there?' he said, leaning back and gazing up at the blue sky. 'Just when you think you've got one thing sorted another thing pops up and—' He broke off as his mobile phone began to ring. 'Sorry. Won't be a minute.'

She waited patiently as he answered the call, peering over to check Hattie was still okay. Her worries were immediately smothered by a lurch of complete and total love as she gazed at her daughter, who was fast asleep, her little hand curled into a fist which she held close to her mouth, while her tummy rose and fell with each precious breath. She was, without doubt, the most beautiful thing Kat had ever seen.

'Right, no problem. I'll be over straight away.' Jonah shoved his phone back in his jacket pocket and groaned. 'Great.'

'What is it?'

'It's Tommy. He's not well. The school wants me to collect him and take him home. Oh hell, I feel awful now. He was grizzly this morning and I was too busy to take any notice of him. I thought he was playing up.' He glanced at his watch. 'I guess I'll have to ring round, cancel work again this afternoon.'

Kat gave him a sympathetic look. 'It never ends does it?'

'Nope. You know, you think it's tough now, while Hattie's a baby? Make the most of it, because it just gets harder and harder as they grow up.' He laughed. 'Sorry, that sounds really depressing. As if you haven't got enough to worry about. Oh well, I'd better get off.'

Kat hesitated. 'Er, if you like I could pick Tommy up for you? I've got nothing else to do all day, so I could take him back to yours and mind him for you while you go back to work.'

Jonah stared at her. 'Are you serious?'

'Why not? That's if you don't mind me being in your house while you're out. And I'll have Hattie with me too, obviously.'

He thought about it. 'Tommy doesn't really know you,' he said slowly. 'I mean, he's seen you around, but he might be a bit wary, especially if he's not feeling well.'

'Okay,' Kat said. 'Well, it's up to you. Like I said, the offer's there.'

Jonah looked at her for a long moment, making Kat's legs go all shaky and weak. She gazed back at him, noting the fine lines around his eyes, and the flecks of gold among the blue-grey, and the thick fringe of black eyelashes, and wondered why it was that men always seemed to get the eyelashes women would kill for.

'Look, how about we both pick Tommy up?' Jonah suggested. 'We can walk him back to my place, and I'll see how ill he really is. Then, if he's okay with being left, I'll get off to work and you can stay at mine until I get home. If he's not okay with it, well I'll make you a coffee for your trouble anyway. How about that?'

Kat tried not to look too enthusiastic about being invited back to Forge Cottage.

'Sure. That's fine by me,' she said.

He beamed at her. 'You're an absolute star! Kat Pennyfeather, I could kiss you!'

She swallowed, anticipation making her heart race. To her disappointment, though, he jumped up and zipped up his jacket instead.

Okay, so he was speaking metaphorically. Well of course he was! For God's sake, get a grip, woman. It's just Jonah!

She took the handles of Hattie's buggy. 'Come on then,' she said stoically. 'Let's go and collect the patient.'

* * *

As it turned out, Tommy had earache. The school secretary advised Jonah that he probably wouldn't need to see a doctor unless the pain hadn't gone away after three days, or if it got any worse.

'Nice warm flannel on his ear and some liquid paracetamol for the pain,' she said, giving Tommy a sympathetic look. 'It's not nice but hopefully he won't need antibiotics. You wouldn't believe how many of our children have been sent home with earache over the years.'

Jonah thanked her but was googling earache before he'd even got out of the school gates.

'She's right,' he said at last, tucking his phone back in his pocket. 'No need for a GP appointment at the moment. Let's just hope it resolves itself.'

He put his arm around Tommy's shoulders. 'We'll soon get you home, mate. I'm sorry I didn't realise you weren't well this morning. I'd never have sent you to school if I had.'

Tommy nodded but seemed disinclined to talk, so they didn't push him, and soon arrived back at Forge Cottage.

'Come in,' Jonah said. 'I think you'll just about get the buggy through the front door as it is.'

Kat carefully manoeuvred the buggy into the spacious hallway and tucked it at the side of the front door, gazing around her as she did and admiring the surprisingly light and airy feel inside the cottage.

She recalled visiting here before, but that had been many years ago, when Jonah's dad was the farrier and his horrible mother lived here. Neither she nor any of her friends had felt the inclination to visit often, having been made to feel as welcome by Mrs Brewster as a dose of shingles.

Jonah steered Tommy into the living room.

'I'll just go and get him some paracetamol and a warm flannel from upstairs,' he said. 'Make yourself at home, Kat.'

Hattie had briefly woken up outside the school, but she'd dozed off again, so it was just Tommy she had to focus on as Jonah headed upstairs.

'Is it both ears, sweetie, or just one?' she asked him gently, noticing he was covering his right ear with his hand.

Tommy said, 'This one,' in a voice that clearly showed he wasn't feeling well. Kat's heart went out to him.

'Bless you. Your daddy will give you some medicine and you'll start to feel better very soon,' she promised him.

Tommy nodded and curled up on the sofa, clutching a cushion to the side of his head.

Jonah was back within minutes, bringing with him a digital thermometer, Tommy's duvet and pillow, and a cuddly Paddington Bear. He took Tommy's temperature and nodded.

'Slightly up but not too high,' he said. He gave Tommy a kindly smile. 'Here we are, mate. Let's get some of this medicine down you, see if it helps.'

He gave Tommy some liquid paracetamol then put the pillow under his head, before tucking him and Paddington under the duvet. What a good father he was, Kat thought, her insides melting as she watched him gently stroke Tommy's dark curls away from his ear before he placed the warm flannel on it.

'That should help,' he said. 'Try to get a bit of sleep if you can. Kat and I will just be in the kitchen, okay?'

Tommy nodded and Jonah motioned to Kat to follow him through into the next room.

She found herself in a large kitchen/diner, fitted with quite modern units and boasting an island of all things.

'I don't remember any of this from the last time I visited,' she said in surprise.

'No, well.' Jonah shrugged. 'I had a bit of work done on the place after Dad retired and moved out, and then Sofia...' His voice trailed off and he filled the kettle with water. 'Tea? Coffee?'

'Coffee please,' she said, slipping onto a stool at the island. 'So, are you going back to work after you've had a drink or not?'

Jonah turned back to her, his face showing indecision. 'I don't know,' he admitted. 'I mean, look at the state of him! I don't feel I should leave him like that.'

'But there's nothing you can do other than what you've already done,' she pointed out. 'Hopefully he'll be asleep most of the afternoon anyway, and if he's not he'll probably only be lying on the sofa. I can be here to take care of him. I'll keep changing the flannel and I'll make sure he's not in too much pain. You can't lose more work, Jonah. You've said yourself you've lost too much already, and anyway, don't you have to be at the racing stables?'

'I know, I know.'

He ran a hand through his hair, leaving it slightly ruffled and stuck up in parts. Kat fought the urge to reach out and smooth it down for him. He would think she'd gone mad if she did that. Perhaps she had. After all, this was Jonah. She'd known him forever and they were friends. This weird feeling she had about him was clearly a post-natal hormonal imbalance. Maybe she should see a doctor.

Obviously blissfully unaware of her secret and highly inap-propriate lust for him, Jonah blithely continued debating with himself whether he should go back to work or not, while he made coffee for the two of them and hunted around for biscuits.

He made Tommy some warm milk as they'd discovered the poor little mite hadn't even eaten his packed lunch and showed no interest in doing so.

Handing the milk to him a few minutes later, Jonah crouched down beside him and stroked his hair.

'How would you feel,' he asked Tommy hesitantly, 'if I were to leave you here with Kat and Hattie while I went off to work for a few hours? Would you mind that?'

Tommy eyed him worriedly, then looked at Kat, who gave him what she hoped was a reassuring smile.

'A nice afternoon on the settee,' Jonah continued. 'You can watch *Paddington* if you like.' He raised an eyebrow at Kat as if asking if she'd mind.

Kat smiled at Tommy. 'I've never seen that series,' she told him. 'We can watch it together if you like.'

'Okay,' Tommy murmured, and Kat wished she could take his pain away.

Jonah got to his feet and sighed. 'Well, I'll get off then if that's all right with you, Kat. You're sure you don't mind?'

'Absolutely positive. We'll be fine, won't we, Tommy?'

Tommy gave a brief nod and Kat's eyes warmed with sympathy as she saw the look of angst on Jonah's face.

'Go,' she murmured. 'Get on with your work. I have your number. At least, I'm guessing you haven't changed it?'

He frowned. 'I changed it about three years ago. Not sure if I gave you the new number.'

'Probably not,' she admitted. 'We don't have cause to text each other, do we?'

'I suppose not.' He looked a bit sheepish. 'Well, have you still got the same number?'

'Same one I've had for about ten years,' she said.

'Great. I'll text you my new number so if anything happens —I mean, if Tommy needs me—just ring me straightaway, okay?'

'Promise.'

He quickly texted her his number and she confirmed she'd received the message.

'If you need anything from the kitchen just help yourself,' he told her. He leaned over and kissed his son gently.

'I'm going now, Tommy, but I'll be back before teatime, okay? Kat will look after you. Just you lie there and watch *Paddington* or have a bit of a nap if you can. Love you.'

'Love you, Daddy,' was Tommy's feeble response.

Jonah hovered for a moment then nodded at Kat and, without saying another word, he hurried upstairs to get changed. Five minutes later she heard the front door close and realised he'd gone to work.

Seconds later, Hattie started crying.

'Here's the remote, Tommy,' she said, handing it to the little boy. 'I'm going to take Hattie in the kitchen so she doesn't disturb you, but when she's had her dinner and settled we'll come back in here, okay?'

Tommy nodded, and Kat got up to fetch her daughter from the buggy. She heard the sound of Netflix starting up, and then the theme tune for *Paddington* began. Smiling to herself, she unstrapped Hattie and kissed her daughter.

'Let's get you sorted and then we've got an afternoon somewhere new for you to explore. Wait until you see how big the floor space is, Hattie. You'll love it!'

SIX

Tommy was no bother at all, having fallen asleep halfway through the second episode of *Paddington*. Hattie was a different prospect, being livelier than ever after her dinner and excited to find herself in new surroundings. She shuffled around on her bottom, exploring various parts of the living room and gurgling to herself in delight.

When she started to get a bit louder, Kat carried her into the kitchen, not wanting her to wake Tommy up.

As she held Hattie in her arms, she gazed around the large kitchen/diner with a gleam in her eyes. Now this was what she called a kitchen! There was not only an island, but a table and chairs, too, and even a sofa. She would kill to have this much space in her own flat.

She made herself a coffee and sat on the sofa, letting Hattie explore for a while. She'd already brought her daughter's favourite toy from the buggy in the hallway, and she kept Hattie amused, squeezing the bear's tummy and making it giggle. When Hattie giggled, too, Kat's heart leapt. Was there ever a lovelier sound than a baby's laughter, she wondered? If there was, she didn't think she'd ever heard it.

At about three o'clock her phone rang, and she felt a quiver of anticipation as she saw Jonah's name on the screen.

'Hi, Jonah.' Did that sound casual enough? She closed her eyes and mentally shook her head. Of course it did. How could he possibly know her heart was beating harder than it had since she was fourteen years old and had first set eyes on Marti Pellow's incredible smile when she saw him on *Top of the Pops*? That's how she felt right now. Fourteen again. It was pathetic.

'Hi, Kat. Just checking up on Tommy. How's he doing?'

'He's fast asleep,' she said. 'He didn't even manage to get through two episodes of *Paddington*. Hattie and I are in the kitchen, so we don't wake him up.'

'Oh no! That's not good. I never thought about that when I brought his duvet down,' he admitted. 'Are you okay in there? Comfy enough?'

'Are you joking? It's smashing in here. This sofa's better than the one I've got at home, and Hattie's fine. She's playing with her toy, and she's had a good look around. What time will you be home?'

'Oh, of course. You'll need to feed her, won't you? Look, I should be back by about a quarter past five, but if she needs her tea just help yourself. Does she eat proper food yet?' he added, sounding worried.

Kat laughed. 'Yes, she eats proper food. She's had some peanut butter sandwiches for her dinner—I hope that's okay? It seemed easiest. She usually has a cup of water with her tea, and a bottle of milk before bed. Shall I get your tea on for when you get back?'

'Don't be daft! I wouldn't expect you to do that,' he said immediately. 'No, just see to Hattie and I'll cook something for Tommy and me when I get back. That's if he wants to eat anything, of course. So he's okay? You're sure?'

'I'll know more when he wakes up,' she said, 'but honestly,

right now he's fast asleep and I wouldn't fret. Just get on with your work and you'll be home before you know it.'

'Thanks, Kat. I don't know what I'd have done without you,' he told her, before hanging up.

She gave a wistful sigh and eyed Hattie, who was gazing up at her in surprise, as if wondering who she was talking to.

'Your mum's gone batty,' she informed her. 'You should be ashamed of me.'

Hattie whooped with joy and Kat laughed, just as the kitchen door opened and Tommy appeared, holding his ear.

'Oh, sweetheart, we didn't wake you up, did we?' she asked anxiously.

Tommy gave a feeble shake of the head. 'Where's Daddy?'

'He's still at work,' Kat said, rushing to his side. She felt his forehead, relieved to find he wasn't too hot. 'Would you like something to drink? Or something to eat?'

'No. When will Daddy be home?'

'In a couple of hours. Shall I get you another warm flannel?'

'Yes please.'

Kat ushered him back into the living room and scooped up the flannel from the arm of the sofa. As Tommy climbed back under the duvet she hurried through to the kitchen and warmed it again before placing it on Tommy's poorly ear.

'Is there anything else you'd like?' she asked him.

'*The Sheep-Pig*,' he said hopefully.

Kat frowned. 'Which channel is that on?'

'It's my book,' he explained. 'Daddy's reading it to me at bedtime. It's on my bedside table.'

'Ah, right. Shall I fetch it?'

'Yes please.'

Kat nodded and collected Hattie from the kitchen, setting her down on the living room carpet with her bear.

'Can you watch her and make sure she doesn't get into any bother while I nip upstairs and fetch your book?'

Tommy said he would so Kat hurried upstairs and found herself on a spacious landing with no fewer than five doors. This cottage was twice the size of Whistlestop Cottage. Tentatively she opened each door in turn. The bathroom was large and beautifully tiled with a walk-in shower and a curved bath. She felt a pang of envy when she thought of her own tiny bathroom, which was no match for Hattie's collection of toys and toiletries.

Next was a decent-sized room which was obviously Tommy's. It was decorated with woodland animals wallpaper, which matched the pattern on his duvet cover downstairs. Kat spotted the book on his bedside table and collected it, pausing as she realised there was a framed photograph next to his lamp.

Sofia.

She swallowed, realising Jonah must have put it there for Tommy, and thinking what a lovely thing it was for him to do, given the circumstances. She gazed into Sofia's pretty face, remembering the few times she'd seen her around Tuppenny Bridge, hanging on Jonah's arm. Auburn-haired and very slender, she remembered. It was such a shame that she'd been taken so young.

She hovered on the landing, wondering if she dared take a peek in the other rooms.

Deciding she'd only regret it if she didn't, she opened the next door, which turned out to be empty. It wasn't quite as big as Tommy's room, but it was decorated in neutral shades of cream and had a thick cream carpet on the floor.

At the front of the house were two larger bedrooms. The first one was also empty. Evidently Jonah didn't have guests to stay at Forge Cottage. As Kat opened the second door she finally found herself gazing into the master bedroom. It wasn't as cluttered as Tommy's, nor was it as stark and masculine as she'd imagined.

With warm grey walls and an ecru carpet it could have

looked a bit cold, but it was warmed up with splashes of burnt orange in the cushions on his bed, the lightshade, and in a couple of pictures that hung on the wall. A knitted ecru throw on the bed and a deep buttoned-back headboard softened the overall look, and made this room feel welcoming and inviting. And that was without Jonah in it.

As Kat gazed at it she suddenly felt ashamed of herself. She had no business looking in his bedroom, which was his own private space. Quickly she shut the door and hurried downstairs, all too aware that she was blushing.

Tommy was peering over the top of the duvet watching Hattie, who was happily bashing her poor, long-suffering teddy bear on the floor.

'Has she behaved herself?' Kat asked him with a wink.

Tommy managed a smile, which was encouraging. 'She's funny,' he said. 'She laughed at me.'

'She can be very funny,' Kat agreed. 'Although sometimes she can be a little monster. Now, I've got your book. Do you want me to read it to you, or can you read it yourself?'

Tommy gave her a feeble look. 'Can you read it to me please?'

Kat settled herself on the sofa next to him and opened the book, finding a bookmark about halfway through.

'Are you ready?' she asked him, as he shuffled onto his back and lay there, the warm flannel pressed against one ear.

He nodded, and Kat began reading to him, occasionally raising her voice, or pausing for a moment, depending on how loud Hattie was with her gurgles and squeals.

After about twenty minutes, Tommy decided he'd heard enough, so Kat put away the book and switched *Paddington* on again. By four o'clock Hattie was beginning to fret, so she carried her back into the kitchen and hunted around for something suitable to feed her. Deciding on scrambled eggs with a slice of toast cut up into 'soldiers' Kat asked Tommy if he'd like some, too.

To her surprise, he said he would, so she made it for both children, serving Tommy his on a tray and setting Hattie's dish down on the floor, after spreading a clean towel out first to protect Jonah's carpet. She sat down beside her daughter and watched patiently as Hattie helped herself to the food—refusing help from Kat, naturally.

Half of the egg landed on the towel, but Kat had already foreseen that, and it didn't worry her. Hattie sucked and munched on the toast and Tommy managed a smile at the mess she'd made.

Kat collected up the towel, tipped the bits of soggy toast and scrambled egg into the bin, and put the towel in the empty washing machine, then gathered up Tommy's tray. She noticed he'd barely touched a thing and hoped he'd soon regain his appetite.

After she'd washed all the dishes she went back into the living room where Tommy was beginning to whimper. She checked the time, making sure it had been more than four hours since his last dose of medicine, then gave him some liquid paracetamol and changed his flannel. Soon he'd fallen asleep again.

Hattie quickly fell asleep in her arms, and she fastened her into her buggy so she was safe, then hunted in the kitchen for something for Jonah's tea. He'd said he didn't expect her to cook, but she thought it would be nice if he had a meal to come home to, and it wasn't as if she had anything else to do with both children asleep.

She boiled and mashed some potatoes and cooked him some sausages, adding garden peas to the plate just as he walked through the door.

'You're just in time!' She beamed at him and motioned to the meal she'd prepared him. 'I hope you like bangers and mash.'

'What's all this?' he asked, looking perplexed. 'I said you didn't have to bother.'

Her smile dropped. Had she done the wrong thing?

'Sorry. I just thought—well, I had nothing else to do with both kids asleep and I thought it would be nice...' Her voice trailed off and she swallowed.

He shook his head as if realising how rude he'd sounded. 'No, I'm sorry. I didn't mean it that way. I'm really grateful. Just surprised, that's all, and feeling like I've taken advantage of you.'

'Of course you haven't. It was my pleasure. I made Tommy some scrambled eggs on toast, by the way, but I'm afraid he didn't eat much. And he's had another dose of medicine.'

Jonah hurried to the sink to wash his hands as she put his plate on the table.

'Thanks so much, Kat. How's he been?'

'Not too bad. He got on well with Hattie. She even made him laugh. He's watched a bit of television, and I read some of *The Sheep-Pig* to him at his request.'

'Really? Aw, that's great. I popped my head around the door and saw him sleeping. Where's Hattie?'

'In her buggy, fast asleep in the hallway. You must have passed her when you came in.'

'Good job I wasn't singing then.'

She laughed. 'Do you usually sing when you arrive home?'

'Depends on my mood. Luckily I remembered Tommy might be asleep, so I behaved myself. Poor Hattie would have got one heck of a shock if I'd burst into song right next to her.'

He sat at the table and eyed the food appreciatively. 'This looks amazing. Just the job after the day I've had. Aren't you having any?'

'No, I need to get home. I just wanted to give you less to do when you got home in case Tommy's earache gets worse.'

'Hell, I hope it doesn't,' he said anxiously. 'Nothing worse than earache, is there? I had it a few years back, after I'd had a bad cold. Honestly, I'd rather have had toothache, that's how bad it was.'

'I know,' she said sympathetically. 'Just keep an eye on him and see how he goes.' She hesitated. 'Look, feel free to say no if you like, but I'm happy to come here tomorrow and the day after, if necessary, to look after him. That way you can go to work.'

He eyed her doubtfully. 'Are you sure? It's a lot to ask of you.'

'No it's not. I'm bored stiff in the flat anyway, and Hattie's enjoyed herself having more space to shuffle around. Plus she seems to like Tommy. Besides, it's not as if he's any bother. He's such a polite little boy, even when he's poorly. I can bring my knitting. It would be my pleasure, honestly.'

'Kat, I don't know what to say.' Jonah looked quite taken aback. 'That's so kind of you. Honestly, it would help me out so much, I'd be forever grateful.'

He got to his feet and rummaged in his pocket, pulling out his wallet. 'Here, you must take this—'

'I most certain must not!' Kat backed away, holding up her hands in protest. 'I don't want any money, Jonah! We're friends, aren't we? I'm just doing a friend a favour.'

'But if you don't take it I won't feel able to ask you again, and that would be a shame since you're such a good babysitter,' he said, tilting his head to the side and giving her a playful grin. 'Go on. You don't want to make me feel like I'm taking advantage, do you?'

There was an answer to that, but she couldn't possibly give it. Reluctantly she accepted one of the ten-pound notes he offered but refused the other one.

'That's more than enough,' she said firmly. 'Anyway, I'll be round tomorrow. Shall we say nine?'

'That would be perfect,' he said gratefully. 'Thanks so much, Kat. I really do appreciate it.'

'No worries. Now, sit down and eat your tea before it gets cold, and I'll take Hattie home. See you tomorrow, Jonah.'

* * *

Jonah was working late on Friday, because Kat had urged him to use the time she was minding Tommy to catch up on the many jobs he'd had to postpone for various reasons.

He'd normally have finished work before three o'clock, but it was almost six when he completed his rounds for the day and loaded the van to go home.

His heart lifted as he thought about the scene he'd got home to these past three nights. Tommy was feeling much better, and he'd clearly bonded with Kat and even Hattie.

Kat had been amazing. She was so gentle with Tommy, and had the patience of a saint, dealing with a poorly six-year-old and a baby who seemed to be into everything. She'd assured him she'd had an easy time of it, and had enjoyed herself, catching up on her knitting when the two children slept. On Wednesday she'd even found the time to wash and iron Tommy's uniform ready for his return to school on Monday and had made tea for them both that evening before she and Hattie had left for home, even though Tommy had eaten very little of it.

Last night she'd stayed longer. She'd sat at the table with him and Tommy, and they'd eaten tea together. He'd forgotten what it was like to have adult company when he got home from work. It was lovely having a proper conversation around the table, going over his day and chatting to her about local news and the sort of things he supposed Tawnie and Keith talked about every evening. He hadn't realised how much he missed it and was almost sorry that Tommy was well enough to return to school on Monday.

Tonight, he'd decided, he was going to treat them all as a thank you to her. Having rung Kat about an hour ago, he'd ascertained that she and Tommy would both love fish and chips for a change and had promised to call at Millican's for it on his way back.

Parking in the market place, he climbed out of his van and checked his pocket for his wallet, then strode purposefully towards the chippy, his stomach rumbling in anticipation.

'Jonah! Long time no see.'

Jonah turned as someone hailed him, and his face broke into a smile as he saw Noah Lavender walking towards him.

'Noah. How are you, mate? It's been a while.'

'I know. I often wonder how we can live in such a small town as this and yet rarely bump into anyone we know. Mind you, I guess we're both busy. I know I seem to spend most of my life behind a desk. Not like you, doing hard manual labour.'

'Yeah, that's why I'm such a hunk and you're so puny.' Jonah laughed at the expression of mock outrage on his friend's face. 'Only kidding, mate. I can imagine it must feel like hard, manual labour looking after all those kids.'

'You're not wrong there,' Noah admitted, as they walked in the direction of Millican's. 'Although they're easier to handle than some of the staff.' He laughed. 'And speaking of kids, how's Tommy? I heard he got sent home on Tuesday. Earache, wasn't it?'

'Yeah. He was in a lot of pain, and off his food. He's perked up a lot though. He'll be back at school on Monday, don't worry.'

'Glad to hear it.' Noah looked Jonah up and down, taking in his work clothes. 'So who's minding him now?'

'Kat Pennyfeather,' Jonah said. 'She's been brilliant.'

'Kat! Fancy that.' Noah was quiet for a moment. 'How is

Kat?' he asked as they reached the fish and chip shop and joined the queue. 'I haven't seen her for ages.'

'Oh, she's fine. You know Kat. She's—well—she's just Kat, isn't she?'

'Yeah.' Noah gave a short laugh. 'And the baby? Hattie, isn't it?'

'Oh, she's lovely. Gorgeous little thing. Tommy's really taken to her. She's been making him laugh apparently. He's trying to get her hooked on *Paddington* but she's not taking much notice at the moment.' He grinned. 'Are you having fish and chips tonight? Didn't think Isobel would go in for all that.'

'No, she doesn't,' Noah said, giving him a wry smile. 'She's visiting her mother for the weekend, so I'm free to buy what I like. I've been looking forward to this all week.'

Jonah saw the wistful expression in Noah's blue eyes and felt a pang of sympathy for his friend. It couldn't be easy living with someone as bossy as Isobel, that was certain.

'So how come Kat ended up looking after Tommy?' Noah asked, as they edged closer to the front of the queue.

Jonah had been eyeing the menu on the wall and was trying not to visibly drool as his nose twitched at the delicious smells emanating from the fryer, and his stomach growled in response.

'What? Oh, she was with me when I got the call from your school secretary about Tommy being ill.'

'Was she indeed?' Noah's eyebrows lifted in surprise. 'Do you both see much of each other then?'

'Me and Kat?' Jonah laughed. 'Not in the way you mean, that's for sure. It's Kat.'

'And?'

'What do you mean, *and*? And what? She's a mate, that's all. Come on, Noah, you know we go back years. We all do.'

'So what? Does that preclude some sort of romantic entanglement?'

'Romantic entanglement?' Jonah grinned and nudged his

friend. 'No wonder you're a headmaster. And in answer to your question, of course it does. It's Kat!'

'So you've said,' Noah said wryly. 'Maybe, as our dear friend William Shakespeare said, "The lady doth protest too much, methinks".'

'I'm no lady,' Jonah said, shaking his head.

'No, but Kat is. Who knows? Maybe you and she could make each other very happy.'

'Don't be daft! Besides, I'm not looking for anyone, thanks very much. Been there, done that. Never again.'

'Never? Never will feel like a long time.'

'So did being married to the wrong person,' Jonah said grimly.

'Well, I understand that. You were badly hurt by Sofia,' Noah acknowledged. 'Even so, you and Kat are both too lovely to be alone. And she's been alone a long time, after all.'

'Not that long,' Jonah reminded him. 'Hattie's only seven months old you know.'

'Hmm.' Noah shuffled forward as another customer left the shop. 'Did you ever find out who the father was? You don't have to tell me, obviously. Just curious.'

'No. I haven't asked her,' Jonah said. 'None of my business. Or anyone else's. But whoever it is, I don't think he's on the scene now. If he was, I'm pretty sure the Lavender Ladies would have sussed him out by now, don't you think?'

'Are you casting aspersions on my dear Aunt Eugenie?' Noah's eyes twinkled in amusement.

'Just stating facts,' Jonah replied. 'You know as well as I do that your great aunt, and Kat's two, are better than bloodhounds when they're on the track of something. If they haven't figured out who the dad is he can't be nearby, that's all I can think.'

'Yes, love, what can I get you?'

The woman behind the counter quickly took Jonah's order and shouted to the man behind the fryer to put more haddock in. She processed Jonah's payment then took Noah's order while the fish was frying.

'Just think,' Jonah said quietly as they stood waiting, 'if things had worked out differently, Kat might have been married to Leon now. Those two might have had kids. Funny how it all worked out.'

'Yes, I suppose so.' Noah sighed. 'I often think about that time.'

'They were good days,' Jonah said.

Noah gave an abrupt laugh. 'Not all of them.'

'Oh?' Jonah stared at him in surprise. 'Why not?'

Noah cleared his throat and rubbed his forehead. 'I, er, I just mean Leon's accident. That wasn't so good, was it?'

'Oh no. Well, obviously. That was... That was horrendous.'

'Nearly fourteen years.'

'Yes. Next month.' Jonah leaned on the counter, staring unseeingly at the menu. 'Can't believe how quickly it's gone.'

'Sometimes,' Noah mused, 'it seems like forever. I expect for Jennifer it's felt like decades.'

Jonah nodded, remembering how Leon's mum had withdrawn from the world after her eldest son's death. She was only now beginning to come out of her shell.

'Selling Monk's Folly was the best thing Ben could have done for his mum if you ask me,' Noah said. 'It can't have been good for them, rattling around that creepy old house with all those memories.' He nudged Jonah. 'Hey, speaking of the Callaghans, are you helping out on Sunday?'

'Oh of course, they're moving into Daisyfield Cottage, aren't they? I'd love to help, but it depends on Tommy and if I can get someone to mind him.' He gave Noah a surprised look. 'Why, are you?'

'Yes, I said I'd be there. I mean, if Isobel was home it might have been trickier, but with her away... I'd like to anyway.'

'Me too.' Jonah rubbed his chin. 'It will be weird not having Callaghans at Monk's Folly.'

'Ross will take good care of the place, don't worry.'

Jonah had no doubt about it. Noah's younger brother was an artist, like their famous ancestor, and he and Miss Lavender were opening the Callaghans' old home, Monk's Folly, as The Arabella Lavender Art Academy, named after Josiah's grand-daughter, herself an artist who had been forbidden to paint by her awful husband.

'Planning permission's gone through then?'

Noah rolled his eyes. 'Can you really see anyone refusing Aunt Eugenie? From what I gather it's pretty much a given, especially since it's not a listed building. The fact that it will provide a few jobs in the area goes in its favour, plus they don't want to change the look of the place from the outside, apart from smartening it up. I think Ross said there was some issue with access, and they'd have to do something about the road to Monk's Folly, but other than that it seems pretty straight-forward.'

'Ross will be in his element,' Jonah said. 'I'll see what I can do. About Sunday I mean,' he added, wondering if Kat intended to help the Callaghans move too.

'I hope you can make it,' Noah said. 'It will be fun, all of us mucking in.'

'Are you sure you're up to it? I mean, you're so used to sitting behind a desk, will you be able to lift furniture? I don't want to have to give you the kiss of life if it all proves too much for you.'

Noah shook his head, amused. 'Aren't you a comedian?'

The woman handed Jonah a wrapped parcel of fish and chips. 'There you go, love.'

'Thanks.'

Jonah nodded at Noah. 'Well, nice to see you, mate. I'd

better get back and dish this out before it gets cold. Enjoy your Isobel-free weekend.'

'Will do,' Noah said, smiling.

'If you're ever at a loose end you can pop round, you know. Any time.'

'Thanks, Jonah. I might just do that. Though,' he added, a smirk on his lips, 'I'd better ring first. Just in case you're busy with Kat.'

'Give over!' Jonah shook his head and laughed. 'If I can make it on Sunday I'll see you there.'

He took the fish and chips back to his van and put them on the passenger seat, then started the engine.

As if he'd be up to anything with Kat! Noah was off his tree even suggesting such a thing. After all, Kat wasn't a woman. Well, she *was* a woman obviously, but not that sort of woman. Not the sort of woman you'd ask out on a date, or curl up with in front of the television, or sit eating fish and chips with...

He frowned. She wasn't the sort of woman you'd get romantic with anyway. She was his friend. She'd been his friend for years. She'd been his best mate's girlfriend for God's sake! She was—well, she was just Kat.

He stared ahead of him in dismay, noticing that there was a new *For Sale* sign attached to the wall of Pennyfeather's Wool Shop.

So they were going ahead with it then? He hadn't really thought they would. It seemed impossible that their shop wouldn't sit in Market Place for at least another eighty years, the way it had for the last eighty. It had been part of his life since the beginning.

As had Kat.

But she was just Kat!

Shaking his head, he drove the van out of the market place and headed for home.

* * *

Kat had already agreed to help the Callaghans move into Daisyfield Cottage on the Sunday, having arranged for the aunties to babysit Hattie. She'd half considered asking Jonah if he planned to help too, but with Tommy being off colour, and not being too sure if he could get childcare, she didn't.

At least, she told herself that was the reason. Although in her more honest moments she had to admit that the thought of spending the entire day with him, mucking in to help their old friends, was too difficult to contemplate.

Being around Jonah, seeing him with Tommy, and pottering around his home the last few days, had only made her feelings for him deepen. He was such a good father, despite all the difficulties he faced, and she couldn't deny he was physically appealing too. And after all, a little bit of eye candy was always appreciated, right?

But putting him in the same space as the Callaghans, with all the feelings and memories attached to that family, would probably be overwhelming.

Jennifer was Leon's mother. Ben and Jamie were his younger brothers. Jonah was Leon's best friend. It was too much. When she was with the Callaghans, she was one version of herself. When she was with Jonah she was another version. She didn't think those two versions should meet. It seemed all wrong, somehow, that she'd be around Leon's family while her secret thoughts would be straying to another man. Especially that particular man.

Not, she thought, that the Callaghans would blame her for being attracted to someone else. She was quite sure they'd be happy if she moved on. After all, they hadn't said a single reproachful word to her about Hattie. It would just—well, it would be different if she was having these thoughts about a stranger, rather than Leon's best friend.

And anyway, it was all academic because Jonah clearly saw her as nothing more than *his* friend—a face from the past. Leon's girlfriend.

As they ate their fish and chips, though, Jonah casually mentioned that he'd bumped into Noah. 'He mentioned the Callaghans move to Daisyfield Cottage this Sunday. Are you planning to help?'

Kat had to admit she was. 'I'm sorry, I should have mentioned it,' she added.

'Why? You don't have to tell me everything you're doing,' he said quickly. Too quickly. She looked at him in surprise.

'I know that. I just mean, if you wanted me to have Tommy on Sunday, so you could help too, I won't be available.'

'Oh.' He nodded, looking slightly embarrassed. 'Yes, I see what you mean. Oh well...'

She hesitated, not sure if she was overwhelmed with guilt, or just downright masochistic.

'Maybe the aunties would look after Tommy? They're having Hattie for me, and I'm sure they wouldn't mind babysitting him too. It's not as if he's any trouble.'

Jonah gave her a doubtful look and she forced herself to shrug, as if the outcome of this conversation didn't matter one way or the other.

'It's up to you. I can ask them, but if you'd rather they didn't—'

'It's not that,' he'd said hastily. 'Just, are they really up to it? I mean, they're getting on a bit, aren't they?'

She gave him an indignant look. 'Do you really think I'd leave my seven-month-old baby with them if I had any doubts about their ability to cope?'

'Sorry, sorry. Of course not. Okay, well if you think they'd be up for it, thank you.' He sighed. 'I'd quite like to be there to help them to be honest—the Callaghans, I mean. It's going to be a big deal for them, leaving Monk's Folly.'

'Especially for Jennifer.' Kat was silent for a moment, thinking about Leon's mother, and all she'd gone through, not only losing her son, but also her husband a year later. Julian had been suffering from cancer for a couple of years. It made her tearful to think about it.

'At least she's moving on at last,' Jonah said comfortingly, as if reading her mind. 'The fact that she's willing to leave that house behind, and that she's accepted a job as cook at the art school when it opens is really positive, right?'

'Yes. And she's been round to dinner with Sally and Rafferty a few times too. Now Summer and Ben are a couple I suppose they'll welcome her into the family. They're like that, and it will do her good to be around such lovely people. Jennifer will be all right, I'm sure. I'm so glad about that.'

'So will you ask the aunties?' Jonah said. 'Or shall I?'

'I'll call them now if you like?'

He looked over at Tommy, who was eating chips, a look of bliss on his face. Kat was glad to see the little boy had regained his appetite anyway.

'What do you think, Tommy? Would you mind being looked after by Rita and Birdie while I help Ben's family move house?'

'The horse doctor?'

Jonah grinned. 'Yeah, the horse doctor. You can help them look after Hattie, too, if you like.'

Tommy had no objections, so Kat had duly telephoned the aunties, who were suspiciously excited that she'd asked them, and had assured her they'd be more than happy to look after Tommy for Jonah.

She ended the call and heaved a heavy sigh.

'What's up? No go?'

'Oh, they're happy to have Tommy,' she assured him. 'It's just...'

'What?' Jonah raised an eyebrow then gave her a crooked

smile. 'Let me guess. They're adding two and two together and making a million. Right?'

'They didn't exactly say anything, but they were clearly excited I was calling on your behalf, and you know what they're like,' she said apologetically. 'Don't be surprised if you hear about a new bet that's running any day now.'

He shrugged. 'Let them do their worst. As long as we know the truth—that we're just friends—it doesn't matter.'

'No,' she said faintly. 'I guess not.'

Kat and Jonah. Just friends. Well, that sorted that out.

SEVEN

Sunday dawned bright and clear, with a distinct nip in the air. The seasons were undoubtedly changing; the mid-September landscape subtly turning from green to gold and orange, as trees began to shed their summer clothing and adopt the autumn trends.

Some of the buildings in Tuppenny Bridge had already been decorated for the new season, with wreaths of tawny and amber leaves and red berries adorning front doors, and garlands strung across shop windows. The residents liked to make an effort, aware that soon the place would be flooded with visitors for the sheep fair at the end of the month, and were keen to make a good impression and show off their town at its best.

Harvest Festival at the church would take place on the second day of the fair, the first of October, and the volunteers who decorated All Hallows were already planning their autumn displays, under the watchful guidance of Miss Lavender, naturally.

A stiff breeze ruffled the trees and hedges as Kat and Jonah headed down Green Lane, having dropped off their children at

Whistlestop Cottage. Ahead of them they could see a few people were already on the riverbank: a small group of middle-aged people dressed for a hike; an elderly couple walking their dogs; a couple lying on their backs on a blanket, gazing up at the sky; a few children sitting with their feet dangling in the water, closely guarded by their watchful parents.

Kat noticed that the summer dresses and shorts and T-shirts of previous weeks had been replaced with jeans and jumpers, and thought it wouldn't be long before the riverbank was more or less empty on Sundays again.

But for now it was still a popular place to be. She knew that in a few hours the beer garden at the side of The Black Swan would be ringing with laughter and chatter as people gathered to spend time together, making the most of the dying days of summer while they could. As they crossed the bridge a group of riders on horses and ponies passed them, smiling and bidding them both a good morning. From All Hallows the church bells rang out, the sound carrying across the town, calling the worshippers to morning service.

She thought how lucky she was to live in Tuppenny Bridge, which must surely be the most picture-perfect place in the world. She couldn't understand her dad moving abroad. The thought that he might have dragged her away from this town if not for the aunties' intervention filled her with horror even now. She had so much to thank Rita and Birdie for, she must remember that, even though she'd seen the For Sale sign on the wool shop had gone up on Friday, when she'd returned home from Forge Cottage after the fish and chips.

Jonah had warned her, but it had still been a shock, and she felt a wave of sorrow for her aunties, knowing it must be even more traumatic for them.

Now, as she gazed up at Monk's Folly, standing alone on the hillside, she thought that soon, like the Callaghans, she'd be

starting somewhere new. She didn't want it to be Whistlestop
Cottage, she really didn't, but she had to admit that she'd rather
be there than leave Tuppenny Bridge.

If that was her only option to stay in this town she'd take it.
Rita and Birdie had saved her from being sent away once before,
and now they were offering to do it again. She just wished she
could think of a way to save their shop for them.

'Looks like they've already started,' Jonah said, nudging her
before nodding towards Monk's Folly, where Kat could see a
furniture van had somehow managed to make its way along the
rough, riverside track and pull up outside the house.

The far side of that stretch of the river was a different thing
entirely to the town side. It was wilder for a start; nature having
been allowed to have its way there. There were no buildings
other than Monk's Folly, and few people ventured along that
stretch of the riverbank, ensuring that trees and shrubs and
flowers flourished undisturbed, providing homes for wildlife.
Although Far Bank, as the locals called it, was just as beautiful
in its way—perhaps more so in some respects—than Near Bank,
Kat thought she wouldn't like to live at that house, so cut off
from the town that lay just across the bridge and a million miles
from it.

She was glad Jennifer was finally getting out of there and
thought the art school was the perfect use for the house. It
would be full of people at last, and those views would keep the
students happy for sure. It had been a brilliant idea of Eugenie
and Ross Lavender's.

When they ventured up the path to Monk's Folly, they
were greeted by two men who were huffing and puffing as they
carried the Callaghans' ancient wardrobe to the van. It must
have been there since before Jennifer married Julian, Kat
thought. Possibly before Julian was even born. She tried not to
judge but thought if it was down to her she'd have left it behind
or burned it.

'Awful, isn't it?'

She spun round, blushing with embarrassment as if her thoughts had appeared in a speech bubble over her head, but relieved to see Sally standing in the doorway, rather than Jennifer.

'Well...'

Sally laughed. 'Don't worry, Jennifer's said the same. It's not going to the cottage with them. The van's here to take the rubbish to the tip, including that awful old wardrobe and several other pieces of furniture that the charity shops turned down.'

'Really?'

'Who'd want them? Let's be honest, would you? Talk about dark and gloomy.'

'You're absolutely right, Sally.' Jennifer came to stand on the doorstep and put her hand on Sally's shoulder. 'I always hated that thing, and I'll be glad to see the back of it. It says it all when you can't even give your furniture away. The van's already nearly full. Our old sofa's in there too, and good riddance.'

She beamed at them all. 'Good morning, Kat and Jonah. It's really good of you to help like this. It's going to be quite a party!'

She hurried back inside, and Sally turned back to Kat.

'Is she all right?' Kat asked. 'I thought she'd be in a bit of a state to be honest, but she seems okay. Or is that an act?'

'Nope, she genuinely does seem to be looking forward to leaving this place for good,' Sally said. 'She's been dead excited buying new stuff for the cottage. Well, it's been that long since she's been able to afford anything, who can blame her? The proceeds from the sale of Monk's Folly have changed her life, even if, strictly speaking, it's Ben's house and Ben's money. It's been a blessing that it moved forward so quickly, but with no chain on either side there wasn't much to hold it up. The sooner she puts this place behind her the better, I reckon.'

At that moment, Ben and Noah came out, carrying a chest

of drawers that, if anything, looked even uglier than the wardrobe.

'Jonah, at last! Thought you were never coming,' Noah said, letting out a sigh of relief as they placed the chest on the ground. 'Hi, Kat. Nice to see you, too.'

'Hiya, Noah. Looks like we've a fun day ahead of us. Where do you want us to start?' Kat asked.

'All the furniture in the living room is for this van,' Ben explained. 'It's all going to the tip. Anything that the charity shop would accept went yesterday, and I've already taken loads of junk in the Land Rover to be disposed of during the last couple of weeks.'

'What are you actually keeping?' Jonah asked. 'And is it going on the van after they've been to the tip?'

Ben shook his head. 'We've bought new, modern furniture for the cottage. It was all delivered straight there, during the last week or two. Mr Eckington was kind enough to let us have the keys before the sale went through, which was good of him. All that's to go to the cottage now is smaller stuff like bedding and Mum's kitchen stuff, Jamie's desk and laptop, that sort of thing, plus our personal stuff obviously.'

'We've had a busy time of it,' Sally confirmed. 'Carpets got fitted on Thursday, didn't they, Ben? And me and Jennifer were hanging curtains all last week. It's been proper exciting, seeing the cottage taking shape.'

Ben and Noah picked up the chest of drawers again and lugged it over to the van. They placed it on the tailgate and stood chatting for a few minutes to the removal men, who were scratching their heads and clearly wondering if all the Callaghans' surplus furniture was going to fit in one journey.

Sally's daughter and Ben's girlfriend, Summer, came to the door. 'Thought I heard voices. Do you want a cuppa before you get started?'

'I think it's time we all had one,' Sally said. 'I mean, we've been hard at work for, ooh, at least an hour. I'll put the kettle on, love. You show Kat and Jonah where they're needed.'

For the next few hours the team worked hard to empty Monk's Folly. Jonah had offered his van, but Ben had insisted there was no need. The removal men managed to take all the surplus furniture to the nearest tip in two journeys, and soon the van was filled with the bits that the Callaghans were keeping.

Various cardboard boxes filled up with remnants of a family's life, now changed forever. There were some light hearted arguments about a few of the items, as not everyone agreed they were worth keeping.

'Your recorder!' Ben laughed and waved the instrument at his teenage brother, Jamie. 'Remember that? Give us a chorus of "Three Blind Mice". Go on, I dare you.'

Jamie pulled a face. 'It wasn't my idea to learn the recorder,' he insisted. 'I mean, it's not exactly cool, is it?'

'Not the way you played it,' Jennifer said, her eyes twinkling. 'I've never heard such a frightful din. If only we'd had noise-cancelling headphones. Even so, I don't want to part with it. I have happy memories of you learning "London's Burning" on that thing.'

Kat smiled, glad to see Jennifer looking so relaxed and happy. She'd worried that leaving Monk's Folly would be a wrench for her, but if anything the prospect of moving seemed to have given her a new lease of life. She looked healthier than she'd looked since—well, a long time.

'Are we keeping this?' Ben asked, a sudden change in his tone. He pointed to a battered suitcase on the floor. 'I know you said you'd think about it but if you want me to take it to the charity shop tomorrow I can.'

'I think we'll keep it,' Jennifer said quietly. 'For now. We've thrown enough of the past away, Ben. Just give me a bit longer, eh?'

He nodded and hugged her. 'Right, this can go in the Land Rover then,' he said, lifting it up and carrying it outside.

Jennifer gave them all a sheepish look. 'I know it's silly,' she said. 'They're only old clothes of Leon's and Julian's, and I should really have got rid of them by now, but I can't quite bring myself to. Not yet.'

Sally put her arm around Jennifer's shoulders. 'You've been amazing, love. You've come on in leaps and bounds. There's no hurry is there? And if you never get rid of them, so what? No law against it, is there?'

'I suppose not,' Jennifer said, giving her a grateful smile. 'Thanks, Sally.'

As she went back upstairs to check everything had been brought down, Kat and Sally exchanged compassionate looks.

'Bless her. I think there's more stuff of theirs here, too, but like I said, she'll get rid of it in her own good time. Or not. Whatever.'

From the corner of her eye, Kat spotted a small box of photograph albums. Jamie spotted it at the same time, and before she'd even realised what he was doing he'd pulled the box over and lifted one of the albums out.

'Look at this!' he exclaimed, glancing up at them all with amusement in his eyes. 'You're all in it. Oh boy, look how young you all look!'

'I suppose you're amazed they're in colour and not sepia.' Noah shook his head. 'How old do you think we are?'

'But look,' Jamie said, holding up the album, 'you've got to admit you've aged a lot since then!'

They all fell quiet as their gazes fixed on the photographs he was showing them. The gang of five. Jonah, Kat, Noah, Isobel—and Leon.

There they were, smiling back at their older selves, not a care in the world. No idea that, in less than four years their lives would be altered forever. Eighteen years old with their whole futures ahead of them.

There was Leon, dark-haired and grinning, his arm draped over Kat's shoulder; Kat, her long, light brown hair in a ponytail, leaning into him, arms folded in a casual, relaxed manner as she smiled for the photographer; Jonah, the tallest of them even at that age, standing in the middle, looking as if he wasn't quite sure what to do with himself; Isobel, glamorous even then with her make-up and blonde hair, looking at Noah as if he was the bee's knees; and Noah himself, sandy-haired and slender, arm around Isobel's waist, beaming at the camera like the cat that had got the cream.

How long ago and far away it all seemed now.

Kat swallowed and turned away, not wanting to look any longer. She wandered outside and moved down the path towards the track. Finally reaching the gate, she leaned on it and gazed down over the river, wondering how many times she'd done the same thing with Leon at her side.

She'd tried to hang on to those memories; days when she and Leon had seemed like the perfect couple. They'd laughed and loved and been so sure that nothing would ever tear them apart. She'd been so proud of him when he started work at the brewery.

'Don't you wish I'd gone to university like Noah?' he'd teased.

'Of course not! I'm glad you're not going. I want you here with me, always.'

He'd kissed her then and she'd been so glad that he'd applied for a job at the Lusty Tup Brewery working with his dad. He was just as bright as Noah, as their A level results had proved, despite Noah's private education, but the academic life didn't appeal to him any more than it appealed to her. It was just one more thing they had in common.

'I don't know how poor Isobel's going to cope without him,'

Kat had murmured, feeling a pang of sympathy for Noah's girl-friend, perhaps for the first time.

'Oh, she'll manage. It will be worth it in the end. You know Isobel's got delusions of grandeur, being a St Egbert's pupil. She's determined Noah's going places. Besides, she's going to college to learn floristry, isn't she? She'll be too busy to miss him much.'

'And Jonah's starting his farriery apprenticeship soon,' she'd said wistfully. 'And here's me, stuck in a wool shop. I won't be qualified in anything.'

'Oh, what does it matter?' He'd put his arms around her and hugged her tightly. 'Each to their own. We're all different, and that's what makes the world go round.'

And he'd been right in his way. They *were* all different, yet somehow they stayed friends. Good friends. Spending as much time together as they could, laughing, having fun...

Until that night.

She shivered, pulling her jacket tighter around her.

'Are you okay?'

Jonah's voice was gentle behind her, and she turned her head, giving him a faint smile as he came to stand beside her, resting his elbows on the top of the gate.

'I'm fine,' she lied. 'Just needed a bit of fresh air.'

'I haven't forgotten,' he told her. 'It gets to me too, you know, even after all this time.'

She nodded. 'I know. Funny how you can go for days, even weeks not thinking about him at all, and then something happens and it's like you're right back there, in that moment.'

'It was always bound to be tricky,' he said. 'You're at his old home, helping his family. It was always going to be hard for you.'

'And you,' she reminded him. 'He was your best friend.'

'But he was your boyfriend,' he said. 'I know how much you two loved each other.'

She looked back at the house. 'We need to go back in, finish up. We're all heading to Daisyfield Cottage in a few minutes.'

He grinned. 'Have you heard about the decorating party?'

'What decorating party?'

'Jamie's idea apparently. He's come up with a cunning plan for us all to meet up at the cottage one weekend. They'll provide the food and drinks, and we'll bring our paintbrushes and old clothes and get stuck in redecorating the place for them.'

'Well!' Kat laughed. 'You've got to hand it to Jamie. He's not backwards in coming forwards, is he?'

It was one of Leon's sayings, and her smile died as she saw the look in Jonah's eyes and knew he'd remembered too.

'Come on,' he said kindly. 'Let's finish up here, shall we?'

She nodded and followed him back into Monk's Folly, her thoughts still with Leon. She knew Jonah grieved for him too of course, but it was different for him. When he remembered his friend, he could do so with warmth and happiness.

Whereas Kat... Her memories were clouded by that one bitter memory of their final meeting—a memory so painful it obliterated most of the happy ones she'd struggled so much to hold on to. She could see it all now, feel those emotions as if it were yesterday: her tears, Leon's face white with shock, their raised voices, the anger within her that she saw and heard reflected in him—an anger that was so unfamiliar, so alien to them that even now she reeled from the memory of it.

She wished, with all her heart, that she could remember Leon with the same ease and acceptance that Jonah did, but somehow she knew she would never be granted that privilege.

And if anyone here today knew the truth, what would they think then? Would it change their memories too? Would it make them look at Leon differently, or would they be so caught up in blaming Kat that they wouldn't see her side of the story at all?

God knows it had taken her long enough to see the picture clearly herself.

Leon and Jonah had been like brothers. If it came to a choice, Jonah was bound to see it from Leon's point of view. If he ever found out, maybe he'd never again see her as a friend. Maybe—just maybe—he'd never speak to her again.

EIGHT

'Happy anniversary!'

Jonah kissed Tawnie on the cheek and murmured in her ear, 'Mum's not here, is she?'

Tawnie laughed and ushered him into her home. 'No, you're okay. She's been and gone, early this morning. Come in and have a celebratory drink with us.'

'I wasn't sure if you'd be going out or something,' he admitted, steering Tommy into the living room ahead of Tawnie. 'After all, sixteen years of marriage is something worth celebrating.'

Keith was sitting in his favourite armchair in front of the television, and raised a glass of beer in Jonah's direction.

'We are celebrating,' he said, nodding at the glass. 'What more do you need really?'

Tawnie tutted and rolled her eyes. 'Ever the romantic. I've told him, he'd better splash out on our twentieth anniversary, and I mean big time. He can start saving now. A glass of beer and a night in front of the telly isn't going to cut it every year.'

Jonah laughed. 'She has a point.'

Keith groaned. 'Don't agree with her! Anyway, I got her a card and some flowers. What more does she want?'

'I'm truly blessed,' Tawnie said. She winked at Jonah. 'I'm guessing you'll want a cup of coffee?'

'Please. If I wasn't driving I'd finish off Keith's beer, but there you go.'

'What about you, Tommy?' Tawnie asked. 'We have some banana milkshake if you'd like some?'

Tommy nodded eagerly, just as Iris and Lilly entered the room.

'Hiya, Tommy. Do you want to come upstairs and watch a Disney film with us?' Iris asked him.

Tommy certainly did, so Tawnie said she'd bring drinks and biscuits upstairs for them in a few minutes.

'Iris is so kind to him,' Jonah observed as he followed his sister into the kitchen. 'You should be very proud of her.'

Tawnie flicked on the kettle and poured three glasses of milkshake, shaking her head slightly as she did so.

'I am, especially when she admitted she'd already done her homework. You know, when you and Mum were here for dinner? She just wanted to escape.'

Jonah raised an eyebrow. 'Escape? From what?'

Tawnie sighed. 'She heard what Mum was saying and she didn't like the way she was talking about you and Tommy. She was worried she'd end up saying something horrible to Mum so she got out of the way. How bad's that?'

'Very bad,' Jonah agreed. 'I wonder how Mum would feel if she realised she was alienating her own granddaughter?'

'Well, she can't say it isn't justified,' Tawnie said with feeling. 'Keith and I felt awful after you left—like we should have stuck up for you more.'

'You did stick up for us,' Jonah reassured her. 'And to be honest, it wouldn't have made a difference. She's never going to accept Tommy. I realise that now and I'm not going to waste any more time trying to get her to change her mind. It's her loss, not ours.'

'I know that. It's a shame. He's such a gorgeous little boy.'

She made the coffees and found a tin of biscuits. 'I'm just going to take drinks and snacks up to the kids,' she said. 'Can you take the coffees through? I only made two because Keith's happy with his beer.'

'No worries.'

Jonah went back into the living room while his sister headed upstairs with refreshments. He put the two mugs of coffee on the occasional table and sank into the other armchair.

'Anything good on?' he asked, nodding at the television.

'Not really,' Keith admitted, 'but I'm sure Tawnie will find some soppy film to watch after you've gone and that will be it for the evening. I'm making the most of it while I'm in charge of the remote.'

Tawnie came downstairs and sat on the sofa. 'They're all watching *Encanto*,' she said fondly. 'The girls really do love Tommy you know. They'll always be on his side.'

'I know, and I appreciate it.'

'So,' Keith said, nodding at the carrier bag Jonah had placed by the chair when he'd first entered the room. 'I spy a present. Is that for us?'

'Keith!' Tawnie shook her head. 'Honestly, he's got no manners, has he?'

'Are you saying you didn't spot it when he brought it in?'

'Well of course I did, but you don't go asking, do you?'

'I don't see why not,' Keith replied. 'It's clearly for us, since it's wrapped up in anniversary paper, so why shouldn't we hurry him along?'

Jonah laughed. 'It's okay. It is for you actually, although don't get your hopes up. It's just something I made a few months ago and put aside for you.'

'Something you made?' Keith looked thoughtful. 'What can

it be? It's not a model of the Taj Mahal made out of lollipop sticks is it?'

'Why would it be that? You do have random thoughts,' Tawnie said, smiling her thanks as Jonah handed her the present. 'Ooh, it's quite heavy. What is it?'

'Only one way to find out,' Keith said.

She unwrapped the present and her eyes widened with delight. 'Oh, Jonah! It's perfect! You made this? Really?'

Jonah's face burned with embarrassment. 'Yeah. Like I say, it's not much but...'

'Not much? It's gorgeous! Look, Keith.'

Tawnie held up the present, her eyes shining.

'Love,' Keith read. 'Very nice.'

'Very nice? It's brilliant!' She gazed at the metal sign on its stand in awe. 'Are all these letters made out of horseshoes?'

Jonah noted her obvious enthusiasm with some embarrassment. To his eyes his efforts weren't a patch on his dad's artwork. Still, this one had taken quite some time to make, so maybe he shouldn't be so dismissive. Tawnie clearly appreciated it anyway.

He'd worked on used horseshoes, turning them into four letters which spelled out the word 'LOVE'. The letter 'O' had been formed in a heart shape. Each letter had been joined to the next, then the whole word had been attached, by the lower points of the heart and the 'V' to another horseshoe, which lay flat and acted as a stand.

Sometimes he drilled holes into the letters instead of putting them on a stand, so people could hang them on their walls, but he'd decided Tawnie had so many family photos on her walls already there wouldn't be room for this, so he'd made it a standing ornament instead.

'They are,' Jonah said. 'I thought I might as well do something useful with them. They took some cleaning up I can tell you. Do you really like it?'

'I love it! I like the way you've replaced the letter "O" with a love heart. When did you start making things like this? Or is this the first one you've made?'

'I've been making them for ages,' he admitted. He hesitated. 'After I met Sofia I wanted to give her something special that I'd made with my own hands, and I started experimenting with different designs. I've got a few in the forge. Then, after she left I had a lot of empty evenings to fill, so I spent them making even more stuff. I do all sorts—lots of things made from recycled horseshoes, and other items too. Candle holders, fireside companion sets, that sort of thing.' He decided not to mention the more intricate objects of art he'd created, far from certain they were worth mentioning.

'Just like Dad used to,' she said softly. 'Why didn't you tell me?'

'It didn't seem that important at the time,' he said. 'To be honest, it was just a way of taking my mind off the empty house. Then, when Tommy came home I didn't have time to do it any longer, so I haven't really made anything for the past year.'

'Well, I think you've got a real talent. Dad would be so proud of you. And, hey, remember how much money he used to make from it? It was a very lucrative sideline as I recall.'

'Dad had time,' Jonah pointed out. 'He spent every weekend and evening in the forge to get away from Mum, didn't he?'

Tawnie laughed. 'I suppose he did. You ought to do something with it; show them to other people.'

Jonah ran a finger under his shirt collar. 'I—I sort of am,' he said awkwardly. 'Fact is, I've taken a stall at the sheep fair. I'm going to try to sell some of them. Well, I've got a whole stack of things just lying around in the forge, doing nothing, and I thought I might as well free up a bit of space. Not that I'm expecting to sell many, but if even one or two go it will be something.'

Keith frowned. 'I thought you were doing a couple of shoeing demonstrations at the show?'

'I am. I'll have to juggle the stall with those.'

'Or,' Keith said, 'here's a radical idea. You could get someone to man the stall for you.'

'Are you volunteering?' Jonah asked in amusement.

'Me? No chance, mate. I can't make it I'm afraid. I'll be away that weekend. My team are playing away.'

Knowing Keith's passion for his football team, Jonah knew there was no contest when it came to choosing between attending a sheep fair or following the team to their next away game. He couldn't blame his brother-in-law for that.

'I could help you out on the Sunday,' Tawnie said hesitantly, 'but I promised to take the girls up to Kirkby Skimmer on the Saturday. There's a new film that they wanted to see at the cinema, and we're going to make a day of it. Unless...'

'Unless what? Please tell me you're not suggesting Mum!' Jonah said, horrified at the thought. She'd hate his designs and would no doubt pour scorn on them anyway. The last thing he needed was the stress of her chipping in with her thoughts and criticisms.

'Actually,' Tawnie said, 'I was thinking of Kat.'

'Kat?'

'Don't say it like that! Why not, Kat? She's been really helpful with Tommy while he was poorly, so I'm sure she'd mind the stall for you. And you said she needs money for a deposit on a bigger place, so surely any extra cash would come in useful?'

'She's got Hattie to look after. Besides,' he added uncomfortably, 'she'll probably want to wander round the show, not be stuck selling, or more likely not selling, a bunch of my old tat.'

'Stop fishing for compliments,' Keith said. 'You know perfectly well it's not tat. Not if this item's anything to go by anyway.' He smirked. 'Bit touchy when it comes to Kat, aren't you?'

'Not at all, but she's probably had more than her fill of helping me out,' Jonah said. 'She spent half of last week looking after Tommy, remember.'

'Which was surprisingly noble of her,' Tawnie agreed. 'Did she and Tommy get on okay?'

Jonah eyed her suspiciously. 'Obviously, or I wouldn't have asked her to stay on until the Friday evening. What's your point?'

Tawnie's eyes widened. 'What point could I possibly be making?'

'I think she's asking if you fancy the girl, Jonah,' Keith said, raising his glass of beer and grinning at him. 'I'd quite like to know that, too.'

'Oh for goodness' sake, not you as well! Look, how many more times do I have to say this? She's just Kat!'

'What's that supposed to mean?' Tawnie demanded.

'It means—it means she's an old mate. I've known her most of my life, and there's absolutely nothing more to it than that. Do you really think I'm interested in any woman after what happened with Sofia?'

He broke off and rubbed his forehead wearily. 'I'm not going down that road again, and it should surely be obvious to you why Kat—of all women—is definitely out of bounds.'

'Because of Leon?' Keith asked, frowning.

'Or because of what happened with Tommy?' Tawnie said gently.

Jonah took a deep breath. 'Take your pick. Both. Anyway, even if neither of those reasons were there it still wouldn't happen. She's just Kat.'

'Oh! If you say *she's just Kat* one more time!' Tawnie playfully punched his arm in exasperation. 'All the same, putting aside any possible romantic thoughts about Kat, you've got to admit she was a godsend to you last week when Tommy was ill.'

'I'm not denying it,' Jonah said with feeling. 'I don't know what I'd have done without her.'

'It's a shame she won't be on maternity leave for much longer, but I suppose she'll be going back to work at the wool shop before too long, right?'

'Not exactly, no.'

'Oh?' Tawnie exchanged glances with Keith. 'Why not?'

'If you must know,' Jonah said, 'it turns out the Pennyfeathers are selling the shop. Apparently it's not making enough money, and that means she's going to lose her job and her home. Not the best news when you've got a baby daughter to support.'

'Oh no! Poor Kat. That's awful.' Tawnie's eyes were full of sympathy. 'Fancy the Pennyfeathers having to sell the shop. It's been in Tuppenny Bridge forever. It won't be the same without it.'

'Maybe not,' Keith said, 'but are you surprised? How many wool shops do you see around these days? I can't imagine any of them making much money.'

'You'd be surprised,' Tawnie said. 'Knitting's always been a big thing in the Dales, and there's been a growing interest lately among the younger generation. Will the Pennyfeathers be staying in the town?' she asked. 'I mean, they're not moving away or anything? It just wouldn't be right without them. They're funny old ducks, but even so.'

'I don't think Miss Lavender would let them move away,' Jonah said, laughing. 'They're her spies on the ground, so to speak. She relies on them to gather intelligence, and of course they do all the dirty work for her, organising the bets so she doesn't have to sully herself with it all, while she no doubt creams off the profits.'

'Well, that's something at least,' Tawnie said.

'Actually, they've offered Kat a room at their home, so she won't be on the streets anyway.'

'Really? Imagine living with Rita and Birdie,' Tawnie said.

'You lived with your mother for long enough,' Keith remarked. 'I should think living with those two would be a walk in the park compared to that.'

'Kat's dreading it,' Jonah admitted. 'Don't get me wrong, she loves her aunts to bits, but their cottage—well, you only have to look at the two of them to picture what their home looks like. Kat can't imagine how bad it's going to be when you add Hattie's things into the mix.'

'No,' Tawnie said slowly. 'I should imagine it will be an awful jumble.'

'She's got that look on her face,' Keith said, giving his wife a knowing look. 'I'd run for it, Jonah. She's up to something.'

'I'm not up to anything,' Tawnie said indignantly. 'Well,' she added as an afterthought, 'maybe I've just had an idea that could help both you and Kat, that's all.'

'He won't let her move in with him, love, so give it up,' Keith advised.

Jonah spluttered coffee in shock. 'Move in with me? I don't think so!'

'Oh, but before you dismiss it out of hand—'

'You're serious? Bloody hell, Tawnie, are you insane? After what I just said!'

'Will you just listen?' Tawnie put her mug back on the table and leaned towards him, her eyes eager. 'I was thinking of a business arrangement. Think about it! Kat needs a job and a home. You need someone to take care of Tommy and the house so you can get back to working full-time hours. Well, let Kat move in and both of you get what you want.'

Keith wrinkled his nose. 'Maybe Jonah doesn't want a baby under his roof for one thing.'

'He won't be responsible for her,' Tawnie protested. 'He

won't have to do anything for her. Besides, Jonah's good with children, you know he is. But he'll be out at work all day anyway, and the baby will be asleep after tea, so he won't have much to do with her. And,' she added excitedly, 'that will mean there'll be someone around at weekends so you can spend time in the forge making more of your designs! That could really take off you know, Jonah. A sideline like Dad's. It would probably pay for Kat's keep right there.'

'It would never work,' Jonah said, gripping his mug of coffee tightly. 'For one thing, why would she want to move in with me any more than she wants to move in with her aunts? The whole point is that she wants a place just for her and Hattie.'

'And maybe one day she'll be able to afford that, but right now her only option is the Pennyfeathers' cottage, and let's face it, Forge Cottage is probably paradise next to that. It's big and airy and modern and nothing like Whistlestop Cottage.'

Jonah frowned. 'Have you ever actually been inside Whistlestop Cottage?'

'Well, once I think. Years ago, when I was about twelve. I can't remember why.'

'I'm sure it's changed a lot since then.'

'Hmm, and probably for the worse, and it was bad enough then. Oh, come on, Jonah, are you honestly telling me that Kat would be better off there than at yours?'

'No, but... What about Tommy? It's not fair on him to expect him to put up with strangers.'

'Except they're not strangers,' Keith pointed out. 'Kat took care of him last week when he was poorly, and if Tommy didn't mind being around her and Hattie when he wasn't feeling too good, I can't see him minding now he's full of beans again. He'll probably love having them there.'

'And just think,' Tawnie added slyly, 'no more rushing around in the morning trying to get him ready for school in time, or worrying if he's ill and can't go in, or taking time off work because it's half term or whatever. You'll be able to get your business back up to full strength. Surely you can see that it's a great idea from your point of view?'

'She's right,' Keith said. 'Sorry, Jonah but it makes sense for both of you. You've got a couple of spare rooms at Forge Cottage, and plenty of living space, and a garden. Kat would have a home and breathing space to look for a job. You'll get peace of mind and the chance to make more than enough money to cover the expense. Plus, you'll have a bit of adult company for a change. That can only be a good thing if you ask me.'

'You see? If even Keith can see how much sense it makes you must realise it too!'

'Oh okay, you've made your point.' Jonah puffed out his cheeks, feeling slightly under attack. 'I'll think about it, okay? Now can we talk about something else please?'

The trouble was it *did* make sense. Everything Tawnie had said added up, and he could see that it would be a great solution for both him and Kat, not to mention Tommy and Hattie.

It wasn't that the arrangement wouldn't suit them that worried him. It was that the arrangement might suit them too much. He couldn't deny the thought of Kat moving in to Forge Cottage permanently had filled him with an excitement he really hadn't been expecting, but that was the problem.

He liked Kat. He'd always liked Kat, even when they were kids and she'd only ever had eyes for Leon. But she was his friend, nothing more, and he'd quite like it to stay that way. He couldn't deny, though, that ever since Noah's remarks he'd been forced to look at her in a different way, and quite frankly it terrified him.

He hadn't been exaggerating when he'd told Tawnie that Kat was the last person he should get involved with. The truth was, after everything he'd gone through with Sofia, he couldn't face it all happening again.

Having seen the way Kat had reacted at Monk's Folly when she'd come face to face with all those old memories of Leon, he realised her heart still lay with him, even after all this time. She clearly only saw him as a friend, and that was what he wanted and needed. So why had seeing her reaction to that old photo given him a feeling akin to a punch in the guts?

He knew he could be very useful to Kat, but could he really trust her not to break his heart the way Sofia had? If he let her into his life it would give her the opportunity to do just that, and he didn't think he could bear it.

Tawnie leaned forward and said quietly, 'She's not Sofia, Jonah. You know that really, don't you?'

He met her gaze and as she eyed him steadily he felt himself relax a little.

She was right. Kat wasn't Sofia. He'd known her forever, and she just wasn't made like his ex-wife. She would never do to him what Sofia had. He could trust her. The question was, could he trust himself?

NINE

Jonah dropped the foot of the bay pony whose hooves he'd been trimming, and straightened as Joseph Wilkinson, owner of Whispering Willows Horse Sanctuary, stroked its nose and told him what a good lad he'd been, standing so patiently.

'That should do him.'

Joseph nodded. 'Ta very much, Jonah. Good job as always. I heard you're going to be doing shoeing demonstrations at the fair again this year.'

'You heard right,' Jonah said, putting the rasp back into his toolbox. 'One on Saturday and one on Sunday afternoon. Will you be there?'

'I might have a wander round,' Joseph said. 'See how I feel.'

Jonah eyed him thoughtfully. Was it his imagination or did Joseph look tired? Obviously, running a horse sanctuary was hard work, and Joseph was in his mid to late sixties, but even so. And he seemed to have lost a bit of weight too.

'Are you feeling all right, Joseph?' he asked, picking up the toolbox and carrying it over to his van.

'Me? Right as rain. Got Little Miss Sunshine to help me out, haven't I?' He grinned and nodded across the yard, where

Jonah could hear Summer Fletcher—who worked at the sanctuary on a mostly voluntary basis in between shifts at The White Hart Inn—singing to herself as she mucked out one of the looseboxes.

Jonah pulled a face. 'Does she often sing?' If, he thought, you could call it singing, which was debatable.

'All the bloody time since she got with Ben Callaghan. Proper Pollyanna she is. It's sickening.' Joseph laughed. 'No, I'm happy for her, for them both. Everyone needs a bit of love in their life, don't they?'

'I suppose so.'

'Mind, I'll stick with horses if it's all the same to you. They're a lot less trouble than women from what I've heard.'

'Yeah... you're probably right there.' Jonah nodded. 'Are we all done then, Joseph?'

'We are, thanks. You've done a good job on Duggie's hooves. I love seeing them start off all mucky and rough and watching the way you peel all that off and leave them all shiny and bright. Proper satisfying to see it.'

'Satisfying to do, too,' Jonah agreed. 'Especially when a horse's feet have been neglected and the hooves are really overgrown.'

'Aye, who needs women?' Joseph laughed. 'Bank transfer all right?'

'Isn't it always?'

'I'll send it over this afternoon. Thanks, lad.' Joseph began to lead the pony across the yard. 'I'll try to pop over and watch one of your demonstrations,' he called over his shoulder.

'Honestly, you don't have to!'

'I'd like to support you. You never know, I might be the only bugger watching.'

Jonah laughed as he packed his equipment back in the van and removed his apron. Well, that was a cheery thought. He felt far more confident now. Not.

As he climbed into the driver's seat and slammed the door shut, he thought about the stall he'd taken, and his stomach turned over with nerves. He'd done shoeing demonstrations before and knew they usually attracted a good audience, but the stall was a different proposition.

What if no one wanted to buy any of his creations? He'd feel such a fool. What had possessed him to take it in the first place? Okay, he'd wanted to clear out some of the items that had been taking up space in his forge for over a year now, but he could have just taken them to a charity shop. Or a tip.

He should have quietly shoved them on the Callaghans' removal van he thought grimly. No one would ever have known, and he'd have been rid of them for good. As it was they were going to be on display for all the residents of Tuppenny Bridge to gawp at and discuss.

He'd already decided how much they were going to sell for, having looked online at comparable items, but now he was wondering if he should lower the prices. He might actually sell one or two if he reduced them to a few quid.

He glanced at the clock on the dashboard and grimaced. Half past two already! He'd need to collect Tommy from school soon, but if he hurried he'd be able to get to Maister's and get something in for tea. Stocks were running low, and he'd meant to do a big shop at the weekend, but Saturday had flown away from him and on Sunday he'd been busy with the Callaghans.

He drove to the small supermarket on Station Road, thinking he really did have to get his act together. There never seemed to be enough time to do anything to his satisfaction.

He ignored the quiet voice in his head that was busily reminding him of Tawnie's suggestion, and instead focused on something his dad had taught him.

'If something seems too good to be true it probably is.'

Having Kat at Forge Cottage seemed like the ideal solution,

but it came with too many risks, and he'd learned the hard way that some risks just weren't worth taking.

* * *

Parking up in Maister's car park, Jonah leapt down from the van, locked the door, and hurried towards the building, grabbing a trolley from the line outside the entrance.

'Don't be busy, don't be busy,' he muttered as he pushed it into the supermarket, his eyes quickly scanning the aisles to see how many customers were milling around. It was Thursday, so it shouldn't be too bad. Jonah could see it was nowhere near as busy as it was on a weekend, which was a relief.

He quickly threw a few items which would pass for healthy into the trolley, then wheeled it down the last aisle, his eyes swivelling left to right as he double checked he didn't need anything else.

'Sodding thing!'

He knew that voice, and as he glanced round his heart leapt upon seeing Kat. She was pushing Hattie in one of the bigger trolleys with the baby seats. At least, she was trying to.

'Uh-oh,' he said, giving her a sympathetic look. 'You've got one with a dodgy wheel!'

Kat looked up and her face broke into a smile, making his already fluttering heart beat even faster.

'Oh hiya, Jonah! Yeah, trust me. I don't know why but I always seem to pick a rogue trolley that just wants to go its own way. It's been a nightmare getting round here.'

'It's usually me who gets landed with one of those,' he admitted. He tickled Hattie under the chin, and she giggled and waved her arms at him.

'How's Tommy?' Kat asked, gritting her teeth as she attempted to manoeuvre the trolley into line.

Jonah took hold of the end of her trolley and helped her

steer it into position. 'He's much better thanks. Back to normal and back at school.' He hesitated. 'I think he quite misses having you around. You and Hattie.'

'Oh bless him. Does he?'

She sounded a bit distracted and he wondered if she was just being polite asking about Tommy, but wasn't really interested at all. He didn't reply, taking his place in the queue behind her.

After a few moments of awkward silence, she turned to face him and he realised, with dismay, that she had tears in her eyes.

'What's up?' he asked, concerned. 'Are you okay?'

'I'm being daft.' She shook her head. 'I mean, I knew it was coming. I just didn't think it would be so soon.'

'What?'

'It's the shop. Someone's coming to look at it today. They're going to be looking round the flat too. What if they like it, Jonah? What if they *buy* it?'

He heard the misery in her voice and his heart went out to her.

'Sabotage the viewing,' he suggested jokily, trying to cheer her up because he didn't know what else to do. 'Tell them there's mould, or damp, or you have mice.'

'I thought about it,' she admitted. 'I was going to leave one of Hattie's killer nappies hidden away behind the sofa or something and tell them it was the drains.'

'Oh, good idea!' he said, almost admiring her ingenuity while worrying a little at how devious she could be.

'Yeah, I thought so. But I can't, can I? I mean, it wouldn't be fair to the aunties. They don't want to sell any more than I want them to, but they have to. They *need* to. So I can't stop them or make it more difficult for them. I'll just have to go along with it and that's that.'

'I suppose you're right. Surely you don't have to be at the

viewing, though? They've got an estate agent seeing to it, haven't they? You could go out.'

'The aunties want me to be there, spying on them to find out what they want to turn the shop into. And Hattie will be asleep anyway, which is another thing. They'll have to keep out of her bedroom, whether they like it or not. Besides it's my flat. For now at least. I don't like the idea of strangers poking about while all my things are there.'

'Fair enough.' He watched, feeling helpless as she began to transfer the contents of her trolley to the conveyor belt. Despite his misgivings, Tawnie's words kept replaying themselves in his mind. Would Kat moving into Forge Cottage be the perfect solution to both their problems?

But what if it went wrong? There were so many ways it could end in disaster, even supposing she wanted to move in with him in the first place. She might hate the idea. She might think even living with Rita and Birdie would be less trouble than living with him and Tommy.

On the other hand, she might be so relieved and glad to have more space and less interference that she'd jump at the chance.

And if she did, and he didn't like it, what would happen then? She could refuse to leave. He'd be stuck with her. She could claim squatter's rights or something. They could end up hating each other.

He mentally shook his head, realising he was overthinking things as usual. Kat would never do something like that. She wasn't, he reminded himself yet again, Sofia.

'Kat—'

'Wow, you really like to cut corners, don't you?'

He blinked, confused, as she pointed at his trolley and laughed.

'Sorry?'

'Bagged salads, prepared veg, ready-made mash, a roast

chicken... It must take you all of five minutes to make tea for you and Tommy.'

He couldn't help but laugh too. 'You've got me. All I do is lay it all out, microwave the mash and veg and boil a kettle to make some instant gravy. Done. Hey, don't judge me. I'm a busy man.'

'Obviously.'

He glanced into her trolley and felt a pang of envy as he saw the food she'd bought. He remembered the meals she'd made for him and Tommy last week and his stomach gave an involuntary growl.

But he couldn't ask her to move in with him now, could he? She'd think he wanted her for her culinary skills.

Well, if they were housemates...

He swallowed. 'Kat—'

'Do you need a carrier bag, love?'

Too late. The woman on the check-out was talking to Kat and had already started scanning her shopping. She'd be too distracted to have this conversation with him now.

He chatted to Hattie while he waited, and smiled as the pretty, blue-eyed baby beamed back at him. He was almost sure Kat had green eyes. Was Hattie's father blue-eyed then?

Without even meaning to he found himself considering all the men he knew in Tuppenny Bridge, trying to remember what colour eyes they had. Ross Lavender had dark eyes, so dark they were noticeable. Noah's were blue, of course, but he definitely wasn't the type to cheat. He had to admit he wasn't sure about anyone else's. Besides, who else was there?

He realised what he was doing and tutted impatiently, annoyed with himself for going down that road. It was none of his business who Hattie's father was. Kat had made it perfectly clear that she wasn't saying, and that was her right. She must have her reasons for it.

Maybe he was married...

'All done.' Kat pulled the trolley towards her and dumped her three carrier bags in it. 'Why haven't you loaded your stuff onto the conveyor belt?'

Jonah realised he'd completely forgotten, and hurriedly unpacked his trolley while the checkout woman gave him an eye roll, as if he'd just confirmed her deepest suspicions that all men were basically useless.

He was surprised and, he had to admit, flattered when Kat waited for him. As he handed over his debit card he turned to her and said, 'I can give you a lift back if you like.'

'Oh no, there's no need. It's not far to walk,' she said. 'Besides, you'll need to pick Tommy up, won't you?'

He nodded. 'Won't take me long to drop you off though.'

'Quicker for you to go straight up Station Road onto Chestnut Lane. Honestly, thanks, but the walk will do me good.'

They wheeled their trollies out of Maister's and into the car park.

'Right,' Kat said with a heavy sigh, 'I guess I'll say goodbye then.'

'Good luck with the viewing,' Jonah said. 'I don't know if I want it to go well or really badly.'

'Same here,' she admitted. She lightly touched Hattie's cheek. 'We'll be okay, won't we, sweetie? As long as we're together what does it matter where we live?'

'Kat—' Having tried to start the conversation twice before and being interrupted both times, he found himself pausing as if waiting for yet another interruption. When she didn't say anything but stood, staring up at him as she waited for him to continue, he gulped, realising he had no choice but to ask her the question now.

'Er, I was wondering. Look, you can say no if you like, obviously, but how would you feel about moving into Forge Cottage?'

Kat's eyes widened and he realised he'd been right. Her eyes *were* green. A really gorgeous light green. He was surprised he'd remembered after all these years. His heart thudded.

'I mean,' he said, 'you *and* Hattie, obviously. I've got two spare rooms so it wouldn't be a problem, and there's plenty of space for your stuff. Tommy would love it, and there's a garden and everything...'

His voice trailed off as she continued to stare at him.

'It was just an idea,' he finished lamely.

'Are you serious?'

'Yeah, but look, you don't have to if you don't want to. I do understand—'

'How much would you charge?'

He blinked, not sure what she was talking about. 'Charge?'

'For rent. Only I won't have a job, and I'm not sure what help I'll get financially to tide me over until I find a new one that fits in with Hattie.' She swallowed as her voice cracked with emotion. 'I'm sorry. It's just when I think about it all it gets a bit overwhelming. I was going to take her with me to work at the wool shop you see. It wouldn't have been a problem. But what other employer is going to want a baby on the premises? And I haven't even started to look for childcare around here, and how I'll afford it is another thing entirely so—'

'I don't think you understand. I mean, I haven't made myself clear. I wouldn't charge you rent, Kat.'

She wiped her eyes and stepped back a little. 'Huh? What do you mean?'

There was a definite note of suspicion in her voice. What did she think he meant? Oh hell, did she think he was propositioning her? Or was he reading too much into it again? He seemed to do that a lot lately. Overthink. Worry. Fret about stuff that wasn't real.

'What I mean,' he said quickly, 'is that I was hoping—if it's okay with you—that you'd sort of do what you did last week.

You know, be there for Tommy after school and at weekends and holidays, maybe do a bit of shopping, cooking, that kind of thing?

'I'd pay you, as well of course. You'd be a sort of live-in housekeeper stroke nanny,' he continued, not wanting to sound as if he'd be taking advantage of her. 'I do realise that it's not your ideal solution. I know you want a place of your own, but I was thinking it would help us both out for now, until you find something better. Not,' he added hastily, 'that I'd be in any hurry for you to leave. But I do see it's probably more to my advantage than yours, so if you don't want to...'

She looked dazed, as if she couldn't believe what he was saying. Was that in a good way or a bad way? Jonah really wasn't sure.

'You do know Hattie has a lot of stuff? There'd be the buggy for a start, which would have to stay in your hallway. And then there's all her toys, and her playpen—although maybe I could set that up in her room if it's big enough.'

'It can go in the living room. It's not a problem.'

'What about Tommy? How would he feel about us living there?'

'I'll talk to him, but I don't think he'll have any objections. He enjoyed having you both round last week. To be honest, I think anything that makes me less stressed can only be good for him, and I'm sure we'd both benefit from your organisational skills. You can't do a worse job than me anyway.'

'What if Hattie's teething and she cries during the night and you've got to be at work in the morning?'

He frowned. 'What if Tommy has a nightmare and wakes you up and you've got to get up early with Hattie? It happens. I'm sure we both know what parenting involves by now.'

She watched him thoughtfully. 'Can I think about it?' she said at last.

He couldn't deny he felt disappointed. He supposed a part

of him had hoped she'd jump at the chance. Then again, he thought it was probably a good thing that she hadn't. When he'd broached the subject of Sofia moving in with him, she'd been installed in Forge Cottage, bags unpacked and her toothbrush in the bathroom before he'd had chance to finish the question.

'Of course,' he said. 'Take all the time you need.' He nodded at the carrier bags in his trolley. 'I'd better go. I've got a frozen cheesecake in there, which was stupid of me since I've got to collect Tommy in—' he glanced at his watch, 'less than five minutes! Bloody hell, I'll have to leave now. Look, just give it some thought and let me know. No pressure, honestly.'

'Thanks, Jonah. I'll do that.'

She smiled at him, and he smiled back, then ruffled Hattie's dark hair in a farewell gesture before quickly pushing the trolley to the van.

Well, he'd done it now. So much for avoiding risks. He supposed it was up to Kat where they went from here.

He really wished he could make up his mind whether he wanted her to accept or decline his offer. No doubt her reply would tell him the answer to that soon enough.

TEN

'Well, I think it's a great idea!' Sally handed Kat a mug of coffee and sat down next to her on the sofa. 'I don't understand why you didn't bite his hand off. It's the perfect solution.'

They were sitting in the living room of the flat above The White Hart Inn. Hattie was playing with some toys on the rug in front of them. Rafferty and Summer were both downstairs, working shifts in the pub. It was just Kat and Sally, and Kat had wasted no time telling her friend about Jonah's job offer the previous day.

'I'm worried I'll end up being his housekeeper for years,' she said reluctantly. 'I mean, I'm thirty-six now, Sally, and what have I done with my life? Worked in a wool shop since I left school and look where that's got me. I want to find a proper job, but how will I fit that around being there for Tommy?'

'I take your point,' Sally admitted. She placed her mug on the coffee table then squeezed Kat's arm in sympathy. 'Aw, look at your face. I can see it's not exactly the perfect solution, but maybe it's perfect for now. Even Jonah said it wouldn't be forever. Just until you find something suitable. And who knows, maybe you'll find a better job that fits in around Tommy. Either way, wouldn't living at Forge Cottage be better than living with Birdie and Rita? I mean, bless them they're lovely, and you know we all think the world of them, but actually *living* with them?' She shook her head. 'I can't see it working out, especially not with Hattie in tow.'

'I know, I know,' Kat said wretchedly. 'I get that, I do. I wasn't looking forward to moving back in to Whistlestop Cottage after all this time, but even so.'

'Even so what?' Sally frowned. 'Am I missing something? It seems to me Jonah's thrown you a lifeline, and I'm amazed you're not grabbing it with both hands.'

'Hey, he'll get just as much out of this as I will,' Kat pointed out. 'Built-in babysitter, meals on the table, clean house...'

'Has he asked you to cook and clean?'

'Not exactly,' Kat admitted reluctantly. 'At least, he didn't mention any cleaning. But what else am I going to do all day? I need to earn my keep and that's another worry. I'm going to feel obligated to him.'

'Okay, okay.' Sally held up her hands in surrender. 'Have it your way. I just don't think Jonah's that sort of man, but if you're not going to accept then what *are* you going to do?'

Kat put her mug on the coffee table next to Sally's and leaned back on the sofa. She clutched a cushion to her chest and rested her chin on it, feeling fed up. 'I don't know,' she admitted. 'That's the trouble.'

'How did the viewing go last night?' Sally smiled and nodded at Hattie as the baby showed her one of her toys. 'Did they seem interested in buying?'

'The woman seemed keen,' Kat admitted. 'Not sure it will happen though. Her brother was supposed to be viewing it with her, but he didn't turn up. It was all a bit awkward, and Mr Rustill—he's the estate agent—was obviously put out about it. Judging by the conversation the woman was having on the phone it seems they're buying the place together, but the brother is having second thoughts. Daisy, the woman, promised to book a second viewing and make sure her brother comes with her next time, but I'm not so sure. She seemed keener on the flat than the shop, too. Did a lot of measuring up. Anyway, someone else has made an appointment to view it so I'm not out of the woods yet.'

'Well, whether it gets sold next week or next month or next year, the fact is someone's going to buy it at some point, love.' Sally tilted her head, watching her with an understanding expression. 'I just think you should give Jonah's offer some consideration, that's all.' Her eyes narrowed suddenly. 'Unless I'm missing something.'

'Missing something?' Kat gave an unconvincing laugh. 'Like what?'

'You tell me.' Sally frowned. 'There *is* something, isn't there? You and Jonah get on all right, don't you? I thought you were mates from years ago?'

'We were! We are!' Kat squirmed, not sure how to explain it.

'Uh-oh!' Sally looked suddenly worried. 'You think he fancies you, is that it? Are you worried he's going to try it on with you?'

'Of course not!' Kat couldn't help but feel indignant on Jonah's behalf. 'He's not like that. It's just—'

'Just what?' Sally tutted. 'You're going to have to fill in the blanks for me here, love, because I'm not seeing your problem.'

Of course she wasn't, because she didn't know half the story, and Kat couldn't possibly fill her in on everything she didn't know. Maybe there was something she could admit though.

'I think—I think something's changed between me and Jonah lately,' she confessed. 'I don't know what it is, but it's like I'm seeing him in a whole new light. It's making me really uncomfortable.'

'In a bad way or a good way?' Sally asked curiously.

'I'm really not sure,' Kat said.

'Well, I mean do you think worse of him now than you did or better?'

'It's nothing bad,' Kat assured her. 'I just—he's always been just Jonah, you know? Like I told you, we've been friends since we were kids, and I never really looked at him before. But lately...'

'Ooh!' Sally's eyes widened in delight. 'You mean you fancy him!'

'I never said that!' Kat gave Hattie an anxious look, as if her baby daughter would be staring up at her accusingly, judging her mother for being a loose woman.

'You didn't have to. It's what you meant, isn't it?' Sally handed her the mug of coffee. 'Here, have a sip of this to lubricate your throat then tell me all about it.'

Kat laughed. 'What are you like?'

'Desperate for gossip. I haven't heard a whisper of this around town you know. Even the Lavender Ladies haven't got wind of it, so when did it start?'

'Nothing's started,' Kat said firmly. 'And it's not like it's anything tangible. Just a feeling that I'm not quite certain of yet.'

'Have you told Jonah?' Sally asked. 'Is that why he asked you to move in with him?'

'No! Bloody hell, no way. I couldn't face him if he ever thought—ever suspected—that I had these feelings about him. I'd die, Sal, honestly I would. He doesn't see me that way. He'd feel terrible if he knew.'

'But how do you know?'

'Because to him I was, and always will be, Leon's girlfriend.'

Sally's smile dropped. 'Aw, I forgot. He was Leon's best friend, wasn't he? But look, love, it was a long time ago. I'm sure he sees you differently now.'

'He doesn't act as if he does.'

'Well,' Sally said with a sigh, 'that's men for you, isn't it? You know what they say about leading a horse to water? Well, in a man's case you not only have to lead him there, but you also have to shove his bloody face in the trough, otherwise he won't even notice there's any water in it.'

'It's not so easy in our case,' Kat said. 'There are—issues. The thing is, Sal, if I do move in with him and he finds out how I feel he might freak out. He could chuck me and Hattie on the streets and then where would we be?'

'As if Jonah would do that! And even if he did—which he won't—you've still got the aunties as a backup plan. What have you got to lose?'

'My pride. My dignity. My friendship with Jonah.' Kat sighed. 'We've known each other so long it would be awful if we fell out over my stupid hormones.'

'Well, that's it!' Sally laughed. 'If it all goes pear-shaped just tell him it was your post-natal hormones and nothing to do with you at all. He'll believe it. Men get very nervous when you mention hormones and he won't want to delve too deeply. He'll just accept your word for it, and it will all be forgotten.'

'You've got an answer for everything, haven't you?'

'Yep. So what's it to be? Whistlestop Cottage or Forge Cottage?'

'Maybe,' Kat said gloomily, 'I should just claim squatter's rights at Monk's Folly while it's standing empty.'

'Except work will be starting there soon, and anyway, would you really like to live in that gothic monstrosity all by yourself?'

'I'd have Hattie.'

'Fat lot of good she'd be fighting off the ghosts of Arabella Lavender and her horrible husband.'

'Blimey, I'd forgotten about old Henry.'

'Lucky you. Anyway, the point is, what answer are you going to give Jonah?'

Now that, Kat thought, was the question.

Kat still hadn't fully made up her mind what she was going to say to Jonah when she pushed the buggy up the path and knocked on his front door early that evening. She had some vague notion that, maybe when she saw him, she'd know what to say.

As it was, when he opened the door and smiled down at her she had no clue whatsoever.

'Kat! This is a nice surprise. Come in.'

He stepped aside, holding the door open for her to push the buggy through into the hallway.

'She's asleep,' she told him in hushed tones. 'Am I okay to leave her in the buggy here? I can't believe she fell asleep to be honest. She's usually awake until around half seven these days. I suppose I'll pay for it later.'

'She'll be fine there,' Jonah reassured her. 'We'll leave the living room door open a little so we can hear her if she wakes up.'

She nodded nervously and followed him through into the living room, where Tommy was kneeling on the floor, his brow furrowed as he leaned over his colouring book, wax crayon in hand.

'Hiya, Tommy.' She smiled at him, and he raised his head and smiled back.

'Hiya, Kat. Look what I've done.' He lifted the book to show her the sterling job he'd made of colouring in a scene from *Encanto*.

'Wow, nice work!'

'Shall I take your coat?' Jonah offered.

'Thanks.' She shrugged it off and handed it to him and he padded quietly back into the hallway and hung it up for her.

'It's definitely turning chilly lately,' he said on his return. 'You can tell October's just around the corner. Would you like a cup of tea, coffee?'

'Coffee would be good,' Kat said. 'Ever since I had Hattie I only drink tea first thing and last thing at night. Unless I have hot chocolate at night, that is.'

Wow, talk about oversharing! As if he cared about any of that. Well, at least if he made her a cup of coffee it would occupy him for a few more minutes and give her a bit longer to work out what she was actually going to say to him.

'Shall we go into the kitchen? Tommy, will you do me a favour, buddy? Will you listen out and let us know if Hattie wakes up please?'

'Okay,' Tommy said cheerfully, as he continued his masterpiece.

Jonah led Kat into the kitchen/diner, where she slipped onto a stool at the island and half-listened as he prattled on about something that had happened at school today while she rehearsed various speeches in her head.

I'm sorry. I can't move in with you, Jonah. I've thought about it, but it just wouldn't work. It's not you, it's me. I'm an ungrateful sod and I'd rather be squashed into Crochet World with my ageing great aunts than live in comfort with you and Tommy. It's your own fault for being so damn gorgeous.

'So all I've heard for the last week is "We Plough the Fields and Scatter",' Jonah said, laughing.

Kat blinked. 'Huh?'

He gave her an odd look. '"We Plough the Fields and Scatter"? Remember that one?'

'Yessss,' she drew out, not sure where he was going with this.

'Well anyway, he's looking forward to it. I remember our harvest festival assemblies, do you? All those hampers we took to the nursing homes! I used to feel so awkward when the other kids brought fresh produce and my mother sent me with a tin of spaghetti hoops.' He laughed, his blue-grey eyes twinkling with amusement.

She had no idea why he was banging on about the harvest festival. She was too busy worrying what she was going to say to him when he inevitably asked her if she'd given his suggestion any thought. He must realise that was what she'd come round for. To say yes or no.

I'd love to move in with you, Jonah. Let's not bother with separate rooms. If you can squeeze your clothes into half a wardrobe I'm happy to do the same. Now let's lock lips and seal the deal.

'Would you like some ice cream?' He sounded awkward now. Clearly, her strange behaviour had made him uncomfortable. Before she could even answer he shrugged and rolled his eyes. 'Of course not, we've just established it's cold out there. Besides, you've probably only just had your tea. We've not long had ours, as you can probably tell from the mess in here. I usually tidy up when Tommy's gone to bed.'

I really can't move in with you, Jonah. Just the suggestion that I do has put this barrier between us, and if I actually lived with you imagine how awful it would be. We've been friends for too long, and what if living together pushes us into something else that neither of us can cope with? I mean, don't get me wrong, you're hot. You're really hot. I honestly don't know how I didn't notice it before, because now that I have, your utter gorgeousness is slapping me in the face every time I see you. You're seriously phwoar material, I mean, really...

'Here you go.'

As he handed her the mug of coffee Kat blurted, 'I'd love to.'

Jonah stared at her. 'Sorry?'

Oh no, no, no! That wasn't what you were supposed to say at all. But look at those baby blues! How can anyone blame me? Oh hell, what am I supposed to say now?

Her eyes fell on a large, half-wrapped package on the table.

'You're wrapping something?'

He gave her a puzzled look, as if he couldn't keep up with her conversation, which wasn't surprising.

'I was halfway through it when you knocked on the door. It's just a little housewarming gift for the Callaghans. Nothing much.'

Nothing much! As he lifted the wrapping paper she saw it was a wine rack, made from eight horseshoes fixed together. With four shoes at the front and four at the back, it would cradle four bottles of wine. It looked amazing.

'I've never seen anything like that,' she said, impressed.

'Hmm, well, it's nothing much. Just something I made ages ago and didn't know what to do with.'

'You *made* it?' Kat's eyes widened. 'Wow, Jonah. You should sell these!'

He cleared his throat. 'So, have you been thinking over what I said? I'm guessing that's why you're here?'

'I never even thought about getting them a housewarming present,' she admitted, feeling rather ashamed both for that and for cleverly skipping over his question.

'You've had enough to think about,' he said reassuringly. 'Besides, you helped them move, and you're going to their decorating party. That's present enough. Like I said, this is just some old stuff I had lying around from ages ago. No big deal.'

You're just a genuinely kind, thoughtful man, aren't you?

Her eyes fell on the washing up waiting to be done in the sink, and she thought about how harassed Jonah often was, and everything he'd had to deal with over the last few years. Even with all that, he could remember thoughtful gestures like housewarming presents, and helping his old friend's family move house.

There was no ulterior motive here. Jonah saw her as nothing more than a friend, and his offer had been made for the exact reasons he'd given her; because she needed a home for herself and Hattie, and because he needed someone to help him take care of Tommy. That was it.

Now that she had it all straight in her mind, there was nothing to stop her from accepting his generous offer, was there?

'If it's all right with you,' she said, giving him her very best smile, 'I'd love to move in.'

He looked genuinely delighted. 'That's great! Well, as soon as we've drunk these I'll show you to your room, shall I? When would you like to move in?'

'I guess the sooner the better,' she said. 'I didn't enjoy watching a prospective buyer plodding around my flat last night, and there's another one lined up next week.'

'I was thinking about you,' he replied sympathetically. 'It can't have been easy. Well, the rooms are available whenever you want them.'

'How about tomorrow?' she asked tentatively. If she took too long to think about it she might change her mind.

'Great! Tomorrow it is.' Jonah sipped his coffee, watching her thoughtfully. 'I'll see if we can get someone to watch the kids. I'll have to park in Little Market Place, what with it being Saturday. Have you told Rita and Birdie yet?'

'No,' she confessed. 'Look, Jonah, there's something I'd better warn you about. The aunties—well, you know as well as I do what they're like. If they find out I'm moving in here you can imagine what they'll think.'

'I can. No doubt there'll be a bet running on us before the week's out.'

'And you don't mind that?'

He shrugged. 'If you don't, why should I? Hey, don't look so worried. I won't hold you responsible for anything your aunties do or say. Look, it's like I told you before. As long as you and I know the truth it doesn't really matter, does it? We know it's just friendship and mutual convenience, so let them speculate. It's about time I gave them something to talk about anyway. It's been a while.'

He'd just confirmed that, whatever she was feeling for him, it wasn't reciprocated, and now that she knew it for sure she wouldn't make the mistake of ever letting him know what was in her heart. She could keep things strictly platonic, and there'd be no awkwardness and no heartbreak when it all went wrong, and he told her he could only ever see her as Leon's girlfriend.

So long as she kept her head and didn't open her mouth they'd be fine. Who knows? Maybe within a few months her hormones would settle down and this would all seem like some silly blip.

Jonah drained his mug and put it on the draining board, then ran a hand through his dark hair.

Kat swallowed. Who the hell did she think she was kidding? He was sex on a stick, and she couldn't blame her post-natal hormones for how her body was reacting to his.

This, she realised with a hint of panic, was going to be tougher than she'd realised.

ELEVEN

Jonah had very kindly offered to help Kat move her stuff over to Forge Cottage on Saturday morning. Ben repaid the favour the two of them had done him the previous weekend by helping Jonah load the bed, the wardrobe, and various other bits of bedroom furniture into the van, then helped him unload it at the other end.

Summer, meanwhile, amused Hattie and Tommy while Kat put away any last-minute items that were coming with them. When Ben and Jonah returned, Summer and Ben took Tommy and Hattie over to the flat above The White Hart Inn for a few hours while Jonah and Kat finished loading the van with the rest of Kat's stuff.

'Although,' Kat said, shaking her head in amazement, 'it's not really my stuff at all, is it? It's mostly Hattie's. How did she manage to take over my life in such a short space of time?'

'Tell me about it.' Jonah slammed the van doors shut and gave her a rueful grin. 'I often wonder what my life was like before Tommy arrived. Forge Cottage must have been almost empty. And I must have been so *bored*.'

'Oh to have the time to be bored now,' Kat said, climbing into the passenger seat.

Jonah laughed and she felt that weird fizzing sensation in her stomach again. It wasn't an unpleasant feeling, but it was an uncomfortable reminder that Jonah had the power to evoke emotions in her that she really shouldn't be experiencing.

Remember, we're housemates now. Not only that, strictly speaking he's my landlord and boss. I absolutely cannot think of him the way I'm thinking of him. Stop it! Stop it right now. He's Jonah, and he's a friend, and he's not interested!

He climbed in beside her and shut the door. Fastening his seatbelt he gave her a sympathetic look. 'All set? I know this must feel strange to you.'

You have no idea.

'All set,' she confirmed. 'Let's go.'

She'd promised herself she wouldn't look back, but as the van edged out of Little Market Place, she couldn't help it. The back view of the flat wasn't anywhere near as pretty as the front, but it still tugged at her heartstrings.

Jonah had parked round the back because it was Saturday and the market was on, so she didn't get that last look at her front window. He drove out of Little Market Place and straight along Station Road, so there was no final farewell to Pennyfeather's Wool Shop either.

It was ridiculous and she knew it. It wouldn't really be the last time she'd see the shop. She could see it any time she wanted. All she had to do was walk into the market place. But it was the last time she'd have seen it as her home. She wouldn't be able to go upstairs to her flat any longer, and in a few months the shop wouldn't be Pennyfeather's anymore.

It was, without doubt, the end of an era, and her eyes blurred with tears at the thought of it.

'Hey,' he said gently, 'are you okay?'

'I'm fine. I'm just being stupid.' She sniffed and wiped her eyes with the back of her hand.

'You're not being stupid. That place clearly means a lot to you. After all, it's Hattie's first home.'

She gazed at him in astonishment. How did he know what she'd been thinking? Even though she'd hoped to move out of the flat to somewhere bigger, it didn't alter the fact that it was the place she'd brought her daughter home to when they'd left hospital. It was, and always would be, Hattie's first home, and therefore would forever hold a special place in her heart. She just couldn't believe that Jonah had thought of that.

She watched him as he concentrated on the road ahead; the relaxed manner with which he drove, those large, masculine hands, so used to hard, heavy work, holding the steering wheel with a light, easy touch.

She gulped. 'You're amazing.'

'Sorry?' He turned to her, one eyebrow raised.

'It's amazing,' she said quickly. 'How attached you can get to a pile of bricks and mortar I mean.'

'Absolutely. But then again, I suppose both our homes have long family histories. Your great grandma started the wool shop, didn't she? And my family have been farriers and blacksmiths for generations, living in Forge Cottage. Mind you, it was half the size in my grandad's day.'

'It was?'

'Oh yes. Then he had the wisdom and foresight to marry the girl next door.' He laughed. 'When her parents died, the cottage was left to her, so they knocked through and made it one big house. That's why we have four good-sized bedrooms instead of two, and why we have a big kitchen/diner as well as a living room.'

'I thought it was odd,' Kat admitted. 'The aunties' cottage is much smaller. That explains it. Your grandad was very smart.'

'Oh, it wasn't a business move,' Jonah said. 'He genuinely

loved Granny to bits. They were very happy.' He drummed his fingers on the steering wheel as they waited in traffic at the junction of Station Road and Chestnut Lane. 'I vaguely remember them when I was little. They were very smiley and cuddly with each other even then. Shame Dad and I didn't have the same luck in our marriages.'

Kat looked at him in surprise. Obviously, she knew his own marriage to Sofia had ended in divorce, but she hadn't realised his parents' marriage had been unhappy. She remembered that not many people liked Mrs Brewster, but it hadn't occurred to her that her own husband hadn't been keen either.

'Sorry,' Jonah said. 'I shouldn't have said that. Anyway, let's not talk about such gloomy things. How are you feeling about moving in? Nervous?'

'Should I be?' she asked, trying to sound calm, even though her stomach was churning just at the thought of living under the same roof as him.

'No, you really shouldn't,' he reassured her. 'I promise I'll do everything I can to make you and Hattie feel at home.' He glanced over at her as the van entered Chestnut Lane at last. 'I really want this to work, Kat. For all our sakes.'

'Me too,' she managed. 'I'm sure we'll get along fine.'

As long as I keep my mouth shut and my feelings (and hands) to myself.

Once they arrived at Forge Cottage, it took depressingly little time to unload the van and get all her stuff inside.

'Not a lot to show for thirty-six years, is it?' she said, looking sadly at the few boxes that belonged to her.

'Well, if you ask me belongings are overrated,' Jonah said. 'We can't take it with us, after all, and you've already left your mark on the world in the form of Hattie. What more do you need?'

'Cheerful thought,' she observed.

'Come on, buck up and be a rabbit. I'll help you carry this

lot upstairs and then I'll see if I can put Hattie's cot back together for her.'

He was as good as his word, and while he set the cot up in Hattie's room, Kat unpacked her belongings in her new bedroom, thinking at least she didn't have to worry about decorating. The room was done quite beautifully already, in neutral shades of cream and taupe, with a duck-egg blue blind at the window.

Her wardrobe, chest of drawers, and double bed were in place, although Jonah said she only had to say if she would prefer them in a different position and he'd move them round for her. She assured him they were fine as they were, and began to make the bed up, then unpacked some of her personal belongings to give it a more familiar feeling.

The buggy, Jonah said, could easily stay in the hallway without causing any obstruction, and Hattie's playpen was portable and could go in any room she happened to be in, so that was all right. The baby's bath things, he added, could go in the bathroom with no problem.

'That's her cot done,' Jonah called. 'Just needs her bedding putting on now.'

Kat walked into Hattie's bedroom and shook her head. 'It blows me away how big this house is. I mean, this is the fourth room and it's still twice the size of her bedroom in the flat. I don't know how to thank you, Jonah.'

'You don't have to thank me,' he said seriously. 'You're the one who's doing me the favour, remember? I can finally relax knowing Tommy will be okay, no matter what, and that I can start to fill my workbook up with more jobs at last.' He smiled and got to his feet, then put his hands on her shoulders. 'I know it's not easy for you, moving in somewhere strange, but I hope you'll be happy here, Kat. I really do.'

She stared up at his kind face and her stomach fizzed again. He was looking at her with such gentleness and sincerity, and she was so tempted...

There was a loud knock on the front door, and she blinked, silently offering a prayer of thanks that someone had stopped her from making a total fool of herself.

Honestly, she'd only been here five minutes and already she'd almost kissed him! She had to be more careful. Keep those raging hormones in check or she'd never make this work.

Jonah cleared his throat and let her go. 'Who can that be?'

He left the room and was galloping downstairs before she could even begin to formulate an answer. Had he realised what she'd been about to do? She'd never live it down, and he'd be throwing her out before she'd even had chance for a cup of coffee.

'Kat, we've got visitors!'

Kat steadied herself, took a deep breath and went to the top of the stairs. She groaned inwardly, wondering why she hadn't guessed who it would be. Standing in Jonah's hallway were the aunties, along with none other than Eugenie Lavender.

'This is a surprise!'

Even as she said the words, she saw the amused look in Jonah's eyes and realised he was thinking, *Really? Is it?*

She ran downstairs and greeted her aunties with a hug, before looking awkwardly at Jonah.

'Is it okay if they come in?'

He laughed. 'Kat, you don't have to ask permission! This is your home now. Of course they can come in. Nice to see you, ladies. I'll put the kettle on.'

'Ooh, isn't he lovely?' Birdie said approvingly, as they all followed Kat into the living room. She nudged Rita and they both beamed at her.

Miss Lavender, meanwhile, gazed around her in obvious surprise. 'I hadn't realised how much difference knocking the two cottages together had made,' she said. 'This is quite spacious, isn't it? I remember George Brewster carrying out the work. We were never invited to have a look at the finished building.'

She said it with clear disapproval, as if she and her parents had had every right to inspect Forge Cottage after the work had been carried out, and Jonah's grandad had committed a grave sin by not allowing them to do so. Kat supposed that even a young version of Miss Lavender would have had a sense of entitlement.

'Look what we've brought you,' Birdie said, handing her a cake tin.

'I can't begin to guess what it is,' Kat said, smiling as she prised off the lid. It was a sponge cake, clearly decorated by her aunties because there was a rainbow of multi-coloured confection sprinkled over the icing, making the cake beneath almost impossible to glimpse. 'Aw, that's lovely. I'll take it through to the kitchen and we can all have a slice with our drinks.'

'Tell Jonah he can have an extra-large piece,' Rita said with a wink. 'We saw him lugging your furniture onto the van. He needs to keep up his strength.'

'He's very—*muscular*,' Birdie added, an appreciative gleam in her eyes.

'Only you could make that sound so disgusting,' Miss Lavender said, giving her a disapproving look. 'For heaven's sake take that look off your face, Birdie Pennyfeather. It's disgraceful at your age.'

'Well, you can't blame us,' Rita said, winking at Kat. 'You've landed yourself a proper hunk there, Kat. We're right pleased for you.'

'No, no!' Kat almost dropped the cake tin in her efforts to persuade them they were wrong in their assumption. 'Jonah and I are just friends. I've moved in here to care for Tommy so Jonah can get on with running his business. It's to our mutual benefit.'

'Too right it is,' Rita said, grinning.

'So you're not together?' Birdie asked wistfully.

Kat was very aware of three pairs of beady eyes watching her, waiting for some weakening of her defences. She wondered if the bet was already up and running or if they were holding off until they'd scouted Forge Cottage and gathered some intelligence.

She fixed them all with a stern look and said, as convincingly as she could manage, 'There's absolutely nothing between Jonah and me except friendship. We are not, and never will be together, so if that's what you're hoping you're sadly mistaken. It—well, it would be weird! I mean, he's just Jonah!'

'Tea or coffee?'

She spun round and inwardly groaned as she saw Jonah standing there. He must have heard every word she said, but he made no mention of it. He simply stood, smiling at the Lavender Ladies as if her statement meant nothing to him at all.

Which it obviously didn't.

'Tea please,' Miss Lavender said, and Rita and Birdie agreed. Jonah headed back into the kitchen, and she wanted to follow him and explain that she'd just said those things to make sure they didn't start running a book on the two of them, but how could she?

As far as he was concerned, she'd been speaking the truth. She'd probably just voiced his own opinion anyway.

'Don't forget to give him the cake,' Birdie said pointedly, and Kat glanced down at the tin in her hands.

'Oh yes, of course. Take a seat, ladies. I won't be a moment.'

She hurried into the kitchen and put the tin on the worktop.

'They've made us a cake,' she said.

He peered at the colourful sponge inside the tin and laughed. 'Well, even if I hadn't known who brought it I'd have guessed. That's got Rita and Birdie all over it.'

'I know it looks awful,' she said, 'but it will taste good.'

'Great. I'm up for a slice if you're offering.'

She took five small plates from the cupboard and put them

on a tray, then placed the cake on a larger plate, along with a knife.

'You go through,' Jonah said. 'I'll bring their teas and our coffees in.'

Kat realised he hadn't asked her if she wanted tea or coffee, and wondered how he knew what she would have chosen.

'You've made me coffee?'

He frowned. 'That's what you like isn't it? Tea at breakfast, coffee throughout the day, and tea or hot chocolate at bedtime, depending on your mood and the weather, I expect. I remembered it right, didn't I?'

'Remembered it...' Kat's voice trailed off. She recalled saying that to him the other day. It had been a throwaway remark, and she was amazed he'd remembered it at all. 'Yes, that's right. Thank you.'

She took the tray into the living room and set it down on the coffee table.

'Help yourselves,' she told them, and they did. At least, Rita and Birdie did, although Miss Lavender seemed reluctant to do so, forcing Kat to cut her a slice and pass it to her, receiving a nod of thanks in return.

'What have you done with the furniture, Kat?' Rita asked, her cheeks bulging with sponge cake. 'We noticed the bedroom stuff going in the van, but never saw anything else.'

'You were watching us, were you?' Kat asked knowingly.

'Oh, we just happened to be in Little Market Place,' Birdie assured her. 'We'd have stopped to help but we knew we'd only get in your way.'

'And Jonah seemed to have everything under control,' Rita added.

Miss Lavender rolled her eyes. 'I expect you won't be needing a lot of your furniture will you, Katherine? Your cooker, for example.'

'No, at the moment they're still in the flat,' she admitted.

'But don't worry, I've put them all up for sale and if I haven't managed to sell them before the flat goes I'll see if a charity shop wants them.'

'You're expecting to be here a long time then?' Birdie asked shrewdly.

Kat sighed inwardly. 'Until I can find somewhere else. Jonah's kindly said there's no rush.'

'Well, it's bigger than our cottage, that's for sure,' Rita said. 'I suppose we can't blame you for preferring to be here than at ours.'

'Please don't take it personally,' Kat begged her. 'It's just, I could be here for months. Years. It all depends how long it takes me to save up for my own place, and you wouldn't want me under your feet all that time.'

Birdie frowned. 'Years? But, Kat dear, surely you realise—' She scowled as Rita dug her in the ribs. 'What the bloody hell was that for?'

Rita glared at her, and Birdie glared back. As Kat watched, Birdie's expression changed, and she looked apologetically at her sister.

'What must I realise?' Kat asked suspiciously.

'Only that you'd be very welcome at our place, however long it took.' Birdie gave her a bright smile and hurriedly sipped her tea, while Miss Lavender shook her head slightly and nibbled on her cake.

'We have another viewing next week,' Rita said sadly. 'We were wondering if you'd be good enough to be there when Mr Rustill shows them around? It's next Tuesday, around lunch time. Would you mind?'

'No, of course not.' Kat broke off a piece of cake and eyed them thoughtfully. 'What about that woman who came the other night?'

'Not heard a thing from her. It was all very odd about her

brother, wasn't it? I'm not holding my breath about those two buying the place.'

'I'm not sure I'd want them to,' Birdie said, nodding vehemently. 'If he can't even be bothered to turn up and doesn't seem to know if he wants it or not then I don't want him anywhere near.'

'Too true,' Rita agreed. 'Pennyfeather's deserves respect at the very least.'

'It's such a shame,' Miss Lavender said with a sigh. 'I can't believe it's come to this. The idea of Market Place without Pennyfeather's Wool Shop is abhorrent. And of course, we have no idea what the next owners will turn it into. It could be anything!' She shuddered. 'It could be a vape shop!'

'Or a tattoo parlour.'

They all turned at the sound of Jonah's voice. He brought in another tray, this time bearing cups of tea and two mugs of coffee. There was a twinkle in his eye that told Kat he was winding the poor Lavender Ladies up.

'Well, quite!' Miss Lavender said.

'Surely there's a law about such things?' Birdie asked.

'I dunno. I'd quite fancy a tattoo myself,' Rita said thoughtfully.

'Over my dead body,' Miss Lavender told her, giving her a look that would have silenced Kat but seemed to make Rita even more determined.

'A heart and a dagger maybe,' she said. 'Or a unicorn?'

'Bit different,' Birdie said, shaking her head. 'Don't do it, Rita. It's all very well getting it done now but imagine how horrible it would look when you got old.'

Since her aunts were already eighty-two, Kat had great difficulty keeping a straight face, and she realised Jonah was struggling not to laugh, too.

'So anyway,' she said, 'lunchtime on Tuesday. I'll be there. Although I'm sure Mr Rustill could do it on his own, you know.'

'We want to know what these people are like, and he'll only be in it for the money,' Rita said darkly.

'And try to find out what they want the place for,' Miss Lavender urged her.

'Maybe,' Jonah suggested, 'you could run a book on it? Get people to place bets on what Pennyfeather's will turn into.'

'Jonah Brewster,' Miss Lavender said, sounding shocked, 'as if we'd do any such thing!'

'That's proper insensitive if you don't mind me saying,' Rita added. 'This is our life, young man. You don't make bets on something that means so much to people!'

Jonah's eyes widened and Kat quickly stuffed cake in her mouth to stop herself from laughing. Considering the bets the Lavender Ladies had run in the past on people's personal lives they had a real cheek expecting the fate of their shop to be exempt.

She braved a quick glance at Jonah, and her heart leapt as he winked at her before reaching for a slice of cake.

She inwardly sighed with pleasure, then her gaze fell on Miss Lavender, who gave her a knowing look before sipping her tea.

Kat knew, in that moment, that any protests she'd made about her feelings for Jonah had just been declared null and void. The Lavender Ladies would be taking bets before the day was out. She really was going to have to be more careful.

TWELVE

Early on Sunday morning, Kat and Jonah headed down River Road towards Daisyfield Cottage. There was a distinct nip in the air, and the sky was almost colourless. Only the gold and orange leaves on the trees added some cheer as they walked quickly, hands in pockets, their coats fully zipped up as protection against the chill of the day.

'I hope Jennifer's got that kettle on,' Kat muttered.

'Me too, although I'm sure we'll soon warm up once we get started on the decorating,' Jonah said.

They were wearing their oldest clothes and were ready for a day spent slapping paint on walls, pasting wallpaper, and hopefully having fun with their friends and neighbours.

Jonah had dropped Hattie and Tommy off at Whistlestop Cottage—along with toys and books and baby paraphernalia, and a whole raft of instructions from Kat—and had returned looking shell-shocked.

'That place is like a time capsule,' he'd said, shaking his head. 'Trouble is, I can't decide if it's stuck in the nineteen-forties or the nineteen-seventies. Either way, it's not pretty. What a dust trap!'

Kat had laughed. 'I know! All that crochet and the hundreds of ornaments.'

'And that awful carpet! And the fireplace!'

'The land that taste forgot.' She sighed. 'Aw, but I do love them. They're such good people.'

'I know,' Jonah said, smiling. 'I know.'

As they neared Daisyfield Cottage, Jonah nudged her. 'Noah's here anyway.'

He nodded towards a smart, black SUV standing outside the Callaghans'. Noah had only got it last year, and Isobel had boasted about their new car to everyone and anyone who'd listen, so they both recognised it instantly.

'You don't think he's brought Isobel with him, do you?' Kat asked, wrinkling her nose at the thought. She could do without her jibes and sarcastic comments today—or any day for that matter.

'Hell, I hope not.' Jonah sounded as horrified at the thought as she was, which cheered her up. 'I can't see her wanting to spend her Sunday decorating though, can you?'

'Probably not,' Kat admitted with some relief. 'Especially not as a favour to someone else.'

'Well exactly.' Jonah frowned. 'If she is there we'll just have to pretend to be pleased to see her. For Noah's sake.'

'And try to keep the peace all day, despite her jibes.'

They knocked on the door, and a few moments later they were ushered inside by Jamie Callaghan, who was clearly in a very good mood.

He led them through to the kitchen, where they found Jennifer brewing up already, while Ben handed out bacon sandwiches.

'We haven't even started yet and we're already being rewarded,' Noah joked, taking a plate from Ben and grinning at Jonah and Kat.

'You've got to have fuel if you're going to be working,' Jennifer said.

Jonah wondered if, like him and Kat, the others had already eaten breakfast for just that reason, but were too polite to say so. He certainly didn't feel able to refuse when Jennifer smiled brightly at him and said, 'Three rashers or four?'

'Just three please,' he said quickly, wondering if he'd be too full to do any work at all at this rate. He was pleased to see Sally and Summer there, as well as a teenage girl he didn't know. He was even more pleased that there was no sign of Isobel Lavender.

'This is Eloise,' Jennifer said, as if noticing his glance at the dark-haired girl who was leaning on the worktop, watching them all with interest. 'She's Jamie's girlfriend.'

'Aw, pleased to meet you, Eloise,' Kat said, giving Jamie a fond look. 'Where did you two meet then?'

'We go to the same school,' Eloise explained.

'Another St Egbert's pupil, eh?' Kat smiled. 'Have you done any decorating before?'

Eloise looked a bit worried. 'No. Does it matter?'

'Not really,' Jamie assured her. 'I've never done any either. We'll learn together.'

She blew him a kiss and Kat gave Jonah an amused look. He smiled back. Young love. It was quite sweet really.

'Rafferty's going to pop along later,' Sally promised. 'He's hoping to be here at around one.'

'But I'll have to leave then,' Summer added. 'Joseph needs some help at Whispering Willows.'

Jonah frowned. 'Is he still under the weather?'

'Apparently the doctor said he's a bit anaemic, which explains the tiredness. He's taking medication so hopefully he'll feel better soon.'

'No Isobel?'

Kat obviously couldn't resist checking, and Jonah could practically sense her holding her breath as she waited for Noah's answer.

He shrugged. 'No, sorry. She's busy.'

'Not to worry,' Jonah said immediately, sensing a sudden tension in Noah's stance. He wondered how things were between the two of them. Even though he and Noah had been friends for a long time, he knew very little about his home life. He was never invited round to their house, and Noah rarely visited him at Forge Cottage. The Lavenders certainly kept themselves to themselves, and Jonah had no idea if Noah was still happy with his wife or not.

He supposed he should try to find out, but it wasn't something he felt comfortable with. It was none of his business really, and surely Noah would tell him if he wanted him to know? Frankly, he couldn't imagine how it would be possible to be happily married to Isobel, but then again, Noah had been madly in love with her since he was a teenager, so he clearly didn't feel the same. Each to their own.

Ben handed Jonah and Kat their bacon sandwiches, then sank into a chair with a sandwich of his own. Summer sat on his knee, and he put his arm around her waist while they ate their breakfast, contented looks on their faces.

'Now,' Jennifer said, carrying cups of tea and coffee to the table, 'how are we going to do this?'

'What exactly are we decorating today, Jennifer?' Kat asked. 'Is it more than one room?'

'I've bought everything we need for the bathroom, the living room, and my bedroom,' Jennifer said. 'The other rooms are absolutely fine, but the living room wallpaper isn't to my taste, and the bedroom and bathroom need repainting.'

'How about we split up then?' Sally suggested. 'We can't all fit in one room anyway. Who's any good at wallpapering?'

Jonah and Noah raised their hands.

Ben shrugged. 'I've only done it once, at Stepping Stones when I helped Clive decorate his flat. I didn't do too bad a job of it. Well, Clive said it was good.'

'Right,' Sally said. 'So how about Jonah, Noah and Ben tackle the living room, with the wallpaper.'

'Me and Eloise will have a go at the bathroom,' Jamie offered. 'It's only painting. I'm sure we can manage that between us.'

'Hmm. Well, you can give it a go,' Jennifer said doubtfully. 'Do you know how to put masking tape on?'

Jamie gave her a withering look. 'No, because I'm six.'

'Don't be sarky. I'll check anyway, just to make sure you're not making it even worse.'

'Charming,' Jamie said, while Eloise simply laughed.

'I'm sure they'll be fine,' Sally said. 'In that case, how about us women do the bedroom? It will be men versus women and we'll see who makes the best job of it.'

'What's the prize?' Summer asked.

'The knowledge that you've achieved something,' Sally said firmly. 'And that should be more than enough.'

'Eloise and I will be neutral,' Jamie said. 'In fact, we can be the judges.'

'Fair enough,' Ben said. 'Just remember who's promised you a Playstation for Christmas.'

'Ben Callaghan!' Summer gasped. 'Stop trying to bribe the judge!'

After finishing their banter-filled breakfast, they all stood, ready to start work. The women and Jamie headed upstairs, and Jonah, Ben and Noah wandered into the living room.

Jonah puffed out his cheeks in relief. 'Oh, you've already stripped the walls! That's saved us a lot of time.'

'Mum couldn't live with it a minute longer,' Ben admitted. 'Apparently the chocolate brown background and the pattern of huge, pale pink roses didn't suit our new look.'

Jonah couldn't say he blamed her. The old wallpaper sounded hideous and would have clashed horribly with the Callaghans' new grey sofa and chairs, and their contemporary light oak furniture.

'I take it we've got everything we need?' Noah enquired. 'Paste, brushes, that sort of thing.'

'All waiting in the cupboard under the stairs,' Ben said. 'I'll go and fetch it all.'

Jennifer had chosen cool grey wallpaper with a gentle metallic floral pattern in the foreground for the feature wall, and a soft, dove-grey textured paper for the other three walls. Luckily, she, Sally, Rafferty, Ben and Summer had already emulsioned the ceilings and glossed the paintwork in every room in the weeks since Mr Eckington had given Ben the keys, so they didn't have to worry about that.

They decided to tackle the feature wall first and began by moving the furniture into the middle of the room and laying dustsheets on the carpet just in case of any paste splodges. Ben and Noah unscrewed the new electric fire suite from the wall and moved that to the other end of the room, then they unfolded the pasting table and got to work mixing up the paste and measuring and cutting wallpaper.

They could hear a radio playing upstairs and Jonah decided the women couldn't have it all their own way. He took out his phone and tapped his music app, and after a brief discussion about what they should listen to they returned to work, accompanied by some classic rock.

Jennifer had turned off the radiators in the rooms they were all working in, but even so they soon warmed up. By lunchtime, Jonah had removed his sweatshirt and was working in his black vest, while Ben had changed his jumper for a T-shirt.

Noah steadfastly refused to take off his jumper, insisting he had nothing underneath it.

'I can lend you a T-shirt,' Ben offered, but Noah shook his head.

'I'm fine as I am. I'm not even hot.'

Looking at his red face and the way some tendrils of his sandy brown hair were sticking to his perspiring forehead, Jonah was convinced he was lying.

Noah caught him frowning.

'Look, do you really think I want to show my scrawny body off to the likes of you?' he joked. 'Your muscles have got muscles. I'm staying covered up thanks very much. I don't need your pity.'

'Don't be daft!' Jonah laughed, but he wasn't sure it was so funny. Was Noah serious? And if so did that mean he had body issues? He recalled joking with him about having to give him the kiss of life when he tried to move furniture and felt ashamed. 'There's nothing wrong with your body, Noah. You know that, right?'

Noah was shorter than Jonah—probably around five ten—and he was quite slender, but he wasn't puny by any means and Jonah hated the thought that Noah was self-conscious.

'Stop looking so worried,' Noah said, clapping him on the shoulder. 'I'm absolutely fine. Can we just get on with the job?'

Jonah nodded but resolved in future never to joke with Noah about his slender build again. You just never knew what people were struggling with, and he felt ashamed that he hadn't picked up on Noah's insecurities sooner.

'I don't know about you,' Ben said, 'but I'm ready for a drink. Anyone for a can of lager?'

The others agreed it sounded like a good idea, but just as Ben was about to head into the kitchen Sally popped her head round the door.

'How are you getting on? Ooh, that looks lovely!' She walked in and stared up at the feature wall in admiration. 'It looks even better up than it did on the roll.' She gazed around the admittedly messy room and smiled at Ben. 'It's going to be lovely when it's finished, love. A far cry from Monk's Folly, eh?'

Ben grinned. 'You could say that, Sally. We're just going to grab a can of lager from the fridge. Do you want one?'

'I've come down to make us all a cuppa,' Sally said. 'Wouldn't you prefer that?'

The three men looked at each other.

'No, it's okay,' Ben said at last. 'I think we're good with the cans.'

'Suit yourselves,' Sally said. 'I'll put the kettle on. I'm gagging for a nice cup of tea.'

'Kat will have coffee,' Jonah called after her without thinking, receiving a brief, 'I know,' from Sally in return.

He saw Ben and Noah exchange glances and shrugged. 'What? She likes coffee during the day. Tea first thing in the morning and tea or chocolate at night.'

'Does she now?' Noah teased. 'Good job you know her so well.'

'I live with her,' Jonah reminded him patiently.

Ben and Noah grinned.

'So you do,' Noah said, his voice heavy with meaning.

'Oh shut up,' Jonah said. 'I've told you. She's—'

'*Just Kat*,' Noah said. 'I know.'

Jonah, his face scorched with embarrassment, lifted the final strip of paper from the pasting table where it had been soaking up the paste, and carried it over to the wall.

'I'll get those cans,' Ben said.

By the time he returned, carrying three cans of lager and three flapjacks, the feature wall was completely finished.

There was a thumping on the stairs and suddenly the living room was full of women.

'You're kidding?' Kat and Summer exchanged glances and Kat put her hand on Jonah's shoulder. 'Seriously? You've taken all morning to do one wall?'

Jonah bristled, annoyed at the women's teasing laughter and also at himself for the weird feeling Kat's touch had given him.

'Don't forget,' Noah said primly, 'that we've had to let the paste soak in, and there's been a lot of adjusting to get it all straight.'

'Plus,' Ben added, 'you bought paste-the-paper wallpaper, Mum, which isn't anywhere near as easy as the paste-the-wall stuff I used at Clive's. Thanks for that.'

'Oh dear,' Jennifer said. 'I never even thought...'

'It's okay,' Ben reassured her. 'The other three walls have got the paste-the-wall paper. I already checked. It will be much quicker and easier this afternoon.'

Relieved when Kat moved away to give Jennifer's new fire suite an admiring stroke, Jonah said, 'Don't tell me you lot have finished already?'

'We've undercoated the bedroom,' Kat said, not looking round. 'Got to leave it to dry now so I'm going to pop back to the aunties' and check on the kids.'

'Do you want me to go?' he offered.

She turned back to him. 'No, it's fine. You carry on with the wallpapering.' She took a mug of coffee from Sally with a grateful smile. 'Thanks, love. I'm ready for this.'

She'd removed the baggy sweatshirt she'd been wearing earlier, and he realised she was in a T-shirt and denim dungarees that were too big for her. He seemed to recall she'd worn them when she was expecting Hattie and supposed she was using them for painting as she had no further use for maternity clothes. She looked smaller, and a bit vulnerable in them, and surprisingly sweet.

A sudden and unexpectedly fierce lurch of longing for her caught him off guard, and he hurriedly took a swig of lager, not sure what else to do with himself.

Where on earth had that come from?

'Has anyone checked on Jamie and Eloise?' Summer asked.

'I mean, for all we know they might be busily painting the inside of the bath.'

Jennifer laughed. 'I peeked in earlier. They're actually not making a bad job of it. They're being very careful, which is probably why it's taking so long. They're clearly determined to prove they're up to the challenge.'

'Bless them,' Sally said. 'So while we're waiting for the undercoat to dry in the bedroom is there anything else we can be getting on with, love?'

'Well...' Jennifer sounded hesitant. 'There's a chest of drawers that needs putting together. I thought it was ready-assembled but it turns out to be flat-pack, and I have no idea what to do with it.'

'I'll do that for you, Mum,' Ben said immediately, but Sally waved a hand dismissing his offer.

'No need, love. You get on with the papering. Me and Summer are dab hands at putting together flat-pack furniture. I'll just drink this and then we'll crack on.'

Kat drained her coffee and grabbed her sweatshirt and coat from the hallway.

'I'll get off to Whistlestop Cottage,' she said. 'I'll be back in about an hour if that's okay.'

Jennifer nodded. 'I'll make sandwiches for lunch and put some aside for you, Kat.'

Kat bid them all a cheery farewell and left the cottage, and Jonah watched her pass by the front window, feeling suddenly empty now that she wasn't there with him.

He didn't understand it. What had just happened? Where had this sudden intense attraction sprung from? She was Kat, his friend from way back. He'd never looked at her in any other way before and he knew she'd be horrified if she had any idea what he was thinking. It would be impossible sharing a house with her if she knew. Things would be far too awkward between them. She might even decide to move out, which wouldn't be fair on her at all.

Somehow he had to push those feelings back to wherever the hell they'd sprung from and never let them see the light of day again. His friendship with Kat depended on it.

THIRTEEN

Every part of Kat ached as she and Jonah walked home at around seven that evening. The sun was setting; the day exhausted and all too willing to hand over to the night. Kat had every sympathy. She was ready for bed, but there was still loads to do—not least fetching the kids from Whistlestop Cottage.

She'd called the aunties earlier and they'd reassured her that both Hattie and Tommy were perfectly fine. Both had been fed and Hattie had been changed and was fast asleep.

'Tell you what,' Jonah said, giving her a sympathetic look as she trudged up Forge Lane, the reluctance in every step clearly warning him that she wasn't feeling great, 'why don't you have a nice hot bath when we get home while I go and fetch the kids?'

'But you took them there this morning,' she protested, not very forcefully it had to be said. The thought of a hot bath was almost irresistible. Even so, guilt forced her to refuse his offer. 'It's my turn. I'm just being a wimp.'

'You're not being a wimp,' he said. 'You've worked hard today, getting that bedroom emulsioned, putting up the light fittings, and moving Jennifer's bedroom furniture around.' He grinned. 'Several times actually until she made up her mind.'

Kat winced, remembering how she and Sally had raised eyebrows at each other but valiantly said nothing as they lugged Jennifer's king size bed and heavy wardrobe to various points in her room, while she tried to decide where they looked best.

'I was hardly on my own,' she pointed out. 'Anyway, you worked harder than I did and look at you. You barely broke a sweat.'

'But I'm used to heavy work,' he reminded her. 'When you've spent the day shoeing horses, and holding their feet up while you trim their hooves, sticking a bit of paper on a wall doesn't bother you in the least, trust me.'

She closed her eyes for a moment as an image of him at work—all hot and sweaty and muscly in that black vest—flashed into her mind. She pushed it away and took a steadying breath.

'Shall we get a takeaway?' he suggested. 'You run a bath, I'll go and collect Hattie and Tommy, we'll put them to bed, and then we'll sit and eat our supper in front of the telly. What do you say?'

Oh God, it sounded blissful. Kat was too tired and pathetic to argue.

'Sounds great.'

'That's sorted then.'

They reached Forge Cottage and Kat pushed open the gate, giving him a guilty look.

'You're sure you don't mind?'

'Of course not. Go and run that bath. Lots of bubbles. I won't be long.'

He smiled and for a weird moment she thought he was going to lean over and kiss her goodbye. She blinked in confusion and saw him walking rapidly away from her. Honestly, her imagination was way out of control.

She stood watching him stride up the road for a moment, noting with some envy that there wasn't a trace of fatigue or pain in his movement. Sighing, she all but hobbled to the front door and let herself in.

As she poured bubble bath into the hot water, Kat thought that their efforts had been worth it at least, even if that treacherous Jamie and Eloise had declared the men the winners. Daisyfield Cottage looked beautiful now, with the fresh paint and wallpaper and the brand-new curtains, carpets and furniture. It couldn't be more different to Monk's Folly, and Jennifer, Ben and Jamie looked so happy.

It was as if they'd been given a new lease of life, and Kat couldn't be more delighted for them. After everything the Callaghans had been through they deserved this new start, and she was glad she'd been able to help in some small way. God knows, she thought bleakly, she owed them that much at least.

She was just about to step into the water when there was a loud knock on the door.

She groaned. Had Jonah forgotten his key? She couldn't imagine who else would be bothering her at this time on a Sunday evening.

Shrugging on her dressing gown she pushed her feet into slippers and hurried downstairs.

The man standing on the doorstep wasn't someone she recognised; around fortyish, with dark hair slightly greying at the temples, and brown eyes that widened in surprise when she opened the door, as if he wasn't expecting to see her. Well, she thought with some embarrassment, she *was* in a dressing gown. And nothing underneath it she realised, pulling the robe tighter defensively, as if he could somehow see through it.

'Can I help you?'

He stared at her for a moment. 'Oh. I'm—I'm sorry. I didn't mean to disturb you.'

'It's okay. I was just about to get a bath but...' Her voice trailed off and her face turned scarlet as she realised what she'd said. It occurred to her that she was vulnerable, standing there half naked in front of a stranger, and that she was alone in the house.

For a moment she was tempted to respond to an imaginary call from Jonah, but realised he was close enough to know there had been no call, and that might make her appear even more vulnerable.

'What is it you wanted?' She hoped she sounded brisk and unintimidated.

He opened and closed his mouth, then gave a nervous laugh.

'I think there's been a mistake. I'm looking for Matilda Demple. She's a friend of my aunt's and I thought this was where she lived. But you're not Matilda Demple.'

'No,' Kat said flatly. 'I'm not.'

'Ah well, never mind. I'm sure she must be somewhere round here.' He shrugged. 'Sorry to bother you.'

With that, he turned and began to walk up the garden path, and Kat frowned. Wasn't he even going to ask her if she knew where this Matilda Demple lived? Not that she did. She'd never heard of the woman, and it wasn't the sort of name you'd forget.

It flashed through her mind that if anyone would know it would be the aunties, but then again, she didn't want to send him to their cottage because he could be a maniac for all she knew. She could ring them, she supposed, but her phone was upstairs...

By the time she'd run through all those thoughts the man was walking up Forge Lane, heading towards the market place.

Kat shrugged and was about to close the door when Jonah arrived at the gate, pushing Hattie in her buggy, with Tommy trotting by his side.

He glanced at the man and then at her.

'Saw him on the doorstep,' he said. 'Who was he?'

Kat opened the door wider to let them in. 'No idea. Some

bloke looking for a Matilda Demple. Said he thought she lived here.'

Jonah frowned. 'Never heard of her.'

'Me neither. Hello, Tommy. Did you have a nice time with Rita and Birdie?'

Tommy nodded. 'We had a game of rounders in the garden,' he told her. 'Birdie said it was her favourite game, but she's rubbish at it. Rita won.'

Kat laughed. 'You had a game of rounders when there were only three of you?' Well, she supposed it was just doable. The thought of Rita and Birdie playing was quite amusing.

'And,' Tommy added, 'we had lemon meringue pie.' He wrinkled his nose. 'I liked the white bit, but the yellow bit was yukky.'

He yawned and Jonah, who was manoeuvring the buggy into position in the hallway ruffled his hair.

'Think it's bedtime for you, young man.'

'What about my bath?' Tommy asked.

'You can have a quick wash instead,' Jonah said. 'A bath can wait until tomorrow night. It's been a long day. I think we're all due an early night.'

Kat closed the door behind them and peered at Hattie who was out for the count. 'Aw, they've put her in her pyjamas, bless them. I'll carry her up with me and then get my bath. Do you want to wash Tommy while I'm settling Hattie in her cot?'

'Yes, and while I do that you can order the food. Have you decided what you want?'

'You decide.' She didn't have the energy to think about it, and carefully lifted Hattie out of the buggy.

'Shall we share a pizza? Pepperoni?'

'Sounds good to me,' she agreed. 'I'll ring them.'

Jonah watched as she carried her baby upstairs.

'So, you don't know that bloke then?'

She stopped and turned to look at him. He was standing at the foot of the stairs and looked a bit puzzled.

'No. Never seen him before.'

'Odd. Why would he think someone called Matilda Demple lived here? My family has been in this cottage for generations. And Matilda Demple? What kind of name is that? It doesn't even sound real.'

Kat made it to the top of the stairs. 'No idea,' she said. 'Are you bringing Tommy up?'

'Yeah, yeah. Come on, mate.' He ushered Tommy upstairs and Kat carefully carried Hattie to her cot and laid her down gently, then took out her phone to order the pizza, stifling a yawn as she did so. She couldn't wait to step into that bath and have a good long soak. The man at the door was already forgotten.

* * *

When Kat climbed into bed that night she thought she'd probably sleep right through until morning. She was so tired. The hot bubble bath had worked a miracle on her aching muscles, and the giant pizza she'd shared with Jonah had left her feeling full and sleepy. Her bed had never looked so welcoming.

She wasn't sure how much time had passed when the sound of Hattie's crying permeated the bliss of sleep. Kat opened one eye, hoping it had been part of a dream already forgotten.

It was all quiet and she snuggled under the duvet again. The second cry was more insistent, and Kat realised, with some reluctance, that she hadn't been dreaming and that she would have to get up to settle her daughter.

She switched on her lamp and checked her phone. Half past twelve. Sod it! She'd only been asleep for half an hour.

Groaning, she forced herself out of bed and, rubbing her eyes, she stumbled onto the landing.

The bathroom door opened and Kat stopped dead as Jonah walked out. He was oblivious to her presence as he towelled his hair, completely naked except for a towel slung low on his hips.

Kat stared at him. Even in her sleepy, befuddled state, she could appreciate a good body when she saw one. Images of Michelangelo's David came into her mind; those chiselled abs and well sculpted muscles—except David wasn't quite as muscular as Jonah, and he was sadly made of stone, whereas Jonah was most definitely flesh and blood. Most definitely...

'Bloody hell!'

Jonah leaned against the wall, the towel he'd been using to dry his hair hanging limply from his hand as he stared at her in shock.

'You scared the bejesus out of me! What are you doing creeping about?' Another wail from Hattie answered his question and he gave her an apologetic look. 'Sorry, I didn't hear her. I was in the shower.'

She arched an eyebrow. 'Really? I'd never have guessed.'

He glanced down at the towel that was covering his modesty and she noticed faint pink spots appear on his cheekbones as he said, 'Er, yeah. Sorry about that. I'll get dressed.'

He almost tumbled into his bedroom and shut the door behind him. Kat puffed out her cheeks and hurried into Hattie's room, telling herself to behave like a sensible mother, rather than the besotted teenager she felt like right now.

Hattie was clearly growing increasingly cross that her darling mummy hadn't answered her demands immediately, and Kat leaned over the cot, gently rubbing her arm and telling her how sorry she was for keeping her waiting.

She checked her nappy, which was clean and dry—not surprising since she'd been changed at eleven after her late-night bottle of milk—and handed Hattie her bedtime companion, a woolly lamb that the aunties had made for her when she was born. It lived in her cot and always soothed the baby when she needed comfort.

Hattie took no notice of Shaun, as Kat had nicknamed him with a breathtaking lack of originality and thought, and continued to grumble loudly, making Kat nervous that she'd wake Tommy up. She didn't want to pick her daughter up if she could help it, as it would make it harder to get her to sleep again. Instead, she talked soothingly to her, hoping that would do the trick.

She heard the bedroom door creak a little as Jonah entered the room.

'Not having it?' he whispered, nodding at Shaun who had been heartlessly discarded while Hattie kicked her legs and let out intermittent cries for no apparent reason.

'Afraid not,' she said worriedly. 'Sorry. Do you think Tommy will hear her?'

'I doubt it. He's fast asleep.'

He moved to stand next to her and they both gazed down at the cross little baby. Kat inhaled Jonah's clean, fresh scent—a mixture of shower gel, toothpaste, shampoo, and *male*—and closed her eyes briefly against the onslaught of emotions it invoked. He was fully covered now, dressed in the blue checked pyjama bottoms and white pyjama top that he'd told her Tawnie had bought him for Christmas.

She couldn't help wondering if he wore them for bed, or if he stripped off before climbing under the duvet. She hoped she'd get the answer to that question one day.

She mentally shook her head, aware that she was embarrassing herself, then blinked back into reality as Jonah asked her, 'Do you think she's still hungry?'

Grateful that he didn't have a clue what she'd been thinking she said briskly, 'I doubt it. She had a full eight ounces an hour ago, and the aunties told you she'd eaten all her tea, didn't they? I don't know what's disturbed her.'

'Maybe she's missed you,' he said gently, smiling at her. 'All day without you. It must have been hard for her.'

'You think?'

'Definitely.'

There was a look in his eyes that made Kat's breath catch in her throat. She swallowed as Jonah leaned over the cot and stroked Hattie's cheek.

'Shh, now little one. No need for all this fuss. Mummy's right here, see? All's well with the world.'

Hattie stared up at him then treated him to one of her killer smiles that always made Kat's heart leap with joy, then waved her arms around, just to show them she wasn't so easily defeated. Her silence, however, spoke volumes. Apart from the odd gurgling sound she simply watched them, as if checking they were going nowhere.

Kat and Jonah rested their elbows on the cot, leaning over her, while Jonah continued to soothe her with comforting words.

Hattie's eyes closed and then flew open again with alarming regularity.

'She's fighting it all the way,' Kat whispered.

'Tough little cookie,' Jonah replied, with obvious fondness.

Kat watched him, hearing the kindness in his tone and seeing the warmth in his eyes as he interacted with her daughter. The ache for him increased. He was the perfect man. Why hadn't she seen it before?

Maybe, she mused, becoming a mum had changed her ideas of what she thought a perfect man should be. Maybe, a few years ago, Jonah would have been too dull for her, as difficult as that was to imagine. Now, a man who knew how to get a baby to sleep, collected her child while she had an indulgent soak in a bubble bath, and made a truly great hot chocolate before bedtime each night, was her idea of dream boyfriend material.

Who needed nightclubs and wild evenings out when a take-away in front of the telly was on offer? Especially in such undeniably handsome company.

She was so busy staring at him that it was quite a shock when he turned to her and caught her looking.

'I think she's asleep,' he whispered.

Kat gazed down at her daughter who, it appeared, had finally drifted off, clutching Shaun to her side. Jonah must have given it back to her without Kat even noticing.

'I don't know how you manage it,' she told him, baffled. 'You seem to have a magic touch with her.'

'It's just luck,' he said.

'It's bloody annoying.' She smiled at him to show him that, actually, she thought it was amazing.

He smiled back and they stared at each other for a moment, while parts of Kat's body misbehaved themselves and she tried not to dwell on the memory of Jonah standing on the landing in his bath towel.

'I think we can leave now,' he said, moving away from the cot.

Damn! She'd known that was coming, but even so.

'I think we can,' she agreed regretfully.

They padded quietly onto the landing, leaving Hattie's door slightly ajar. Jonah's hair, she noticed under the landing light, was still damp, and rather tousled, as if he'd merely run his fingers through it instead of combing it.

'Time for bed,' he said quietly.

Kat gulped, then realised what he meant.

'It's still quite early,' she said. 'I could make us both another hot chocolate if you like?'

He shook his head. 'School tomorrow, and you know what Monday mornings are like at the best of times. I should...'

She nodded. 'Yeah, me too.'

They stood, facing each other, suddenly awkward.

'Night then, Kat.'

Jonah didn't even wait for her response, as he opened the door and headed into the sanctuary of his bedroom, away from her gaze, closing the door firmly behind him.

Kat burned with embarrassment. Had she given herself away? Why else would he rush off like that? Oh hell, and tomorrow she'd have to face him over the cornflakes as if nothing had happened.

Why, oh why, was she so bad at concealing her feelings?

FOURTEEN

The couple from Lancashire had an appointment for one o'clock on the Tuesday, so Kat made sure she was ready and waiting for them by twelve-thirty.

Birdie and Rita were already behind the counter in the shop, and they looked as nervous as she felt.

'I'm not sure about this, Kat,' Birdie confessed. 'I mean, it doesn't seem right, does it? Lancashire! Why do they want to set up a shop in the Yorkshire Dales? It all sounds a bit suspicious to me.'

Kat laughed. 'Lancashire's not that far away, Birdie! You do know part of Lancashire falls into the Yorkshire Dales?'

Birdie tutted. 'You don't have to tell me that! Doesn't make it right, does it?'

'Funny how you never complain about parts of Cumbria being in the national park too,' Kat said wryly.

'Old rivalries, dear,' Rita said, tapping the side of her nose as if she knew some great secret. 'I have nothing against Cumbria. The red rose and the white rose, however, should never meet.'

'Except in a Tudor rose?' Kat said mischievously. 'You'd think after all these centuries it would be time to let it lie.'

'It's more about sport these days,' Birdie admitted. 'Eugenie's not happy about a Lancastrian couple buying the shop, but then again she does love her cricket.'

'The main thing,' Kat reminded them, 'is that whoever buys this shop adds something to Tuppenny Bridge. If they're going to make a success of it then we should be supporting them. It really doesn't matter where they're from, does it?'

'I suppose not.' Rita sighed. 'It's such a sad day. I know we have to sell the place so I want them to love it, but then again I'd rather they didn't so we wouldn't have to say goodbye just yet.'

Kat gave her a sympathetic hug. 'I know just how you feel,' she said. 'I feel exactly the same.'

The couple in question—whose ears, Kat thought, must surely have been burning—arrived ten minutes early with the estate agent in tow.

Eddie Haygarth, as Mr Rustill introduced him, was a large, ruddy-faced man, whose size could have been intimidating if it hadn't been for the way he constantly deferred to his wife—a sharp-nosed woman called Pauline, with small, dark eyes and a permanent sneer on her face.

She looked around the shop as if she thought it should be demolished.

'Well,' she pronounced, not two minutes after setting foot in the place, 'this is a lot pokier than it looks online. I understand there's a good-sized room at the back,' she added, turning to Kat without so much as a glance at the aunties, who she'd clearly dismissed as irrelevant the moment Kat introduced them. 'Though if by "good-sized" you mean as big as this room I think that might be a bit of an exaggeration.'

'The room in the back is a bit bigger than this one,' Mr Rustill said eagerly. 'Although this is quite a good size actually.' He eyed the shop doubtfully. 'It's just a bit—cluttered.'

Kat tried to see it through the Haygarths' eyes, and knew that Birdie's and Rita's habit of shoving things rather haphazardly in every available space had left the shop looking extremely untidy, and a lot smaller than it actually was.

While Kat had been on maternity leave they'd clearly taken the opportunity to rearrange the shelves to their taste and it definitely showed. No wonder Pauline was having trouble seeing past the mess.

She gave the aunties a wry look and followed the Haygarths and Mr Rustill into the back room—the Lavender Ladies' sacred space.

Eddie rubbed his hands in obvious glee. 'Well, this is more like it, isn't it, my love? Nice big room here.'

Pauline blinked, puzzled. 'What do you use it for?'

Kat could hardly say it was where her great aunts and their friend gathered to exchange gossip and information about the residents of Tuppenny Bridge, so she merely shrugged.

'We don't really.'

'You don't use it?' Pauline wrinkled her nose. 'What a waste of space.'

Kat couldn't deny it.

Mr Rustill nodded eagerly. 'But imagine what use you can put it to, Mrs Haygarth. There's a small kitchen just to the side of the shop. Would you like to see that and then I'll show you upstairs.'

Pauline pronounced the kitchen poky, and the staff toilet basic at best, before following Mr Rustill up to the flat, Eddie lumbering behind her with a silently fuming Kat trailing behind.

'As you can see, it's got a decent-sized living room and kitchen,' Kat said, thinking how much bigger it looked now that Hattie's paraphernalia had gone. 'There are two bedrooms, and a bathroom. The second bedroom is a bit smaller than the main one,' she admitted. 'Would it just be the two of you or—?'

'Oh good heavens, we wouldn't be living here!' Pauline

laughed scornfully. 'We have a five-bedroomed house in Clitheroe if you please.'

'Oh, right,' Kat said, nonplussed. 'So what will you do with it then?'

Pauline shrugged carelessly. 'God knows. I suppose it could be a stock room. Or we could rent it out to someone. I suppose there are always people looking for accommodation at the lower end of the social scale, however poky it is.'

Kat bit her lip to contain her annoyance. If that woman used the word poky one more time she'd show her how poky she could be, by poking her right in the bloody eye.

'Would you like to look around the bedrooms?' Mr Rustill suggested.

Eddie nodded, but Pauline flicked back her jet-black hair and announced it wouldn't be necessary.

Kat's mouth fell open as Pauline practically pushed her out of the way and headed back downstairs. Eddie gave her an apologetic look and followed. Mr Rustill gave Kat a despairing look and trailed behind them.

Birdie and Rita were waiting in the shop and their eyes darted between the Haygarths and Kat, as if trying to read their expressions.

'So what did you think?' Birdie asked eventually, as Kat didn't trust herself to speak.

'It's er, very nice,' Eddie said, nodding kindly. 'A bit smaller than we expected I think.'

'To say the least,' Pauline snapped. 'It's overpriced, that's for sure.'

'I think,' Mr Rustill said firmly, 'that you'll find it's a very fair price.'

'Well you would say that!'

There was that irritating tinkling laugh again. How, Kat wondered, could a mere laugh convey utter contempt the way

Pauline's did? It was quite a skill, and right now she wished she shared it.

'It's the Yorkshire Dales,' Kat said with some difficulty. 'You're in the national park here. Prices are at a premium.'

'Clearly.' Pauline shook her head. 'I should tell you we own a shop in a beautiful village in the Lake District, and if you'll forgive me for saying so I think that's probably a bigger draw than this little town in Yorkshire. It pulls in the crowds all year long. We're swamped in the summer. And yet we bought that shop for a lot less than you're asking for this place. I think we'd need to knock at least forty thousand off the asking price, and that's just for starters.'

Kat glanced at Mr Rustill but he seemed to have lost the power of speech.

'Do you mind me asking what it is you actually sell?' Rita ventured.

Pauline blinked. 'Well, what do you think? Fudge.'

'Fudge?' Rita and Birdie exchanged glances. 'And you can afford four shops by selling fudge?'

Now it was Eddie's turn to look affronted. 'It's not just any old fudge. You must have heard of Haygarth's Olde English Fudge Company? Surely...' He gazed round at them all, obviously baffled by their blank faces. 'No? Seriously?'

'I don't think I've ever seen your stuff in town,' Kat admitted. 'The gift shops and sweet shops around here tend to stock Carroll's. A Yorkshire company.'

'Oh, Carroll's!' Pauline's lip curled. 'But they diversify! They also make chocolate and rock and boiled sweets and toffee. You know what they say: Jack of all trades, master of none. We purely concentrate on fudge. It's what makes our product so much better. We've won awards, haven't we, Eddie?'

'We have,' Eddie said, nodding furiously. 'Our fudge is second to none.'

'When Haygarth's Fudge arrives in Yorkshire you'll never

look back,' Pauline said confidently. 'Carroll's won't know what's hit them.'

Kat's heart sank as Mr Rustill asked hopefully, 'So you're definitely interested in the shop then?'

Pauline and Eddie exchanged doubtful looks.

'We've got a few other places to look at,' Pauline explained. 'We're keen to expand into Yorkshire, having had such success in Lancashire and Cumbria, but I'm not convinced Tuppenny Bridge is the right place to start. At least, not in these particular premises.'

She hitched her handbag higher on her arm and sniffed. 'We've got an appointment for another viewing in Skipton in an hour and a half. We'd better be going. Eddie!'

She was already heading for the door, and Eddie followed her, raising a hand to them all as he reached it.

'Thanks for showing us around,' he said, seeing as Pauline had already left the shop. 'We'll be in touch.'

Mr Rustill sighed and shrugged, then followed them outside.

The door closed behind him, and Kat let out a long breath.

'Somehow,' Birdie said shrewdly, 'I don't think they'll be in touch.'

'Bloody good job too,' Rita said. 'What a horrible woman! And he was worse than useless. Only came to life when he talked about fudge.'

'Sodding fudge,' Kat said.

They all looked at each other and burst out laughing.

'But it's Haygarth's Fudge, don't you know?' Birdie said, imitating Pauline's faux posh accent perfectly.

Kat sighed, remembering that the whole point of the day had been to sell the shop. 'I'm sorry it didn't work out. We're not having much luck, are we?'

'Oh well,' Birdie said. 'It's early days still. I'm sure someone will want this place. It's just got to be the right person, and these people weren't right for it. I'm glad they didn't want it. They can bugger off back to Clitheroe and keep their rotten fudge, because personally, we prefer Carroll's here.'

'Absolutely!' Kat hugged her aunts to her, glad they were coping with another failed viewing so well. 'We'll find the right buyer eventually. Don't worry.'

Birdie swallowed. 'The trouble is, Kat, I don't want to find them. I don't want to sell.'

Kat stepped back, heartbroken to see tears in Birdie's eyes. Rita's eyes looked suspiciously shiny too.

'I'm so sorry,' she said. 'If there was anything I could do...'

'We know, dear. We know.' Rita patted her arm. 'It is what it is. Pennyfeather's must be sold and that's an end to it. We must be brave and find our Yorkshire grit.'

'We must,' Birdie agreed. 'The fact is, there's nothing more to be done.'

She was right, but Kat wished with all her heart she could find another solution to the problem. If she could save Pennyfeather's for her aunts she would do so in a heartbeat. Whatever it cost.

* * *

It had been a long, hard day at work, and Jonah had been working late. By the time he got home, tired and hungry, it was nearly seven o'clock, and both Tommy and Hattie had been fed and bathed. Hattie was already upstairs asleep, and Tommy was in his favourite pyjamas, watching *Paddington*, although he soon forgot about that in his rush to greet Jonah when he walked through the door.

Jonah had a shower and got changed then read Tommy a bedtime story. As he gently closed the book, Tommy was half asleep, and Jonah kissed him on the forehead and murmured goodnight, before turning out the main light and heading downstairs.

Something smelled good. Really good. His nose twitched in appreciation as he followed the scent to the kitchen, where he found Kat dishing up two big platefuls of her home-made shepherd's pie.

'Sit down,' she said, smiling at him. 'I'm just mashing the tea.'

He raised an eyebrow. 'You've made it in the pot? Are you having tea?'

'Yeah.' She shrugged. 'I thought why not, since you were. Seems daft making tea for you and coffee for me.'

She put the plates on the table, and he sank into a chair, wondering if it would be rude to dive straight in without waiting for Kat.

'Tuck in,' she told him, pouring tea from the pot into their mugs, and Jonah needed no further invitation.

'Oh my God, this is so good!' He'd had her shepherd's pie once before, and the memory of it had lingered in his mind. Now he closed his eyes and chewed blissfully.

'It will warm you up.' Kat put two mugs of tea on the table and took a seat next to him. 'It's a bit nippy tonight. The nights are definitely drawing in.'

'It is officially autumn,' he pointed out. 'I just hope the weather holds for the weekend. It would be a shame if the sheep fair was rained off.'

Kat nodded and spooned up some shepherd's pie, gazing out of the window at the gathering darkness.

'Something on your mind?' he asked, noting that she wasn't her usual chatty self.

She sighed. 'Just thinking about the aunties and the wool shop.'

'Oh, of course. You had a viewing today, didn't you?' He felt bad for forgetting. 'How did it go?'

Kat pulled a face that told its own story, but she filled in the details for him as they ate, clearly still smarting from Pauline Haygarth's rude and condescending attitude.

'Sounds to me like we've all had a lucky escape,' he said, taking a sip of tea. 'Who wants people like those two in Tuppenny Bridge?'

'I know, I know. We definitely don't,' she said. 'Trouble is, it means we're no closer to selling Pennyfeather's, and even though we don't want to it doesn't solve our problems, does it?'

'The right buyer will come along sooner or later,' he assured her. 'Try not to worry.'

'But I do worry. Rita and Birdie were so upset today. They don't want to lose the shop, you know. It's as plain as day. I just wish I could do something to help.'

'I know.' He prodded his shepherd's pie, not sure what to say to cheer her up. He hated seeing her so down.

'Oh, forget it,' she said, clearly making a huge effort to switch on a smile. 'You don't want to listen to me rabbiting on about the shop. How was your day?'

He didn't mind her talking about the shop as long as she wanted, but he sensed she was eager for a change of subject, so he obligingly started to tell her about the jobs he'd done during the day, including paying a visit to some racing stables over in East Midham.

'You're doing a shoeing demonstration on Saturday, aren't you?' Kat asked.

He nodded, scraping up another spoonful of shepherd's pie, sad to see that he'd almost cleared his plate.

'Yeah. And on Sunday.'

'Oh, you'll be busy then.'

'They don't take long,' he told her. 'Are you planning to go?'

'Of course. I'll take the kids. I'm sure Tommy would love to see you at work. Besides, the sheep fair's always fun, isn't it? It's great to see all the sheep in the market place, and the shearing demonstrations. Then there are all the stalls to visit from visiting traders.'

'Hmm.' His stomach tightened as anxiety hit him. He still hadn't told her about the stall, but since he needed her help he supposed he'd have to. 'Thing is...' He prodded the remaining shepherd's pie nervously. 'Thing is, I've taken a stall there myself.'

Her eyebrows shot up in surprise. 'You have?'

'Yeah. I—I thought it would be a good way to get rid of some of the ornaments that are cluttering up the forge.'

'You mean like the wine rack you made for the Callaghans?'

'Yes, and other bits and bobs. I might as well make a few quid from them if I can, rather than just chucking them away. I mean, they might not sell anyway, but it's worth a shot, right? Dad used to sell his and he did quite well out of it. Mind you, he was a lot better at it than I am.'

'I'd love to see them,' she said. 'You say they're in your forge?'

Nerves made him almost drop his fork. He cleared his throat. 'That's right.'

'May I see them? I've never even set foot in the forge before.' She grinned at him. 'I remember your dad telling us off when we dared to venture near, remember? He had a right go at Leon because he wanted to watch him working. Said he wasn't there for entertainment, and we should bugger off and do something useful with ourselves for a change.'

'That was Dad all over,' Jonah said, laughing at the memory. 'He sounded all gruff and cross, but he was a softie really.' He sighed. 'I suppose I could show you, if you really want to look.'

'Well, only if you're sure. You don't sound too enthusiastic.'

He pushed away his plate. 'Oh no! It's not that, honestly. Just, it's nothing special and you'll probably be disappointed. And the ornaments—they're just me messing about, that's all. Don't expect anything great, will you?'

Kat's eyes were warm with understanding. 'Don't be so hard on yourself. If they're anything like the wine rack I'll love them. Anyway, I only want to look at them. You don't have to try to sell them to me.'

'Come on then,' he said, getting to his feet.

'Have you finished the shepherd's pie?' she asked, noting he'd left a couple of spoonfuls.

Funnily enough, his appetite had deserted him.

'It was delicious,' he assured her. 'But I'm absolutely stuffed now. Come on, let's get this over with.'

Before I change my mind.

He led her outside and round to the forge which was attached to the cottage. Unlocking the door, he ushered her inside, flicking on the light as he did so. She gazed around at the stone floor, huge hearth, and large, solid anvil.

'Hmm. It looks a bit like a medieval torture chamber,' she laughed, nodding at the multitude of tools hanging from the bare stone walls. 'I expect it looks less intimidating when the forge is lit and you're at work here.'

Her eyes fell on the collection of metal objects in the far corner, and she hurried over to them, glancing back at him with excited eyes.

'Jonah! You made these? Oh wow.'

She held up one of the metal signs like the one he'd given Tawnie and Keith.

'This is fabulous,' she told him. 'I love it!'

'I can make them with other words, like home or someone's name,' he explained. 'I used to take orders before...'

His voice trailed off and Kat watched him for a moment, as if waiting for him to finish the sentence. When he didn't, she turned back to the stack of ironware and continued looking through it all.

'Candle holders?' she asked, holding up another item.

Jonah nodded.

'There's all sorts here,' she said. 'Wall sconces, letter racks, fireside companion sets, lucky horseshoes… What's this?'

'It's a hoof pick made from a horseshoe,' he said. 'And that shoe heart there is a photo frame. I can personalise stuff, too, of course. I made a memorial for someone when they lost their pony a few years ago. Two horseshoe hearts entwined, with hair from the pony's mane braided into the shoes and its name engraved on them.'

'I'm so impressed,' she said. 'Seriously this is so good. You'll have no trouble shifting them at the sheep fair. Trust me.'

'You really think so?' he asked uncertainly, wondering if she was just being kind.

'Of course I do. You know, you ought to start a website. I'm sure you could start selling online.'

'Oh, I don't know about that. I was wondering,' he said hesitantly, 'if you'd do me a favour. It's a big favour though, so feel free to say no. I won't be offended.'

'What is it? If I can help I will, of course.'

He turned away, not wanting to see the reluctance in her eyes. 'I wanted to ask you if you'd be able to man the stall for a little while on the Saturday and Sunday. It's just while I do the shoeing demonstrations, that's all.'

'Oh.'

He heard the disappointment in her voice and spun round. 'It's okay. If you don't want to do it that's fine. I'll find someone else.'

Though God knows who.

'It's not that,' she said. 'Honestly, I'd love to help you on the stall. I'm quite happy to do that. It's just…'

Her face had gone pink, and he realised she was embarrassed about something.

'Go on,' he urged. 'You can tell me the truth.'

'Well,' she said, 'to be honest, I was kind of looking forward to watching you do the shoeing demonstration. I've never seen you at work before, and I really wanted to see what it was like.'

'Oh.' It was his turn to feel embarrassed. He managed to grin at her. 'It's just me banging a few nails in, remember?'

Kat laughed. 'Oh yes. Sorry about that. I really would like to see it though.'

'Really?' He couldn't imagine why, and he was also aware that his stomach had just flipped over with a sudden attack of nerves at the thought. 'Well, Tawnie said she might be able to watch the stall on the Sunday, though I don't think she was planning on coming to the fair really. She was never all that keen on it. I suppose I could close up for a little while...'

'We'll figure something out,' she said. She ran her hands over two iron hearts, looped together on a stand. 'These are going to be so popular,' she told him. 'You're quite the romantic deep down, aren't you?'

He watched her fingers stroking the metal and imagined what it would feel like to have her touching him in the same way. He jerked guiltily when she dropped her hand and turned to look at him, her green eyes warm and admiring.

God she was so beautiful! How had he never noticed all these years when they'd been living in the same small town, walking the same streets, even hanging out together? What had he been thinking?

Somehow, she'd entirely escaped his attention. Well, in that way at least. Always there, he'd seen her almost every day. Yet he hadn't, had he? Seen her. Not properly anyway. She'd been the cheeky kid who lived at The Black Swan, the ponytailed teenager who everyone felt sorry for because her mum had died, and the besotted girlfriend of his best mate, who was a bit of a curiosity because she lived with the batty Pennyfeather sisters.

Then she'd been the grieving partner of Leon. And it had all got awkward, sad and too bloody difficult to deal with. So he'd backed away from her.

Well, not just him. The gang had broken up after Leon's death, he remembered. Isobel and Noah spent all their time as a couple, and had got married a year later; he'd thrown himself into work, not wanting to think about how lonely he was without his best friend, nor how much he missed him.

Kat had been devastated, and he hadn't known what to say to her. It had come as a huge relief to him when she went to stay with her dad in Dorset to get over the trauma. He supposed when she finally came back to Tuppenny Bridge he'd expected that she'd got over it. He'd hoped she had because that let him off the hook.

He felt ashamed remembering. He hadn't been there for her at all. Too bloody caught up in his own misery to consider hers. Somehow, they'd gone from seeing each other almost every day to nodding greetings when they passed in the street.

Now they were adults with children to care for and a whole heap of responsibility. Kat wasn't that young ponytailed girl any longer. And one thing was for sure, she was no longer just Kat.

It hit him, as she stood there, a half-smile on her lips, that she'd become central to his life in a way he'd never expected. After Sofia, he'd honestly thought he was done with romance, and having Tommy to focus on had convinced him his life was complete, and he didn't need anyone else.

But the longing for her was too overwhelming to be denied, and he felt a clutch of panic as he realised his feelings for her had entirely changed. He was in severe danger of falling in love, and that would be the worst thing he could do.

He'd been here before, after all. Sofia had been a vulnerable single mother, too. She'd seen Jonah as a meal ticket for life and had fooled him completely with her declarations of love. He couldn't go through all that again, and even though his heart was telling him Kat was different, his head was warning him that the circumstances were too similar, and he'd be a fool to ignore the signs.

'Don't look so shocked,' she said, a puzzled look in her eyes as he continued to stare at her. 'Your secret's safe with me. I won't tell anyone.'

'My secret?'

'About you being a romantic at heart,' she said, nodding at the iron hearts.

He let out a long breath. 'Oh, I see. Yeah, keep that quiet. I wouldn't want anyone getting ideas.'

Not that it was likely. If Kat hadn't noticed how he felt about her while he'd been standing there gawping at her like an idiot, there was little chance that she'd get ideas. He was reading far too much into all this. Kat wouldn't be interested in him anyway.

For all he knew, Hattie's father could still be on the scene.

He remembered the man she'd been talking to at the door. She'd been wearing nothing but a robe and had seemed perfectly relaxed considering he was supposed to be a stranger. And that story she'd told him about him thinking someone called Matilda Demple lived there. Was it likely? The Brewsters had lived in Forge Cottage for generations, so why would he have thought that?

His stomach tightened. Could he be Hattie's father? Had she sent him away, knowing Jonah would be on his way back?

He honestly didn't know, and it was none of his business anyway. It just proved to him, if he needed more proof, that developing feelings for Kat was a bad idea and it was time to put the lid on his emotions. Fast.

FIFTEEN

Saturday dawned at last. Looking out of the bedroom window Kat realised the rain had held off overnight and the day was cloudy but mercifully dry.

She felt a bubble of excitement rising within her. She'd always loved the sheep fair. It was the highlight of Tuppenny Bridge's calendar really, popular not only with the residents of the town, but with people far and wide.

The market place was out of bounds to cars, naturally, since it was full of sheep pens during the fair. Cars, therefore, were directed to the council-owned pay and display car park on Bankside, just past The Black Swan, or to the private car park, which was actually a field behind the pub, owned by the people who ran it. She remembered her dad had considered that field a real asset during his years as landlord, yielding a tidy profit for no effort during events such as this.

She'd had a word with Sally and had been grateful beyond words when her friend had offered to man the stall while Jonah did his shoeing demonstration and Kat watched. Summer had volunteered to help in any way she was needed.

'Are you sure you don't mind?' Kat had asked, feeling she was taking advantage of their good natures.

'Don't be daft, love.' Sally had dismissed her fears with a wave of the hand. 'Rafferty's working on Saturday any road, so it's not like I'd have been wandering round with him. And Ben's on duty, checking the sheep and judging some of the classes with Clive, so Summer's in the same boat. We'll be happy to help.' Her eyes had narrowed at that point, though. 'Never thought I'd see you so keen to watch a horse being shoed.'

'It just interests me,' Kat said, squirming with embarrassment. 'I've never seen it done before, and I'd like to know what Jonah actually does all day when he's at work.'

'And being all manly and professional.' Sally giggled and Kat nudged her.

'Behave yourself! It's not like that.'

'Oh, I wouldn't be so sure about that,' Sally said. 'You're a bloody awful liar, Katherine Pennyfeather. I can see that gleam in your eye. You're imagining him in his work clothes, all hot and sweaty, with those muscles flexing and...' She wiped her forehead. 'Bloody hell, is it me or is it hot in here?'

Kat burst out laughing. 'What are you like?'

'I wouldn't blame you, you know,' Sally said, the smile dropping from her face. 'He's a lovely fella. I can't get over the way he's taken Tommy on the way he has. And let's face it, he's pretty easy on the eye too.'

'It's not like that,' Kat repeated, shaking her head.

'But why not? You're both single, you're both single parents, you're even sharing a sodding house. What more do you need? What's stopping you?'

'Well, for a start, he doesn't see me in that way,' Kat said firmly.

'Oh? And you're sure about that, are you?'

'Of course I'm sure. I'd know if he did. To him I'm just the girl he's known forever, and Leon's girlfriend.'

'Hmm. Do you think he's guessed how you feel about him?'

Kat blushed. 'Honestly, I'd rather die than admit it to him,'

'Maybe he already knows.'

'Of course he doesn't.' She shifted uncomfortably. 'Well, I don't think he does anyway. I thought maybe I'd given myself away a couple of times but...' She shook her head determinedly. 'No, he definitely doesn't. He wouldn't be able to look me in the eye if he did and he's been carrying on just as usual.'

'So if you're convinced he hasn't guessed how you feel about him, what makes you think you'd guess if he felt the same about you?'

Kat's mouth dropped open. 'Well... I mean, I would, wouldn't I?'

'How?'

'I just would. I live with him!'

'And he lives with you, but you're pretty certain he hasn't got a clue how *you* feel.' Sally shook her head. 'What if you both feel the same way and neither of you has the courage to tell the other one? This could go on for years. Don't waste time, Kat. If you like him in that way, tell him.'

'But what if he doesn't feel that way about me? How could we go on living together after that? It would be too awkward. Impossible. I'd have to leave.'

Sally sighed. 'All I know is, it was a similar situation for me and Rafferty. I nearly left anyway because I was that fed up with it all. I was constantly trying to guess how he felt, but neither of us had the guts to say it out loud, so in the end I nearly finished us. But when we finally said it—' She shrugged. 'Well, you know how that turned out. You were at the wedding. I just think if he matters that much it's worth the risk. Think how much fun you could both be having instead of dithering.'

As Kat hastily got dressed, she thought about what Sally had said. Was she right? Was it time for her to be brave and tell

Jonah that her feelings towards him were no longer strictly platonic?

Feeding Hattie her breakfast twenty minutes later she wondered what she'd been thinking. Seeing Jonah hurriedly buttering toast and slathering on peanut butter for Tommy, she thought he couldn't possibly look less like a man in love. He seemed far too busy for that; his thoughts clearly focused on the day ahead. Yes, he had a lot to think about, but surely if he had romantic feelings towards her there'd be something? A lingering look perhaps, or a tender smile in her direction...

She sighed inwardly and gave Hattie another spoonful of porridge.

Jonah placed a mug of tea in front of her. 'I'm going to load up the van with the stuff,' he said, sounding distracted.

'Already?' She frowned. 'Do you need a hand?'

He shook his head. 'I can manage. I've got plenty of time. You've got enough on your plate seeing to these two anyway.' He hesitated. 'Are you still going to watch the shoeing demonstration?'

'Yes, I told you. Sally and Summer are minding the stall, and I'll bring the kids to watch you at work. I think Tommy will love it.'

Tommy, who was munching his peanut butter on toast, gave an enthusiastic nod.

'Okay. If you're sure.' He gave her a faint smile. 'Right. I'd better make a move.'

'You haven't had breakfast yet,' she pointed out.

'I can grab something later at the fair,' he said. 'They'll be serving breakfasts soon enough. You know how popular they are with the farmers.'

Kat nodded. She used to love watching the market place getting ready for the fair from the window of her flat. Preparations would start on the Friday evening, when the pens were erected, ready for the arrival of the sheep the following morning. By now, she knew, the market place would be a hive of activity, and the air would be heavy with the smell of sizzling bacon and sausages, with participants queueing up for their breakfasts and catching up with fellow stallholders and farmers.

It was another thing to miss about the shop. This house was beautiful, and she loved living here, but it was tucked down a quiet lane and she was used to the bustle of Market Place.

Jonah ruffled Tommy's hair and told them not to worry if he wasn't back because he might be needed to give people a hand, and he had his stall to get ready.

'You're sure you can manage with these two?' he asked worriedly.

'Don't be daft. Of course I can. Go on and get ready, and I'll see you later,' Kat told him cheerfully.

'Thanks, Kat,' he said, and hurried out of the kitchen.

She sat back in her chair and puffed out her cheeks. Tommy looked at her and grinned.

'Are you excited to watch Daddy putting shoes on the horses, Kat?'

She smiled. 'I am, Tommy. Are you?'

'Yes, but I've seen him do it before. He took me to a farm once and I had to stand with this girl while Daddy got the fire out of his van and melted the shoes, so they'd fit her pony. They're not like our shoes, you know.'

Kat raised her eyebrows in mock surprise. 'Are they not?'

He shook his head. 'Nope. They're metal. And Daddy has to cut their hooves before he puts the shoe on, but don't worry because it doesn't hurt. Daddy says it's just like cutting our toenails.'

'Fancy that.' Kat gazed at him. 'Well, you learn something new every day. Thanks for that, Tommy.'

He shrugged. 'S'all right.'

'Are you nearly finished eating? Because if you are you can run upstairs and clean your teeth, then we'll get you dressed.'

'In my new woolly jumper?' he asked eagerly, and she nodded, smiling.

Tommy slid out of his chair and obligingly headed to the bathroom. Kat eyed Hattie's porridge-smeared face.

'Right, young lady. Time to get you washed and changed. It's going to be a big day, Hattie. I can feel it.'

Hattie waved her arms in delight and beamed at her mum. It was almost, Kat thought hopefully, as if she sensed it too.

All the sheep had to be in their pens by ten thirty, but even though Kat had arrived in the market place an hour early, it was, as she'd known it would be, absolutely heaving. The entire square was full of sheep of all sorts of different breeds, while the pavements teemed with tourists, farmers, and residents, exchanging news, taking photos, or hanging over the pens to admire the sheep.

Several food stalls were doing a roaring trade, and in Little Market Place, a trailer had been parked in front of the Town Hall for the sheep shows. From past experience, Kat knew that the three shortlisted sheep of each breed would be brought onto the trailer at several points throughout the day, to be shown off by their handlers, while a man with a microphone explained to the crowd what the judges were looking for and what made a champion sheep.

The local school, All Hallows' Church of England Primary School, would soon be open for people to wander in and check out the harvest display in the hall. In the church, the flower festival was due to take place from ten forty-five, with displays from local gardeners and florists, including Isobel, naturally.

Even though it was the same thing every year, it never ceased to fill Kat with wonder. Tommy was delighted to see the sheep in their pens, and Hattie lunged forwards in her buggy, clearly also excited to see these new and interesting creatures.

'Isn't it wonderful?'

Kat spun round and smiled as she saw the Lavender Ladies beaming from ear to ear. Eugenie Lavender looked elegant as always in a pale grey dress and white cardigan, with smart but sensible shoes. Rita and Birdie, meanwhile, had no doubt disgraced themselves again in her eyes; their ensembles could hardly be called elegant, featuring a clashing palette of oranges, pinks, greens and purples, the crocheted waistcoats that had definitely seen better days, and the usual garish adornments in their dyed red hair.

Whatever Eugenie thought of them—and Kat could well imagine—to Kat they were just her great aunts, and their appalling taste in clothes was yet another reason to love them. She gave them both a big hug, and smiled a welcome at Miss Lavender, who nodded graciously in return.

'I must say the market place is looking wonderful,' the old lady said, glancing around with pride, as if she'd been personally responsible for the entire thing. 'We have a record number of entrants, you know. And all proceeds going to such good causes.'

Any money raised, once costs had been covered, was donated to the Tuppenny Bridge Fund, which had been set up decades ago by Eugenie Lavender's father. Throughout the year people could personally donate or hold charity events for the fund, and each year after the Harvest Festival celebration the money was divided between local causes, voted for by the townspeople.

This year the residents had voted to donate some money to Whispering Willows Horse Sanctuary, some to the local primary school, and the rest to the church to help pay for the running of its much-valued Community Club, which was held twice-weekly at the Town Hall.

'Tommy!' Rita ruffled the little boy's hair in delight. 'What a fabulous jumper.' She beamed at Kat. 'Did you make that for him?'

Kat nodded as Tommy grinned up at her aunt.

'It's got a sheep on it,' he informed her, as if she hadn't spotted the big woolly animal on the front of his dark green jumper. 'Kat knitted it and I helped her with the wool, didn't I, Kat?'

'You certainly did,' she said, smiling fondly at him. 'Your daddy hasn't seen it yet, has he? It's a surprise for him.'

'Is Jonah not with you?' Birdie asked, sounding and looking disappointed.

'Er, no he's not,' Kat said with deliberate nonchalance, knowing any hint that she would have liked him to be would only fuel the Lavender Ladies' thirst for gossip. 'He's actually in the field behind the churchyard right now, setting up his stall.'

'His stall?' Rita was wide-eyed with excitement. 'What stall is this? What's he selling?'

'A squeeze of his biceps with any luck,' Birdie said, with a naughty chuckle.

'Really, Birdie,' Miss Lavender said sharply. 'Is there any need to be so coarse?'

'You should have heard what I was going to say until I toned it down,' Birdie retorted, a gleam in her eye.

Miss Lavender sucked in a breath and rolled her eyes to the heavens, as if asking for patience from above.

'But what is he selling?' Rita persisted. 'He's never taken a stall at the fair before.'

'Well,' Kat said, feeling undeniably smug that she knew something they didn't, 'you'll have to wander over there and see for yourselves, won't you?'

'We shall, shan't we?' Rita asked the others.

'Too right,' Birdie agreed.

'I'm sure we'll be over that way at some point during the

day,' Miss Lavender said coolly, although Kat could tell she was dying to know. It was quite amazing that she didn't already. Eugenie Lavender had so many fingers in so many pies that Kat wouldn't have been at all surprised to discover that every single stallholder had to be personally approved by her.

'Are you doing anything in particular, Miss Lavender?' she asked politely. 'Have they asked you to cut a ribbon or anything?'

Miss Lavender eyed her doubtfully, as if not entirely sure whether she was being mocked.

'I'm firing the starting gun at the sheep races later,' she said cautiously. 'And tomorrow, naturally, I'll be one of the judges at the craft fair in the Town Hall.'

'Naturally.'

'Isn't Jonah doing one of his shoeing demonstrations this year?' Rita asked, sounding disappointed.

'He is,' Kat said, feeling ashamed that she'd never bothered to watch one before. 'I'm looking forward to seeing it.'

'Oh, so am I,' Rita assured her. 'It's always so interesting to see our local tradesmen at work. We were thinking of going on one of the brewery tours, weren't we, Birdie?'

The Lusty Tup Brewery organised tours regularly but held special events during the weekend of the sheep fair. The tours always proved popular and raised lots of money, not only for the brewery but for the Tuppenny Bridge Fund, too. Kat had never been able to bring herself to go on one, knowing it was where Leon had worked. She'd never set foot inside the place and had no desire to do so.

'Well, enjoy it if you do,' she said. 'Now, I'm going to wander round the market place and show the children the different breeds of sheep, because Tommy's itching to have a look at them all. Have a lovely day, ladies. I'll no doubt bump into you again.'

'No doubt. Have a wonderful time. Here.' Miss Lavender

rummaged in her bag and pulled out her purse. She handed Kat a twenty-pound note. 'For the children.'

'Oh, Miss Lavender,' Kat said, surprised and deeply touched. 'There's really no need.'

'I'd like to,' Miss Lavender said. 'Treat them to something. Have a lovely day, Katherine.'

Without thinking, Kat leaned over and kissed her on the cheek. 'That's so kind of you. Thank you.'

Miss Lavender brushed off her thanks, but Kat could see the gleam of pleasure in her eyes, and it left her with a warm, fuzzy feeling as she pushed the buggy deeper into the market place, Tommy holding on to the buggy handles as they walked.

Although there were stalls and events throughout the day, the focus of the weekend was always the sheep. It was an important day, not only in Tuppenny Bridge's calendar, but in the calendar of the local farmers too. Not just from Skimmerdale either, but from all across Yorkshire and beyond.

Today's showing events alone had fourteen sections, each with five or six classes. Kat had bought a programme for two pounds, and could see today's events were for Texels, Herdwicks, Kerry Hills, Wensleydales, Suffolks, and many other breeds. Tomorrow's shows would include the Swaledales, the Rough Fells, the Blue Faced Leicesters, and—her own personal favourites—the Jacobs.

People who thought sheep were all the same had no idea, and Kat agreed wholeheartedly with Tommy as they stood looking at a pen of black-faced Suffolks when he pronounced them beautiful, and just like the one on his jumper.

'What a smashing jumper that is,' a woman said, nodding approvingly at it. She peered at Kat hopefully. 'Can I ask you, where did you buy it?'

Kat felt a little embarrassed. 'I made it actually,' she admitted.

'You never did! Well, aren't you clever. I wish I could knit, but no one ever taught me and I'm too old to learn now,' the woman said with a sigh.

'You're never too old to learn a new skill,' Kat assured her. 'There are plenty of books on the subject. Or you could watch videos on YouTube.'

The woman wrinkled her nose. 'I'd never follow all that. Wish my mother had taught me but she was too busy working in a factory all day, bless her.' She nudged Kat. 'You ought to sell them jumpers, love. I'd buy one for my grandson like a shot. You could have made a fortune here today, what with all these sheep lovers being here.'

Kat laughed, thinking it was hardly likely. Still, it was nice of the woman to say so.

As the woman moved off, Kat gazed around while Tommy and Hattie stared in wonder at the sheep. She spotted Summer walking arm-in-arm with her best friend, Clemmie Grant, who worked in the local bookshop. Dolly Bennett, who was Clemmie's aunt and boss, must have given her the morning off to have a wander around.

She realised Ben and senior vet Clive were in the process of looking over the Kerry Hills and watched, smiling, as the girls stopped beside the pen in which they were working, and Ben leaned over and planted a kiss on Summer's lips.

It was so good to see the two of them happy. Ben was like a different man since he and Summer had got together, and since he'd finally shed the burden of Monk's Folly. She wondered if Jennifer would pay a visit to the fair at some point over the weekend. Kat had never spotted her there before, but things were different now after all. She hoped so. There was nothing she wanted more than Jennifer's happiness.

'Kat!'

She waved as Ava Barrington, the vicar's wife, strolled up with Bluebell from Cutting it Fine, the local hair salon, at her side.

'Aren't you working today, Bluebell?' Kat asked, glancing quickly at the salon but not able to tell if it was open or not.

'Am I buggery,' Bluebell said cheerfully. 'No one's going to come in for a haircut today, are they? And I'd have had a mutiny on my hands if I'd asked Clover and Buttercup to work through the sheep fair,' she added, referring to her two daughters who worked in the salon with her. 'Besides, I'd rather be here having fun. Aw, look at them bairns. Do you like the sheep, Tommy?'

Tommy nodded. 'I like that one best,' he said, pointing to a Suffolk sheep that stared back at him before turning to nudge its neighbour out of the way.

'Smashing,' Bluebell said approvingly. 'Ooh, it's like the one on your jumper! Very nice. So where are you off to next?'

'Are you going to watch the duck trials?' Ava asked, her dark brown eyes sparkling. 'I love it! Watching the ducks waddling along while the sheepdogs round them up. So funny.'

'She's playing truant,' Bluebell confided. 'Should be in the church showing people around the flower exhibition and smiling and nodding like the dutiful vicar's wife. It's me. I've led her astray. Zach will be very cross with her. She'll have to say ten Hail Marys tonight.'

Ava nudged her. 'That's a different crowd,' she said, giggling. 'I'll make it up to Zach somehow.'

'I'm sure you will,' Bluebell said, waggling her eyebrows. 'And talking of hunky men, where's that Jonah of yours?'

Kat blushed and immediately checked that Tommy wasn't listening. 'He's not *my* Jonah,' she muttered, embarrassed. 'Don't say things like that around here. You know what will happen.'

'Oh, darling, if you mean the Lavender Ladies running a bet on you two getting together you're way too late,' Ava said cheerfully. 'That's been going ever since you moved in with him.'

'You're kidding!' Though why, Kat wondered, was she even surprised? 'Anyway, I haven't moved in with him. Not like that.

I'm sort of working for him as a babysitter and housekeeper, and accommodation comes with the job.'

'I'd like a job like that,' Bluebell said dreamily. 'Mind you, knowing my luck I'd end up getting hired by Joseph Wilkinson or someone like that.'

'Don't be so beastly,' Ava chastised her. 'Joseph's a lovely man.'

'Course he is, love, but I ask you, would you rather have his face staring at you every day over your morning cornflakes, or Jonah's? Be honest.'

'Will you be quiet!' Kat shook her head, smiling, then nodded meaningfully to where Tommy was crouched down, chatting through the bars of the pen to a bored looking sheep about goodness knows what. 'I don't want him repeating stuff like that to his dad, now do I?'

'Might give him a nudge,' Bluebell suggested. 'That is, unless you've already nudged him yourself.'

'It's not like that...' Kat sighed, knowing she was on a hiding to nothing. Once the people around here got something into their heads it was hard to shift. 'I suppose you've had a bet.'

'Too right I have,' Bluebell said comfortably. 'I reckon Harvest Festival should do it.'

'That's tomorrow!' Kat gasped.

'How much time do you need?'

Ava patted her on the arm. 'Don't worry, sweetie. There's no pressure. I've given you until Halloween.'

'Oh for goodness' sake!' Kat shook her head. 'Right, I'm afraid I'll have to say goodbye. I'm going to the field now to browse the stalls and watch the demonstrations. And that's the real reason before you start.'

'We believe you.' Ava winked at Bluebell. 'We'll be heading that way later ourselves. We'll come and say hello—to you, or to Jonah, or maybe to both of you. Who knows?'

Grinning, they walked off and Kat rolled her eyes and took a reluctant Tommy's hand.

'Sorry, but it's time to go and see Daddy,' she told him, which cheered him up immediately.

She couldn't help wondering, as she headed towards All Hallows, if all the locals had been gossiping about her and Jonah, and how many of them had placed bets on when the relationship would change from platonic to romantic.

And, she had to admit, she also couldn't help but wonder if someone stood to make a profit on their bet, or if every single one of those hopeful punters was on a hiding to nothing.

SIXTEEN

After spending the rest of the morning in the field beyond the churchyard, watching some of the events that were taking place there with an excited Tommy, and a thankfully sleepy Hattie, Kat headed towards Jonah's stall, realising as she drew near that he wasn't alone. He was talking to Ross Lavender, who as usual had a pretty woman hanging off his arm.

'Hello,' Kat said, trying to smile naturally as her heart thudded just at the sight of Jonah standing there, looking all gorgeous in jeans and a checked shirt.

'Hello yourself,' he replied, smiling back, and holding out his arms as Tommy rushed to greet him.

He scooped his son up and kissed him. 'Have you had a good morning? By heck, what a smashing jumper that is!'

'Kat made it for me. We saw the sheeps and some of them looked just like this one!' Tommy told him, pointing excitedly to the one on his jumper. 'There were loads of them. And there were ducks, and the dog was chasing them, but he didn't eat them.'

'I'm relieved to hear it,' Jonah said, laughing.

'I love the duck trials,' Ross admitted. 'Always fun to watch.'

'How are you, Ross?' Kat asked, realising she hadn't really spoken to him for ages. Years ago, when they'd both been regular guests at Monk's Folly—she as Leon's girlfriend and he as Ben's best friend—they'd talked regularly, even if it had been about silly, minor things. After Leon's death they'd not really seen each other except to pass on the street or to exchange smiles and waves at local events such as these.

It was a shame. She'd liked Ross, who—if she was being honest—had always been much nicer than Ben back in the day. Of course, Ben had grown up and become a lovely man, whereas Ross had turned into a lady-killer who didn't seem to hang out with anyone much. Then again, he was heavily into art, and she supposed that was his real passion. It certainly didn't seem to be any of the women he dated, who came and went with remarkable frequency.

'I'm fine thanks, Kat. How about you? I hear you're working for Jonah now.'

Kat shuffled awkwardly. 'I suppose I am, yes,' she mumbled, just as Jonah hastily said, 'Not working for me as such. Helping me out, that's all.'

'Just while I find something else to do,' she added, reluctantly forced to acknowledge to herself that she didn't want to be known as Jonah's childminder and general dogsbody. 'You heard about the wool shop I suppose?'

'Of course. Aunt Eugenie's always going on about it, and the For Sale sign is up for everyone to see, which is awful. I'm sorry. I'll be sad to see it go.'

'Yes, me too.' She looked pointedly at his companion who'd been listening to their exchange with interest. 'Hello. I'm Kat.'

Ross cleared his throat. 'Sorry. This is my friend, Nina.'

His *friend*? Yeah, right. Kat held out her hand and Nina shook it limply, while shooting Ross a look that showed she hadn't liked that description one little bit.

'Pleased to meet you,' Kat said, while thinking it would

probably be the one and only time she ever saw her. Everyone knew that Ross never dated any woman more than once or twice.

She turned to Jonah. 'How's it going anyway? Have you managed to sell anything?'

'A few bits,' Jonah said with a shrug.

Ross burst out laughing. 'You're too modest! I've just been telling him how well he's doing, because I've seen quite a few people walking around with his works of art sticking out of their bags.'

'Works of art! Hardly,' Jonah said, looking embarrassed.

'But they are.' Ross turned to Kat. 'They're really good. I'm impressed. I was just saying, if he's interested we'd like to display some of them at the academy when it's up and running. Maybe Jonah could do demonstrations to the pupils if we took them to the forge. I'm sure some of them would love to watch an artist blacksmith at work.'

'I'm hardly that,' Jonah protested. 'I'm a farrier first and foremost.'

'With a real talent for art,' Ross said. 'I mean, look at this!' He held up a small sculpture of a bat, its wings folded around itself like a cape. 'You can't tell me this isn't art!'

'Jonah!' Kat exclaimed. 'I didn't see that in the forge. It's beautiful. You made this, really?'

He gave a short laugh. 'Yeah, but if you knew how long it took me to make it and how many of them went wrong...'

'Stop putting yourself down!' Ross eyed him sternly. 'There's going to be a shop and gallery at the academy when it opens, and if you want to sell any of your stuff there you only have to say. We're looking to showcase local art in all its forms, and this is perfect. Think about it, okay?'

Jonah nodded and Ross sighed.

'Have a word with him, Kat,' he said. 'He doesn't realise how good he is.' He put the bat back on its stand and turned over the price ticket, shaking his head. 'You've got to be kidding me. Don't let this go for less than seventy pounds. I mean it!'

'Seventy—' Jonah began, clearly shocked, but Kat interrupted him.

'I won't,' she said firmly. 'Thanks, Ross.'

'Can we go and get something to eat now?' Nina whined, and Ross draped his arm carelessly over her shoulder.

'Yes, of course. Come on then. See you later, guys. Good luck!'

Jonah put Tommy back on the ground and ruffled the little boy's hair. 'This jumper's smashing, Kat. Thanks so much. What do I owe you?'

'You don't owe me anything. Don't be daft. I've just had a woman telling me I should sell them,' she added, feeling a bit embarrassed to admit it. 'She reckons I'd have done a roaring trade at the fair.'

'So you would. Maybe next year?' He crouched down in front of Tommy. 'So, have you had anything to eat?'

He looked up questioningly at Kat who nodded. 'We've had sandwiches and cake at the café. What about you?'

'Not had time,' he pointed out.

She rummaged in her bag. 'That's what I thought so I brought you these.'

He straightened and peered into the paper bags she'd given him. 'Cheese sandwiches and a slice of Bakewell tart. Just the job! Thanks, Kat.'

'You're welcome.'

She glanced round, smiling, as Summer and Sally arrived.

'Thought we'd come early so you can tell us what we need to know,' Summer said. 'So come on, fill us in.'

There wasn't really that much to tell, and Jonah quickly ran through the basics. While he was talking to them, Kat had a quick look at the price tickets and, like Ross, she was shocked at what she saw.

'Jonah, you're seriously under-pricing these,' she told him. 'I think you should triple them at least.'

'They'd never sell,' he protested. 'They're not worth that much!'

Sally and Summer had a look at the tickets on some of the items.

'She's right, love,' Sally said. 'You're practically giving them away at these prices. I'd triple them too, if I was you.'

He hesitated. 'Double them,' he said eventually. 'That's as high as I'm prepared to go, though. Okay?'

'Deal,' Kat said, glad he'd seen sense, even if she was sure he could have asked more. 'You'd better get off anyway. Find somewhere quiet to eat your lunch then get yourself ready for the shoeing. Tommy and I will be there watching. Good luck!'

Jonah nodded and, after a hug from Tommy, he strolled away, paper bags in hand.

'Wow, these are really good,' Summer said, sounding surprised as she gazed around the stall. 'Have you seen these, Mum?'

'I know. Lovely, aren't they?' Sally lightly ran a hand over some of the sturdier pieces. 'Man of many talents that Jonah, isn't he?' She gave Kat a knowing look and Kat responded with an almost imperceptible shake of the head.

Summer, however, had clearly noticed. She grinned.

'If that warning was for my benefit, you needn't worry. I already know all about this sizzling romance that's going on under the roof of Forge Cottage.'

'What sizzling romance?' Kat demanded.

'Come on now, Kat. The Lavender Ladies are running a bet on when it will become public knowledge, so it must be true.'

Sally laughed. 'Don't be mean, Summer! It's all right, love, we've all been there, remember? We know how this works. Then again, you can't say their track record doesn't speak for itself. They were right about me and Rafferty, and they were right about Ben and Summer, so maybe...'

'Has Ben heard about this?' Kat asked anxiously.

'Of course he has. Why?'

'Well... Leon.'

Summer looked surprised. 'Don't be daft. Ben's really rooting for you.'

'He hasn't told Jennifer, though? I wouldn't want her to get the wrong idea.'

'Aw, Kat, love,' Sally said, shaking her head, 'you've got to stop worrying about all that. Jennifer would want you to move on and be happy.'

'But he hasn't mentioned it to her?' Kat persisted.

Summer shrugged. 'Not that I know of, no.'

'Please,' Kat begged, 'tell him not to. It's just gossip, nothing more than that, and not worth upsetting her with.'

Summer and Sally exchanged puzzled looks.

'Please?'

'Okay,' Summer said, sounding uncertain. 'If that's what you want. I'll tell him.'

'Can we watch the sheep races?' Tommy asked, peering up at Kat with a pleading expression.

'Sure we can,' Kat said, glad of a change of subject. 'But your daddy's shoeing demonstration comes first. The sheep race starts after that.'

'If you like,' Summer offered, 'I can stay at the stall while the races are on, and Jonah can watch the races with you. I'm sure *Tommy* would like that.'

Kat decided not to rise to the bait. 'That's lovely of you. You'll have to ask Jonah.' She remembered about the prices and picked up a bunch of spare price labels that were lying behind the counter. 'Have either of you got a pen? I'm going to change these prices before he comes back to tell me he's changed his mind.'

* * *

The shoeing demonstration was about to start, and Kat led Tommy over to where a young woman had led a large, hairy, coloured cob into the field, next to where Jonah's van was parked, its doors open and the portable forge inside clearly visible.

There was a camera on a tripod and a large screen set up so that people would be able to see what Jonah was doing. Kat felt nervous for him as he stood waiting while a man in tweeds tested the microphone to make sure people could hear him clearly. He was going to be explaining what Jonah was doing to everyone. No wonder he'd been nervous!

Jonah was wearing his apron over his jeans, although Kat felt the term "apron" was misleading. It looked more like short leather chaps, with big pockets on each side. She couldn't help but feel a stab of pride as she watched him, especially when she heard two young women close by say how gorgeous he was.

He didn't look at the crowd, which didn't surprise her. No doubt he would be trying not to think about them, focusing instead on the job in hand. He spoke to the young woman holding the horse and stroked the horse's muzzle before getting to work.

Kat watched as he put the horse's hoof between his knees and reached for a hammer and another tool from his toolbox.

The man with the microphone explained that the first thing Jonah was doing was removing the old shoe. The nails were removed and then Jonah used what looked like giant pliers to pull the shoe away from the hoof.

He worked swiftly and surely, taking a curved knife to the hoof, scraping away chunks of it and making Kat wince, although the horse seemed totally unflustered by the experience, so it clearly wasn't bothering him. The man explained that Jonah was paring away the excess sole and dead frog, allowing healthy tissue to breathe. Kat presumed a frog was part of the foot and not an unfortunate amphibian that the horse had trodden on.

He then used what the man said was a nipper to trim the hoof wall to the required length. Kat watched, fascinated, as Jonah went through a variety of tools just to get the hoof ready for shoeing. She'd had no idea there was so much to it, and her mind whirled as the man informed them of all the different tools he was reaching for throughout the demonstration: nipper, rasp, tongs, pritchel, and so many types of hammer, each of which apparently had a different use.

Bit by bit, Jonah peeled away layers of dirty hoof, revealing a fresh, white surface. He then took a rasp, which was just like a giant nail file, and Tommy looked up at her as Jonah filed the hoof firmly and assuredly, bits of it showering down on the ground around him.

'It's okay,' he whispered to Kat. 'It doesn't hurt the horse at all, promise.'

Her heart melted as he took her hand in his and clasped it tightly, as if to reassure her.

Using tongs, Jonah took a horseshoe from the forge on his van. It was glowing red hot, and he placed it on the anvil, where he got to work shaping it and brushing it with a large, stiff brush, to remove any loose filings.

He then placed the horseshoe on the hoof, and steam poured from it, making Tommy gasp, even though he'd seen it all before. It was Kat's turn to squeeze his hand, and she was gratified when he rewarded her with a happy smile.

Jonah removed the shoe several times to shape the edge of the hoof around the imprint of the shoe, scraping bits away before pressing the hot shoe against the foot again.

Eventually, he seemed satisfied and began to nail the shoe to the hoof using what the man called a driving hammer. It looked like a claw hammer, and after Jonah had banged each nail in he used the claw end to break off the ends of the nail that were protruding through the hoof wall.

He used a variety of tools to make sure the nails were flat against the hoof and rasped them again, before brushing them down with what looked like a long nail brush. Kat glanced at the screen and saw a close-up of the finished hoof, clean and gleaming, with a shiny new shoe in place.

There was a round of applause as Jonah dropped the cob's foot and gathered up his tools, giving a brief nod to acknowledge the crowd while the man with the microphone pointed out what a skilled job being a farrier was, and how long it took to train, and informed them that anyone interested in becoming a farrier would find more information in the leaflets at the rural careers stall.

The young woman spoke to Jonah for a few minutes while he packed his things back in the van, then she led the cob away. Kat beamed at Tommy.

'Wasn't that amazing? Isn't your daddy clever?'

Tommy nodded. 'Can we watch the sheep races now?'

Kat sighed inwardly. There was no pleasing some people. 'Let's see if your dad wants to watch them too, shall we?'

Tommy was quite pleased by that idea, so as the crowds drifted off towards the fenced off track near the churchyard fence, grandly nicknamed the racetrack, Kat led him over to the van, where Jonah had just slammed the doors shut.

He turned, smiling when he saw them.

'You watched then?'

'Didn't you see us?' Kat asked. 'We were front row, cheering you on.'

'I didn't hear anyone cheering,' he said, laughing.

'Okay, well in our heads we were cheering you on.' She didn't tell him what else had been in her head, nor how her body had reacted to seeing him looking so capable and professional. She'd almost melted on the spot, but there was no way she could tell him that. Instead she said cheerfully, 'You were really good. I was impressed. Would you like to watch the sheep racing with us?'

They followed him to the side of the van where he opened the driver's door and said, 'I'd love to, but I've got the stall to see to.'

'Summer said she's happy to cover if you want to come with us,' Kat told him quickly. 'What do you think?'

He hesitated then nodded. 'Why not? Give me five minutes to shift the van and I'll meet you at the racecourse.'

She thought he probably had no idea how the thought of spending another half an hour in his company thrilled her. She hadn't realised it herself until that moment. There was no denying it any longer, though. She was totally, one hundred per cent, head over heels in love with Jonah Brewster. Now what was she supposed to do?

SEVENTEEN

Sunday was colder—much colder. Jonah turned over the page on his Country Year calendar to reveal October's photograph, which was appropriately autumnal. Today was the second and final day of the sheep fair, and the day would begin with the Harvest Festival service at the church.

He hadn't intended to go, thinking he'd be busy on the stall, which had, to his astonishment, been a resounding success. He couldn't believe how much money he'd made yesterday, as he'd fully expected sales to drop after Kat doubled the prices. They hadn't, and he had to admit it had boosted his confidence, knowing that so many people were willing to pay so much for the things he'd made.

Kat was taking the children to All Hallows because she told him she loved the service, and went every year with her aunties, at which point Sally, who'd been standing with them offered to man the stall for an hour or so if he wanted to go to the church with them.

When he'd declined her offer, thinking it too much of an imposition, she'd assured him it was no bother at all.

'And I'm sure it would mean a lot if you went,' she'd added. 'To Tommy.'

He supposed it would be nice if he could be there for his son, rather than leaving him in Kat's capable hands yet again. And, if he was being really honest with himself, it would be lovely to attend church with Kat and Hattie, too. So he'd said yes to Sally's offer, and he couldn't deny he was looking forward to it.

Kat was just slipping a cardigan on Hattie when he brought Tommy, fully dressed and teeth cleaned, downstairs. Jonah watched her for a moment, thinking.

'Did you knit that, too?' he asked, nodding at the chunky grey-blue cardigan that looked lovely and warm on the baby girl.

'Sure did,' Kat said, buttoning it up despite Hattie's wriggling. She glanced up at him. 'Why? Do you like it?'

Jonah sat down next to her on the sofa. 'You know, maybe that woman at the fair had a point. You know, the one who said you should be selling jumpers yesterday? She reckoned you'd make a killing, and I think she could be right. These are good, Kat. Really good. Have you ever thought about setting up a knitting business?'

Kat frowned. 'Are you serious?'

'Why not? Think about it. You're always knitting in your spare time anyway. You've told me yourself you love it, you've loved it since you were a little kid. You could sell them online. Maybe even get a market stall once you've built up your stock. What do you think?'

She hesitated, clearly uncertain. 'I suppose it's a thought,' she said slowly. 'It would certainly bring in some extra money, and it would fit around Hattie and Tommy, too. I'm not sure how much I'd make though.'

'Well, just think about it,' he urged, taking Hattie from her knee. 'Come on, get your coat and let's get off to the church.'

All Hallows was packed when they arrived, looking particularly lovely with the flower displays on view. A variety of foodstuffs was already laid out on the altar steps. They added a bag of apples, some tinned soup, and a packet of pasta to the other offerings, knowing that after the service the provisions would be boxed up and delivered to the elderly residents of Tuppenny Bridge.

Glancing round, Jonah could see quite a few of the locals were there. Harvest Festival was probably the most popular church event after Christmas, so it wasn't surprising, and it was no wonder that Zach Barrington, the local vicar, beamed round at them all in delight, clearly pleased to see such a full church.

The service was one of thanksgiving, and a reminder to them all that everyone owed a great debt to the food producers in the world, who in turn owed much to the mercy of God. Zach also took the time to point out that not everyone was so blessed, and that there was a great deal of hunger and poverty, including in their own community, and led prayers for the well-being of those less fortunate.

There were several readings, and the congregation sang three of Jonah's favourite hymns: *We Plough the Fields and Scatter*; *Come, Ye Thankful People, Come*; and *All Things Bright and Beautiful*.

After the service there was tea, coffee and biscuits, and everyone milled round, exchanging news and admiring the floral displays.

'Wonderful service as always, vicar,' Miss Lavender said. She was the only person Jonah knew who ever referred to Zach in that way. Everyone else just used his name, which he preferred, but there was no swaying Miss Lavender. 'So good to see so many donations. There'll be quite a haul for the elderly.'

'Does that include you, Miss Lavender?'

Some cheeky teenage boy had the nerve to ask her that, and Jonah had to admire his courage.

Miss Lavender gave him an icy stare. 'Hardly, young man.

And I wouldn't mock if I were you. One day it will be you whose door the church is knocking on and you might well be grateful for the donation. So think on that.'

Jonah grinned as the boy was dragged away by his embarrassed mother, and Miss Lavender gave a satisfied nod before hurrying off to supervise the tea and coffee service, because apparently whoever was in charge of that was being far too slow.

'What would we do without her?' Zach said in his broad Yorkshire accent, so unlike his wife's cut-glass tones.

'Probably relax a bit more?' Kat suggested, her eyes twinkling.

'Well, there is that,' Zach agreed. 'Still, we'd be lost without her. She's done so much to help and I, for one, am very grateful.'

'Plenty of donations I see,' Jonah remarked, nodding towards the altar steps.

Zach smiled as he glanced behind him. 'Definitely. People have been lovely. I know it's not been an easy few years for most people, and there are too many struggling financially, so it's heart-warming to see them donating what they can to help.'

'Reckon the Tuppenny Bridge Fund will be down on other years then?' Jonah asked, knowing that the vicar was one of the committee in charge of the fund.

'It's hard to say. There haven't been as many donations throughout the year,' Zach admitted, rubbing his chin. 'Like I said, it's been a tough few years so it's not surprising. But the sheep fair has been very busy this year, and we've had record entrants for the classes, plus even more stalls than usual. Maybe we'll make more from that. And then of course there's the annual donation from the Lavender Ladies to come.'

Kat and Jonah exchanged surprised looks.

'The Lavender Ladies?' Kat asked. 'They make a donation?'

Zach looked astonished that she didn't know. 'Well of

course they do. What do you think they do with the profits from the bets they run?'

Jonah shrugged. 'To be honest, I thought they just pocketed it.'

Zach laughed. 'I believe that would be illegal. Miss Lavender would never permit it.'

Kat pulled a face. 'Reckon the aunties would.'

'Well, maybe...' Zach winked. 'But you know Eugenie Lavender. Everything above board. She made sure, from the day I arrived in this town, that I was aware of the, er, sideline they had going, and that I had full access to their records. Every penny they make goes into a special account, and each year they hand it over to the Tuppenny Bridge Fund. They've donated a small fortune over the years. Naturally I can't condone gambling in any form, but even so, I have to admit it's been a blessing for the fund. Their profits have helped a great many causes in this town.'

'Well I never,' Kat murmured. 'I had no idea.'

'Oh yes,' Zach said, his eyes twinkling. 'So all those courting couples finally getting together are doing some good for Tuppenny Bridge. Remember that.'

He placed a hand on each of their shoulders and grinned at them, then headed off to speak to Rafferty Kingston.

Realising what he'd meant by that last remark, Jonah felt his face heating up. He hardly dare look at Kat, wondering if she was aware that there was a bet running on them. He really hoped not, but it would be a miracle if that had escaped her notice in this town.

Luckily, at that moment, Tommy announced he wanted a biscuit, so Kat led him away to get one. She left Jonah with Hattie, who was sitting in her buggy, staring wide-eyed at everyone milling around her, and receiving the occasional pat on the head and adoring smile from various members of the congregation with surprising calm and grace. There were several admiring comments about her cardigan, which Jonah took great pleasure in passing on to Kat when she returned.

As the church emptied, Jonah announced he'd have to head back to the stall.

'You're sure you're okay with Tommy?' he murmured. 'I know it's a lot to ask—'

'It's not a lot to ask at all,' Kat said. 'Stop worrying. I'm taking them to the market place now because the Jacobs are being shown today and I do love to see them. I'll catch you later.'

Jonah nodded and dropped a kiss on Tommy's cheek, then he bent down and took Hattie's little hand in his and squeezed it gently.

'Behave yourselves, you two,' he told the children. 'I'll see you all later.'

He straightened, and his gaze landed on Kat. For one horrifying moment he almost leaned forward to kiss her too, but thankfully caught himself in time and stepped back as if he'd been slapped.

'You okay?' she asked, looking puzzled.

'Fine. Just lost my balance for a moment.' He shrugged. 'Must be getting old. I'll see you soon.'

With that, he strode away as fast as possible without actually breaking into a jog. Where had all these feelings for Kat come from? Why now?

This, he reflected with rising panic, was getting serious. Something was going to have to be done about it.

* * *

Summer and Clemmie joined Kat and the children as she wandered towards the sheep pens, keen to watch the Jacobs being judged.

'No Dolly?' Kat asked as they walked beside the buggy

towards Little Market Place where the judging was taking place.

Being Sunday, The Corner Cottage Bookshop was closed for the day, so she'd assumed Dolly would be attending the fair.

Clemmie, a pretty twenty-six-year-old with fair hair and blue eyes, wrinkled her nose. 'Edits,' she said briefly.

Dolly Bennet was an author of wartime sagas, as well as owning the bookshop, and Kat knew all too well that her writing schedule took priority over everything else. It possibly explained why Dolly wasn't married or seeing anyone, although according to her she had no time for all that *romantic tosh* and saved it instead for her fictional characters.

'What a shame. It's been a great fair so far,' she said. 'What a pity she's had to miss out.'

Clemmie laughed. 'Well, sheep aren't really Dolly's thing anyway. She's not that bothered. To be fair, I feel pretty much the same. We've enjoyed the races and the duck trials and browsing the stalls, but I can take or leave the sheep.'

'Not that you can miss them,' Summer added, glancing around the market place which was jammed with pens full of various breeds of sheep. The sound of bleating filled the air, and a loudspeaker announced the various classes at regular intervals, so Kat had to agree with Summer's statement. Whatever else was going on, this event was definitely about the sheep first and foremost.

'Are you going to watch the judging?' she asked doubtfully, wondering where else they would be going in this direction.

'Nope. We're off to the Lusty Tup Brewery on a tour,' Summer told her. 'I've heard loads about it, but I've never been. There's a bus running from Station Road in five minutes for the next tour, so Clemmie offered to go with me. Ben's not keen, but he's too busy checking over the animals and judging anyway. Even if he wasn't I don't think he'd come. He's a bit funny about Lusty Tup, what with his brother and everything.' She went pink suddenly. 'Oh! Sorry, Kat. I didn't think.'

'It's okay.' Kat gave her a reassuring smile. 'It was a long time ago.'

Although she felt pretty much the same as Ben. The brewery was the last place she felt like visiting.

'We'd better hurry if we're going to catch the bus,' Clemmie said.

Summer nodded. 'See you later, Kat.'

'Have a good time,' Kat called after them, as the two girls hurried away. 'Don't sample too many of the freebies!'

She saw the pen of Jacob sheep and nudged Tommy. 'Look! Those are my favourites. Aren't they lovely?'

The Jacobs were, she thought, a joy to behold. With dense, piebald fleeces and impressive horns they looked more like goats than sheep. Some of them had brown patches while others had black, and most of them had four horns, although some had two. They were known for being sharp-witted and alert and didn't have the more docile expressions seen on some of the other breeds of sheep.

Tommy agreed that the Jacobs were beautiful, although he wasn't so keen on the horns, and it was clear he'd preferred the hornless Herdwicks and Suffolks yesterday.

Right now, the Rough Fells were being judged, and Kat wheeled the buggy closer to the trailer outside the Town Hall, where the top three were being examined to decide which prize they'd be awarded.

'I'm glad I bumped into you,' said a voice beside her, and she spun round, wrinkling her nose as she fought to remember the name of the young woman who'd come to view the shop, but whose brother hadn't bothered to turn up.

'Are you? Why's that?' Daisy! That was it. Relieved, Kat smiled at her. 'Don't tell me your brother's changed his mind?'

'He says we can book another viewing,' Daisy revealed. 'If

that's okay.' She looked anxious. 'You haven't sold it yet, have you?'

'Not yet,' Kat replied, deciding not to add that they hadn't even come close. 'When were you thinking?'

'Wednesday evening?' Daisy suggested. 'Do you think it could be just us? No estate agent, I mean. He might get pushy, and I don't want to scare them off. Tom's girlfriend's coming with us too.' She didn't sound too keen on the idea. 'I'm sorry we messed you about last time. Tom's been living in a city for a long time, and he's a bit reluctant to move back to the Dales. It's his girlfriend who's keener, although she's never lived in the country before. She's got this fantasy I suppose. She watches too many rural property programmes. To be honest, I don't care if she loves it or hates it once she gets here, as long as she persuades Tom to buy the shop. I'll worry about what happens later after we've bought it.'

'You really want it then?' Kat asked doubtfully.

'I really do,' Daisy admitted. 'I'm sick of living in the city and now Dad's gone there's nothing to keep me there. We're from Upper Skimmerdale originally, you see. Dad had a sheep farm up there. I'm a country girl at heart. Couldn't resist the sheep fair, and I...'

She broke off, staring at the trailer where the judging of the rough fells was in its final stages, transfixed.

'He only used to breed Swaledales.'

'Sorry?'

'Ignore me. I was thinking out loud.' Daisy nodded towards the trailer. 'See the farmer with the sheep on the right? I know him. Well,' she gave a bitter laugh. 'I *used* to know him.'

Kat saw a tall man with dark, curly hair and a face that reminded her of Aidan Turner.

'Oh? You don't see him any longer?'

'We were neighbours,' Daisy said, her voice suddenly brittle. 'He's a sheep farmer too. I used to help him out with the children after his wife died.'

Kat glanced uncomfortably at Tommy. 'Right. So you're friends then?'

Daisy wrapped her arms around herself. 'We were. I thought—I thought we were more than that. I used to cook for him, see to the kids, do the washing, get them to school. Well, as much as I could. I had a job, and the farm, and my dad to see to, but...' She sighed. 'Anyway, it turned out I was just a helpful neighbour in his eyes. Someone new and prettier came along and that was that.'

'Oh.' Kat felt subdued. 'I'm sorry.' She felt it best not to say anything else, as it was clearly a sore subject. To her surprise, though, Daisy seemed keen to continue. It was as if a torrent of hurt was pouring forth.

'It was my own fault. I let myself be pushed into the friend zone, and it's always a mistake. Plus I was too bloody helpful. I made it easy for him. When someone came along who challenged him a bit he was a pushover. They're married now,' she added. 'I don't think she's here though. No doubt she'd be hanging off his arm if she was.'

'How long ago was this?' Kat asked, sensing that Daisy was still hurting.

'Oh, about six, seven years.'

Crikey! And she still hadn't moved on, clearly. Kat gripped the handles of the buggy as Daisy turned to her and she saw tears in the woman's eyes.

'I left it too late,' she said flatly. 'I should have told him how I felt, but I kept putting it off. In the end he'd stopped noticing me. I was just there. I shouldn't have let us get so comfortable.' She nodded at the trailer. 'He's won, look. Thought he would.'

Kat watched as the judges shook the farmer's hand. He was rather good looking, she thought. She could understand Daisy falling for him. What a shame he'd only seen her as the help...

Daisy's face reddened suddenly, and there was a hint of panic in her voice as she said, 'He's seen me! I've got to go. I'll see you later, Kat.'

She hurried off, melting into the crowd, and Kat saw the farmer scanning the hordes of people as if looking for her. She had a feeling that, if he went looking, he wouldn't find her. Daisy clearly didn't want to bump into him again, even though she'd obviously been besotted with him at one time. Probably, she thought sadly, she still was.

She turned the buggy around and took Tommy's hand, leading him away from the crowd. Her interest in watching the Jacobs being judged had waned, and she thought it might be time to take the children home instead.

Daisy had given her food for thought. Like Kat, she'd stepped in to help with the children when this man had lost his wife, and like Kat she'd fallen for the bereaved father. But she hadn't told him how she felt, and her chance had passed when he'd met someone else—someone he didn't see as simply a kind friend who'd helped him out, but someone new and exciting. Someone he could fall in love with.

What if that happened to her and Jonah? What if Jonah met someone else who he talked to about other things, rather than whether Tommy's school uniform needed washing, or if they'd run out of peanut butter for his packed lunch?

Frowning, she headed towards Forge Lane. She'd been the one who'd insisted that she was simply staying at the cottage as a glorified babysitter. That she and Jonah were just friends. But if she repeated that often enough it might be something Jonah himself could never get past. The more she reinforced it, the greater the chance that he would never be able to see her as anything other than the hired help.

She'd thought she had time. Plenty of time. She'd thought her feelings towards Jonah were something she could bury.

Pretend it wasn't happening. There was always tomorrow after all.

But what if he met someone this very afternoon? What if someone stopped by his stall and admired his work and they got talking? What about the young woman who'd lent him the cob to do his shoeing demonstration with yesterday? It could, she realised with increasing alarm, happen any time.

She didn't want what had happened to Daisy to happen to her.

She had to tell him how she felt. He might be horrified. He might tell her that he didn't feel the same way and never would. But at least then she'd know she'd tried; that she didn't have to live with the same regrets Daisy had.

Whatever the outcome, it was now or never.

EIGHTEEN

Jonah had expected Kat to turn up at the stall at some point during the day, so when she didn't, his heart sank. He told himself she had enough on her hands with the children, and anyway, why would she want to stand and talk to him when she could see him any day of the week, and probably had far better things to do with her time?

He imagined her in the market place, laughing and chatting with their friends and neighbours. Maybe Ross Lavender had sidled up to her and she was talking to him? He wasn't sure why that thought had popped into his head, but he wished it hadn't.

Nina, he was sure, was already yesterday's news, and Kat was an attractive woman. Okay, she was seven or eight years older than Ross, but what was that in the scheme of things? He'd bet Ross had dated women a lot older than that. They'd seemed to get on well yesterday when they were talking at the stall and...

He shook his head. What the hell was wrong with him? He was acting like some daft bloody kid!

Hattie and Tommy had already had a long day at the sheep fair yesterday and expecting them to cope with another full day was probably unfair. Kat had no doubt taken them home because they'd had enough. He needed his head read if he thought it was anything more than that.

As the field beyond the churchyard emptied, he drove the van close to the stall and began to load what was left into it. He was pleased there was very little to take back. He'd sold most of the artwork and had made a tidy profit, far beyond his expectations.

Thanks to Kat persuading him to up the prices. She had more faith in him than he had in himself.

There she was, in his head again. She seemed to live there almost permanently these days. He closed the van doors and leaned against them, wondering what the hell he was going to do about it.

This, he thought wretchedly, was the last thing he needed. He blamed Noah for putting the idea into his head in the first place. He would never have seen Kat as anything but a friend if not for him and his stupid comments.

An image flashed into his mind. The Market Café. Baby vomit dribbling down his jacket. Kat dabbing at his chest with paper napkins. Her gaze lifting to meet his. The way his heart had pounded most unexpectedly...

Had it happened then? He'd dismissed the way his body had reacted and told himself it meant nothing, and somehow he'd convinced himself it was true until Noah opened the whole can of worms again. Maybe he couldn't blame his friend for his feelings after all. But it didn't matter whose fault it was anyway.

What mattered was what, if anything, he was going to do about it.

A warm glow crept through him as he remembered her reaction yesterday when they'd got home. She'd been full of praise for him—delighted he'd sold so many items on the stall—chatting excitedly about how clever he was with horses, and how amazing it had been, watching him shoe the cob, and how brilliant he was at his job.

It occurred to him that she'd seemed proud of him, which made him proud of himself. She'd also made him feel good about himself, and it had been a long time since he'd felt that way.

He ran a hand through his hair and groaned. He had to tell her how he felt. There was no running away from this, not any longer.

But what about Leon?

The thought stopped him in his tracks. Leon had been his best friend, and he'd loved Kat so much. How would he feel if Jonah made a move on her?

Another thought occurred to him, and he tried to quell the queasiness in his stomach. How would Kat feel if the best friend of her one true love told her *he* was in love with her? What if she was disgusted with him?

But it had been fourteen years. He closed his eyes briefly as he realised that, actually, it would be exactly fourteen years a week from today. October the eighth. A day never to be forgotten.

Would it be tactless and appalling if he even broached the subject so close to the anniversary?

Of course it would! What the hell was he thinking?

Jonah muttered a curse and climbed into the van, slamming the door shut.

If he wanted to drive Kat away for good, now would be the perfect time to tell her that he loved her. Idiot. He was going to have to keep a lid on his feelings for now. There was nothing else for it.

He was about to drive up Forge Lane but changed his mind. He'd leave the van in the car park of The White Hart Inn tonight. He needed a drink.

* * *

Kat had spent the afternoon preparing a hearty chicken casserole for tea, thinking it would be nice to have a family meal around the table. By six o'clock, however, she'd had to admit defeat, and gave Tommy and Hattie theirs, then bathed them, and got them both into clean pyjamas.

By seven, Hattie was fast asleep in her cot, and by eight—knowing he had to be up for school tomorrow—Kat had tucked Tommy into bed and read him a story, assuring him that Daddy was absolutely fine and was just busy putting away the stall, and that he'd see him tomorrow at breakfast.

She went downstairs and stacked the dirty crockery and cutlery in the dishwasher, eyeing the casserole dubiously, hoping she wouldn't have to keep it warm for much longer.

She cleared away Hattie's things and double-checked Tommy's school uniform was ready for tomorrow. Then she checked she had everything for his packed lunch, even though she already knew she had.

With the house clean and tidy, the children asleep, and the tea ready to go, Kat sank onto the sofa and gazed unseeingly at the television, wondering where on earth Jonah had got to. It couldn't take him this long to load up his van.

Her mobile rang and she grabbed it, feeling guilty at her disappointment that it was Sally's name flashing on the screen, rather than Jonah's.

'Hiya, Sal. How's it going?'

'Hiya, love. Just thought I'd ring you and give you a head's up that Jonah's here.'

'Here? You mean the pub?'

'I do. And I've got to tell you he's standing at the bar, staring into a pint of beer, and looking like he's got the weight of the world on his shoulders. Rafferty's been trying to get out of him what's up but he's not in the mood to talk evidently. Anyway I thought you'd like to know, in case you were worrying where he was.'

'Thanks, Sal. Bloody hell, I wonder what's happened?' Kat frowned, anxiety turning her stomach. 'He was fine earlier. I've been expecting him home. I've made our tea and the kids are in bed.'

'Maybe,' Sally said, after a moment's hesitation, 'you should come and collect him.'

'Don't be daft. How can I? I've got the kids.'

'Our Summer and Ben are here doing nothing. I'm sure they'd mind them for you if you wanted to pop round and collect him.'

'Yes, maybe I should. Are you sure they won't mind?'

'Course not, love. They've finished their meal, so I'll pop over and ask them now. Expect them in ten minutes.'

She ended the call and Kat stared at the screen, chewing her lip as she wondered what on earth had made Jonah seek refuge in the pub. He wasn't a *drowning your sorrows* sort of man, and anyway, what sorrows did he have to drown? As far as she was aware he'd had a good day. A good weekend in fact. Something had clearly gone wrong after they'd parted company earlier.

Ben and Summer arrived within ten minutes, as Sally had said, and they didn't seem at all surprised that Kat was on a mission to save Jonah from himself.

'I saw him hunched over the bar,' Summer admitted. 'He looks proper miserable.'

'He got like that once before,' Ben said. 'When Sofia left. He was on a real downer for months, but then he pulled himself out of it and he's been great ever since.'

'Bluebell was in,' Summer told her. 'She said she hadn't seen him drinking alone in a pub since he got custody of Tommy, so she's a bit worried about him. I can't think what's wrong with him.'

'Me neither,' Kat said anxiously. 'Thanks for looking after the kids. I won't be long.' Silently, she added, 'hopefully,' to that statement and left Forge Cottage, wondering exactly what lay ahead of her.

* * *

Jonah was, indeed, propping up the bar at The White Hart Inn, and Kat headed straight for him, nodding an acknowledgement to Sally and Rafferty who were serving customers but managed, nevertheless, to wave to her as soon as she walked in.

'There you are!' she said, standing by Jonah's side and attempting a casual, faux jolly tone. 'I was wondering where you'd got to. I've got a chicken casserole at home with your name on it.'

Jonah sprang up looking guilty. 'Sorry. I was...' He shrugged and gestured to his half-empty pint glass. 'Well.'

'Are you drunk?' she asked, trying not to sound as if it were an accusation. It was up to him if he got drunk, obviously, although she did think it was a bit rich when he knew she had the kids to see to. He could, at the very least, have rung her to warn her he'd be late, especially since she'd been so knotted up with anxiety as she prepared to tell him how she felt. Not that he could have known that, to be fair.

'Do I look drunk?' he asked, puzzled.

She had to admit he didn't. Even so, that didn't mean he wasn't.

'How many of those have you had?'

'This is my first one,' he said, his eyebrows knitting together. 'Any more questions?'

'Sorry.' She had to admit she was a bit baffled. Sally had made it sound as if he was weeping into his beer, and Summer and Ben had insinuated he was in a right state. He seemed perfectly fine to Kat, other than the fact he'd gone to the pub after finishing work rather than going straight home.

She glanced over at Sally who quickly turned away and started serving another customer.

Okay, something funny was going on here. Why had they made such a big drama of Jonah having a simple drink?

'I think I've been played,' she said heavily, leaning on the counter next to him.

'Played?'

Briefly she explained what had happened and why she was here. Jonah's mouth fell open as he listened, and he shook his head.

'Bloody hell! There's no such thing as a private life in this town. Fancy making out that I was legless. I bet you thought I'd be swaggering down the street singing "Nellie Dean".'

Kat wrinkled her nose. 'What's "Nellie Dean"?'

'Buggered if I know,' he admitted. 'But it's what people are supposed to sing when they're drunk, isn't it?'

'I've no idea. I have to say I'm relieved to find you sober. I wasn't sure I was going to be able to get you home. I reckon the best I could have managed was to bundle you into your van and leave you there for the night.'

'Fair enough,' Jonah said. 'If I'd got myself into that much of a state I guess it would be all I deserved. Now you're here, would you like a drink?'

Kat hesitated. 'Best not,' she said. 'I've got Summer and Ben babysitting and the casserole's keeping warm. If you want to stay here I'll eat mine and put yours in the fridge for tomorrow. Or you can have it later if you're hungry.'

So much for the big confession. Oh well, maybe tomorrow…

Jonah pushed away his beer. 'I might as well come home with you,' he said. 'Imagine what people would say if I stayed here on my own. You don't want to get another phone call at eleven o'clock telling you I'm on the verge of being arrested for being drunk and disorderly, when what they really mean is I've had two whole pints and I took my jacket off.'

She laughed. 'Come on then. Let's go home.'

'Let's give them something to talk about,' he said mischievously, and linked his arm through hers, which sent a bolt of electricity through Kat immediately.

'See you later, Sal,' she called, satisfied to see Sally's look of surprise as she and Jonah walked arm in arm out of The White Hart Inn.

They crossed the road and headed slowly up Forge Lane. It was a cold, still night, and Kat was glad she'd worn her winter coat. She glanced at Jonah, who was wearing *the jacket*, and thought he looked bloody gorgeous. She wished she had the nerve to have that conversation with him right now.

'Are you warm enough in that?' she asked doubtfully.

'You're kidding. It's boiling,' he told her. 'Mind you, my ears are freezing.'

She reached out a hand and touched them. 'Crikey, you're right. They'll be snapping off soon if you're not careful. You'll have to wear a hat in future.'

'Fat chance,' was his fervent reply.

They walked in silence for a few moments, then Jonah said, 'I'm sorry you got dragged out on a wild goose chase.'

'It's okay. It wasn't your fault. I'm just glad you're all right. I was worried about you.'

'Were you?'

'Of course. I thought something had happened. Something awful to upset you.'

'No, no. Nothing happened. I just fancied a beer, that's all.'

'Good.' They reached Forge Cottage and Kat pushed open the gate. 'If you ever fancy a beer again, could you let me know so I'm not worried?'

He nodded, not looking at her. 'Promise.'

Summer and Ben looked a bit surprised when Jonah and Kat walked in.

'Oh!' Summer said. 'We weren't expecting you back so soon.'

'Are you okay, Jonah?' Ben asked, peering at Jonah with obvious concern, which made Kat suspect that he'd genuinely thought there was something wrong with his friend.

'I'm absolutely fine,' Jonah reassured him. 'I had half a pint of beer, that's it. I don't know what all the fuss is about.'

'But Mum said...' Summer's voice trailed off and she swallowed, before glancing nervously at Kat.

'Yes,' Kat said heavily. 'I can imagine she did.'

'Well,' Ben said defensively, 'you did look miserable, standing at the bar staring into your glass.'

'What were you expecting me to do?' Jonah enquired. 'Jump onto the counter and start a singsong? How do you look when you're standing at the bar alone having a drink?'

'I've never done it,' Ben admitted. 'So I wouldn't really know.'

'I'll throttle my mother,' Summer said.

'You know what she's like,' Kat soothed, not daring to look at Jonah. 'Tell her from me I'm a big girl now and I can sort my own life out.'

'Maybe she's put a bet on with the Lavender Ladies,' Jonah suggested. 'She might as well. Every bugger else in this town has.'

'Don't you mind?' Ben asked, surprised.

'Not now I know it all goes to charity, no. Fill your boots is what I say. It's all in a good cause.'

'It goes to charity?' Ben sounded astonished.

'Oh yes.' Briefly, Kat explained what Zach had told them earlier.

'Who'd have thought it?' Summer said, puffing out her cheeks in surprise. 'I never realised it was illegal to make a profit from a few friendly bets like that. I'll bet Rafferty knew all about the fund though, because he's an ex-barrister, and I'll bet he mentioned it to Zach. Zach must have put his mind at rest, or I don't think he'd have allowed it to carry on.'

'Come on,' Ben said, nudging her. 'I'll walk you home. Let's leave these two to enjoy their supper. Sorry about all the drama.'

'Thanks for babysitting at such short notice,' Jonah said, clapping him on the shoulder. 'Sorry you were dragged out of that warm, cosy pub.'

Ben and Summer waved goodbye, and Kat closed the door behind them and leaned against it for a moment, thinking how embarrassing this all was and wondering how she was supposed to behave around Jonah now.

Sally had made it obvious that she was matchmaking. Clearly Rafferty knew about it. Ben and Summer knew, too. And there was the bet running on their relationship, which Jonah was obviously aware of. What on earth was she supposed to do? How was she supposed to act?

She'd got herself all fired up to tell him how she felt but Sally had spoiled it. Oh, of course she hadn't meant to. No doubt she'd thought she was helping Kat out — giving her a gentle nudge in the right direction. She wasn't to know that she'd effectively ruined her big moment. She was far too embarrassed to say anything now.

Right, just act normally. Go in there and dish out the casserole and make small talk. Ask him how the day went on the stall. Ask him about today's shoeing demonstration. Ask him how much money he thinks the fair has raised this year. He'll be mortified too. He won't want to think about it. So talk about any bloody thing except us. Me and Jonah. This. Whatever this is.

She walked slowly back into the kitchen. 'Ready for your tea?'

He smiled. 'Sounds great. I'll just grab a shower.'

Fifteen minutes later they were sitting at the table with plates of food before them, eating awkwardly.

Kat could hardly wait for the meal to be over. This wasn't what she'd envisaged when she'd made her resolution to tell him the truth. Bloody Sally Kingston. She'd be having words with her tomorrow.

'Well, this is awful, isn't it?'

Jonah's question jerked her back into the moment and she stared at him in dismay.

'Is it?' She splashed her spoon into the casserole. 'Is it over-cooked? I did have it keeping warm a long time, I suppose.'

'I wasn't talking about the casserole,' he said gently.

Kat's face burned. 'Oh.'

Were they really doing this now? She steeled herself for the polite, *It's not you, it's me*, conversation. She supposed she'd had it coming.

'They weren't entirely wrong,' Jonah mumbled.

Kat frowned. 'Sorry? I didn't hear you properly.'

He cleared his throat. 'I said they weren't entirely wrong. I *was* miserable. I went into the pub because I felt—' He pushed away his plate and leaned back in his chair. 'Sorry. I don't know how to start this.'

'Maybe start with telling me why you were miserable?'

'It's Leon's anniversary next week,' he said flatly.

Kat's heart sank. As if she needed reminding! Was this what all the misery was about? If that was the case, it was a good job she hadn't spoken about her feelings to Jonah. He'd have been horrified that she could even think of such a thing when the anniversary was so close.

'Hmm,' she said, not knowing what else to say.

'Thing is,' he said, 'it's been fourteen years. That's a long time.'

'I know.' She moved some chicken around her plate, making no attempt to spoon it up.

'Well, I mean, things happen, don't they? Life goes on. We might not want it to, and I suppose at first we feel guilty when it does. I mean, I felt guilty for ages, for just being alive when Leon wasn't, and I'm sure you felt the same.'

Oh, you have no idea how I felt when Leon died, believe me.

When she didn't reply he hurried on. 'But the thing is, how long do you go on feeling guilty? That's the question, isn't it? When is it okay to move on with your life? And then,' he added, leaning forward as if warming to his theme, 'you have to ask what exactly is it okay to move on with? I mean, are there limits and boundaries, even fourteen years later? Or is it okay to do whatever you want after that? Is it ever okay to do some things? What do you think?'

Kat blinked. 'I think,' she said slowly, 'that I have no idea what you're going on about.'

He sighed and ran a hand through his damp hair. 'I'm making a proper pig's ear of this, aren't I?'

'Yeah, you are really,' she agreed. 'Whatever "this" is.'

'Thing is,' he said, trying again, 'since Leon died, I got married, adopted a little boy, got divorced.'

'So you did,' Kat said, completely bewildered by where this was going.

'And you,' Jonah said carefully, 'had a relationship, got pregnant, had Hattie...'

He stared at her, and she stared back, not knowing what to say to that.

'So, in a way, we've both already moved on from Leon, haven't we?'

'I'll never forget him,' Kat said uncertainly. 'And I'm sure you won't either.'

'I won't!'

'But you're right. A lot's happened in fourteen years. We've both moved on with our lives. We had to. There's nothing wrong with that.'

'No! That's what I think. There's nothing wrong with moving on with your life. Nothing at all.' He sounded eager. 'And of course, life can take you in unexpected directions. I mean,' he gave an abrupt laugh, 'who'd have thought we'd end up under the same roof?'

'Who indeed?'

'But now that we are, and it's all working out really well, and we all get along great... I mean, we do get along great, don't we? You and Tommy, me and Hattie, Hattie and Tommy.' He hesitated. 'You and me.'

'Like one big happy family,' Kat said, hardly daring to hope that this was going in the direction she thought it was going. 'Jonah, what are you trying to say?'

'I suppose—well—it's all a bit dodgy and bad timing really, because I realised something this weekend, and it seemed amazing and brilliant, but then I remembered the date and I thought, uh-oh, because of all the times, this was the worst. But the thing is, if I don't say it now I might not ever have the courage to say it at all, and that would be a shame, because I really don't think—and I've given this a lot of thought, Kat, believe me—but I really don't think he'd mind. Leon, I mean. I really think he'd be happy about it, because he'd want us to move on. Don't you think?'

Kat stared at him. 'Jonah, will you please tell me what it is Leon wouldn't mind?'

He swallowed. 'You can tell me if I'm out of order.'

'I will, don't worry.'

'And you can tell me I'm being a fool if that's what you think.'

'I shall. If I think it.'

'And I won't be offended, and you needn't worry about having to move out.'

'Okay. Well, that's good news.'

'And if you—'

'Jonah,' Kat cried desperately, 'will you just bloody tell me!'

'I think I'm in love with you!'

There it was, out in the open and hanging between them like a flashing neon sign, or words written in fireworks, sparking left right and centre over the table.

'You *think*?' Kat asked him.

'I know,' he said firmly.

Kat took a sip of water, pushed away her plate, and walked slowly and deliberately to his side. She sat on his lap and kissed him gently.

Jonah pulled her close and kissed her back, not so gently, which Kat was, in actual fact, rather glad about.

'Is that okay?' he whispered.

'I thought you'd never say it,' she whispered back.

Five minutes later they headed upstairs, leaving the ill-fated chicken casserole to quietly congeal on their plates.

NINETEEN

Joseph Wilkinson narrowed his eyes as a whistling Jonah loaded his tools into his van and turned to beam at him.

'You do know it's October?'

'Monday October the second,' Jonah confirmed, his eyes sparkling. 'What a beautiful day it is, too.'

Joseph glanced up at the grey, miserable sky, which held a definite threat of rain. 'Oh, aye? Is that a fact? Well, as long as you're aware of the month, cos I thought you'd mistaken it for April.'

'April?'

'Full of the joys of spring, aren't you?' Joseph shook his head as he patted the Exmoor pony, Barney, whose feet had just been nicely trimmed. 'Anyone would think you were in love.'

'That's because he is,' Summer said, leaning over the door of the loosebox she'd been mucking out and grinning at them as they stood in the yard. 'I'm right, aren't I? Mum's matchmaking did the trick!'

Jonah shook his head. 'Fancy asking me a question like that. I'm a gentleman, and a gentleman never kisses and tells.'

'Ooh, so we're right, Joseph!' Summer clapped her hands in glee. 'Jonah and Kat have got together.'

'About bloody time,' Joseph said. 'Barney was the last of them, lad. I'll send the money over later today.' He took the pony's halter rope and began to lead him away. 'Clive'll be annoyed though. He's put twenty quid on you two getting together at Christmas, so you've jumped the gun a bit there.'

Jonah shook his head, amused at the thought of all those people betting on his relationship with Kat. To be honest, he was amazed anyone had. He wouldn't have put any money on it. It had seemed like a wild and impossible dream, but now it was reality. His reality. He could barely believe it.

Last night had been better than he'd ever imagined. He'd worried at first that he was rushing her, but she'd been quick to reassure him that she'd been in love with him for ages and had just been trying to pluck up the courage to tell him.

They'd both agreed they'd waited long enough, and it had been a night to remember, although Kat had talked nineteen to the dozen at first, clearly nervous.

'What if I don't live up to your expectations?' she'd asked, eyeing him with uncertainty as he peeled off his shirt. 'I mean, look at you! You're so fit, and I'm...'

'What expectations?' he'd asked, frowning. 'Kat, I haven't got any expectations, but even if I did I'm sure you'd more than live up to them.'

It had taken her a while to get undressed, and he did everything he could to reassure her. She was clearly embarrassed by the tracks across her stomach for one thing.

'They weren't there until I got pregnant with Hattie,' she'd said, peering down at them in dismay. 'And look how soft my belly is! I'm not exactly supermodel material, am I?'

'Your body is perfect,' he promised her. 'It's just grown a baby! How amazing is that?'

'Well, I know, but—' she began, and he kissed her gently to

stop her from making any more derogatory comments about herself.

'You're beautiful,' he told her, meaning it. 'Please stop apologising. Believe me, your body is having an incredible effect on mine.'

She'd laughed then, seeming to accept he was being completely genuine, and before too long she'd forgotten all about her worries and focused on what was happening between them, which had, he thought with a wide grin on his face, been a revelation to them both.

Kat had made sure she crept back to her own room in the early hours, just in case Tommy woke up and wandered into Jonah's bedroom. Neither of them wanted to confuse him until they were both absolutely certain this was a relationship that was going to last.

Although, personally, he couldn't imagine how it wouldn't. Kat was perfect for him. He couldn't believe it had taken him so long to realise it.

He was still grinning as he watched Jonah leading the Exmoor to the paddock behind the stables, Barney walking slowly and steadily to keep pace with him, but a moment later his smile dropped. He frowned, then leaned over the loosebox door where Summer was raking up hay.

'Summer, how's Joseph doing?'

She straightened and gave a sigh. 'Not too good, if I'm honest. I've switched a few shifts at the pub so I can be here more. I'm practically full-time now, here during the day and working four evening shifts at the pub. Ben has to spend his nights at The White Hart Inn or he'd never see me, poor thing.'

'That can't be good for you both.'

'Oh, he understands. He's worried about Joseph too. He's spoken to Clive about it, and Clive keeps insisting it's just anaemia and age, but Joseph's not that old. Not really. About sixty-seven I think.'

'And he's seen a doctor?'

'Yes. Lots of times. He's been to the hospital a few times, too. Clive went with him the last time. He told Ben that Joseph just needs to get more rest and make sure he's taking his medication. That's why I upped my hours here. Joseph wasn't pleased because he couldn't pay me any more money, and he didn't think it was fair on me, but I think deep down he was relieved. He didn't argue much, and that's not like him.'

Jonah nodded. 'Well, I suppose if Clive went with him...'

'I know, that's what I thought. If there was anything seriously wrong Clive would know and he'd tell me, so Joseph must have been telling me the truth. I wish we could afford another stable hand so he could do even less. It worries me. I don't want him to give up Whispering Willows, but if it all gets too much for him... I mean, there's only so much I can do, even with the best will in the world.'

'I know. You work very hard.' Jonah knew all too well how much effort went into keeping the horse sanctuary running. It was hard to believe there was much left of Joseph's inheritance, and it was no wonder the place looked so shabby. Maybe it would be better all round if he sold Whispering Willows. Then again, what if a new owner didn't want to run it as a sanctuary? What would happen to all these horses, ponies, and donkeys? It didn't bear thinking about. He wished he could come up with a solution to it all.

'Maybe there'll be a decent donation from the Tuppenny Bridge Fund,' he said hopefully. 'Joseph might be able to pay you from that.'

'I wouldn't take it. I'd rather it went on the horses. Anything helps, doesn't it?' She leaned on the rake handle as she surveyed him. 'I'm really pleased for you, you know. Kat's so lovely. She's been such a good friend to Mum ever since she and Rafferty moved here, and I'll never forget that. You're lucky to have her.

Then again, she's lucky to have you too. I hope you'll both be very happy.'

Jonah's smile returned, unable to stay away for too long, despite his worries.

'Thanks, Summer. I know we will be.'

'When are you going to go public so the Lavender Ladies can pay out?' she asked, her eyes sparkling mischievously.

'No time like the present,' he said. 'Spread the word for all I care. Oh!' His smile faltered and he said, 'Maybe not just yet. It's the eighth on Sunday and—'

'Leon's anniversary.' Summer nodded understandingly. 'Yeah, maybe wait until that's out of the way. Kat was worried about Jennifer's reaction, I know that.'

'We haven't forgotten him,' he said anxiously, keen to make her aware.

'I know that, and so does Ben,' she assured him. 'They'll all be thrilled for you both, I'm sure of it.'

'But Kat's right. What about Jennifer?'

She sighed. 'I know. Jennifer's going to have a hard time of it this week. I'm sure she'll be happy for you and Kat, but you're right. Maybe this isn't the time to announce it. It can wait, though, can't it?'

'It can,' he said, smiling again. 'We've got all the time in the world.'

* * *

'I bloody knew it!' Sally handed Kat a mug of tea and sat in the armchair, a wide smile on her face.

They were in the living room of the flat above The White Hart Inn, and Hattie was playing with her toys on the floor. Sally's face was a picture of happiness, and Kat couldn't help laughing at her friend's expression.

'Oh, did you?' she asked. 'Clairvoyant, are you?'

'It wasn't that difficult to work out,' Sally said, rolling her eyes. 'Soon as you walked in I said to myself, Sally, love, there's only one thing that puts an expression like that on a woman's face, and that's a bloody good seeing to. Thank God he's finally put you out of your misery.'

'What a way to put it!' Kat said indignantly.

'Am I wrong?' Sally demanded.

'Well, no...'

'There you go then. Drink your tea. And there's another thing! You drinking tea in the afternoon. What happened to only drinking coffee during the day? Let me guess, Just Jonah drinks tea so now you do too.'

'Just Jonah.' Kat giggled at his nickname. 'Anyway, you're making it sound so pathetic, and it's not like that at all.'

'Aw, love,' Sally said, sounding mortified, 'I didn't mean it as an insult. Honest! I think it's lovely. You two are welding together like a proper couple. It's only natural that you start picking up each other's ways. I'm right happy for you both, I really am.'

Mollified, Kat sipped her tea.

'Well, go on then,' Sally said eagerly. 'Give me all the gory details.'

'That's private,' Kat said primly.

'Private? It wasn't private when you were asking me to fill you in on me and Rafferty, last Christmas Eve. You were like a dog with a bone, wanting to know every bloody detail as I recall.'

'Which you refused to tell me!'

'I told you enough, though! Come on, don't be mean. Just tell me if it was worth the wait.'

Kat couldn't wipe the smile off her face at the memory. 'Too right it was, Sal. Bloody hell, he's absolutely lovely. Honestly, it was amazing.'

'Aw, I'm so pleased for you,' Sally said. 'It's nice when the first time goes well.'

'And the second time,' Kat said, her eyes twinkling. 'And the third.'

'Third! Bloody hell, who is he, Superman?'

'It was only twice last night,' Kat explained. 'But he came home from work at ten this morning—just to see how I was—and one thing led to another...'

'In front of Hattie?'

'Of course not! She was having a nap. What do you think we are?'

'Part rabbit by the sounds of it. He'll never be at work at this rate.' Sally chuckled and handed Kat the biscuit tin. 'Here, you'd best keep your strength up.'

'Thanks.' Kat helped herself to a Jammie Dodger.

'Have you told Rita and Birdie yet? They're going to be over the moon for you, bless them. Not just because of their bet, but because they'll be so happy that you're happy.' She crunched into a chocolate HobNob. 'How are they anyway? Any news on selling Pennyfeather's?'

'Nope. Not heard back from the Haygarths, thank goodness,' Kat said, dabbing crumbs from the side of her mouth. 'I hope we don't either. Awful woman. I bumped into Daisy at the sheep fair, though.'

'Daisy?'

'Daisy Jackson. She and her brother are considering buying Pennyfeather's, remember? She's the one who turned up, but her brother didn't. Anyway, they're all coming for another viewing—her, the brother, and the brother's girlfriend. According to Daisy the brother's not so keen but the girlfriend is, so we'll see.'

'When are they viewing it?'

'Wednesday. Day after tomorrow.' Kat sighed. 'I really don't want them to buy it, but I also really do for the aunties' sake. It's difficult. I wish I could think of another solution.'

'What do they want the shop for, do you know?'

'Not really. I don't think it's bloody fudge, though, so that's something.' She managed a smile and Sally laughed.

'It will all work out for the best in the end, love,' she said. 'Things have a habit of sorting themselves out, whether we worry about them or not. Look at you and Jonah.'

Kat took another sip of tea, her stomach fizzing with excitement at the thought of what lay in store for her tonight. Once the kids were tucked up in bed asleep…

Life had definitely taken a turn for the better.

TWENTY

Things were getting heated. Too heated.

With great difficulty and immense willpower, Kat pulled away from Jonah and forced herself to be strong.

'I have to go to the shop, remember?' she said, wishing she hadn't agreed to show the Jacksons around Pennyfeather's now. There were so many more interesting things to do at home, after all.

Jonah groaned. 'Really?' He put his arms around her again and she wriggled free, laughing.

'Honestly, if I don't leave now I won't leave at all, and you know it.'

'Would that be such a bad thing?' He raised an eyebrow and Kat melted.

Kissing him again she wished she could stay here forever. The kids were fast asleep, and they could easily lock the doors and...

She stopped kissing him and stepped away. 'I don't want to leave but I promised. Honestly, I'm obsessed. What have you turned me into?'

'Will you be long?' he asked, reluctantly letting her go as he clearly accepted that she wasn't going to cancel the appointment with the Jacksons.

'About an hour at the most. Maybe less. Fingers crossed.' She fastened her coat and eyed him with longing. 'Ohhh, this is awful. I just want to drag you to bed.'

'I'm happy to be dragged,' he said hopefully.

'I know you are, and I'm happy to drag you.' She shook her head determinedly. 'No, this has to wait. Duty first.'

'I know. I'll be waiting when you get back,' he promised.

'You'd better be. I want you in bed, completely naked by the time I get home,' she told him, not entirely joking. 'See you soon. Wish me luck.'

He kissed her lightly on the lips. 'Good luck.'

For a moment she was tempted to kiss him back again, but knowing where that would lead she quickly turned and left Forge Cottage. She did, after all, have a job to do. Hopefully this evening she'd manage to secure a promise that the Jacksons were going to buy the wool shop.

They were waiting outside as Kat arrived at Pennyfeather's, and she quickly unlocked the door and let them in, switching on the light so she could see them properly and introduce herself.

So this was the missing brother? She eyed him curiously. He seemed a bit older than Daisy, but he had the same dark hair, brown eyes, and round face. He smiled a greeting and she realised he didn't share her dimples.

'Pleased to meet you, Miss Pennyfeather,' he said. 'I'm sorry about the last time. Bit of a mix-up at work I'm afraid. Anyway, we're here now.'

Daisy looked awkward, all too aware that Kat knew he was lying.

'Pleased to meet you, too, Mr Jackson,' she said, deciding to let him off the hook. 'You can call me Kat.'

'And you can call me Tom,' he said. 'This is my partner, Andrea.'

'Andi,' the woman said. 'Only my mother calls me Andrea.'

She gazed around the shop uncertainly, and Kat wondered what she was thinking. A city girl, Daisy had said, and Kat could believe it. She wasn't a farm girl anyway, unlike Daisy. Those elegant hands and carefully manicured and polished nails didn't belong to someone who worked the land. She was beautifully made up and had expensive-looking highlights in her hair. Kat wondered if she was planning to open a salon or a nail bar, because if she was she'd have stiff opposition from Bluebell.

'It's a bit...' Andi's voice trailed off and she lifted her eyebrows at Tom who gave a slight cough.

'What Andi means is, it's rather difficult to see how big the shop is, what with all the, er, excess stock.'

'You mean the clutter?' Kat smiled. 'My great-aunts are lovely, but they do tend to keep a messy-looking shop, I agree. However, it's a good size. You have the dimensions from the estate agent's, I take it?'

'I do,' Andi agreed, 'but it's hard to get a clear picture under all this junk.'

Kat tried not to feel offended. There was no junk in this shop. Andi was beginning to sound uncomfortably like Pauline.

'Maybe if I take you into the back room, that will help you get a better idea,' she offered. 'It's all but empty, and it's only slightly bigger than this room so that should help you work out the overall size.'

She led them into the back room and Andi and Tom stared around while Daisy nibbled her thumb nail, clearly anxious.

'Sorry,' Kat said, 'but you never mentioned what your plans were for this shop? I take it you're not planning to keep it as a wool shop?'

'Partly,' Andi said. 'I want to turn it into a crafter's paradise.'

Well, that was unexpected! Andi didn't look the type.

'This is already a craft shop really,' Kat said. 'That is, it used to just sell wool, but in recent years we've added other ranges, such as dressmaking patterns and material, needlework kits, that sort of thing.'

'Oh yes, but that's barely scraping the surface,' Andi explained. 'My idea is to sell everything for the crafter and the artist, all under one roof. We'd have to knock both rooms into one, of course, but I think it would be a reasonable space to do what we want to do.'

'Are you sure?' Tom asked, sounding doubtful. 'I visualised something much bigger.'

'If you could pop by during the day,' Kat suggested, 'you could go to The Corner Cottage Bookshop. It's the same size as this building, and they've used the whole thing as a shop. You can see for yourself how large it is. They even have books upstairs, so if you wanted to—'

'I have plans for the upstairs,' Daisy said quickly. 'That's where I come in, you see. I've always wanted to run my own little teashop, and we thought a craft café would be perfect for the first floor. I'm sure it would help bring customers in, and we could have demonstrations upstairs, too. Maybe even crafting clubs.'

Kat thought about the woman she'd spoken to at the sheep fair. The one who'd admired Tommy's jumper and had regretted that she'd never learned to knit. Maybe a craft café would be the perfect place to hold knitting classes? She'd be happy to teach anyone who wanted to learn. She thought about the clothes she'd made for Hattie, and the patterns she'd designed for her baby knitwear and Tommy's jumper. Maybe she could design patterns for her student knitters? And for more advanced knitters? Maybe the Jacksons would let her sell them in their shop? Maybe...

She realised they were all staring at her, waiting for her reaction. She cleared her throat. 'That does sound good,' she said. 'We used to have a craft café in the town, but it wasn't anywhere near as big as this place, and when the owner died a couple of years ago it was turned into an estate agent's, so there's definitely a gap in the market.'

'Would there be a problem?' Andi asked. 'Turning a flat into a café, I mean.'

'I wouldn't have thought so,' Kat said. 'This row of buildings was never supposed to be residential. In fact, mine is the only flat in the entire row, not like the shops on the other side of the square. As I said, the bookshop's upper floor is part of the shop, and I know the chemist's is used as a storage space, while the upstairs of the surgery is a consulting room and toilets. I don't think you'd have any trouble getting permission to change it back to business use. And for a town this size, with so many visitors, we're desperately short of cafés.'

Especially in the market place, she thought, with its one and only drab café that hardly appealed to anyone.

'Hmm.' Andi sounded surprisingly downbeat about that.

'Is there something else worrying you?' Kat asked politely.

'It's just—well—when Daisy said a town, I pictured something a bit less...'

'Rural?' Kat suggested.

'Exactly,' Andi said gratefully.

'You said you wanted to live in the country,' Daisy said, a hint of resentment in her voice.

'Oh come on, Daisy.' Tom draped his arm around his sister's shoulders. 'I warned you that she was living in a fantasy world. It's all very well sitting on the sofa watching *Escape to the Country* on a loop, but I knew as soon as she saw the Yorkshire Dales for real she'd have second thoughts. You must have too.'

'Surely,' Kat said puzzled, 'you've been to the Dales before? You live in Leeds don't you?'

'Yes, but we only ever visited on sunny days, and I've never stayed here before.'

'Stayed here?'

'We've rented a little cottage in Lingham-on-Skimmer for the week,' Tom explained. 'I thought it best that Andi get a real taste of the country if she was intent on moving here, and that she should see it outside of the summer months too.'

'That's why I was here for the sheep fair,' Daisy explained. 'Tom and Andi were there too, but they were in the pub when I met you. We spent the afternoon at the fair though, didn't we?'

'Yes,' Andi said glumly, 'we did. So many sheep! The craft fair was interesting, though.' She fixed Kat with an astonished gaze. 'Mind you, I had no idea there were so many dead animals in the countryside. It's a bit off putting if I'm honest.'

'Dead animals?'

'She means roadkill,' Tom said. 'She was a bit shocked, weren't you, love?'

'Every few yards there's another squashed badger or summat,' she said, looking disgusted. 'And no one cleans them up, so *things* can happen which are absolutely vile.'

'I told her about the crows and foxes feeding on the carcasses before the council gets to them,' Tom explained. 'It's been a bit of a culture shock. I think Andi's beginning to realise that maybe city life is more her style after all.'

'I'm not being funny,' Andi said, 'but that hair salon across the square looks like somewhere my gran would go for her shampoo and set. It's not exactly Toni & Guy, is it? And where are all the clothes shops? I mean,' she added, looking doubtfully at Kat's jeans, jumper, and winter coat ensemble, 'you must have some decent ones *somewhere*.'

'There's a train station,' Kat pointed out. 'You can always go back to Leeds, or to York, or Harrogate.'

'Kind of defeats the object though, doesn't it?' Andi said.

'And I'm very worried you'd be bored,' Tom added. 'It's all right for me. I'm an accountant, and I can work from home at all hours. Besides, I'm used to the country in all seasons. Andi would find it proper dull.'

'She'll be too busy working to be bored,' Daisy protested. 'We've got a business to set up, remember?'

'All work and no play,' Tom said coolly.

'Who do you think you're kidding?' Daisy burst out. 'This isn't about Andi. This is you not wanting to move back to the Dales.'

'Well, can you blame me?' he asked. 'Didn't we suffer enough when we were kids on that miserable farm? I couldn't wait to get out and you know it.'

'But this isn't a farm, and you promised!' she said, her eyes shining with tears.

'Because you kept going on and on about it,' he said, sounding annoyed. 'And then you recruited Andi into this mad scheme, and I knew there'd be no dissuading her. She had to see it for herself. Now I think she has.'

'But you know how much I want to come back here,' Daisy pleaded. 'I can't stand it in the city, Tom, and now Dad's gone there's nothing to keep me there. And this is a market town, it's not exactly the middle of nowhere.'

'As good as,' Andi said with a shudder. 'Perhaps Tom's right, love. I'm not so sure this is the place for us after all. Maybe we'd be better off looking for business premises in Leeds. What do you say?'

'I don't want to live in a city,' Daisy said. 'I've told you that. Please, just look around properly. Think what we could do with this place.'

'I'm sorry,' Tom said, to Kat rather than his sister. 'I think we've been wasting your time, but we won't take up any more of it.'

'Hang on a minute, I never said no, did I?' Andi scolded him. 'Stop making decisions for me. Honestly, bloody men, it's always about them, isn't it?'

'But you just said!' Tom said, sounding outraged.

'I said I wasn't sure,' Andi pointed out. 'I haven't made my mind up yet. I need more time.' She tilted her head at Kat. 'Is that all right?'

'Of course,' Kat said reluctantly. 'Though of course, if we get an offer in the meantime there's no guarantee my aunts won't accept it.'

'Point taken, and that's fair enough. Come on, Daisy,' Andi urged her. 'Let's go back up to Lingham-on-Skimmer and I'll treat you to a Chinese. That's if they do such a thing up there.' She rolled her eyes at Kat. 'It's like the back of beyond, honestly. Can you believe there isn't even a McDonald's?'

They politely shook Kat's hand and turned to a clearly distraught Daisy.

'We'll wait in the car,' Tom said. 'I'm sorry it's not been an outright yes today, Daisy, I really am. Like Andi says, we just need more time. We'll be in touch.'

After nodding at Kat, he and Andi headed out into the market place, no doubt highly relieved that their true feelings were finally out in the open.

Kat looked at Daisy, feeling nothing but sympathy for the poor woman.

'I'm so sorry,' Daisy said, wiping her eyes as they walked back into the front of the shop.

'It's okay. It's not your fault. I'm sorry it didn't work out for you.' Sorry for her aunts, too, and for Tuppenny Bridge. Kat had to admit the *crafter's paradise* and the craft café sounded like real assets for the town, and possibly for her. It was a shame it probably wouldn't be happening.

Daisy sniffed and looked longingly around the shop. 'I never even got to go back upstairs. I had such plans for this place. I've wanted to run a café for ages. I love baking, you see. It's the one thing I'm really good at.'

'He hasn't said no yet,' Kat said.

Daisy looked far from convinced. 'I can see the way this is going,' she said. 'It will take a miracle to save me now.'

'Isn't there any way you could buy this place on your own?' Kat asked hopefully.

Daisy shook her head. 'That's always been the problem. You see, when Dad died, we finally got to sell the farm. Crows-car's been in our family for generations, but Tom didn't want to farm, and I never wanted to go back up there because...'

She fell silent for a moment, and Kat remembered the sheep farmer she'd been watching at the fair. She could guess all too well why Daisy didn't want to return to Upper Skimmerdale.

'Anyway, while he was in the nursing home in Leeds, Dad would never sell the place, but after he passed we got rid of it as quickly as we could. Sounds mean, but we weren't exactly happy there. Dad had left everything to Tom, which was bloody unfair because Tom cleared off and left him to it years ago, whereas I stayed and took care of him, and put my own life on hold...'

She swallowed down her tears and Kat wanted to hug her. Poor Daisy. It sounded awful.

'But Tom was decent about it. He signed half of everything over to me. Said it was only fair. Thing is, together we could buy this place, just about, but with just my own share it wouldn't come close. If the farm had been a thriving concern when we sold it, it might have been a different story, but we'd already sold the stock and some of the land to pay towards Dad's nursing home fees so by the time we could get rid of the house and the rest of the land there wasn't as much money as we'd hoped.'

'And you don't know anyone else who'd be willing to become a partner?'

Daisy shook her head. 'No one. I'm sorry, I really am. I'll do my best to persuade them both, I promise, but I'm not feeling very confident.'

'It's me who's sorry. I can see how much this all means to you,' Kat said gently.

'Bloody men!' Daisy said bitterly. 'One way or the other

they've ruled my life for as long as I can remember. Dad made me miserable, with his bullying, and Tom abandoned me—just left me to deal with Dad alone. Then Eliot... Well, he wasn't what I thought he was, and I wasted far too many years mooning around after him, being his unpaid childminder and housekeeper. And now Tom again, letting me down, just when I needed him most. God I hate being dependent on them! They're so selfish and unreliable. Well, I guess that's a lesson to me. From now on I'll have to look after myself.'

'What will you do?'

'I have no idea, but I'll think of something. For now, though, it's back to Kirkby Skimmer for a Chinese takeaway. Whoopee doo! And on Friday we go home, back to Leeds, and back to my job in the supermarket. Fabulous.'

'Oh, Daisy.'

'I'll be fine, don't worry.' Daisy tilted her chin defiantly. 'Like you said, it's not over yet. They haven't one hundred per cent turned it down, and until they do I'll keep trying.'

'But if we do get another offer—'

'I know. I understand that.' Daisy opened the shop door. 'Thanks, Kat, for being so nice about all this. I know we've messed you about loads. I really will keep the pressure on. I so want this shop.' She glanced around it again. 'It really is lovely. I think I'd be very happy in Tuppenny Bridge.'

'So do I,' Kat agreed. 'I'll keep everything crossed for you.'

As the door shut behind Daisy, Kat heaved a heavy sigh. Poor woman had clearly had a rough time of it, and whatever she said, it didn't sound as if any amount of pressure would persuade Tom and Andi to change their minds.

It seemed Daisy had been forced to rely on men who'd consistently let her down. That was the trouble with being dependent on them, she supposed, and the thought jerked her back into the realities of her own life.

She and Jonah were happy—happier than she'd ever

dreamed possible—and she really wanted that to continue. All the same, this had shaken her. Right now, she was totally dependent on him. He was not only her—well, what did she call him now? Boyfriend? Partner? Lover? She felt a thrill at the thought and refused to be distracted by it. The point was, he was also the man who'd put a roof over her head, and that didn't feel right.

She needed to earn some money. She needed independence. She needed a career of her own. If she'd had any doubts about that before, this conversation with Daisy had just clarified matters once and for all, and she thought knitting might be the answer to her problems. She'd have to go home and start making plans straight away.

Well, perhaps not straight away.

She smiled and flicked off the light, then left the shop, locking the door behind her. Planning her new business venture could wait until tomorrow. She had bigger plans for tonight.

TWENTY-ONE

Jonah felt quite lost. He was so used to having Kat around that the cottage felt empty without her. It was ridiculous. She was, after all, only at Daisyfield Cottage. She and Sally, along with Ava Barrington and Dolly Bennett, had decided to spend the evening with Jennifer.

With the anniversary of Leon's death fast approaching, they were all too aware that she might slide back into the depression that had dogged her for years and had sworn to do all they could to prevent that from happening.

He thought it was nice of them. Ben had taken Jamie to the cinema in Kirkby Skimmer and intended to take him for something to eat afterwards, so hopefully it was going to be a fun, girly evening.

Jonah wasn't sure what that entailed, and frankly he dreaded to think, but he thought it would probably do Jennifer the world of good. It didn't stop him missing Kat, though.

Hattie was full of beans and showed no signs of sleepiness, so there was plenty to keep him occupied as he tried to entertain her. It took him back to the early days of his relationship with Sofia, when Tommy had been very small. That had been a steep learning curve, but he'd soon bonded with the little boy, and he felt as if he'd already bonded with Hattie, too. It was impossible not to love her, with her cheeky smile and stubborn, affectionate nature.

He'd forgotten, though, how much hard work caring for a baby was, and with two children to care for he and Kat were often exhausted by the end of the day. Not that either of them would have it any other way.

Kat obviously adored Tommy, and as for Jonah—well, he was starting to think of Hattie as his own daughter. She and Kat were a package, and he loved them both dearly. He was thoroughly enjoying being part of this new blended family.

He supposed they'd been very lucky, because Tommy hadn't seemed remotely jealous of Hattie, and had accepted her presence with no problem at all. In fact, Jonah reflected, Tommy seemed to be much calmer and happier these days. He supposed it was down to Kat's steadying influence. There were no more mad rushes in a morning, no more last-minute ironing of the school uniform, no panic over the packed lunch.

He watched fondly as Tommy concentrated on his newest colouring book, looking up now and then to grin when Hattie giggled. He'd already decided that hearing her laugh was one of the best things ever and spent a great deal of time trying to entertain her, which Jonah thought was the sweetest thing.

Hattie was having a great time, picking up her plastic bricks and putting them to her mouth before banging them on the rug. She seemed to love smashing her toys onto the floor lately. She was babbling a lot, too, making lots of unintelligible sounds which amused Tommy no end.

Jonah thought he heard rain outside and wandered over to the window, pushing the blind aside to get a look. Sure enough, there were raindrops on the glass. He knew Kat had her winter coat on and wondered if she'd taken an umbrella. Maybe Dolly or Ava would give them all a lift home if it was raining when they left.

A slight movement made him turn his head and he realised someone was standing on the pavement by the gate. It was hard to see with the light behind him as he peered into the darkness, but he was almost sure there was a shape. Was it a man?

He frowned and leaned closer to the glass. Whoever it was suddenly turned and hurried away, just as a car pulled up outside Forge Cottage. It couldn't be Kat getting a lift home already, surely? It was far too early.

He groaned as he realised his visitor was none other than his mother. What the bloody hell did she want?

He dropped the blind and turned to look at the two children, feeling a sudden flash of panic as he took in the state of the living room, with Tommy's colouring pencils scattered all over the coffee table and Hattie's toys taking up most of the floor.

Then he straightened, annoyed with himself. This was his home, and the children's home, and if it was too messy for her taste, then tough. He hadn't asked her to come here. Why had she anyway?

He bit his lip in annoyance as he heard her try the handle of the front door and was glad he'd dropped the latch after Kat left. The way things were between him and his mother she had no right to assume she could just walk in.

He heard the sharp rap on the door and knew she was annoyed already. Great.

'Daddy, someone's at the door,' Tommy informed him, sounding surprised about it.

'Yeah, I know.' Jonah hesitated. Should he clear away Hattie's toys at least? But then, she was happy and settled playing. It wasn't really fair to take them from her just yet, and it was another half hour till bedtime.

Oh sod it! At another, even louder bang on the door, he

reluctantly opened it, his heart sinking as his mother pushed past him, her lips pursed and a sour expression on her face.

'You took your time. Do you realise it's chucking it down out there?' she demanded.

'Good evening to you too, Mother.'

'Hardly good, unless you're a duck.' She shrugged off her coat and handed it to him.

Struggling already, he silently hung it up on the hook and followed her through into the living room, waiting for her reaction.

'So it's true!'

He steeled himself as she stared down at Hattie, who lifted her cherubic face and gaped at Mrs Brewster in surprise.

'My God! I heard you'd taken another one in, but I couldn't bring myself to believe even you'd be that bloody daft. Yet here you are.'

Jonah seethed. 'Shall we go into the kitchen?' He glanced over at Tommy who was looking a bit worried. 'Hey, mate, can you keep an eye on Hattie for me? She should be okay, but just in case. I'm just going to make—' he couldn't bring himself to say Grandma so finished, '—my mother a coffee. Okay?'

Tommy nodded and Jonah took his mother's arm and steered her into the kitchen.

'Well,' she said, as he flicked on the kettle, 'you want your head read, you really do.'

He said nothing, aware that she wouldn't listen anyway, not until she'd said her piece. He dutifully made two coffees while she ranted at him.

'Another single mother looking for a meal ticket! It would be laughable if it wasn't so bloody infuriating. How much more time and money are you going to pour away on other people's kids, Jonah? So who's this one's father? Another one living the life of Riley while you scrimp and save to pay for his kid's upbringing, I suppose.

'And who's this woman you're shacked up with? Please don't tell me you've put a ring on her finger already. My God, they see you coming, they really do. Why don't you give up the farrier work and open up a bloody refuge for single mothers and their kids and have done with it?

'Your father would be turning in his grave if he could see what's happened to you and this cottage since he passed. All that hard work to build up a business and make this a beautiful home, and you hand it all over to some scrounger who's never heard of contraception.'

Jonah banged the coffee down on the table and glared at her.

'Have you finished?'

'I haven't even got started,' she hissed. 'When are you going to wake up and see sense, eh? What's wrong with you? Is it some weird fetish you've got going on?'

'I'm not even going to dignify that with a response,' he said flatly. 'Who told you anyway?'

'Are you joking? As if you can keep anything quiet around here.'

'You don't live in Tuppenny Bridge now,' he pointed out.

'I shop here sometimes,' she said. 'I go to the doctor's here. I go to the library.'

And yet you never once call in to see us. He didn't say it out loud, though, because he didn't want to guilt trip her. Not because he cared, but because he didn't want her to start popping in. God forbid.

'So who is she? Where did you meet this one?'

He took a steadying breath. 'I've always known her. You have too.'

She frowned. 'I have? Who?'

'Kat,' he said, cradling his mug of coffee as if drawing on warmth to keep the chill of her icy stare at bay. 'Kat Pennyfeather.'

She stared at him incredulously. 'Katherine Pennyfeather! You mean Stephen Pennyfeather's girl? Her who used to live at The Black Swan?'

'That's right.'

His mother shook her head, dazed. 'What the bloody hell are you playing at? She's got family here, not like the other one. Let them take care of her. Bloody Rita and Birdie Pennyfeather, nutty as a fruitcake the pair of them, but they're her blood relatives. They should be paying for her brat, not you!'

'Hattie's not a brat!' Jonah glared at her. 'She's a lovely baby girl, and what kind of woman are you to be so horrible about two innocent children who've never done a thing to harm you?'

'Except bleed my son dry of course,' she retorted. 'Katherine Pennyfeather. Well, I've heard it all now. And how did she manage that little trick, eh? What sob story did she spin you? So go on, you must know. Who's the father?'

Jonah's grip on the mug tightened. 'None of your business.'

'Oh come off it. No doubt I could ask anyone in this town and they'd tell me straight away, so you might as well spill the beans.'

'I sincerely doubt it,' he said, aware that she'd have no hesitation in doing just that.

Her eyes narrowed. 'Are you telling me no one knows?'

He shrugged and she let out a peal of laughter.

'Well, if no one in this town knows then that can only mean one thing. She doesn't know either! Well, isn't that just charming. You really know how to pick them, don't you? You're a bloody fool, Jonah Brewster. Your father would be ashamed of you.'

'Somehow I doubt that. My father always had what you lacked. Compassion.'

'Compassion! Who are you kidding? I'm as compassionate as the next person. I donate ten pounds to Children in Need every single year, so don't make out I don't care about other people. I have compassion, Jonah, but I save it for those who deserve it. And that doesn't include women who see my son as an easy meal ticket.'

'Kat's not like that, but I don't suppose you'd believe me even if I tried to explain,' he said.

'Oh, you don't have to explain. I remember her when she was a teenager. Soon got her claws into Leon Callaghan didn't she? Had her eye on Monk's Folly, no doubt. Not surprising, really, after she moved in with Dumb and Dumber at Whistlestop Cottage. Who'd want to live there? No, Monk's Folly was the prize she had in mind, and I'll bet she was gutted when Leon had that accident and she lost her chance—'

'Stop it! Just stop it right now!' Jonah leapt to his feet and banged his fist on the table. 'You know nothing about Kat, or what she's been through. She loved Leon, and she was heart-broken when he died. Monk's Folly had nothing to do with it.'

'Soon moved on though, didn't she? So no one knows who that child's father is? Interesting.'

'Soon moved on? It's been fourteen bloody years,' Jonah gasped. 'Hattie's eight months old. How long did you expect her to mourn?'

'Oh, not long,' she said drily. 'Not long at all.'

'You're a horrible woman, Mother, do you know that?'

'You can say what you like about me, Jonah,' she said. 'It's water off a duck's back to me. I'm only doing my job, trying to protect you. If you can't see that then it's you who's got the problem, not me.'

'I asked Kat to move in with me,' he said, struggling to keep his voice even. 'I was having problems getting Tommy to school on time, and I couldn't work late because I had to pick him up at three. Kat needed somewhere to live and a job, so it was the easiest solution. She takes care of Tommy which means I can take on more work. She has her own room. It's a professional arrangement.'

He was all too aware that he was lying to his own mother, but sometimes the ends justified the means. Besides, it was none of her bloody business what went on between him and Kat. She was the last person he'd confide in.

She stared at him for a moment, then leaned forward, her eyes boring into his.

'You wouldn't have needed anyone to help you if you hadn't fallen for the oldest trick in the book in the first place.'

'Not Sofia again!'

'It all started with her. If you hadn't taken her in, along with her illegitimate offspring, none of this would have happened. Now look at you, stuck not only with the first kid, but now saddled with another one, and paying for the bloody privilege. Honest to God, you couldn't make it up!'

'Right,' Jonah said heavily, 'you've had your say. If that's everything you might as well leave now.'

'I haven't drunk my coffee yet,' she said pointedly. 'Besides, I want to meet Kat. Get her side of the story. Oh yes,' she said, nodding furiously, 'I definitely want to hear her take on all this. Where is she anyway? Out clubbing with her boyfriend, no doubt.'

'Where she is is none of your concern,' he said. 'And as for waiting for her, I don't think—'

He broke off at another knock on the door.

'You'd better get that,' his mother said coolly. 'It's probably a desperate single mother with twins, wondering if you've got a bed for the night.'

'Oh, bugger off, Mother,' he snapped, and hurried to the front door.

Normally he'd have been quite happy to see Birdie standing on the doorstep, but tonight it was the last thing he needed. He could hardly turn her away, though, as the rain was pouring down and she was beaming up at him, looking so pleased to see him that he'd need a heart of stone—or of his mother—to send her packing.

'Jonah, lovey,' she said, 'I thought I'd pop round and make sure you were okay since our Kat's out, and I brought you this, look. Apple pie! Me and Rita have had half but there's too much for us, and we thought you and Tommy might like to share what's left for supper.'

'That's very kind of you,' Jonah said, ushering her in and closing the door behind her. 'You really shouldn't have. Not in this weather.'

'Oh, a bit of rain never harmed anyone,' Birdie said cheerfully. 'No, I won't stop, lovey. No need to take off my coat. Is it okay if I just pop my head round the door and say hello to the kiddies? Is Hattie still awake?'

She was already in the living room before he could reply, and he heard her cooing delightedly at the baby and calling a cheery greeting to Tommy.

Really, he thought, she couldn't be more different to his mother if she tried and he felt a wave of sadness at the knowledge that the children would never be loved by Maureen Brewster, no matter how much time passed.

Hattie, he noticed, was looking tired. It was almost her bedtime. He needed to make up a bottle for her and change her nappy before taking her upstairs. If only his bloody mother hadn't turned up he could have asked Birdie to keep an eye on the kids while he made the formula, but he didn't dare ask her to stay now. The sooner she left the better. He certainly didn't want her crossing paths with his mother.

'Well, well, well, look who it is.'

He groaned inwardly as the woman herself stepped into the living room, arms folded and lips tight as she surveyed Birdie.

Birdie's smile faltered a moment, then she said brightly, 'Why, it's Maureen Brewster. How are you, dear? I haven't seen you for ages.'

'No. I'm rarely invited round these days,' Jonah's mother said coldly. 'Unfortunately, my son's way too busy looking after other people to spare any time for me.'

'Is he?' Birdie looked at Jonah, clearly puzzled by the remark. 'Oh well, it's nice to see you now anyway. I've just brought them the remains of an apple pie Rita and me made earlier. It's proper tasty, if I say so myself. Maybe you'd like a bit?'

'No thank you.' Her lip curled at the suggestion. 'So I hear your Kat has moved in with my son.'

Jonah winced as Birdie, who'd apparently forgotten all about heading straight back home, settled herself on the sofa and beamed at him.

'That's right, and it's all going really well, isn't it, love? They're a proper family. Kat's got everything running like clock-work, and Tommy and Hattie get on so well, it's like they're brother and sister already.'

'Is that so?'

His mother didn't sit down, but surveyed Birdie with interest.

'Does—' She stared down at the baby and said, with obvious reluctance, '—Hattie have any real brothers or sisters?'

Jonah flashed her a look of warning which she ignored. Birdie put the apple pie on the coffee table and shrugged.

'Kat's only got one child.'

'But the father? Perhaps he's got other offspring?'

She was as subtle as a brick, and Birdie clearly understood what was going on.

'Buggered if I know, Maureen. No idea who he is, and I don't really care either. What does it matter, eh? Kat's happy. Hattie's happy. They've got Jonah and Tommy. Happy endings all round.'

'You think so?' was Mrs Brewster's flinty response.

'It's really kind of you to bring this pie for us, Birdie,' Jonah said desperately. 'Maybe you should be getting back now before the rain gets any heavier?'

She eyed him steadily then nodded. 'All right, Jonah. You're right. I don't want to have to swim home, do I?'

With some difficulty, she bent down and kissed the top of Hattie's head, then planted a kiss on Tommy's cheek, telling him she hoped he enjoyed the pie.

'Nice to see you again, Maureen,' she said, heading into the hallway.

Jonah was dismayed to see that his mother had followed them. Did the woman never give up?

'I see that thing's taking up most of the hallway,' she said, nodding at the buggy which was sitting next to the front door.

'Hardly,' he muttered. 'There's plenty of room.'

'Looks expensive,' she replied, her voice heavy with meaning. 'Must have cost Kat a fortune.'

'Oh, Kat didn't buy it,' Birdie said brightly.

That was news to Jonah, too, but he said nothing. His mother couldn't resist asking the question, though.

'She didn't? So who did?'

Birdie shrugged. 'No idea. It's a mystery to us all, love. She found it on her doorstep. Literally. It had been delivered to her flat, can you believe it? No label to say who it was from. She asked everyone she could think of, but no one knew anything about it. Rita and me thought maybe Eugenie had bought it for her, because who else can spare that kind of money? But no. She swore she hadn't, and knowing Eugenie she'd have made bloody sure we all knew if she had.

'Anyway,' she finished with a flourish of the hand, 'whoever it was had good taste. Top quality that one. It's one of those that converts from a pram into a carrycot, buggy, and car seat. We checked at the pram shop when we went to Harrogate for the day, and it's one of the best. Whoever bought it for her clearly had a few quid, and a very generous heart.'

'Now isn't that interesting?' his mother said, giving Jonah a look that said it all.

'I think it's probably time you went, too,' he said, handing her her coat. 'I need to make up Hattie's bottle, and it's bedtime for the kids, so I'm going to be busy. Thanks, both of you, for coming over.'

His mother's mouth fell open, but he was in no mood for her objections. He practically bundled her onto the street behind Birdie, who thankfully took the opportunity to link arms with the woman and almost drag her to the gate. He would have to remember to give Birdie a big hug when he next saw her, he thought, as he closed the front door.

Even so, what she'd said worried him.

Someone had bought Kat that expensive buggy and hadn't revealed who it was from? That made no sense. Unless...

It surely could only have been a gift from Hattie's father, and if that was the case he was obviously aware that Kat had a child. His child. So where was he now?

They'd never really discussed it before. Jonah had always considered it was Kat's business and if she wanted to tell him she would. But this was different. Now they were a couple, she should surely tell him if the father was still on the scene?

And why the big secret? He could only assume that, whoever he was, he was married. Why else would there be such a need to keep things quiet? Yet he'd bought the baby a buggy, so clearly he cared. Was he still in touch with Kat? Did he still see Hattie?

He thought about the man she'd been speaking to the other night on the doorstep. She'd come up with a really crazy excuse, which made no sense to him. And then there was the man who'd been standing outside the gate tonight. Jonah hadn't seen him clearly, so he had no idea who he was, but there'd been someone. He'd only moved away when Jonah's mother had pulled up in her car. Was it the same man? Was he hoping to see Kat?

Did he still have feelings for her?

And did she still have feelings for him?

It was hard to believe, given the way she'd been with Jonah over recent days, but then again, hadn't Sofia...?

He shook his head as Hattie's wail drifted into the hallway and Tommy called, 'Daddy, Hattie's crying!'

'Coming!'

This was all his mother's doing. She'd dripped her poison into his mind and he was being stupid enough to listen to her. Kat wasn't Sofia, and he had to trust her. What sort of future would they have together if he didn't?

TWENTY-TWO

It wasn't often that Jonah worked from the forge. In his father's day, and even more so his grandfather's day, the place would be a hive of activity, as locals brought their horses and ponies to have their feet cared for and shoes replaced.

These days, most of his work was mobile. He had a portable gas forge for the van, and he travelled around visiting local horse owners, whether they were racing stables, sanctuaries, farms, or individuals with one small pony to care for.

It seemed to him that the forge was wasted space, and he wished he could make more use of it. He would have liked to take on an apprentice at some point, train someone up so he could give a little more time to the blacksmith side of things. He enjoyed the process of creating artwork, and he liked being in the forge. Whenever a horse was brought to him to shoe from there it was a rare treat.

Today was one of those days, because a young girl who only lived a few doors down the lane from him had brought her pony in to have a loose shoe removed and a new one fitted. It wasn't worth firing up the big forge, so he used the portable one. Even so, it was nice to be working from the building he'd spent so much time in when he was younger, watching and learning from his father and grandad.

Better than driving around all day anyway. He spent far too much time in that van for his liking, but his catchment area was large, covering a huge area of Skimmerdale, and even straying into several other nearby dales, thanks to word of mouth and recommendations.

His grandad had worked constantly from the forge. The local farms had relied on heavy horses to do the work that was done by machinery these days, several Tuppenny Bridge residents had ponies to pull traps, and there had been an active riding and hunting community here at one time, so there'd been plenty of work for him to do in the town. Now none of the farms had heavy horses, people drove cars everywhere, fox hunting had mercifully ended, and there were far fewer children taking up riding.

It was a shame, because it meant he had to go further and further afield to make a living. Not all things, in his humble opinion, could be viewed as progress.

As his neighbour's daughter led her pony away, Jonah looked around the forge and sighed. Yep, definitely a waste. His mother, he recalled, had wanted to convert it into an extension to the cottage, but his dad had refused, saying the forge would never die while he had breath in his body. Well, his dad was gone, but the forge was just about ticking over. Just about.

'Ahem.'

He glanced up, surprised to see a man standing at the door, watching him. Something about him was familiar, and the skin on Jonah's arms prickled in warning. Where had he seen him before?

He was possibly in his early forties, with dark hair that was going grey, and dark eyes that watched him with a trace of anxiety.

'Can I help you?'

'Jonah Brewster?'

'That's right. What can I do for you?'

The man puffed out his cheeks. 'Sorry. Now I'm here, face to face with you, I really don't know how to start.'

Jonah stared at him. 'You've been here before,' he said flatly.

The man talking to Kat on the doorstep! It could only be him. Even though he hadn't had a clear look at him every instinct was telling him it was the case.

'I have,' the man admitted, rather shamefaced. 'I was going to knock on your door last night but then you got visitors and I thought... Well, this isn't really something I can talk to you about in front of company.'

Jonah's stomach churned. Was this Hattie's father after all? Had he come to stake his claim? To warn Jonah that, whatever was going on between him and Kat, he was the little girl's dad, and Jonah had better remember that.

Or was it something even worse? Did he want to warn Jonah that he had feelings for Kat and that she had feelings for him?

No, that was rubbish. He knew it, deep down. Kat had made it very clear that she was in love with Jonah. She couldn't fake that. It wasn't the same as it had been with Sofia, he knew that instinctively. This must be about Hattie, and Hattie alone.

He picked up his phone from the shelf he'd left it on and glanced at the time.

'I can spare half an hour,' he said gruffly. 'That's all, though. I have another job to get to and I'll be cutting it fine as it is. We can go inside, though I warn you, Kat's not in. She's just gone to do the shopping, and she'll be a while.'

The man looked puzzled. 'Sorry, who?'

'Kat.' Jonah sighed. 'Maybe you know her as Katherine?'

'I don't know who you mean,' the man said, then his face cleared. 'Oh, do you mean that lady in the bathrobe who answered the door? I take it she's your partner? I wasn't expecting to see a woman, and it threw me. I'm afraid I made up some stupid excuse and left.'

'Matilda Demple,' Jonah murmured. It was his turn to look puzzled. The man clearly wasn't here about Hattie then if he didn't even know who Kat was. So what the hell did he want?

Curiosity got the better of him and he led his visitor into the cottage kitchen, where he washed his hands then put the kettle on while the man sat politely at the table.

'So,' Jonah said, taking out two mugs from the cupboard, 'what's this about?'

The man rubbed his face. 'Perhaps I should introduce myself. My name's Phillip Corcoran. I believe you'll recognise the surname.'

Jonah paused, teabag hovering over his mug. 'Corcoran?' he asked faintly. 'As in, Chris Corcoran?'

'That's right.' He looked faintly embarrassed. 'My brother. I see by your face that this is something of a shock to you.'

'You could say that.' Jonah hastily made the tea and carried the two mugs over to the table. He realised his hands were shaking as he put the tea before his guest, and he cursed himself for it as he sank into the chair opposite Phillip Corcoran, the brother of the only man he'd ever truly loathed.

'I'm sorry to intrude and I realise you must be a bit taken aback that I'm here. Especially after all this time.'

'Why *are* you here?' Jonah asked, not able to bear the small talk any longer. He just wanted the man to get to the bloody point and go. He couldn't imagine what he had to say to him anyway. As he'd said, it had been quite some time…

'It's about my mum and dad,' Phillip said quietly. 'I'm here on their behalf really. They—this is so difficult—they really would like to see Tommy.'

So there it was. The thing he'd feared.

'After all these years? You've got to be kidding me! I think they gave up their right to see him when they wanted nothing to do with him after he was born. No better than their precious son, who didn't even bother hanging round long enough to be there at the birth.'

'It's really not as simple as that,' Phillip began, but Jonah wasn't having it.

'You've got a bloody nerve, you know that? Where have you all been for the last six years? Where were you when Tommy was born? Where were you when Sofia—' He swallowed and gulped down unexpected tears, whether of sorrow or rage he wasn't sure '—when Sofia passed away? I didn't see any of you stepping forward or showing any concern for him then. And now you turn up here, telling me they want to see him? Over my dead body.'

'You really don't understand,' Phillip said desperately. 'I know how it looks, but the thing is, Jonah—may I call you Jonah?—the thing is, they've only recently found out that Tommy existed. Until last month they had no idea they had a grandchild. I had no idea I had a nephew. You must believe me about that.'

Jonah stared at him. 'Are you for real?'

'I know it sounds incredible, but it's true. Chris didn't breathe a word of any of this. If we'd known, believe me, we'd have done something about it long ago.'

'You really didn't know that Tommy existed?'

'I swear to you.'

Jonah sipped his tea, hardly able to take it in. 'Why now? Why did Chris suddenly feel this great urge to confess this big secret to you all?'

Phillip sighed. 'Honestly, who knows? He's a law unto himself and I've never been able to fathom him out. I'm not going to make excuses for him, Jonah. He's one of the most selfish people I've ever known. Always has been. Mum and Dad have despaired of him many times, but this—this is a new low, even for him.'

'So is he expecting to see Tommy, too?' Jonah couldn't deny it to himself. The thought of that man having access to Tommy was unbearable, even though he was his biological father. He didn't deserve to see his son.

'God, no! Chris has got zero interest in Tommy. He only spilled the beans because he was about to leave the country.'

'Leave the country?' Hope flared in Jonah's heart. Good riddance to bad rubbish!

'He's moved to Spain with his wife,' Phillip explained. 'They're a perfect match to be honest. She's as bad as he is. I hate to say it about my own flesh and blood, but we were all glad to see the back of the pair of them. He'd hoped for a farewell gift of several thousand pounds from Mum and Dad and got quite a nasty shock when they refused to give him any more money. Anyway, he took the opportunity to tell us all what he thought of us. It wasn't pretty. Dad told him to clear off and not come back, and that's when Chris dropped the bombshell. He knew what would hurt them the most, I guess. He was right. They're devastated.'

Jonah ran a hand through his hair, imagining how it must feel to find out you had a six-year-old grandson you had no idea existed. He couldn't help but feel a pang of sympathy for the couple, even though part of him was insisting that it made no difference. It was too late for any family reunions now. Tommy was a Brewster, whether they liked it or not.

'So he told you about me? Me and Sofia?'

Phillip nodded. 'We'd never even heard of her. We don't know anything about her, except that Chris didn't want to know and that she'd met you not long after she had Tommy, and you'd adopted him.'

'That's right,' Jonah said. 'I adopted him. All official. Chris didn't care. Said he wasn't bothered one way or the other what happened. You can't overturn that. Tommy is officially Tommy Brewster and there's no going back from it.'

'I'm really not trying to take him away from you,' Phillip said earnestly. 'This isn't about that. Honestly. Mum and Dad—me too, if I'm honest—would love to meet him, that's all. Be part of his life. We don't expect you to hand him over, and all we're really asking is that you allow us to get to know him. It would mean so much to Mum and Dad. My wife and I can't have children, so this is probably the only grandchild they'll ever have. You understand?'

He understood all right, but fear made him unyielding. He knew he had the official documents which said he was Tommy's father, but he didn't trust this. They might take him away. How did he know they weren't working in cahoots with Chris Corcoran? They might whisk his son off to Spain and then he'd never get him back.

'I'm sorry we never got to meet Sofia,' Phillip said quietly. 'Sorry we weren't able to help her when she needed us most. If we'd known... Chris said she'd passed away.'

'That's right,' Jonah said briefly. He had no desire to give any details to this man.

'How awful. She can't have been very old?'

'She was thirty-three.'

Phillip hesitated, as if waiting for Jonah to expand on the subject. When he didn't he said slowly, 'I believe that you two had divorced by then.'

'Wow.' Jonah gave an abrupt laugh. 'He didn't leave much out, did he?'

'It's none of my business,' Phillip said.

'No. It's not.' Jonah took a large gulp of tea.

Phillip sighed. 'Will you at least think about it? I know it's a lot to take in, but Mum and Dad really don't deserve this. They're good people, Jonah, and they're heartbroken that Chris has treated his son this way.'

'Tommy's not his son,' Jonah growled. 'He's mine.'

'Well, you know what I mean. Biologically—'

'Biology means nothing.' Jonah banged his mug down on the table. 'A dad is someone who's there for a child, no matter what. Who puts his own needs and wants to one side to make sure that kid has everything *he* needs and wants. A dad doesn't just run away because he can't be bothered, or he's got better things to do with his time. I'm Tommy's dad, and that's all there is to it. Chris Corcoran was just a sperm donor.'

Phillip winced, then got to his feet. He handed Jonah a business card.

'I'll leave you to think it over. I realise it's a lot to ask, but I hope you'll give it serious thought. Please, ring me when you've reached a decision.'

'And if it's a no? What then?'

Phillip hesitated. 'Well, I hope it won't be. We'll have to cross that bridge when we come to it, won't we?'

'You mean legal action?'

'I'm not your enemy, Jonah. I'll get off and leave it with you. It was nice to meet you.'

'Wish I could say the same,' Jonah muttered, showing his visitor out.

He didn't even bother to say goodbye but shut the door firmly behind him. He was shaking with anger and didn't trust himself to say another word. But beneath the anger there was something much worse. Fear. What if the Corcorans tried to take Tommy away from him? Would they have a case?

Losing Tommy was something he couldn't even contemplate. He wasn't going to let anyone take him away. Just let them try.

TWENTY-THREE

Kat wasn't back by the time Jonah had to set off to his next job, so he didn't get the chance to tell her about Phillip Corcoran's visit. He spent the afternoon working at various stables, his stomach churning with anger and misery as the memory of the conversation he'd had with that man kept replaying in his mind.

He was glad to get home and find refuge in Kat's arms. Her warm and welcoming hug was just what he needed after the shock he'd received.

'Hey,' she said, stepping back after holding him for what felt like ages, 'are you okay?'

He hadn't wanted to let her go at all. He just wanted her to hold him and make it all go away. Tommy was in the next room, though, and he couldn't go into everything he'd been through now. It would have to wait until the kids were in bed.

'I'll tell you later,' he promised her, and she nodded, looking worried but thankfully not pushing him.

'Okay. You go and have a long soak in the bath, and I'll have tea ready for when you come downstairs.'

The evening seemed to drag on for ages, and it felt like an

eternity before Tommy and Hattie were both finally asleep in bed.

Kat curled up on the sofa beside him and said, 'Okay, are you going to tell me what's wrong now?'

He stroked her hair and kissed the top of her head. 'It's been a hell of a day.'

'I guessed that by your face when you got home. What's happened?'

'You really won't believe this.'

'Try me.'

She listened quietly as he explained all about his unexpected visitor, and the emotions it had stirred within him: the anger he felt towards Chris Corcoran; the fear that Tommy would somehow be taken away.

'And they never knew any of it?' Kat shook her head, amazed. 'How awful for them. This Chris bloke sounds like a right nasty piece of work.'

'He is. Didn't stop Sofia from loving him though.'

'Well,' Kat said quietly, 'we all make mistakes.'

Was she talking about Hattie's father? He realised his insecurities were getting out of hand and pushed the subject away. He had more than enough to worry about already.

'She kept on making them, though,' he said bitterly. 'Right 'til the end.'

Kat twisted round to look at him. 'What do you mean?'

'I never told you about me and Sofia, did I?'

'No. And I didn't like to ask.'

'Maybe it's time you knew the truth,' he said. 'The whole sad, sorry story.'

'Sounds ominous.'

'It's pathetic.' He sighed. 'I met her in a pub over in Wensleydale. I'd been working that way, and I dropped in for something to eat, to save me cooking when I got home. She was waitressing there. She was nice. Friendly like. We got chatting. Well,' he shrugged, 'you know how it goes.'

Kat nodded. 'Go on.'

'We'd been seeing each other for three months before I found out she had a baby son.'

'Three months?' Kat sounded shocked and he couldn't blame her. It had been quite a shock to him, too.

'Yeah. That should have warned me. She told me she'd been afraid I wouldn't want to know her if I knew she had a baby. It turned out she'd been in care most of her life. Never knew her own father, and her mother didn't want to know. She was a mess. So vulnerable. Of course, by then I'd fallen for her, and I pushed any misgivings to one side.'

'Misgivings? About the baby?'

'About her lying to me,' he said. 'I really didn't mind about Tommy, but it upset me that she'd kept it from me. She seemed so scared I'd walk away, though, and I couldn't do that to her. It was what she said she'd dreaded, and I wasn't going to prove her right. Anyway, Tommy was a cute little thing. Sixteen months old, and already bright as a button. We bonded pretty quickly, and Sofia was thrilled that we got on so well.'

'It would make all the difference,' Kat agreed. 'I couldn't have looked twice at any man who didn't accept Hattie.' She reached up and kissed him. 'You passed that test with flying colours, my love.'

He smiled absently, his mind far away as he remembered those early days with Sofia and Tommy.

'It wasn't long before she started dropping hints about moving in. To be honest, I couldn't blame her. She was in a tiny little flat, and it was hard work getting a buggy up all those stairs. Plus the rent was high, and her wages and benefits didn't leave her much spare, and then there were childcare costs, and everything a baby needs at that age. Well, I put it to her, quite offhandedly, that it might make more sense if she moved in with me one day.' He gave a bitter laugh. 'She almost bit my hand off. Honestly, she was installed the next day and that was that.'

'I remember we all thought it was a bit sudden,' Kat admitted. 'We didn't even know you were dating anyone. And then, of course, you got married almost immediately.'

'She proposed to me. Well, it wasn't even a proposal. More a, "Shall I book the registry office or will you?" sort of statement. I thought she'd seen my offer for her to move in as a statement of intention. But, you know, I loved her, and I thought she loved me, and we both loved Tommy, so what was the harm in it?'

'Not really a great reason to get married,' Kat said thoughtfully. 'I think I'd be pretty hurt if all I heard was, *what's the harm in it?* It's hardly romantic.'

'No,' Jonah agreed. 'It isn't. But you see, it all felt like a mad rush that I couldn't keep up with. I wasn't sure what the hell was going on. She almost called it off the day before, you know.'

'She never did!' Kat took his hand, clearly astonished. 'Why?'

'At the time she said it was just nerves. I found her crying on our wedding morning, and she admitted she'd almost cancelled the registrar. I told her if she needed more time we could easily postpone, but she got all panicky and said it was just her being silly, and she was simply anxious about saying her vows in front of all those people. Which in hindsight,' he admitted, 'was ridiculous. There were only about six guests, and two of those were Tawnie and Keith.'

'So was there more to it?' she asked gently.

'Yeah. I found out later—much later—that she'd been to see Chris. Told him it was his last chance and begged him to take her and Tommy back. He wasn't interested. I was just the safety net, nothing more.'

'Oh, Jonah! I'm so sorry.'

'It was all a lie, Kat,' he admitted, his face burning with shame as he recalled how easily he'd been taken in. 'Right from the start it was about making him jealous, hoping he'd want to step up and do the right thing by her if he thought another man was taking her and Tommy away from him. Of course it didn't work. He'd made it very clear to her from the moment she told him she was pregnant that he didn't want anything to do with the baby. He'd never wanted kids. Sofia didn't stand a chance of changing his mind.'

Kat was silent, her face pensive. He squeezed her hand, and she forced a smile.

'Poor Sofia,' she murmured.

'Well, maybe so, but she had no right to lie to me and use me like that,' he pointed out, somewhat testily.

'Of course not! I didn't mean that. Just... Well, if she loved him, and he didn't want to know.' The expression in her eyes hardened. 'Tommy was as much his responsibility as hers. It takes two to make a baby. If he really didn't want children he should have made sure it didn't happen.'

'I agree,' he said. 'But we're talking about Chris Corcoran here. Nothing's ever his fault. And yet, somehow, she kept falling for it.'

Kat's eyes widened. 'You mean, even after the wedding?'

'The whole time. I found out later that she'd been seeing him the entire course of our relationship. I can't tell you how devastated I was.'

'I'm so sorry,' she said. 'I had no idea you were going through all that. If I'd known—'

'I didn't want anyone to know,' he admitted. 'I was humiliated. I'd been made a fool of, and I was angry, Kat. So bloody angry. I caught them together you see, and he couldn't wait to tell me the whole truth. Made me feel like such an idiot, and I had to stand there and listen to him gloating about how she'd never loved me, and it was all about him.'

'What did you do?' she whispered.

'Threw her out. I was so furious I couldn't think straight. I told her to go to him and see how happy he made her. I even changed the locks on the doors. I wouldn't answer the phone to her. I blocked her number actually. I was beyond angry, I really was.'

'And what about Tommy?'

'That,' he said, rubbing his face wearily, 'is what I regret most of all. I just handed Tommy over to her without any fight. I thought, *Well, if they want to be a family, let them be. I've been stupid for long enough.* But the truth is, Chris hadn't changed. Once he got Sofia away from me he lost interest again, and Tommy was never part of his plan. Sofia ended up staying at a friend's place, sleeping on a sofa while Tommy shared a room with her friend's kid. They were really struggling financially, and of course, Sofia was heartbroken all over again. Not about me,' he added hastily. 'About Chris.'

'How awful,' Kat said. 'The whole thing's horrible. I mean, don't get me wrong, I understand why you were so angry, but even so. It seems to me Sofia had been through enough, and she and Tommy were having a bad time of it, too.'

'I know,' Jonah said. 'I came to my senses after about a month. I was worried about them. I made enquiries, found out where they were living, and I went to see her. We had a long talk. She told me she loved me in her own way, and that she was sorry, wanted another chance, but I couldn't go there again. I loved Tommy, and I wanted the best for him, so I agreed to help her out. I gave her the deposit for a decent flat and gave her money for Tommy every week. Of course, once the divorce started I was paying her official child support anyway, but I always gave her extra, and if Tommy needed anything on top of that I'd pay for it. But the thing that really got to me was the way she'd blackmail me.'

'Blackmail you? How?'

'If she wanted something—maybe she needed an electricity bill paying, or Tommy needed new shoes—she'd always threaten to stop me seeing him if I didn't pay up. There was no need for her to be like that. I'd never refused to help her financially, so why do that? What was the point? It just made me despise her.'

'Maybe,' Kat said thoughtfully, 'she was testing you, to see how much you wanted to see Tommy? Or maybe she didn't trust you to keep your word? After everything she'd been through with this Chris bloke, not to mention the way her own parents had treated her, you can hardly blame her for not believing in other people's promises.'

'I'm not Chris,' he said immediately. 'I'm nothing like him.'

'I know that,' she said. 'And I'm sure Sofia did, too, deep down.'

'Well anyway,' he said, 'she didn't make it easy for me to see Tommy. There were lots of missed weekends until I took her to court for proper access. I didn't want to do that, but I had to make her see that Tommy needed me as much as he ever had. Whatever had gone on between me and Sofia, I genuinely loved Tommy, and I knew he loved me. Why Sofia acted that way I've never fathomed. She'd say no to me having him for the weekend, even though it had been agreed, and then she'd go out and leave him with a neighbour or something.'

'It sounds like she was trying to exert some control,' Kat suggested. 'Maybe because she'd had so little control in everything else. And maybe it was partly about punishing you.'

'For what?' Jonah asked, aghast. 'I did everything I could for them both.'

'Except take her back,' Kat said gently.

'Can you blame me for that?'

'No, I can't. I don't. I'm just seeing it from her side, that's all.' Kat squeezed his hand tightly. 'You've been through a lot, Jonah. I can see that. You did the best you could in terrible circumstances.'

'And then of course she died,' he said quietly. 'It was so unfair, Kat. No warning, nothing. She didn't deserve that.'

Kat nodded. 'An aneurism, wasn't it? I remember how shocked we all were. She was far too young. The only thing to be thankful for is that she didn't suffer.'

'But she'd had such a rotten life. I wish I could have been her happy ending... Well anyway, there was all the guilt to deal with on top of learning that I was now solely responsible for Tommy. It's been quite a learning curve.'

'But you've done him proud,' Kat said, 'and I'm certain that Sofia would be so grateful and happy for the way you've looked after him. You know, I think you're wrong about her in a way. I think she did love you. And I think she trusted you, too, far more than she'd ever trusted Chris. Think about it. She adored Tommy, and was a good mother to him, and she chose you to be his adopted father. She clearly knew that she could rely on you to be there for him if the worst should happen. That took a lot of courage and faith, Jonah. Don't underestimate her feelings for you.'

He hadn't thought of it that way before and was surprised to feel a little comforted by her words.

'Maybe so.' He ran a hand through his hair. 'Doesn't help with the Corcoran situation though, does it? I can't believe I'm here after all this time, dealing with his bloody family and their demands.'

'Are you really so against them seeing Tommy?' Kat asked. 'I mean, if what Phillip says is true—'

'*If*,' Jonah reminded her. 'You can never be sure you're getting the truth from a Corcoran.'

'Okay, but if it's true that they've only just found out about Tommy, it doesn't really seem fair that they're denied access to him, does it?'

'I don't want them to have access,' Jonah protested. 'He's nothing to do with them. It's not my fault their precious son threw away his rights, is it? I adopted Tommy legally. He's not a Corcoran and he never will be.'

Kat bit her lip, and his eyes narrowed.

'You don't agree?'

'I just think, well, it seems harsh. They're his grandparents. Don't they deserve to get to know him? None of this is their fault.'

'It's not mine either!'

He couldn't believe she was taking their side in all this. Hadn't she heard a word he'd just said? Chris Corcoran had made his life a misery, and he didn't want Tommy to be involved with his family in any way. Why couldn't she see that?

'I just think they sound decent. Not like Chris. He clearly told them about Tommy to hurt them, and if he knew it would do that then obviously they're nothing like him. If they were, they wouldn't be bothered about seeing Tommy, would they?'

'And what if it's a scam? What if they're planning to whisk him abroad?'

Kat waved the question away. 'Well, is that really likely?'

'I can't believe you're not taking this seriously,' he said, pulling away from her.

'I am,' she said, turning round to fully face him. 'It's just— well, don't you think it would be a shame for Tommy to never know his grandparents? Especially since Sofia's parents will never know him, not to mention the way your mother treats him. The more loving people a child has in his life the better, don't you think?'

He got to his feet, pacing the floor as he tried to make sense of what she'd said.

'They could be awful people,' he pointed out. 'Look at the boy they raised! Why would I want people like that around my son?'

'You can't automatically blame the parents for the way the

man turned out,' Kat said, shaking her head at the idea. 'It's like blaming you for the way your mother is.'

'It's nothing like that! I didn't bloody bring her up, did I?'

'No, but she brought you up, yet despite it all you're nothing like her. So why assume the Corcorans are anything like Chris, especially when Phillip seems completely different, and they sound like a decent family. I'm sorry, I don't want to argue with you, but I just think it would be cruel to deprive them of their grandson, and cruel to deprive Tommy a chance to get to know his grandparents.'

Jonah felt icy cold. 'Really?' he asked. 'So how often does Hattie get to see her grandparents?'

'My dad's abroad,' she said, bewildered. 'You know that.'

'I meant her paternal grandparents,' he said. 'How much contact do you allow them with their granddaughter?'

Kat paled. 'I can't believe you just said that to me.'

'Why? It's the same thing.'

'It's not the same thing at all. It's nothing like it.'

'Why isn't it? Because Hattie's father still sees her?'

Kat got to her feet. 'I'm going to bed,' she said stiffly. 'My own bed. I'll see you in the morning when, hopefully, you'll have had a chance to calm down.'

All the fire and rage within him subsided immediately, and he stared at her bleakly, all too aware that he'd hurt her.

'Kat—' he began, but she ignored him and headed out of the living room without looking back.

He sank onto the sofa and put his head in his hands. Bloody Corcorans, causing trouble for him yet again!

But he couldn't hide behind them. For once, this wasn't their fault. It was he who had hurt Kat. No one else. What a bloody mess.

TWENTY-FOUR

Kat usually looked forward to Saturdays, when Jonah wasn't working, and Tommy wasn't at school. Today, though, as she looked out of the window at the dark sky, seeing yet more raindrops pattering on the glass, she thought this particular Saturday was going to be anything but fun.

She couldn't believe Jonah had attacked her like that—dragging her own circumstances into their argument to make a point. She'd only been trying to help him. He had no right to bring up Hattie's parentage.

She wiped away tears as guilt swept over her. *Hypocrite!*

She couldn't go there again. It was too much to deal with. Time to get on with the day. Fifteen minutes later she crept downstairs to make herself a cup of tea. It was still early, and Hattie and Tommy probably wouldn't wake up for another hour. As for Jonah—he tended to be up early during the week, but weekends were his time for a lie-in. He would get up when the kids did most likely. Maybe now would be a good time to start planning her knitting empire.

She went into the kitchen and stopped dead, her heart

racing as she saw Jonah sitting at the table, a mug of tea in front of him.

'You're up early,' she said coolly, trying to strike a balance between *I'm not really talking to you* and *I'm not ignoring you completely*.

'I didn't sleep well,' he admitted, and a quick glance at him confirmed he had dark shadows under his eyes. Despite herself, she felt a pang of sympathy for him. This Tommy business was really worrying him.

She sighed and checked the kettle. The water was lukewarm. He must have made that tea ages ago.

'Would you like a fresh brew?'

'If it's no trouble. Thank you.'

'Don't be daft.' She took his half-empty mug from him and, on impulse, bent to kiss the top of his head. 'It will all work out, you know. It's your decision. They can't force you to let them see Tommy, but if you do decide to let them there's nothing stopping you from being present the whole time to make sure everything's above board.'

'Right now,' Jonah said heavily, 'I'm more worried about me and you.'

Kat sat down opposite him. 'What about me and you?'

'The way I spoke to you yesterday. I'm so sorry, Kat. I never meant to hurt you.'

'No, I don't suppose you did,' she admitted. 'Even so, you managed it.'

'I know. I don't know what got into me. You were only trying to help.' He gave her a sorrowful look. 'I really am sorry. I missed you last night.'

'I missed you, too. Why do you think I'm up so early?' She smiled at him. 'Pair of daft buggers, aren't we?'

His face lit up and her heart skipped as she squeezed his hand. 'Cup of tea coming right up.'

Ten minutes later they sat on the sofa together, making the most of this precious peace before the children woke up.

'I've got something to tell you,' Kat said. 'About my search for a proper job.'

He raised an eyebrow. 'You've found one?'

'Not exactly. I'm thinking about starting my own business,' she admitted, feeling almost shy as she put her thoughts into words. It was a big leap after all. Was she capable of being her own boss? Or was she fooling herself?

'Your own business? Well, that's, er, impressive. What were you thinking of doing?'

'Promise you won't laugh?'

He tilted his head at her. 'As if I would.'

'Okay, well, it's knitting.'

Now he really did look confused. 'Knitting?'

'Remember what you said about selling jumpers like Tommy's? Well, that's one idea. I also thought about baby clothes. When I made Hattie's little bootees and matinee jackets and hats, I got loads of compliments. People said they rarely saw such traditional little baby clothes for sale these days, and wished they could get hold of them. Well, maybe I could knit those, too.'

He nodded. 'I'm sure they'd sell. You mean online, like I suggested? Or were you thinking of a market stall?'

'I'm not sure yet,' she admitted. 'But it's more than that. I was thinking about designing my own patterns and selling those, too, so people could knit their own. Which led me to another idea. I'm considering giving knitting lessons. Things have changed. Kids used to be taught to knit by their mothers and grandmothers, but that seems to be dying out. I'm thinking I could be the one to teach them.'

'Adults or kids?' he asked.

'Both. Adults to start with I think, but later... I'd have to get a criminal record check, I think, to work with kids, and I'd have to think of easy patterns and yarns for them to work with. And of course, there's the matter of figuring out where to hold the classes.'

Briefly, she explained to him what Daisy had in mind for Pennyfeather's.

'I'm not sure that will happen now,' she said sadly, 'which is a shame. But maybe Barbara at Market Café will let me hold classes there? It's not exactly thriving, is it? Or maybe I can rent a room at the Town Hall if it's not too expensive?'

When he didn't reply she said hesitantly, 'Obviously, there's a lot to work out, and it's still in the planning stages, but... What do you think?'

'I—I mean, I can see it would be good for you if it works out.' He didn't sound too sure, though. 'If there's the demand.'

'It will take time to build up,' Kat admitted. 'I'm not saying I'll suddenly make a fortune or anything. But at least I'll be bringing some money in. Paying my way at last.'

'Paying your way? But you're already earning your keep here! You earn your wages and more. I couldn't manage without you.'

'Is that what's worrying you?' she asked. 'Look, that's the beauty of being self-employed. You should know. I can work around the kids. I'll still be there to take Tommy to school and pick him up, I promise.'

'It's not that,' he said slowly. 'If needs be, I can go back to working fewer hours again. Tommy's my responsibility after all. It's just...'

'Just what?' she asked, puzzled. Then she sighed. 'You think it's a stupid idea, don't you? You think it will never take off and I'm kidding myself.'

'No! No, Kat, it's not that at all. Honest. I just—' He shrugged. 'I know it sounds daft, but, well, everything feels so perfect at the moment. Why would you want to change it? I thought we had a good little set-up here, but it sounds like this is no longer enough for you. Aren't you happy?'

'Of course I'm happy,' she said immediately, shocked at his insecurity. 'How can you question that? But I don't want to be dependent on you for everything, Jonah. We're a partnership, and that means I need to contribute to this family myself, without relying on you for money. I can't put all my eggs in one basket. I have to think of Hattie. Besides, I need something of my own. Something I can build and be proud of. You understand, don't you?'

He kissed her forehead. 'Yeah, I understand. Of course I do. I'll help you any way I can, and I think it sounds like a great idea. Let's hope Daisy's brother comes through with the craft shop idea, eh? It would be the best place for your new empire to start.'

Relieved that he seemed to be reassured she sipped her tea, her mind wandering to all the possibilities that lay before her. She would keep everything crossed that the Jacksons wanted the shop, but if they didn't maybe Miss Lavender could pull a few strings and help her get a room at the Town Hall? She'd have to look into running a market stall, too. Or maybe she should focus on online sales at first?

'Kat,' Jonah said uncertainly, 'can I ask you something?'

'Go on.'

'The buggy...' Jonah looked awkward, clearly nervous about proceeding with the question. 'Birdie mentioned that you didn't buy it. That it was an anonymous gift.'

Kat tensed. She'd known by his tone that this was a question she might not like. Even so, she'd known it was coming at some point, and after his confession yesterday she felt she owed him some honesty.

'That's right.'

'So, did you ever find out who bought it?'

'No. I didn't.'

He nodded. 'Ah, right.'

She eyed him for a few moments, seeing the struggle he was having not to ask her anything else. Finally, she took pity on him.

'Why don't you just ask the question?'

He looked startled. 'I'm sorry?'

'You want to know something else, don't you? I can see it in your face. Why don't you go ahead and ask?'

He took a deep breath. 'Okay. Could it be from Hattie's father?'

'No.'

She saw the uncertainty in his eyes and sighed, then placed the mug on the coffee table. Pulling her knees up under her chin she put her arms around them and faced him, albeit reluctantly.

'There's no chance it could be from Hattie's father, Jonah, because he has no idea where Hattie is, or that she even exists.'

'You never told him?' he said, his eyebrows shooting up in surprise. She saw a fleeting glimpse of disapproval in his face and knew it was time to be honest.

'Hattie doesn't have a father. Not in that sense. If you really want to know, she was conceived by medical means. I went to a clinic, chose a donor, had the procedure done there. There's no doting daddy waiting to burst out and demand to see her if that's what you're worried about. No ex-lover about to make a claim on her, or me. It's just me and her, the way I wanted it.'

Jonah stared at her in clear shock. 'I never even thought...'

'No. Evidently not many did. Have you any idea how many bets were taken on who the father was by the Lavender Ladies? You were on the list, by the way,' she added, giving him a wary smile.

How exactly was he going to react to this, she wondered?

He'd had enough shocks during the last couple of days. It was anyone's guess how he'd take this one.

'Why, Kat?' he asked, sounding genuinely bewildered. 'Why would you do that?'

'I'm thirty-six now, Jonah. How much time do you think I had left to conceive naturally? There was no man in my life—hasn't been since Leon really, let's face it. I've had a few short-lived relationships, but nothing serious. Certainly nothing serious enough to produce a child. But I wanted a baby so badly. It was all I could think of for the last few years. I was lucky. The aunties charged me so little rent that I could save a bit. It took me years, but I finally had enough for one shot at getting pregnant. Just one chance, Jonah, and it worked. You can't imagine...'

She shook her head, her eyes glistening with tears as she remembered that moment when she'd realised it had been successful. The overwhelming joy and relief, tempered with the fear that something could go wrong, because did she really deserve to be so lucky?

'Who else knows?' he asked. 'Surely you told your aunties?'

'Nobody knows. You're the first person I've ever told. That should tell you a lot.'

'Thank you,' he said quietly. 'For being so honest with me, I mean.'

'Well, you told me the truth about you and Sofia, so it was the least I could do. Besides, I could see it was eating you up, and you have enough on your plate with Tommy's family turning up out of the blue. The last thing you need to worry about is some angry father landing on our doorstep demanding rights to Hattie.'

He shuffled closer to her and put his arms around her. 'I'm glad you could be so truthful about everything. I'm also glad I told you about Sofia. No secrets between us, Kat. I love you and I really want this to work.'

'I want it to work, too,' she told him. 'I love you so much.'

As he held her tightly, she blinked away tears. She hadn't been as honest with him as he thought, and one day she'd have to tell him the whole truth. But when that happened it would devastate him, and she just couldn't bring herself to do it.

TWENTY-FIVE

They'd agreed to meet in the churchyard: the Callaghans, Kat, Jonah, Sally, Rafferty, Summer, Noah, and Isobel. It was Sunday October the eighth, and fourteen years to the day that Leon had died in the car accident.

Jonah knew it was going to be tough. His own heart swelled with grief whenever he thought about his best friend, and that grief was exacerbated by his guilt over living with Kat. He could only hope that Leon would understand and forgive.

His own feelings didn't matter, though. He couldn't begin to imagine the grief Kat was feeling, and as for Jennifer, Ben, and Jamie... Well, it was different for Jamie, he supposed, because the poor lad had barely known his brother. He'd only been a baby himself when Leon died. Ben, though, had been a teenager, and had been forced to grow up overnight, since Jennifer had gone to pieces and was already having to cope with a dying husband.

It had been a terrible time, and it had taken Jennifer years to let go of Monk's Folly and her suffocating grief. She definitely needed support today, and he was determined that he'd be there for her. It was, he reflected, as he finished shaving, good that they lived in such a close-knit and caring community. Jennifer wouldn't have to face this awful day alone.

'Do you think Isobel will turn up?' he asked Kat, as they walked hand in hand down Forge Lane towards All Hallows.

She looked pale, he thought, and felt a pang of compassion for her.

'I don't know,' she said briefly. 'Who *can* know with Isobel?'

He tightened his hold on her hand, trying to reassure her that he was there for her, and they walked through the open gates of the churchyard and turned right towards the Garden of Ashes.

Some people were already sitting on the benches nearby. As they drew nearer they realised Sally and Rafferty were there with Summer.

'You all right, love?' Sally asked Kat, as her friend sank onto the bench next to her. She put her arm around her. 'I know it's a sad day for you.'

'And for you, Jonah,' Rafferty added. 'I never knew Leon, obviously, but I know you were good friends. It seems he was a well-liked young man.'

'He was the best,' Jonah said firmly. 'I was lucky to have him as my friend. I still can't believe he was taken so soon. It just doesn't seem fair.'

They all glanced at Kat who gave a strangled sob, and Jonah's heart sank. He understood all too well how she was feeling, but he couldn't deny that it worried him a bit that she was still so devastated after all this time. He had no illusions that she could ever love him the way she loved Leon, who had, after all, been the love of her life, but he'd hoped maybe one day... Looking at her now he wasn't so sure he'd ever mean that much to her, and it was painful to acknowledge.

As Sally comforted Kat, Summer said, 'Who's got the kids? Rita and Birdie?'

Jonah nodded, not trusting himself to speak.

Rafferty gave him an understanding smile, and Jonah wasn't sure if it made things worse. The last thing he needed was anyone's pity.

'Miss Lavender was just leaving when we got here,' Summer said. She nodded over at the stone that marked the place where Leon's ashes were buried, and Jonah noticed a spray of lilac and white flowers lying there. 'She left those.'

'That's nice of her,' Jonah said, still watching Kat worriedly.

''Ey up,' Sally said, over Kat's shoulder. 'Here comes Noah and Isobel. Ooh, what's happened to her?'

Kat pulled away from Sally, wiped her eyes, and looked round. Jonah glanced over at the path, where the Lavenders were walking slowly and solemnly towards them. Noah was carrying a bunch of flowers. Isobel, he realised, was wearing a sling. As she drew nearer he saw two of her fingers were strapped together and she was also wearing a Velcro wrist splint.

'Morning,' Noah said quietly.

'Morning, love. Aw, Isobel, what on earth have you done?' Sally asked, eyeing Isobel's injury with concern.

Isobel glanced at Noah. 'It's all very silly really,' she said. 'I fell yesterday—tripped over something—and I put my hand out to save myself and broke my little finger.'

'It's a metacarpal neck fracture,' Noah explained. 'Quite a common injury. She'll be fine. It just needs a bit of TLC for a while.'

'Ouch,' Sally said, wincing. 'That sounds ever so painful. Bless you. Well, it's good of you to be here in the circumstances.'

Noah put his arm around his wife. 'I told her she didn't have to come,' he said.

Jonah noticed Isobel edging slightly away from him. 'And I told him it was only right I did. After all, Leon was my friend, too. We were all like a family really, back in the day.'

She glanced down at Kat. 'How are you bearing up?' she

asked, sounding surprisingly sympathetic. 'I know this must be an awful day for you.'

Kat straightened. 'I'm fine,' she said. 'It's Jennifer we should be thinking about now. If this is bad for us imagine how awful it is for her.'

'And Ben, too,' Noah added. 'Yes, today must be all about them, not us. I see someone's already laid some flowers.'

'They're from your aunt,' Summer told him.

'Yes, she ordered them from me the other day,' Isobel said. 'I forgot to mention it. Sorry.'

'It's okay,' Noah said. 'It doesn't matter, does it?'

'Here they are!' Rafferty said, sounding relieved to break the sudden awkward silence that had fallen on the group.

They all waited solemnly as the Callaghans headed towards them, Jennifer carrying a bouquet of white roses and lilies. She looked sad but carried herself straight, facing them with dignity and dry eyes.

'Thank you all for coming,' she told them, managing a smile for them. 'It's so kind of you all to be here.'

'It's something we all wanted to be part of,' Isobel assured her. 'Leon meant a lot to us all.'

'Oh, Isobel, what on earth happened to your hand?' Jennifer gasped.

'Honestly, it's nothing. Just a little accident last night.'

Summer put her arms around Ben and held him tightly. Jonah had a sudden need to hold Kat, but it would look odd if he did so now, given they'd agreed to keep their relationship from Jennifer until this day was over. He didn't want her to think they were disrespecting Leon's memory, especially at this time of year.

'Now we're here,' Jennifer said, gazing down at the flowers they'd all laid on the stone, which had spilled over onto her husband's neighbouring stone, too, 'I don't really know what to say. I'm used to coming here alone throughout the year when it's just me and him. Well, and Julian, too, of course.' She gave a faint smile at her husband's stone. 'What does one do on occasions such as this?'

They all looked at each other awkwardly.

'Speaking for myself,' Sally said eventually, 'I just wanted to come here to show that none of you need grieve alone. We're here for you, and you're here for each other. Leon must have been really special to inspire such loyalty and love all these years later.'

Jonah glanced at Kat who had her head down. He noticed a tear trickling down her cheek and, unable to help himself, he took hold of her hand. They'd been friends for years, after all. Surely Jennifer wouldn't suspect anything untoward by him comforting a friend?

To be fair, everyone seemed too preoccupied with their own thoughts. They all stood quietly, gazing down at the stone, and Jonah's mind wandered back to the days when he and Leon had hung out together. They'd been best friends since primary school, and he'd imagined them growing old in each other's company.

Leon would have been best man at his wedding, he thought. Although, maybe if Leon had been alive, he would never have married Sofia in the first place. Maybe his friend would have talked some sense into him. Maybe he'd never have started dating her at all if he'd still had his best mate around. Who knew?

There was, he realised, no point in dwelling on it. Leon had died and that was that. He'd had to find the courage to go on without him. They all had. And somehow they'd managed it: Jennifer, Ben and Jamie leaving Monk's Folly with all its memories behind to start a new life in Daisyfield Cottage; Noah and Isobel getting married and building a life together; Kat taking her destiny into her own hands and having a baby alone.

His eyes misted with tears at the thought of it. That

someone like her hadn't found someone else to love after Leon. That she'd ended up visiting a clinic to have the baby she longed for. It didn't seem right. Would she and Leon have had kids together one day? He supposed they would have if fate hadn't been so cruel.

'You know,' Jennifer said thoughtfully after a few moments of silence, 'maybe next year we should do something more formal. What do you think?'

Ben frowned. 'What do you mean by more formal?'

'I was thinking, it will be fifteen years next year. We should have some sort of service of remembrance for him. Would Zach help us, do you think?'

'You mean, a memorial service in the church?' Rafferty asked. 'I'm sure he'd be pleased to do that, Jennifer.'

'I think that's what we'll do,' she said, nodding. 'A proper memorial service. This whole community mourned when Leon died, and they should all have the chance to remember him. And really, when I look back, I barely remember his funeral. It was all such a blur. I'd like to do this for him. It would mean a lot to me.'

'Then that's what we'll do,' Jonah said firmly. 'I think it's a great idea.'

Everyone murmured their agreement. Jonah noticed that Kat didn't respond verbally, although she nodded. He wondered if she was too upset to speak. His thumb gently stroked the base of hers as he tried to convey that he understood her grief, but her head remained bowed.

Finally it was agreed that it was time to leave.

'If you want to come back to the pub,' Rafferty said, 'the drinks are on the house. Let's raise a glass to Leon's memory.'

'Oh, that's lovely of you,' Jennifer told him, smiling. 'Thank you, Rafferty.'

They all made their way out of the churchyard.

'Are you okay?' Jonah murmured to Kat as they trailed behind the others.

She finally looked at him, and he saw her eyes were red with crying. His heart plummeted.

'It's been a difficult day,' she said, her voice sounding thick with emotion.

'I know, love. I know. If you want to go straight home—'

She shook her head. 'No, it's fine. Let's get this done.'

'Kat,' he said hesitantly, 'if you want to talk about Leon any time, I'm here for you. You know that, don't you?'

She gently stroked the side of his face. 'I know that, but honestly there's no need.' She glanced at the Garden of Ashes then turned back to him, a determined look on her face. 'There's really nothing else to say.'

TWENTY-SIX

Jonah had been working flat out for over a week. His appointment book was full, and he'd spent the weekend after Leon's anniversary in his forge, having decided to replenish his stock of artwork.

He knew he wasn't being entirely fair to Kat, who'd been left alone in the cottage with the kids, but he needed space to get his head straight, and when he was with her his thoughts became a tangled mess.

On the surface, they were getting along fine, but he couldn't help but feel that something had shifted between them. She had a pensive look on her face when she thought he wasn't watching her, and he couldn't shake the feeling that she was keeping something from him.

He couldn't deny he was worried. He'd always known Leon was his competition, even so long after his death, but he'd been knocked sideways by how upset Kat had been at the church-yard. It was since that day that she'd seemed different. Had she realised that she'd been fooling herself? That no man could come close to Leon, no matter how much she tried to tell herself otherwise?

After all, wasn't that why she'd had Hattie by artificial insemination, or whatever it was they called it these days? Because she didn't want a baby with any man other than Leon, and with that option gone she'd resorted to a donor, whose face she would never have to look upon, and whose name she would never know. Maybe she'd kidded herself that Hattie was Leon's after all. Who knew what grieving people told themselves?

He had every sympathy for her, but where did it leave him? He'd been here before. Sofia had always been in love with another man, and it had made it impossible for her to love Jonah, no matter how hard she tried.

Chris had beaten him, even though in Jonah's humble opinion he'd been the poorer man. Yet Sofia had chosen him, despite his terrible treatment of her and Tommy.

With Leon it was even worse. How could Jonah possibly compete with the memory of Kat's lost love? He knew all too well how good their relationship had been. He'd been a witness to it. He knew Leon was a wonderful man, a hundred times better than Chris Corcoran.

Was he destined to be second best yet again? He thought he'd loved Sofia, but what he felt for Kat was so much stronger than anything he'd ever felt for his ex-wife. He wasn't sure he could stand living in Leon's shadow. He'd done all this before. It wasn't fair to expect him to go through it again.

Then there was the worry of her business idea. He wanted her to be happy, and to succeed in whatever she chose to do, but he had to admit there was a little part of him that was afraid. What she'd said about putting all her eggs in one basket... Was she planning to leave one day? It hadn't sounded as if she expected their relationship to last, or why would she need an escape fund? Was she already comparing him to Leon and finding him a poor second best?

He realised he was pulling away from Kat, but he couldn't help it. It was hard to see the tension and sadness in her face, so it was easier to stay out of her way. Forging artwork gave him something else to focus on, and even though he knew it wasn't going to solve his problems he clung to his work, even knowing he was simply putting off the inevitable. At some point he'd have to talk to her. He couldn't go on thinking the worst like this. Maybe she needed help. Grief counselling or something. Maybe.

On the Monday evening, eight days after the anniversary, he ate his tea and, feeling guilty, stacked the dishwasher and helped her get the kids to bed.

'Do you mind?' he asked her, as she settled herself on the sofa. 'I'm just...' He held up the keys to his van and she stared at him.

'You're going out?' she asked.

'Yeah. I thought I'd go and see Tawnie. I haven't been there for a while. Time to have a catch up.'

'We should invite her round here,' Kat said hesitantly. 'I'd like to see her again after all these years, and I've never met Keith, or the girls.'

'Maybe. Soon.' He smiled at her. 'That would be nice. I'm sure she'd love to meet you. So, you don't mind her knowing about us then?'

She looked surprised. 'Why would I?'

'Well, it's just...' He shrugged. 'You changed your mind about telling Jennifer. I thought we were going to announce it to the world. Let the Lavender Ladies collect on their bets. But you decided you didn't want it out there officially yet, so...'

'That's different,' she said, turning away from him. 'Jennifer isn't Tawnie. You know that.'

'She's got to know some time, Kat,' he said gently. At least, she did if they were serious about each other. Were they? He just didn't know any more.

'What time will you be home?' she asked, then pulled a

face. 'God, listen to me! I sound like a nagging wife. Come home whenever you like. No hurry.'

'Are you sure you don't mind?' he asked uncertainly. 'I can leave it for now if you'd rather I stayed.'

'No, it's fine. I'm going to work on a new knitting pattern anyway,' she assured him.

Feeling bleaker than ever he nodded and bent over to kiss her. She gazed up at him.

'I love you,' she told him.

'I love you, too,' he said, grasping at her words with a mixture of relief and doubt. Did she mean it? Or was it just something she said? 'I won't be long.'

* * *

Tawnie was delighted to see him.

'Hello, stranger! Where the hell have you been?'

'You know where I live,' he pointed out, heading past her down the hallway and into the living room. He gazed around, surprised to find it empty. 'Where is everyone?'

'I've been abandoned,' she said dramatically. 'Keith's taken Lilly swimming, and Iris is at her friend's house. Honestly, I never see her these days. She's growing up so fast, and hanging around with her parents no longer holds any interest for her. It's quite sad really. Wait until Tommy gets to her age. You'll see.'

He nodded glumly and sank into the armchair that Keith usually occupied.

'Blimey,' Tawnie said. 'You look happy. Not. What's rattled your cage?'

'I don't even know where to begin,' he admitted. 'What a bloody mess this all is.' He rubbed his face. 'How did I end up here, Tawnie?'

'Where's here?' she asked gently, sitting opposite him.

'Come on, Jonah, it can't be that bad. Why don't you start from the beginning?'

And so it all came tumbling out. How he and Kat had finally got together, the visit from Phillip Corcoran, and the revelation he'd had in the churchyard at Leon's anniversary gathering.

Tawnie listened without interrupting, her face expressing a mixture of emotions as his story went from happy to angry to sad. When he finally stopped talking she leaned back in her chair and puffed out her cheeks.

'Whew!' she said. 'No wonder you haven't had the time to visit. That's quite a ride you've been on, Jonah.'

'I really don't know what to do,' he admitted.

'About?'

'Any of it. The Corcorans have no business being around Tommy, and I don't owe them anything. Do I? And as for Kat—how the hell do I compete with the memory of her perfect boyfriend? I can't, can I? And I've been here before, remember?'

'Chris Corcoran wasn't dead,' she reminded him. 'And he was far from perfect.'

'No, but he was a bloody saint in Sofia's eyes. It didn't matter how badly he behaved, she still adored him. And Leon never behaved badly. That's the trouble. He was a good bloke, Tawnie, you know that. I loved him. I still miss him myself.'

'And maybe that's all it is with Kat,' she suggested. 'Maybe you're mistaking her natural grief and sense of loss for something else. I mean, come on, Jonah. It's the anniversary month. She's bound to be remembering and feeling a bit low. It doesn't mean she doesn't feel just as much love for you.'

'But you didn't see how she was in the churchyard,' he persisted. 'And something's changed since that day. She's different. Distant. I can't seem to reach her.'

'Have you actually tried?' she asked pointedly. 'From what you've just told me you've spent every day since working to keep out of her way. Not very supportive or understanding if you don't mind me saying so.'

She was right and he knew it. 'I think,' he said slowly, 'that I'm avoiding her in case...'

'In case she tells you you're right and she can never love you as much as she loved Leon?' Tawnie shook her head. 'Have you any idea how paranoid that sounds?'

'Does it?' Jonah sighed. 'I wish I knew what to think.'

'If you hadn't been through all that with Sofia you wouldn't even be questioning this,' Tawnie said. 'You're still bruised from that experience, and you're casting Kat in the same light. Plus, you've got all this worry about the Corcorans now, and that's adding to your misery, making it harder for you to look at things rationally.'

'I really don't know what to do about them,' he told her. 'I've been expecting another visit from Phillip Corcoran every day. So far he's kept away, but how long will that last? He might be planning to take legal action for all I know.'

'Would it be so bad if the Corcorans did see him?' she asked. 'Don't look at me like that! It's just a thought. I mean, what harm can it do?'

'It could confuse Tommy. They might hurt him. I have no idea what they're like.'

'And you'll never know if you don't give them a chance. They sound like normal, decent people who've had a shock. Imagine finding out you've got a grandchild somewhere in the world and you had no idea he even existed. Poor things.'

'You feel sorry for them?'

'Jonah,' she said patiently, 'of course I do. Don't you?'

He hesitated, then nodded glumly. 'I suppose I do. If they're as decent as this Phillip fellow made out.'

'Don't judge them by Chris's standards,' she urged. 'How would we feel if we were judged by Mum's?'

'Hell, that would be bad,' he acknowledged, managing a wry smile. 'Actually, Kat said the same thing.'

'There you go then! And look, you can be with Tommy the whole time. I'm sure they wouldn't expect you to just hand him over to complete strangers. It would be supervised access, and you'd take it at your own pace. Yours and Tommy's. Whatever he's comfortable with. He does know about Chris?'

'Oh yes, of course. He remembers him, but...'

'You've never talked about him?'

'Not since he came to live with me after his mum died,' he admitted, shamefaced. 'I never wanted to, and he never brought him up. We've talked about Sofia a lot of course. He loved her and there was a lot to unpack emotionally after her death. But the subject of Chris never came up, and I was glad about that.'

'Maybe you need to have a little chat with him then. Explain about the Corcorans. See how he feels about meeting them.'

'You're right,' he said wearily.

'Of course I am. I'm your big sister.' She grinned at him. 'Coffee?'

'Yeah, go on. A biscuit too, if you've got one.'

'I can do better than that. I've got a chocolate cake in the kitchen. We can eat that while we figure out how you're going to broach the subject of the Corcorans to Tommy, what you're going to say to Phillip Corcoran, and, just as importantly, what you're going to do about Kat.'

TWENTY-SEVEN

'That's a... surprise,' Sally said, staring at Kat with eyes that revealed exactly how much of a surprise it really was. 'I've got to admit, love, it never occurred to me. A sperm donor! Well, I don't reckon anyone will have won their bet on that one, do you?'

She was leaning against the kitchen worktop, holding a glass of white wine. Kat was hovering in the doorway, so she could keep an eye on Hattie who was fast asleep on the sofa in the next room, having exhausted herself playing peek-a-boo with Sally and hurling building blocks across the room.

They were in the flat above The White Hart Inn, and Sally had had to switch the light on. Outside was dark and gloomy, even though it was only early afternoon. The sky was grey and swollen with rain, and Kat thought the miserable weather this month hadn't helped her mood.

'Are you disappointed in me?' she asked, aware that her news might have made Sally see her differently.

Sally's eyebrows shot up. 'Why the hell would I be disappointed in you? What difference does it make how Hattie got here? The main thing is she's here, and aren't we all glad about that?' She gazed through the open door at the sleeping baby and smiled. 'Bless her. Don't you go worrying about what people think, love, least of all me.'

'Thanks, Sal.' Kat almost slumped in relief.

'What I don't get,' Sally said, pulling out a chair and sitting at the table, motioning Kat to join her, 'is why you felt the need to tell me now, after all this time. What's brought this on?'

'Because,' Kat said, setting her wine glass down opposite Sally's as she sat, 'I told Jonah the other day, and I thought if he knew it was only fair you did, too. You are my best friend, after all.'

'Aw, love. That's really nice of you to say. Thank you. I won't tell a soul, you know that, don't you?'

'Of course I do.' Nervously, Kat took a gulp of wine.

Sally's eyes narrowed. 'So how did Jonah take it?'

'I'm not really sure,' Kat admitted. 'Things have been a bit—awkward—lately.'

'Aw no! Don't tell me there's trouble in Paradise already! You've only been together five minutes. What's gone on?'

'If I tell you something, will you promise not to tell anyone, even Rafferty? I know it's a big ask, but you see it's not my secret to tell. But if I don't tell you I can't really explain everything else.'

'Love, honestly, I promise you I won't tell anyone, even Rafferty. Hey!' Sally reached for her hand. 'You look as if you're about to burst into tears. What on earth's the matter?'

'I told Jonah about Hattie because he told me about Tommy. About Sofia. About their relationship. It's not what I thought, Sally. It's really sad, actually.'

Briefly she explained about Chris Corcoran and Sofia's betrayal of Jonah. Sally listened attentively, her head tilted in sympathy as Kat poured out how Jonah had caught them together, and discovered Sofia had been seeing her ex the entire time.

'Poor love,' Sally said when Kat finally finished. 'What a terrible thing to go through. No wonder he's in a state about this Phillip Corcoran turning up.'

'We had a bit of an argument about it,' Kat admitted. 'I thought he should let the family see Tommy and he was against it.'

'That's a shame,' Sally agreed. 'I think Tommy needs to know who his real family are, even though his father sounds like a waste of space.'

'Jonah's his real family,' Kat said firmly. 'And his real father.'

'Aw, I know that, love. I didn't mean anything by it.'

Kat sighed. 'I know. Sorry. I guess I'm just a bit on edge.'

'So what happens next?'

'Well, Jonah went to see his sister and she apparently persuaded him that I was right, and he should let Tommy see the family.'

'Ooh, well that's good then, isn't it?'

'He said he was going to call Phillip Corcoran and see if they could all meet at The Black Swan on Saturday.'

Her voice faltered and Sally peered at her, concerned. 'And?'

'He didn't ask me to go with them.'

'Oh, well.' Sally leaned back; her expression thoughtful. 'I suppose I can understand that.'

'Can you?' Kat couldn't hide the hurt she was feeling. 'I'm not sure I can. Are we a family, or are we two separate units—him and Tommy and me and Hattie?'

'I'm sure he didn't mean it like that, love. It's a lot for Tommy to deal with, and he's probably just trying to make it as simple as possible for him. Besides, maybe he's not sure you'd want that? For one thing, you haven't even come clean about your relationship yet. You were going to tell everyone after the anniversary of Leon's death, but you still haven't. Maybe Jonah's worried it's you who's got the doubts?'

Kat considered the matter. 'I suppose that's a possibility…'

'You sound really pissed off with him,' Sally observed. 'Is there something else going on?'

Kat hesitated. 'He's been working in the forge all hours,' she said. 'I hardly see him these days. And he's—oh, I don't know, Sal—distant. I don't understand it. Maybe he's more shocked about Hattie's conception than I'd realised. I have no idea what's in his head, but I do know he's different.' She took another gulp of wine. 'I think he's going off me.'

Sally laughed. 'Don't be daft! He's besotted with you, anyone can see that. Why would you think he was going off you?'

'When I talked to him about setting up my own business he was far from keen. I could see it in his eyes. I told him I'd work around the kids, but it was pretty obvious that he was worried he'd be losing a housekeeper and nanny. It made me wonder. Is that what I am to him? I mean, I know we're together and everything—well, sort of—but is it more out of convenience for him? Has he told himself he's in love with me because it makes everything so much easier? Maybe finding out I want to change that has made him realise that's all he really wants me for.'

'You don't really believe that? To be honest, love, it's you who seems to be pulling away from him, rather than the other way round. I don't get why you didn't tell Jennifer about your relationship. It's like you're ashamed of it. And if I'm confused imagine how Jonah's feeling.'

'I didn't think it was the right time, the way things have been between us lately. I thought, why should we put her through all that when it might be over and done with in a few weeks anyway?'

Sally shook her head. 'You're really overthinking all this, you know. Jonah's bound to be worried about the kids, but that doesn't mean that he sees you as the paid help. And as for Jennifer, why are you so worried about telling her? It's been fourteen years, love. She knows you've had Hattie, and as far as she's aware that means you've had sex with someone, and it hasn't bothered her, has it? No one in their right mind would expect you not to find another bloke after all this time.'

'Maybe not, but Jonah's not just another bloke, is he? He's Leon's best friend.'

'So what? I should think that would make it better if anything. She knows neither of you will ever forget him, but it's nice that you've found comfort in each other.'

'You think?' Kat couldn't help rolling her eyes and Sally put her elbows on the table and leaned forward again.

'Are you serious about all this? The doubts about Jonah, I mean?'

'I couldn't be more serious, Sally,' Kat admitted. 'I'm even thinking it might be better to move out again.'

'No way!'

'Just to put some distance between us for a while. Sort out this mess with the Corcorans. Maybe it's too much, me living with him so soon. It might work better if I live somewhere else and we just date for a while.' She gave a mirthless laugh. 'That's a joke in itself. We haven't even been on a date. Can you believe that?'

'What, never?'

'Nope. Hardly romantic, is it?'

'Well do something about it then! Ask him on a date. I'll mind the kids for you if that's what's stopping you.'

'It's not what's stopping me,' Kat said sadly. 'Maybe it was before, but now I just think, is it worth it? I don't know what Jonah wants, Sally. I don't know how he feels. I thought I did, but he's pulling away from me. I can feel it. And you know what occurred to me the other day? He got landed with a child because of Sofia—a child he loves with all his heart, don't get me wrong, but not his own child. Not his flesh and blood. Not a child he was prepared for or wanted. And now I've landed on his doorstep with Hattie, another child that's not his and that he never expected. All because he has a kind heart and knew I needed somewhere decent to live. Just like Sofia. What if he's starting to realise that he's landed himself in exactly the same situation? It would be enough to put anyone off, surely?'

'Right,' Sally said firmly, 'that's more than enough of that. You have to talk to Jonah about all this, Kat. Whatever's going on his head can't be any more tangled than what's going on in yours. Communication, that's what it takes! Tell him all your worries and let him reassure you.'

'Or not.'

'I'm sure he will. But if he doesn't, at least you'll know the truth, won't you?'

But that was the trouble, Kat thought. She wasn't sure she wanted to know. And if she expected him to tell her the truth, shouldn't she tell him *her* truth, too? Sometimes, she thought bleakly, ignorance really was bliss.

TWENTY-EIGHT

The Black Swan was busy, even for a Saturday afternoon, and Jonah thought it was a good job he'd booked a table, or they'd have had no chance of eating here.

As he settled Tommy into his chair, he gazed out of the window at the beautiful view of the River Skimmer and thought what a lovely place this was. He seldom visited this pub and wondered why. He supposed because, in the summer, it was heaving with tourists.

It would, he thought, be a lovely place to bring Kat. Or would it be too sad for her since she'd grown up here? That's if she wanted to go out for dinner with him of course.

As the thought entered his head, he realised that the two of them had never been on a date before and jolted upright in shock. How had that happened? They were in a new and what should have been romantic relationship, but where was the romance? God, he'd completely failed her. He would have to do something about that. If she wanted him to...

He wished she was here with him now. She'd have put him at ease, and she'd know what to talk to the Corcorans about. They'd no doubt love her. Who wouldn't?

He'd hoped she'd offer to come with him to The Black Swan, but she hadn't, and he hadn't liked to ask. Maybe he was too afraid she'd refuse. It would feel like another nail in the coffin of their relationship.

He couldn't deny he'd been desperately hurt when she told him she'd rather they delayed revealing their relationship to everyone.

'But I thought we'd agreed?' he'd asked, feeling sick that she'd changed her mind. 'After the anniversary we said. You were going to tell Jennifer and then we were going to let the whole town know.'

'I know, I know. It just...' She broke off and shrugged. 'I don't know. It's early days. Let's just leave it a while longer. Give Jennifer time to get over the anniversary.'

Was that really the reason? How long, he'd wondered bitterly, were they supposed to let Leon dictate the course of their own relationship? Then he'd felt ashamed of himself for being so horrible about his best friend.

The truth was, he didn't know what to think any longer. His thoughts were all over the place, and he seemed to be in a permanent state of anxiety. Was Kat just making excuses because she had no intention of staying with him? Maybe she no longer saw a future with him at all. Maybe he'd been kidding himself. It wouldn't be the first time he'd turned a blind eye to the facts staring him in the face, would it?

As his worries overtook him again, he sat down next to Tommy and tried to focus on his son. This was a huge day for him, and although he didn't seem nervous, who knew how he would react when he finally met his grandparents and uncle for the first time?

Tommy had taken the news of the Corcorans with surprising ease.

'Do you remember a man called Chris?' Jonah had asked

him gently, not entirely sure how Sofia had referred to him in front of Tommy.

Tommy had considered. 'Do you mean my other daddy?' he asked eventually, which had hit Jonah like a punch in the stomach.

Forcing himself to smile, he'd nodded. 'That's right.'

'Mm. He made mummy cry,' Tommy told him. 'I didn't like him much. He was mean.'

Jonah closed his eyes for a moment, wondering how much Tommy knew or remembered. It didn't bear thinking about.

'Well,' he said at last, ruffling his son's hair, 'maybe he was mean, but that doesn't mean everyone in his family is mean, does it? And the thing is, buddy, Chris had a brother, and a mum and dad of his own, which means you've got an uncle and a grandma and grandad. They're so excited to know about you, and they'd really like to see you.'

Tommy looked confused. 'But not my other daddy?'

Jonah blinked away tears. 'Your other daddy has gone away to another country, and they don't see him anymore. But hey, what do you think about seeing your grandparents and uncle?'

'I've never had a grandad,' Tommy said, sounding excited for the first time. 'Marcus in my class says grandads are cool. His grandad takes him fishing and gives him three pounds pocket money every week.'

Jonah managed a laugh. 'Well, that does sound pretty cool,' he said. 'So what do you think, eh? Do you want to see them or not? Because if you don't,' he added, 'I won't make you. No one's going to force you to do anything you don't want to do. But if you would like to see them, I'll be there with you. What do you say?'

Tommy nodded. 'I'd like to have a grandad. And another grandma. Do you think this grandma will like me better?'

Jonah swallowed down the lump in his throat. Tommy had

never mentioned Jonah's mother's obvious dislike of him, but clearly he'd noticed. It almost broke his heart.

'I think anyone who doesn't love you is a complete fool,' he said, his voice thick with emotion. 'So shall I ring them and tell them we're going to meet them?'

Tommy nodded. 'Okay, Daddy.'

So Jonah had made the call, and now he could only hope that these people were as decent as Phillip had made out.

'Here you are!'

An overly jovial cry made him look round in dread. There was Phillip Corcoran, all smiles as he held out his hand for Jonah to shake. Behind him, a man and a woman, probably in their mid-sixties, gazed at Tommy, drinking him in as if they couldn't believe he was actually real.

'Jonah, it's good to see you again,' Phillip said. 'This is my mother, Evelyn, and my dad, Vince. Mum, Dad, this is Jonah Brewster. And this,' he added, smiling at his nephew, 'must be Tommy.'

Evelyn and Vince managed to drag their eyes away from Tommy for a moment to shake hands with Jonah, who motioned to them to sit down. There was a general awkwardness as chairs were pulled out and people sat, facing each other in polite silence.

'Well,' Phillip said finally, 'it's good to meet you at last, Tommy.'

Jonah glanced at Tommy, who was watching the newcomers with interest, but didn't seem too worried. His gaze fell on Evelyn, and he was touched to see she was in tears. Even Vince looked dangerously close to crying. He cleared his throat, feeling uncomfortable.

'Tommy, are you going to say hello to everyone?'

'Hello,' Tommy said.

'Hello, Tommy.' Evelyn's voice was thick with emotion. 'It's so good to see you. What a beautiful boy you are.' She turned to her husband. 'Look at those dark curls, Vince. Aren't they gorgeous?'

'They certainly are. Puts me in mind of myself when I was a boy,' Vince said. He nodded at Tommy, a kindly smile on his face and a twinkle in his eye. 'I had curls just like yours until I turned forty, then it all started to drop out, and look at me now.' He patted his almost completely bald head and Tommy stared at him, his dark eyes huge.

'Don't be scaring the poor boy,' Evelyn scolded him. 'Your grandad didn't mean it, Tommy. I'm sure you won't lose your hair.'

The word *grandad* grated on Jonah, and his hand tightened on his glass of water. Well, isn't that what he was after all? Tommy's grandad. At least they seemed nice. Their feelings for Tommy were genuine, he thought. Surely no one could fake the look in their eyes as they beamed at their grandson?

'It's a lovely place,' Vince said, glancing around the pub in approval. 'And a beautiful location, too.'

'We've never been to Tuppenny Bridge before,' Evelyn confided. 'We live just outside York, and we've visited the Dales before lots of times, but never this place. It's a pretty town, isn't it? I can't imagine how we've missed it.'

'And you're a farrier, I believe, Jonah?' Vince asked. 'That's a skilled job. Is there much call for it round here? We don't see a horse round our way from one year to the next.'

'Plenty of work,' Jonah assured him. 'I'm kept very busy.'

'Daddy's brilliant at it,' Tommy told them. 'He showed everyone how to put shoes on the horses at the sheep fair, and everyone clapped him, didn't they, Daddy?'

It was the first time that Tommy calling him Daddy had ever felt awkward to Jonah. He shifted nervously, waiting for some reprimand from the Corcorans, but none came.

'Did they? Well, I wish I'd seen that,' Evelyn said, while Vince nodded enthusiastically.

'I'd have loved to go to a sheep fair,' he said. 'I love sheep. I do love these rural events, and I'd have enjoyed watching your daddy shoeing horses, I'm sure.'

He smiled at Jonah, who finally began to relax.

'Should we order?' Phillip said cheerfully. 'I don't know about you, but I'm hungry, and I'll bet Tommy's ready for his lunch, aren't you?'

'I want chips,' Tommy said firmly. 'And can we have pudding, Daddy?'

'Always,' Jonah told him, smiling.

'Pudding is the best part of any meal,' Evelyn agreed, laughter in her eyes. 'We must always save space in our tummies for that.'

'Do you like apple pie?' Tommy asked her. 'Auntie Birdie and Auntie Rita make great apple pie. Auntie Birdie brought us some round, didn't she, Daddy? We didn't have custard though. I like custard with it really.'

'Love custard,' Vince agreed. 'Unless it's got a skin on it. Now that makes me feel queasy.'

'Ugh! Me too! I stayed for school dinners once and we had pudding and custard and it had skin on it! It made me feel sick. I don't have school dinners any more. Kat makes me a packed lunch.'

'Kat?' Evelyn enquired.

'Daddy's girlfriend,' Tommy said nonchalantly. 'She's at home looking after Hattie. Hattie's my new sister,' he added.

Jonah stared at him. He'd had no idea Tommy had cottoned on to the fact that he and Kat were an item, and as for accepting Hattie as his sister—as easy as that!

'I had the pleasure of meeting Kat a couple of weeks ago,' Phillip told his parents, his eyes sparkling with amusement, no doubt at the memory of her in her dressing gown on the doorstep. 'She seems like a lovely lady.'

She is, Jonah thought bleakly.

Tommy made it sound as if they were one big happy family, but he was no longer sure that was the case. Why couldn't he shake the fear that he was losing her already?

* * *

Kat was relieved to see that Tommy was smiling when he and Jonah arrived home later that afternoon. She glanced warily at Jonah, but he seemed fairly relaxed, although she thought sadly that she detected signs of tension when he greeted her.

'How did it go?' she asked, taking Tommy's coat from him and hanging it up in the hallway.

Jonah shrugged off his own jacket and smiled down at Tommy. 'It was all right, wasn't it, mate? They were nice, weren't they?'

Tommy beamed up at Kat. 'I had sausage and chips and beans, but I left most of the beans. And then I had treacle sponge and custard. Nearly two bowls! Grandma couldn't eat much of hers, so she let me have it. I made her laugh because she didn't believe I could eat all that, but I did, didn't I, Daddy?'

'You certainly did,' Jonah agreed. 'I have no idea how you fitted it all in, but I don't think you'll be wanting much for tea tonight.'

Tommy considered. 'Maybe I could just eat some crisps for tea?'

'Nice try,' Kat said, laughing, and Tommy grinned before running into the living room to turn the television over for *Paddington*.

'So it went all right?' she asked, turning back to Jonah.

He tucked his hands in his jeans pockets and nodded. 'Yeah, it did. They seemed nice enough. Friendly. Didn't object to Tommy calling me daddy, which I thought they might.'

'Why would they? You *are* his daddy!'

'Maybe, but I thought they'd struggle with that, seeing who

their son is.' He paused. 'Tommy told them all about you and Hattie. He explained that you were my girlfriend, and Hattie was his new baby sister.'

Kat felt surprisingly touched. 'He never did! Wow, and we've been so careful not to give him any ideas about us.'

'He's not daft. Evidently we weren't careful enough.' He put his hand on her shoulder. 'Kat, I think we need to talk.'

Kat's stomach lurched with dread. Is this what she'd been fearing? Was she about to get the whole 'It's not you, it's me' talk? But, she realised, he was right. They couldn't go on like this with whatever it was simmering away between them. She wanted it back the way it had been, and if they couldn't fix it, maybe it was better to agree that it hadn't worked and go their separate ways.

She couldn't give any head space to how terrible that made her feel.

'Okay,' she said reluctantly. 'But not now.'

'You agree then? There are things to discuss?'

'I think we both know that,' she said. 'But not while the kids are up. Wait until they're in bed. Then we'll talk.'

He stared at her for a moment, then nodded. 'I'll put the kettle on. I'm ready for a cup of tea after all that drama.'

TWENTY-NINE

By the time Tommy and Hattie were asleep in bed that evening, Kat had worked herself up into a state of dread. Was this the day when he finally told her he couldn't be a surrogate father to yet another child? She wasn't entirely sure if Hattie was his problem, but something was. If not Hattie, then it was definitely all her. Either way, she couldn't stay in a relationship that felt so awkward and strange. How had they come to this?

He brought her a glass of wine and himself a beer and settled himself on the sofa looking pensive.

'So what's this about?' she asked, after a few moments of uncomfortable silence.

'I don't really know where to begin,' he admitted. 'It's been a weird kind of day all round.'

'Were the Corcorans really as nice as you said in front of Tommy?'

He nodded. 'I wish I could say they were awful. It would make things a lot easier. Truth is, they seemed like decent people, and they were obviously mad about Tommy. They got quite emotional talking to him at various points, and I did feel sorry for them in the end, knowing how much of his life they've missed out on.'

'I'm sensing a but,' she said cautiously.

He gave a short laugh. 'That obvious?'

'What are you worried about?'

'Does it make sense if I say they were too nice? Too accommodating. Tommy kept calling me daddy, and they didn't even flinch.'

'But you are his daddy!'

'Yeah, but only—' He closed his eyes for a moment, as if the thought was painful. 'Only by adoption. What if they think blood trumps that? What if they believe that, no matter what any court says, Chris is and always will be Tommy's dad, and that means their rights over him are greater than mine? What if all this is some ploy to lower my guard until they launch a legal challenge?'

Kat took his hand. 'I don't think you have to worry about that at all. Even if that's what they wanted to do I don't see how they could. Tommy was adopted by you when he was three years old. He loves you. His life is here with you. He doesn't even know these people. Besides, grandparents don't have many rights even when their grandchild is with its natural parents, so I honestly don't see this as an issue.'

'But they might try, and we could be caught up in a legal nightmare that drags on for years!'

'You're overthinking this,' she said. 'Just because they've asked to see Tommy doesn't mean they want to take care of him. I'm sure they understand all too well that Chris gave up all rights to his son, and by extension he gave up their rights, too.'

'And you don't think that by letting them see him I'm taking a risk?' he asked, his eyes anxious as he waited for her response.

'No,' she said firmly. 'I really don't. Look, Jonah, why don't you try to see it as it is? The Corcorans understand that Tommy's yours now, but they would like to play a small part in his life, and would it hurt if they did? You told me once how upset it made you that your own mother wanted nothing to do with him. Sofia's parents weren't on the scene and never will be. Don't you think it would be lovely for him to have his grandparents in his life—people who love and care for him almost as much as you do? I know you've been through a lot, but so have they. Chris sounds like an absolute nightmare, and Phillip can't have children. Why deprive them of Tommy?' She blinked away tears. 'I just think it would be cruel, and I know you're scared, but you're not a cruel man. Trust them.'

'I guess I've got a bit of a problem with trust,' he admitted grudgingly.

'Well, that's hardly surprising. And you're not the only one, you know. I struggle with it a bit myself.'

He looked at her, clearly surprised. 'You do? Why?'

She shrugged, half wishing she hadn't said anything but knowing, deep down, that now was the time to open up.

'I suppose Hattie complicates everything. I wouldn't trust her welfare to just anyone. I've been determined, ever since I knew I was pregnant, that I would be the one to take care of her. I never wanted anyone to look at me and think I was failing her. You can't imagine how devastated I was when I heard about Pennyfeather's, because it was my responsibility to provide for Hattie, and knowing I was about to lose both my job and my home terrified me.'

'I can understand that,' he said slowly. 'But you haven't failed her. She's happy here, isn't she?'

'But for now that's down to you,' Kat said desperately. 'Don't you see that? That's why my knitting business is so important to me. When I was talking to Daisy the other week about her not being able to buy the shop alone, I realised how precarious it is, depending on someone else. Hattie's home and her security could be snatched away from her at any time.'

'How?' he asked, perplexed. 'You can't think for a moment that I'd throw you out?'

'This thing between us,' she said unhappily, 'can't you see that it puts me in a vulnerable position? If we were to break up I'd have nothing, and how do I care for Hattie then?'

'You think we're going to break up?'

'No one can predict the future, Jonah,' she said. 'And the way things have been between us lately...'

'Meaning?'

'There's a distance between us. You must have noticed. Why else did you say we needed to talk? I'm right, aren't I? And that just confirms that everything Hattie and I have depends on you, and that's not good.'

'Is that why you want to start the business?' he asked, his brow furrowed. 'Because you thought that would give you some security?'

'Of course it is! Well, that and because I need something of my own to be proud of. Like you, being a blacksmith and a farrier. You've achieved something. I want to do the same.'

'So it's not because you're getting sick of us—me and Tommy? It's not because we're not enough for you?'

Her eyes widened. 'Is that what you thought? Of course you're enough for me! But I need to earn my own money outside of this house. That doesn't mean I don't want to take care of Tommy. Look at it from my point of view, Jonah. This is your house. I need to contribute to it—not just by cleaning and cooking. You do almost as much as I do in the house anyway. I mean financially. If not, how can I ever feel equal? How can I ever feel as if I'm doing right by Hattie?'

'I understand that,' he said. 'I really do. But you never have to worry about Hattie, you do know that? I love her, too, and—'

'Do you?'

He dropped her hand. 'Are you seriously asking me that question?'

'You've never said.'

'I didn't think I had to! I thought it was obvious. She's part of my life now, and I can't imagine not having her around. She's—well, she's Tommy's little sister, and I feel like she's my...'

'Your what?' Kat asked.

'I don't want to sound pushy or presumptuous,' he said hesitantly, 'but she feels like my daughter.'

Kat slumped and he eyed her worriedly. 'Too much, too soon?'

'I thought, maybe you felt resentful of her,' she admitted.

'Why the hell would you think that?'

'Because you've already had one child foisted on you that you weren't prepared for, and I thought maybe you'd struggle with another. Oh, I'm not saying you don't love Tommy now, obviously, but at the beginning his very existence was a shock to you. You had no idea what you were getting into. And then when Sofia died...'

He was quiet for a moment, and she waited, not sure how he was going to respond.

Finally he said, 'You're right. Tommy was a shock, and I wasn't expecting to become a father figure to someone else's baby. But it didn't take me long to fall in love with him, and now I wouldn't have it any other way. He might not have come into my life by conventional means, but it makes no difference to me. He's my son and I love him. As for Hattie, well, that was completely different. I knew all about her, and I went into this with my eyes open. I was more than willing to accept her into my life. You didn't "foist" her on me. I invited you both in, remember?'

'So you had no reservations about us at all?' she asked doubtfully. 'After everything you went through with Sofia you weren't worried you were being used in the same way?'

He opened his mouth to reply but paused, as if rethinking

his answer. Kat barely breathed, her stomach churning as she waited for him to respond.

'If I'm honest,' he said at last, 'I was a bit worried at first, yes. You're right. I've avoided relationships ever since Sofia because, well, trust is hard to rebuild after you've been used in that way. I don't ever want to be second best again, Kat. I don't want to be someone's safety net.'

'Of course you don't,' she said. 'You deserve way more than that.'

He looked troubled. 'Do I?'

'You know you do!' Her eyes narrowed. 'What is it? What aren't you telling me?'

'I know you'd never deliberately do anything to hurt me,' he said. 'I know that because I know you. You're a good person with a good heart, and you're kind and generous and compassionate and—'

'Okay, you're not writing me a character reference,' Kat said, trying to sound jokey. 'What are you trying to say?'

'Leon's anniversary,' he said reluctantly.

Kat stiffened. 'What about it?'

He bit his lip, not speaking, and she hooked her finger under his chin and lifted it, forcing him to look at her.

'What about it, Jonah?'

'I saw the way you were, Kat. I saw how heartbroken you were. You could barely hold back the tears, and you couldn't even speak. After fourteen years!'

He gave her an anguished look. 'I understand how much you loved him, I really do. I loved him too. Not in the same way, but maybe almost as much as you did. He was my best friend, and I'd never want to do anything to hurt him or disrespect him, so please don't misunderstand me. God,' he raked his hands through his hair, clearly wishing he'd never started the conversation. 'Have you any idea how sickened I am by my own feelings?'

'Your feelings for me?' she whispered, shocked.

'No! Never that! My feelings for *myself*.' He grabbed her hands. 'I love you, Kat, I really do. But seeing you so devastated after all this time—it broke my heart. I was jealous! Can you believe that? Jealous of my own best friend. Jealous of a dead man. I'm sorry, but there it is. I wouldn't blame you for despising me for it, because I despise myself for it, but I can't help it. I don't want to be second best again. I know I can't ever expect to compete with the love of your life, but it's a struggle that I maybe wasn't prepared for. I'm sorry. I really am. I know this is my problem not yours, and I swear it's one I'm trying to work on, but—'

Kat stood up and walked over to the window. She pulled the blind aside a little and stared out into the dark night.

'I'm so sorry,' she heard him say. He sounded bleak and broken.

She had so much to tell him, but if she did would that make things worse for him or better? As he'd told her many times, he loved Leon. The question was, did he love Leon more than her? What would hurt him most, the pain he was in now, or the pain she would cause him when she told him what had happened that night? That awful night. The night that had changed everything.

She gazed into the darkness, silently appealing for an answer. She'd never wanted to hurt Jonah. She'd never wanted to hurt anyone, but somehow she'd managed it, even if the people concerned didn't know it. She'd carried her guilt for so many years, and it had coloured most of her adult life.

It had stopped her forming meaningful relationships, forced her to have Hattie alone, made her doubt she deserved such happiness. It had driven her to believe it was her and her daughter against the world; that it was entirely down to her to care for Hattie, and she had to prove to everyone that she was good enough to be a mother.

It had made her pull away from the Callaghans, just when they'd needed her most. It had driven her from Tuppenny Bridge and back to her father in Dorset. It had turned the close bond she'd had with Jonah and Noah, and, to a lesser extent Isobel, into a casual friendship that amounted to nothing more than nods and waves in the street and the occasional conversation at social gatherings.

Jonah's love and acceptance had begun to change all that. She'd felt herself opening up again, putting aside all that pain, grief, and guilt. Being around him had brought her back to life in a strange way. She'd even found the courage to hang out with the old gang again. It had soothed her, helping the Callaghans to move house, helping them decorate. Made her feel useful, as if she was, in some small way, making amends.

She'd never told anyone the truth, and she'd always thought that was the best thing all round. Who would it benefit? It was all too late now anyway. What was done was done, and there was no reason to rake over the past again.

But falling in love with Jonah had changed that. She'd known from the beginning that it would, but she'd been unable to stop herself. If she'd ever hoped that they could be happy without him knowing, today had proved that she'd been fooling herself.

Jonah needed to know. He deserved to know.

But by telling him she would ruin something precious. His life would never be the same again.

'Kat,' she heard him say, as if from a million miles away. 'Please. Talk to me.'

She dropped the blind and spun round to face him.

'Jonah,' she said heavily, 'there's something I need to tell you.'

THIRTY

Jonah was clearly bracing himself for some dreadful revelation, and Kat wished she could reassure him that it wasn't as bad as he feared. The truth was, though, it was probably worse. Much worse.

She sat down next to him, her weight on one hip so she was facing him, even though her instinct was to hide from him. If she could have told him from behind the sofa she would have done. She was dreading seeing the look on his face.

She reached for the glass of wine and downed it in one nervous gulp.

'Wow!' Jonah laughed nervously. 'This is obviously big news. Should I drink my beer first?'

'Maybe a little,' she said, handing him the bottle.

He took a sip and watched her, clutching the bottle tightly in his hand. 'Go on,' he said nervously. 'Let's get this over with.'

She could tell immediately that he'd got the wrong idea.

'This isn't about you,' she said, trying to reassure him on that point at least. 'It's not about us, I mean. You and me. Jonah, before we go any further I have to tell you one thing. You're wrong. Leon isn't the love of my life. You are. And you have to believe that. I *need* you to believe it. Please.'

'You don't have to say that, Kat,' he began, shaking his head. 'I know—'

'But you don't know,' she said desperately. 'That's my point. I'm telling you here and now, as clearly as I can, that *you* are the love of my life. And you're the one person I wish I could avoid hurting, but I have to tell you something now that's going to hurt, and I'm sorry, believe me. I'm really sorry.'

He put the beer back on the coffee table and took her empty wine glass from her hand, placing it next to his bottle. Then he took hold of both her hands.

'After what you've just told me, I can deal with anything,' he said. 'I'm listening.'

'I did love Leon,' she said quietly. 'You know that. We were together from high school, and he was everything to me. Oh, I know we hung around in a gang. The four of us, and later on Isobel too. But Leon was always special to me. Sorry,' she added, aware that sounded insensitive.

'It's okay,' he reassured her. 'It's nothing I didn't know.'

'Honestly, Jonah, I thought life was all mapped out for us. You had your apprenticeship, and Isobel was training to be a florist, and Noah was off at university doing his degree. Me and Leon, we were different in that way. We just went straight into earning a living—me in the shop, and him at the brewery. It seems silly now, but at the time it seemed to confirm we were meant for each other. We told ourselves it was just one more thing we had in common.

'We had plans. We were going to save up, travel. We talked about buying a camper van and going off together in the holidays. We used to look at maps. We wanted to visit the Highlands and islands of Scotland, go to Snowdonia, visit Ireland. We talked about taking the van over to France, Germany…'

Tears clouded her eyes and she blinked them away. 'Basically, all our thoughts for the future were for *our* future. Together. We never made individual plans. It was always me and Leon, and what we were going to do one day. It's odd, but after—after what happened—I've never had the slightest inclination to travel anywhere. Tuppenny Bridge is home, and it's where I feel safest. Funny, isn't it?'

He nodded, but didn't speak, and she saw his own eyes were glassy with tears, and warm with sympathy.

She swallowed. 'Anyway, you know what they say about the best-laid plans and all that. I—well I guess you could say I threw a gigantic spanner in the works.'

She wiped away a tear and he cupped her face gently. 'Take your time. There's no rush.'

'If I don't say it now I might not ever say it,' she said. 'I got pregnant, Jonah.'

For a moment he didn't move. Then he leaned back slightly and blew out his cheeks.

'I had no idea. You and Leon were having a baby? He never said.'

'No, well.' She couldn't help it any longer. Without warning she burst into tears, and Jonah pulled her to him, stroking her hair and murmuring soothing words to her.

'It's all right, Kat, it's okay.'

'It's not okay,' she sobbed. 'It's anything but okay.'

He let her cry until she was ready to move on, and she wiped her eyes and sat up again.

'Sorry.'

'Don't be. Take your time. You don't have to say anything else if you're not ready.'

'I do, Jonah. Honestly, I do. You have to know now because if you don't there's no point.'

'O-kay,' he said uncertainly. 'Well, whenever you're ready.'

She picked up a cushion and hugged it close to her chest. 'It was a surprise when I got a positive test,' she admitted, gazing down at the cushion to avoid seeing Jonah's face. 'We'd taken precautions, so I thought we were safe. I don't know to this day how it happened, but to be honest, I wasn't too upset. Leon and I were madly in love, and although a baby hadn't figured in our plans I thought we could handle anything that came our way. I thought—I actually thought that he'd be pleased.'

She felt, rather than saw, Jonah straighten. 'Are you saying he wasn't?'

She spluttered with bitter laughter, then gasped in horror. 'Oh, God! My nose is running now. Have you got a tissue?'

He jumped up and hurried into the kitchen and returned almost immediately with some kitchen roll.

Blushing, she wiped her nose and tucked the tissue into her sleeve. 'How attractive,' she muttered.

'It doesn't matter,' he reassured her. 'Are you okay? Do you want a break? Another glass of wine? Tea? Coffee? I could make you a hot chocolate if you like?'

She managed a smile and squeezed his hand. 'You're so lovely, you know that?'

He looked confused and a bit worried. She knew he was anxious about Leon's response to her news and didn't think it was fair to keep him waiting.

'In answer to your earlier question,' she said, feeling a little more composed suddenly, 'no, Leon wasn't pleased. Far from it.'

'But...' Jonah seemed shocked. 'I expect it was just so unexpected, that's all. When he calmed down he must have—'

'He didn't want a baby, Jonah,' she said firmly. 'At least, not with me anyway.'

Now she really had shocked him.

'What are you saying?'

'I'm saying Leon was seeing someone else. He was cheating on me.'

Jonah seemed unable to take it in. 'But—but he adored you!'

'Yeah, that's what I thought, too.' Suddenly the tears were

flowing again, and she knew she had to tell him about that conversation. That awful, anger-filled conversation. The last time she'd spoken to Leon.

'He was horrible to me, Jonah! He told me he didn't want a baby. Accused me of getting pregnant deliberately to trap him. I didn't understand. I asked him why I needed to trap him into anything. We were together, weren't we? We loved each other. What exactly was I supposed to be trapping him into? He just looked at me, really coldly.'

She shivered, remembering. 'I didn't recognise him. I'd never seen him look at me that way before. He asked me if I knew. If I'd found out. I didn't know what he was talking about, but he didn't believe me at first. He kept throwing accusations at me, saying I knew and that was why I'd got pregnant, to make him give her up. That's when I finally understood. He was seeing someone else and he thought I'd found out and was using a baby to make him end the affair.'

'Leon...' Jonah seemed unable to formulate a sentence. He looked completely shell-shocked.

'I asked him who she was and how long it had been going on, but he wouldn't tell me. He actually said it was none of my business. I was hysterical, I'll admit it. I was thumping him on the chest, screaming at him. I couldn't believe it. I asked him what I was supposed to do now, and he just stared at me and said, "Get rid of it."'

'No!' Jonah got to his feet. He stared at the floor, one hand on his waist, the other cupping the back of his neck as he struggled to make sense of what she was telling him. 'He wouldn't do that. Not Leon.'

'That's what I thought,' she said quietly. 'Guess we both had him wrong.'

'He never told me anything about any other girl,' he said, swinging round to face her at last. 'I promise you that. I never knew.'

'I believe you,' she said. 'I never thought you did.'

He dropped back onto the sofa, staring at her. 'He actually told you to...'

She nodded. 'We were in the churchyard,' she said, shivering. 'It was dark, but we were shouting so loud it's a wonder we didn't wake the residents up. I've always hated that bloody place ever since. I never go in there if I can help it.'

'He didn't even offer to give this woman up? He didn't—I don't know—do something? Say *anything* to comfort you?'

'Far from it,' she said. 'Basically, it was my fault and my problem. I had to deal with it. He'd planned to break up with me and this had just brought things forward. Honestly, Jonah, he didn't even sound like himself. I couldn't get through to the Leon I'd known and loved. I was scared witless and absolutely heartbroken. I—' She swallowed hard. 'I told him I hated him, and I wished he was dead, then I ran home and left him to it.'

He put his arm around her shoulders and pulled her to him. 'I just don't know what to say. Leon wasn't like that. He was a good man. He was the best.'

He tilted her chin and looked down at her, his eyes pleading with her to give him any crumb of comfort that would prove Leon wasn't as bad as she was making out.

'When you saw him the next day, or whenever it was, what did he say? Surely he'd calmed down by then—had chance to think?'

'I never saw him again,' she said tearfully. 'That night he went to fetch Ben from the party, and...'

'It was that night?' He swallowed and let her go, burying his head in his hands. 'Oh my God.'

She couldn't say anything, watching him dumbly, wondering what the hell was running through his mind.

They both sat in silence for what felt like ages, each lost in their own thoughts.

At last, he looked up and slowly asked the question she'd been waiting for.

'The baby?'

She tried to steady her nerves. 'I couldn't keep the baby, could I, Jonah?'

'Leon's child,' he said sadly.

'It was too much,' she gabbled, desperate to make him understand. 'Even if Leon had lived he didn't want to know. I was heartbroken that he'd betrayed me. And then when I found out about the accident... I can't begin to describe the pain. The grief, the anger, the confusion, the sheer desolation. I couldn't cope with it all.'

He didn't seem to be listening. 'I just don't understand. I don't understand any of it. Leon wasn't that person. He was a good man.'

'That's what everyone says,' she said, unable to keep the bitterness from her voice. 'Oh, Leon Callaghan, he was such a good man, the best. They've turned him into a saint since he died. Well, yes he was a good man, but he wasn't perfect, was he? And that night he was a monster. A cold, unfeeling, selfish monster, and I hated him! I wished him dead, Jonah, and I meant it, and I've had to live with that ever since.'

'The accident wasn't your fault, Kat,' he said, sounding numb.

'I never thought it was,' she said. 'I've never blamed myself for that. But have you any idea how it feels to love someone so much, and miss them so desperately, and hate them with a passion at the same time?'

He looked at her bleakly. 'Yes. When Sofia left that's exactly how I felt, and when she died I lived it all over again. So yes, I do know how it feels. But Leon wasn't Sofia, and I can't believe he said and did those things.'

Was he calling her a liar? She eyed him worriedly. Did he think she was making it up? Exaggerating even? She knew how much Jonah loved Leon, but surely he would believe her? She'd been afraid of telling him what had happened, not wanting for a moment to trash his best friend to him, not wanting to tarnish his memories of Leon, the way hers had been tarnished. It hadn't occurred to her, though, that he'd doubt her word.

She'd been about to tell him the rest of it—the most important bit in a way—but realised she couldn't. He was already devastated, and the way he was looking at her... How would he look at her if she finished her story?

Too late, she realised that he really wasn't ready to hear all this. He hadn't wanted to hear it. He'd been better off not knowing. Now she'd destroyed his beliefs about the one man he'd always idolised. He and Leon had been friends since primary school and she'd just told him he never really knew him at all. What had she done?

'Are you okay?' she asked, knowing it was a stupid question.

He stood. 'I—I think I need some fresh air,' he said. 'I'm going for a walk. I'll be back soon.'

She didn't try to talk him out of it.

He wasn't the only one who needed to be alone right now.

THIRTY-ONE

Jonah hadn't decided to head to the churchyard, yet as he blinked into awareness, he realised that was where he'd ended up.

He found himself standing in the darkness, staring in the direction of the Garden of Ashes, knowing that the remains of his best friend were buried there.

He sank onto the bench and closed his eyes. The night air was cold, and a wind blew through the almost-bare branches of the trees. If he was of a more suggestible nature he could have convinced himself that the spectres of everyone buried here were prowling around him, watching.

But Jonah had never been a believer in the supernatural, and he wasn't afraid of the dark, or of churchyards, or of graves or their occupants.

He had other things to worry about, other monsters to deal with.

Leon.

He could barely take it in. He remembered the day they'd met at primary school: how they'd chummed up almost immediately, bonding over their mutual liking for painting pictures, their mutual loathing of sums and the teacher who forced them to do them.

They'd been inseparable for years. Even when Leon started dating Kat in high school, it hadn't shaken their bond. Kat had just joined their gang, along with Noah, who'd been a timid, quiet sort of boy who they'd pretty much overlooked until Kat told them she felt sorry for him. He was a 'posh boy' from St Egbert's and they wouldn't normally have had anything to do with him, but she'd brought him into their group, so then there were four of them, but even so he'd always known that he and Leon were still best friends. They told each other everything. Everything.

He'd been the sounding board for Leon's frustrations with Ben, who'd turned into a teenage tearaway, and was causing no end of angst to their parents. Leon had wanted to throttle his younger brother. Maybe he would have if he hadn't been able to rant to Jonah.

He remembered when Julian Callaghan had been diagnosed with cancer. Leon had been absolutely devastated, sobbing his heart out in Jonah's garden. Luckily, his mother hadn't been in, but Jonah's dad had heard them from the forge, and he'd ushered them both inside and listened as Leon poured out his fears and sadness.

Jonah had felt helpless, but his dad had been great, and made Jonah see that just being there for his friend was enough. It might not seem much, but it would mean everything to Leon.

Neither of them could ever have foreseen that Julian would outlive his own son. But that awful night in October, fate had robbed Jonah of the man he considered his best friend in the world. The man he could honestly, hand on heart, say he loved like a brother. The man he'd looked up to.

Leon had seemed so incredible to him: working hard at the

brewery, intent on working his way to the top there; taking the pressure off his parents by dealing with Ben's bad behaviour; being strong for his mother who was crumbling under the strain of living with her terminally ill husband.

He'd admired him. Considered him perfect. An example to follow.

Yet he'd been cheating on Kat and had been so vile to her when she'd needed him most.

He hadn't had a clue. Leon had been seeing some other woman and he'd never confided in Jonah. Never so much as hinted. Then again, he supposed that was inevitable. Jonah wouldn't have let him get away with it. He'd have forced him to come clean to Kat. He couldn't abide secrets and lies.

He wondered who she'd been, and a faint memory came to him of a woman he'd seen Leon with once. It had seemed innocent enough. Jonah had gone to pick Leon up from the brewery one night because Leon's car had gone in for its MOT. As he'd pulled into the yard, he'd spotted Leon talking to some pretty brunette. They'd seemed friendly, but he hadn't thought anything of it.

Leon had said she was just someone who worked with him, and he'd had no reason to give it another thought. Now, though, he remembered that she'd been one of the brewery workers who'd turned up for the funeral and that she'd cried. A lot. Even that hadn't sounded an alarm, though, because many people were crying, including a number of his co-workers. It was all circumstantial and he couldn't be certain. Pointless to speculate because he'd never know. He'd never be able to ask Leon, would he?

He hauled himself to his feet and turned on his mobile phone torch. He trudged over to Leon's memorial stone and stared down at it. As the light flashed onto his name, he gave a low moan, as anguish once again overtook him.

'Why didn't you tell me, you bloody idiot?'

The flowers had all gone, no doubt removed by someone—probably Jennifer—as they wilted. It was just a cold, hard stone lying there on the ground. He was tempted to stamp on it in frustration and anger.

'You could have had everything!' he cried. 'A woman who loved you, heart and soul, and a child of your own. You ruined it all, and for what?'

If he'd reacted better to Kat's news, maybe the two of them would have sat and talked, and maybe someone else would have gone to pick up Ben that night.

He felt a sudden chill as the thought occurred to him that, just maybe, Kat would have gone with him, and they could both have been killed. It didn't bear thinking about. Who could tell why the cards fell as they did? Life was all ifs and buts and maybes. Leon had made his decision and he wasn't here to justify it or explain it. They would never know why he'd reacted as he did.

'It wasn't like you,' he whispered, sinking onto his knees. 'You were kind. Why did you treat her like that? Was it this woman? Were you in the grip of some obsession? Was it because you were at your wit's end with Ben and your dad's illness? Was there something else going on? Why aren't you here to tell me?'

There was no answer, except for the wind blowing through the branches behind him.

'I never really knew you at all, did I?' he said sadly, as he got to his feet again.

He stared down at the stone for a moment, then switched off his phone torch and walked slowly out of the churchyard.

* * *

Kat was trembling as she heard the front door open and close again. She listened intently, hearing the key turn in the lock, and the sound of the latch dropping. She heard the living room door open and close, and Jonah's footsteps in the hall as he entered the kitchen, searching for her.

Inevitably, within moments, she heard him coming upstairs, and pulled the duvet up higher, as if protecting herself from him.

The bedroom door next to hers opened, and she heard a light being switched on. Then there was a faint tap on her own door and light from the landing flooded her room as he pushed it open and stood there, looking uncertain.

'Kat?'

She sat up, still clutching the duvet, and switched on the lamp so he could see her properly.

'What are you doing in here?' he asked, walking slowly towards her and sitting on the edge of her bed.

'I thought it best for tonight,' she admitted. 'We've both been through a lot this evening, and I thought maybe you needed time to think things through.'

'Like you said,' he murmured, 'we've both been through a lot this evening. Maybe the last thing we need is to be alone tonight.'

'I know you've had a shock,' she said. 'And I can understand if you don't believe me—'

'Don't believe you?' He raised an eyebrow. 'What do you mean?'

'You said you didn't believe it,' she managed, feeling choked. 'What I told you about Leon.'

He shook his head and reached for her hand, managing to loosen her grip on the duvet, and take it in his.

'Of course I believe you,' he said gently. 'It's just—that's not the Leon I know, and you have to understand that it's a shock to learn he could behave like that towards you. But I believe you one hundred per cent. It breaks my heart, but I don't doubt you, not about any of it. I'm so sorry you went through all that, Kat. I wish I'd known. I wish I'd been able to help you.'

'I know,' she said. 'Thank you.'

'Don't sleep in here tonight,' he pleaded. 'Come back to our room and let me hold you. I think we both need a cuddle, don't you?'

He was so kind, so understanding. There was nothing she'd like more than to be held by Jonah. He could make all her worries go away. But she couldn't do it.

He'd wanted them to be honest with each other, and she'd tried, she'd really tried, but she'd failed. She couldn't bring herself to shatter what was left of his heart. She didn't want to see the look of disgust on his face when he knew the truth. Even if he accepted it, it was too much of a burden for him to carry. How could she put that weight on his shoulders, along with everything else she'd done to him tonight?

'Jonah,' she said heavily, 'I think I'm going to move back to Whistlestop Cottage for a little while.'

The expression on his face changed, the warmth and compassion changing to shock and dismay.

'Why?' he asked, tightening his hold on her hand. 'After everything...'

'I just need some space,' she said desperately. 'I think we both do. Things have changed and you can't deny it. We need time to think things through. Apart.'

'I don't understand.' He let go of her hand, looking bewildered. 'We love each other, don't we?'

She nodded dumbly, staring miserably at the duvet.

'Well then! The worst part's over with, Kat. You've told me the truth. We've got no more secrets between us now.'

She raised her gaze to his, unable to speak.

His expression hardened. 'Are there?'

'Jonah,' she said sadly, 'please just let me go.'

'What aren't you telling me?' he begged. 'Whatever it is, we can work it out between us. It can't be as bad as what you've already revealed.'

'I promise you won't have to worry about Tommy,' she said. 'I've spoken to the aunties and it's all arranged. I'll pick him up from school every day and take him back to Whistlestop Cottage, and either Rita or Birdie will drop him home when you finish work. And I can make sure he's got pack up and his uniform's washed. You can still work as normal.'

'As normal?' He got to his feet. 'As normal? What's normal about this? What's going on? What are you keeping from me?'

'I have to go, Jonah,' she said. 'I'm not saying it's forever, but I need some time to think.'

'Oh, do you?' His voice sounded cold suddenly. 'Well, that's all that matters then, isn't it?'

'Don't be like that,' she pleaded.

'Like what? Upset? Hurt? Totally bloody confused? Sorry, Kat, some demands are too hard to meet. I thought we were in this together. I thought we were a family. What the hell could possibly be so bad that you'd leave me rather than tell me? As if finding out Leon wasn't anything like the man I thought he was isn't bad enough, are you seriously saying there's something even worse? What am I supposed to do? How am I supposed to react to all this?'

'You're just going to have to trust me that it's for the best,' she said, forcing herself to sound calm and in control. She couldn't let him see she was weakening. If he kept pushing she might well give in, and that would be the end of them.

He stared down at her. 'You're not going to change your mind, are you?' he asked at last.

'No.' She plucked at the duvet with nervous fingers. 'No, I'm not.'

He stood quite still for a few moments, and she hardly dared breathe as she waited for his next words. But none came.

He suddenly turned and walked out of her room, closing the door quietly behind him.

She heard him go back downstairs. Heard the living room door open. Heard the faint sound of the television being switched on.

Then she buried her head in her pillow, and all she heard was her own muffled sobs.

THIRTY-TWO

'All I want to know is, do you want steak and kidney pie for tea, or would you prefer chicken and vegetable?' Kat leaned against the counter in the wool shop and shook her head as her aunts exchanged looks and refused to give her an answer. 'It's really not that difficult a decision. I wish I hadn't bothered to ask now. I should just have gone to Maister's and got what I fancied.'

'It's not that easy,' Birdie said. 'Personally, I prefer chicken and vegetable, but we had chicken on Tuesday, and it does get a bit samey. But as for the steak and kidney—well, it all depends which brand you're talking about.'

'Does it matter?' Kat asked patiently. 'They all taste the same really. The only difference is the packaging and price.'

'That's just not true, Kat dear,' Rita began. 'I could tell you some stories that would make your hair curl. Once I got a cheap pie from—'

She broke off and they all turned as the shop door was pushed open, and Daisy walked in.

'Daisy! It's good to see you,' Kat said, smiling at her. Not only was it good to see her, but it was a welcome relief to be spared Rita's hair curling story about a cheap pie. 'How are you?'

Daisy, it had to be said, didn't exactly look as if she were dancing with happiness. She looked, if anything, downright miserable, and Kat's heart sank as she guessed why.

'Sorry,' Daisy said, as she sidled up to the counter, giving Hattie a brief smile as she gazed up at her from the buggy. 'I thought I'd better come and tell you in person. It's only fair.'

'Oh dear,' Rita said as she and Birdie exchanged concerned looks. 'Does this mean what I think it does?'

'It's a no, I'm afraid,' Daisy said flatly. 'I've tried everything, believe me, but Tom was never going to change his mind, and when he promised Andi a hot tub for the garden if we stayed in Leeds—well, it was a done deal. I'm so sorry we wasted your time.'

'You didn't,' Kat assured her. 'It's not your fault.'

'I expect it will soon sell anyway,' Daisy said. 'Have you had any offers yet?'

Birdie looked at Rita, who shuffled uncomfortably.

'To be truthful, lovey,' Birdie said, 'we have had an offer, yes, although we haven't accepted it yet.'

Kat gasped. 'You never said!'

'No, well, we were hoping we wouldn't have to take it,' Rita admitted. 'It's the Haygarths. They've decided they want to open that bloody fudge shop here after all.'

'Oh no,' Kat said, dismayed. 'Anyone but them.'

'I know, dear, but it's the only offer we've had. We were so hoping Daisy would want the shop, but if she doesn't, what choice have we got? Mr Rustill says it's the wrong time of year now for buying and selling. He says things might pick up in the spring, but it's a long time to wait. The way things are, we'd already decided that if we hadn't sold the place by December we were going to have to shut it down anyway, and let it stand empty until we found a buyer. The Haygarths would at least save us from that. It's a shame, but there it is. We can't afford to run it any longer, what with the price of electricity and gas, and everything else going up. It's a worry.'

'It is a shame,' Rita agreed. 'We hoped it would be sold by now. Not that we want to part with the place of course. It's going to break our hearts when it finally goes, but we wanted to pay off our debts and give Kat the money to buy herself a nice little place round here.'

'Rita!' Birdie gasped.

Rita's hand flew to her mouth as Kat stared at her in surprise. 'Oops!'

'You were going to give me the money?'

'Well of course we were, dear. What would we need it for? That little flat upstairs is lovely, and it's served you well for years, but Hattie's growing and you need more space. We knew you'd have to move out, but how could you ever afford it on your wages? Any money we make from the sale of this place is going to you. It will give you a good deposit on somewhere decent.'

'But...' Kat was speechless, as Daisy smiled at her.

'Close your mouth, lovey, you're catching flies,' Rita observed.

'Why didn't you tell me?' Kat asked. 'I was so worried about being homeless, and you let me think I'd be living at Whistlestop Cottage forever!'

'No, we offered you a room at Whistlestop Cottage while the sale went through and you found somewhere of your own. You just assumed we meant forever,' Birdie said.

'You didn't correct me!'

'We were going to, but then you got that offer of a room at Jonah's, and we thought, why spoil things? If you'd known about the money you'd probably have refused his offer, and we didn't want that, did we, Birdie?'

'No, we didn't.' Birdie sighed. 'We hoped you and Jonah

would make a go of things. It's such a shame that things didn't work out. He's the perfect man for you, Kat.'

'We've been through all this,' Kat said. 'Let's not drag it up again.'

'But you love him!' Rita protested. 'We can see it in your face. You're miserable without him. And having seen him in the fish and chip shop the other night, we're pretty sure he's miserable without you, too. Whatever happened, surely it can be put right?'

'Have you broken up with your boyfriend?' Daisy asked sympathetically. 'I'm so sorry. I didn't even know you were dating anyone.'

'Kept it quiet,' Birdie explained. 'Thought we didn't know. As if she could hide that from us! She lit up like a Christmas tree whenever he was near her. Looks like she's had a power cut since she left him.'

'So we're both bloody miserable then,' Daisy said with a sigh.

'What you two need is a good old gossip and a moan,' Rita decided. 'Why don't you go over to The White Hart Inn, Kat? Take Daisy with you. I'm sure Sally would like to see you, and you can drown your sorrows while you commiserate with each other.'

'I've got shopping to do,' Kat reminded her. 'Pie. Remember?'

'Oh!' Rita waved her away. 'I don't want pie for my tea anyway. We've got some chops in the fridge. I'd rather have those. You two go to the pub and I'll mind Hattie. She'll be no bother. Go on.'

Kat looked doubtfully at her watch. 'I'll have to be back by three,' she reminded them. 'I've got to pick Tommy up from school.'

'Still gives you a couple of hours. Go on. Go and let your

hair down. Have a bitch about men. Do you both good if you ask me.'

Kat glanced at Daisy who shrugged.

'Fine by me,' she said.

'Okay.' Kat sighed heavily, knowing when she was beaten. 'You're sure?'

'Positive.' Birdie beamed at her. 'Go on. We'll see you later.'

The White Hart Inn was mostly empty, and only Chloe and Rafferty were behind the bar.

'Is Sally not working this afternoon?' Kat asked. 'Daisy and I are on a mission to have a womanly chat about the foibles of men, so it would have been good to have her company.'

Rafferty laughed. 'She'd have nothing to say on the subject. She's married to the perfect man.'

'I'm sure she could dig deep and find something,' Kat said wryly, remembering only too well Sally's experiences with her ex.

Rafferty turned round and handed her a bottle of wine. 'Here, take this upstairs to the flat,' he said, giving her a wink. 'I'm sure that will jog her memory, and she'll be glad to see you. She's supposed to be cleaning the bathroom this afternoon, and everyone deserves an escape route from that little task.'

'Cheers, Rafferty,' Kat said. 'You're a diamond.'

'Oh, I wouldn't go that far,' he said. 'Anyway, I think she's got something she wanted to tell you. She was going to call you later, so you've saved her a job.'

He ushered them through the door marked private behind the bar and they hurried upstairs, knocking on the Kingstons' door and waiting.

Sally opened it after a few minutes, and she beamed when she saw Kat holding a bottle of wine.

'Ooh, just what I want to see on a miserable Friday afternoon,' she said. 'Come in, love, and save me from myself. I was going to call you later. I've got some news for you that you might —Oh, who's this?'

'This,' Kat explained, as they walked into the flat, 'is Daisy. You remember, Daisy Jackson? The one who wanted to buy the shop?'

'Oh yes! Pleased to meet you, love,' Sally said, holding out a hand before withdrawing it hastily as she remembered she was wearing rubber gloves. 'Make yourselves at home while I get rid of these. Shan't be a tick.'

Kat motioned to Daisy to sit down while she went into the kitchen and got three glasses from the cupboard. She carried them back into the living room and set them down, then opened the bottle of wine.

'Right,' Sally said, returning minus the rubber gloves. 'To what do I owe this pleasure?'

'We're drowning our sorrows,' Daisy said shyly. 'I hope you don't mind me tagging along.'

'Bless you, if you're drowning your sorrows you're in the best place. We've done that a few times in here, haven't we, Kat?'

'If these walls could talk,' Kat agreed. 'What were you going to call me about anyway?'

'Oh, I'll get to that in a minute. Has something else happened? With Jonah, I mean,' Sally said, taking a glass of wine from Kat and nodding her thanks.

Kat handed Daisy her drink then screwed the cap back on the bottle. 'No. I haven't seen him,' she said briefly. 'The aunties have taken it in turns to take Tommy back to Forge Cottage this week, and Jonah's kept his distance as I asked him to. Nothing to report.'

'I still don't see why you left,' Sally said. 'I don't understand it when you seemed to be getting on so well.'

'I had my reasons,' was all Kat would say, feeling so miserable she felt like downing an entire bottle of wine rather than just a glassful. If she hadn't had to pick up Tommy at three she might well have done just that.

'There's always a reason where men are concerned,' Daisy agreed. 'They're never what they seem to be, and you can't rely on them.'

Except, Kat thought sadly, Jonah was exactly what he'd seemed to be. Kind, thoughtful, understanding. He'd been lovely to her, and it was she who'd messed up. She'd been the one to hurt him, not the other way around, and the worst of it was she couldn't even tell him why. Poor Jonah.

'So what's happened to you, Daisy?' Sally asked, clearly recognising that Kat had nothing else to say on the subject of Jonah. 'Are you buying the shop or not?'

'Believe me,' Daisy said, 'if I was buying the shop I wouldn't be here drowning my sorrows. My brother, in his wisdom, has decided it's a no-go. I'm stuck in Leeds for the foreseeable. God knows what I'm going to do with myself now. Carry on working in that bloody supermarket I suppose. Maybe buy myself a cheap flat in town. I don't fancy living with Tom and Andi any more anyway. I think watching them wallowing in their fancy new hot tub might just bring on a stroke.'

Sally giggled. 'Can't say I blame you, love. Can't be doing with hot tubs myself. Ugh! So you think you can afford a flat then?'

'I reckon so,' Daisy said. 'I just didn't want to buy a home because I'd rather invest in a shop.'

'So if you *had* bought the shop, where would you have lived then?' Sally asked, puzzled.

'With Tom and Andi, as I do now. They were going to sell their house and buy somewhere around here with the proceeds. The money for the shop was coming from our inheritance,' she explained.

'Right.' Sally nodded and sat back in the armchair.

'The aunties are gutted,' Kat said. 'Do you know, they were

planning to give me the money from the sale? I never knew. They didn't say a word. They were going to pay off their debts and whatever was left was for me to put a deposit down on a place to live. How lovely is that?'

'Very generous,' Sally agreed. 'And how come they kept it quiet?'

'Because they wanted me to accept Jonah's offer of accommodation and a job,' Kat explained, her spirits sinking as the subject of Jonah resurfaced. 'Anyway, now that's over there was nothing to stop them telling me.'

'So when the shop sells you'll have the money to find somewhere to live at last,' Sally said.

'Yes, although I'll need a bit to set up my knitting business,' Kat pointed out. 'And that's without the problem of finding somewhere I can afford locally. It's swings and roundabouts, Sal. Honestly, I'm sick of it all going round in my head.'

Sally sipped her wine, eyeing them thoughtfully.

'What is it?' Kat asked suspiciously. 'You look as if you're plotting something.'

'Not plotting exactly,' Sally said, 'but I do have an idea, and if it worked it would solve all your problems. Well, most of them anyway. Just let me get this straight in my head.'

She closed her eyes for a moment, and Daisy and Kat exchanged bemused glances.

Suddenly, Sally's eyes flew open and she sat forward. 'Yep! That could definitely work.' She put down her glass. 'Come on, we're going out.'

'Going out? Where to?'

'To see Birdie and Rita first of all,' Sally said, grinning widely. 'And then, if that goes the way I think it will, we're going to pay a visit to Cutting it Fine. Remember, I said I had something to tell you? Well, you'll never believe this. Talk about perfect timing!'

* * *

The sign on the door of Pennyfeather's Wool Shop had been turned to Closed, but Kat thought everyone in Market Place must be aware that it wasn't empty. The racket coming from the shop was so loud she marvelled that Hattie, who was asleep in her buggy in the back room, hadn't woken up and screamed the place down.

What had started as a quiet meeting had turned into a celebration. Sally had rushed back to The White Hart Inn, returning with three bottles of sparkling wine and a bottle of champagne. She and Bluebell had wasted no time pouring everyone a glass and raising a toast.

'To Pennyfeather's Crafts and The Crafty Cook Café!'

Kat and Daisy had been all too happy to join in with the toast, along with two giggling aunts who couldn't have looked more delighted.

'I can't think why we didn't think of it before,' Birdie admitted. 'We could have saved Daisy and Kat all this worry. Thank goodness you were on the ball, Sally.'

'And how wonderful that you'd spoken to Bluebell,' Rita added. 'It just shows you. If it's meant to be, it will happen.' She gave a sigh of contentment. 'How marvellous.'

It had been Sally's idea of course, but the aunties were right, Kat thought. Everything had slotted into place beautifully. The aunties were selling the flat to Daisy, who would turn it into a café.

'The Crafty Cook Café,' she'd announced proudly. 'I've had that name in mind for years.'

As for the shop—they were signing that over to Kat, lock, stock and barrel. The only proviso was that it kept its name, Pennyfeather's, but given that was Kat's name too it was hardly an obstacle.

'Instead of Pennyfeather's Wool Shop, it will be

Pennyfeather's Crafts,' Birdie said, with satisfaction, 'but I think Mother would have approved of that.'

'Are you absolutely sure this is what you want to do?' Kat asked worriedly. 'It feels like a lot to ask, just being given the shop like that.'

'Don't be silly,' Rita said. 'And with the money we get from the sale of the flat we can pay off our debts and have a bit put by for emergencies, and the rest can be used to turn this shop into the crafter's paradise you're dreaming of.'

'I'll knock this room through into the back,' Kat said, gazing around her in delight. 'We'll have so much more space to stock everything.'

'And you can hold your knitting classes in the café,' Daisy said eagerly.

'And sell my own patterns in my own shop.' Kat closed her eyes, imagining it all.

'And meanwhile, Daisy will be sitting pretty in the flat above my salon,' Bluebell added, pouring herself another glass. 'You know, I was fuming when my tenant buggered off without giving me notice, but it's all worked out for the best. Sal was thinking it would be perfect for Kat, but this is even better. I'm so glad you liked it, Daisy.'

'I love it,' Daisy told her, her eyes shining. 'My very own place! You know, I've only ever lived with my dad or brother before. This will be the first home I've ever had of my own. I'm so excited.'

'We'll speak to Eugenie tomorrow about turning the flat upstairs back into commercial property,' Birdie promised her. 'I really don't think you'll have any problems, but it's always good to have her on side. She knows everyone on the council, and they're all terrified of her. Did you know the academy's going ahead? Eugenie's got a firm signed up to do the work on the access road, and they're hoping to have the art school open by spring.' She shook her head admiringly. 'You've got to hand it to her. She makes things happen.'

'This is going to be amazing,' Sally said, tipping her glass towards Kat. 'I'm so happy for you, love. A new venture and I just know it's going to be a big success.'

Kat sipped her wine, but the fizz of excitement was flattening by the minute. How much sweeter would this moment have tasted if she'd been able to share it with Jonah? She longed to tell him all about it and wondered how he'd feel. Somehow she was sure he'd be over the moon for her. He'd probably have gathered her into his arms and hugged her tightly, wishing her every happiness and success.

But Jonah wasn't here, and the way things stood she wasn't sure she'd ever get a hug from him again.

'Chin up,' Sally whispered. 'This is one big problem sorted. Now we're going to focus on the other one. Let's get you and Jonah back together, eh?'

Kat didn't think it would be so easy, but she smiled anyway, aware that, for now, this was a celebration, and she should be enjoying herself.

'The main thing,' Bluebell said firmly, 'is that we're finally going to get an alternative to that bloody awful Market Café.'

'No, no, Bluebell,' Birdie said immediately. 'The main thing is that there will still be a Pennyfeather's in Tuppenny Bridge.'

Six glasses clinked loudly, as they all agreed they'd drink to that.

THIRTY-THREE

Jonah tilted his head to one side and eyed his latest piece of artwork critically. He'd spent every evening this week working on various versions of it while Tommy slept next door, and he'd been refining this effort all day today. He wondered why he was bothering, but something drove him on.

He supposed it was a distraction. This had been the longest week of his life, and sitting in front of the television every evening wasn't an option. It allowed his mind to wander, and that was the last thing he needed. Being forced to focus on his latest piece of art had helped take his mind off his misery. Well, mostly.

It was good of Kat to have Tommy today. It had been her idea, put to him via Rita. Having spent an agonising Saturday stuck in the house all day, watching *Paddington* while the rain poured down outside and thoughts of his broken relationship ran through his head, he knew he'd have been climbing the walls if he'd had to endure the same again today.

But Kat had wanted to spend Sunday with Tommy, and Jonah had been happy to oblige, weak with relief that she still wanted to be part of his son's life, even if she'd washed her hands of him.

His stomach churned as he remembered what else Rita had said to him when she came to pick Tommy up.

'Kat wondered if it would be okay for her to bring Tommy home herself later. She's got something she wants to tell you.'

'Yes. I mean, of course. Of course it's okay.' He'd frowned at Rita, unable to hide his anxiety. 'What is it she wants to tell me?'

'Well, if I told you she wouldn't have need to, would she?' She'd patted him on the shoulder. 'Don't look so worried, Jonah. It's nothing bad.'

He couldn't help wondering what Rita's definition of bad was.

There was a tap on one of the double doors at the front of the forge and Jonah hurried over and pulled it open. Vince Corcoran, of all people, was standing in the lane, gazing with open admiration at the cottage next door.

'Vince.'

'Hello, Jonah.' Vince smiled at him. 'I'm just looking at your lovely home. By heck, our Phillip said it was a picture and he wasn't kidding. Like something off a jigsaw puzzle. Mind you, this whole lane's beautiful. Like stepping back in time.'

Jonah tried to smile but was too worried about the reason for his visit to manage it successfully.

'Can I have a word with you?' Vince enquired.

Jonah blinked and stepped aside. 'Come in. Tommy's not here,' he added, in case that was what Vince had been hoping for.

Not wanting to admit she no longer lived with them he added, 'He's out with Kat today while I do some work.' Well, it wasn't exactly a lie, was it?

'This is quite some place,' Vince told him, gazing round in

open delight. 'I didn't know the old smithies' forges still existed. Tuppenny Bridge is a rare old wonder, isn't it?'

'What can I do for you, Vince?' Jonah asked, steeling himself for the bombshell.

'Well now, there's no need to look so worried,' the elderly man said with a smile. 'I'm not here to cause trouble if that's what you're thinking. As it happens, I've come here to thank you.'

'Thank me?'

'Me and Evelyn were only saying the other day about all you've done for Tommy. Where would he have been without you, eh? The little lad could have ended up in care if not for you, Jonah, because I doubt very much our Chris would have done anything to prevent it. It makes our blood run cold at the thought of him being all alone in the world after his mum died. We're so grateful to you.'

Jonah stiffened. 'You don't have to be grateful to me,' he said. 'Tommy is my son and my responsibility. I did what any dad would do.'

Vince rubbed his chin. 'I think I'm phrasing this badly, and I'm sorry. We know that, Jonah, honest we do. But I can see why you're so wary of me. You must have a very bad impression of our family, and who can blame you? But look at this!' He waved his arm, gazing around the forge. 'This cottage, this town, this life you've given him. All that love. Because, make no mistake, we can see it, clear as day. You and Tommy adore each other, and we couldn't be more thankful for it. And that's what I wanted to say, because me and Evelyn, we realised we hadn't said it that day at The Black Swan.'

'There's no need,' Jonah said, his tone softer this time as he realised Vince was genuine.

'There's every need,' Vince insisted. 'We want you to know how much we appreciate you letting us into your lives like this. I know it can't have been easy for you, and you could have said no. Truth is, we'd have had to lump it if you had. You know as well as I do that we have no right to see him, so I can't tell you how much we owe you.

'But Phillip told us that you were worried, and we wanted to reassure you. We've no intention of taking you to court, or anything like that. Like I said, we'd have no chance, and we all know it, but even if we had we wouldn't do it. All that matters to us is Tommy's happiness, and he loves you to bits, anyone can see that. We're just glad he has you, and if we can be a small part of his life, whenever it suits you, we'll be happy with that.'

He held out his hand and Jonah shook it. 'I'll not keep you any longer. I just wanted you to know how we felt, and to put your mind at rest.'

'Thank you,' Jonah said quietly. 'I appreciate that more than you'll ever know. We'll arrange another get together very soon. I'll call you during the week when I've spoken to Tommy.'

'That'd be grand,' Vince said, smiling. 'Well, I'll be off. See you soon, Jonah. Give our love to Tommy.'

After he left, Jonah leaned against the anvil, so pleased and relieved he could have cried.

Now it was just Kat he had to win back, but that was easier said than done. He had no idea why she'd left, other than there was something she wasn't telling him. Some secret she felt unable to share with him. He'd racked his brains, but he couldn't think for a moment what could be so bad. Unless she'd tampered with Leon's brakes, he knew he'd forgive her anything. He just wanted her back.

Give her time, he'd told himself over and over, when the urge to rush round to Whistlestop Cottage had almost over-whelmed him. *Don't push her. Let her deal with whatever it is she needs to deal with, and then maybe...*

Or maybe not. That was the fear. He couldn't bring himself to accept the possibility, and perhaps it was the need for denial that drove him back to work, desperate to take his mind off it at all costs.

* * *

Kat's legs were growing increasingly wobbly as she wandered down the lane with Tommy, and by the time they reached Forge Cottage she was so anxious she thought she was going to be sick.

She hadn't seen Jonah for what felt like ages, even though it had only been a week. She missed him so much, and while part of her was longing to set eyes on him again, there was another part of her that dreaded it. What if it just weakened her resolve? She couldn't give him what he wanted, but she might well be tempted as soon as she gazed into those grey-blue eyes.

When he opened the door her heart thudded so loudly she was sure he must hear it.

'Tommy!' he said, pulling his son to him for a hug. His voice, though, sounded strained, and as he stared at Kat she could see he looked tired, as if he wasn't sleeping. She knew how that felt.

'Hey, Kat.'

She nodded at him before giving him a faint smile. 'Is it okay if I come in for a moment?'

As he ushered her inside she tried not to give in to the pang of homesickness that attacked her. How odd that she'd only lived here a matter of weeks. It felt like this had always been her home, somehow.

She was all too aware of Jonah giving her worried glances while Tommy babbled on to him, telling him all about his day. She knew he was anxious about what she was going to tell him, and tried to reassure him that it was good news. Well, for her at least.

'I just thought I'd pop in,' she said, hoping that sounded

suitably casual and would put his mind at rest. 'I've got some exciting news about the shop.'

Jonah visibly slumped and she wasn't sure whether that was from relief or disappointment.

'Ah, right. I wondered what the big secret was,' he said. 'Rita said you had something to tell me.'

He turned to Tommy.

'Hey, we've got half an hour before bath time. Do you want to watch television until then? Just while I talk to Kat about something.'

Tommy nodded and sidled up to Kat, taking hold of her hand. 'Are you coming home now? I want you and Hattie to live here again.'

Kat gulped down the tears. 'We'll see, sweetheart,' she said, unable to promise him anything but not wanting to destroy his hopes. Or hers. Or Jonah's for that matter. If it was up to her...

'Shall we go in the kitchen?' she asked Jonah briskly, before she could start sobbing at the pleading look on Tommy's face. 'I won't stay long.'

He handed Tommy the remote and as soon as his son was settled on the sofa he led her into the kitchen. He didn't offer her a drink, but stood gripping the island, his face set as he waited for her to speak.

'It's quite exciting really,' she told him, hoping he'd be pleased for her. 'At least, I think it is.'

As succinctly as she could she told him about the sale of the flat to Daisy, and about their plans to go into business together, running a craft shop and café.

'So Pennyfeather's will remain in Tuppenny Bridge after all,' she finished nervously, 'and I'll be able to do my knitting classes upstairs in the café. And Daisy will only be living across the market place in Bluebell's flat, so it's all worked out perfectly.'

She bit her lip and waited, then her shoulders sagged in relief as he pushed away from the island and embraced her.

'I'm so happy for you, Kat. That's perfect. What a brilliant solution for you all.'

'Really?' She gazed up at him, wondering if he was as pleased for her as he seemed to be. After all, he'd had his doubts about her setting up her own business. 'I'll still be able to pick Tommy up from school, don't worry about that. We're figuring out the details, but we're thinking of taking someone else on in the afternoons. That way I can do a knitting class straight after dinner and leave work at two thirty to be there for Tommy and Hattie. The aunties are happy to look after Hattie at their place in the mornings so it will all be okay. You don't have to worry.'

'I'm not worried about that,' he assured her as he stepped back from her. 'I'd have figured something out. It's not your problem. I just want you to be happy. I'm so proud of you, Kat.'

'Are you?' She smiled up at him through tear-blurred eyes. 'Really?'

'Of course. You deserve this, you really do. I know it's going to be a massive success.'

'What you said about Tommy,' she managed, 'about him not being my responsibility...'

'Well, he's not, is he?' He shrugged. 'That's the way it is. I understand that.'

'Jonah...'

He dug his hands into the pockets of his jeans. 'Yes?'

'Tommy means everything to me. You know that, right?'

'And Hattie means everything to me.'

She nodded. 'It's a bit of a mess, isn't it? I wish things could be different.'

'So do I. I wish I knew why they weren't.'

'If I could...' She shook her head. 'I'm sorry. Maybe—maybe we'll figure it out.'

'I hope so, but it would really help if I knew what the problem was, Kat.'

She couldn't deny that, and wished with all her heart she could explain.

'I'd better get back to Tommy,' he said heavily, obviously realising she wasn't about to answer him. 'Monday tomorrow, and you know how busy Monday mornings are. I'd better get him bathed and ready for bed. Thanks for having him today.'

'It was a pleasure,' she said. 'I'd better go.'

She turned away and he followed her to the front door.

'I won't say goodbye to Tommy,' she told him. 'Just in case it upsets him. Tell him—tell him I love him, and I'll see him tomorrow.'

'Will do.' As he opened the front door he added, 'I really am pleased for you, you know. It's brilliant news. You're going to be amazing.'

She didn't mean to do it but somehow she couldn't stop herself from reaching up and kissing him on the cheek.

As she pulled away he caught her hand and whispered, 'I'm not giving up on us, Kat. I can't. Please don't ask me to.'

Unable to think of a suitable reply she turned and ran down the path, her heart breaking as she heard the door of the cottage click shut behind her.

THIRTY-FOUR

Tawnie had really gone to town on the Halloween decorations. Her house was festooned with plastic skeletons with glowing eyes, swooping bats, fake spider webs, and witches on brooms. Jonah thought it looked funny, but Tommy was enchanted. At least he wasn't scared, which was something, although Tawnie seemed slightly disappointed that he wasn't.

Jonah was just glad to see his son smiling, although he'd looked a little wistful earlier when he'd asked why Kat and Hattie weren't going to Auntie Tawnie's, and enquired, yet again, when they were coming home.

They'd been invited round for tea before they all went trick or treating. Iris had dithered about joining them, considering herself far too old and mature to bother with such things, until she'd learned that her friends were looking forward to dressing up and making the rounds, when suddenly it became completely acceptable for her to take part.

Having eaten an early tea, they'd all hurried to get dressed up, and the house became a scene of chaos as they fought for mirrors and changing space.

Iris was dressed up as Wednesday Addams, and Jonah had

to admit she looked impressive. Lilly, meanwhile, had dressed up as a witch, and looked harmless enough, even though she insisted she was Bellatrix Lestrange from the Harry Potter franchise.

'She's really not,' Tawnie whispered to Jonah. 'The label on the costume said *generic witch*, but don't tell her that for goodness' sake!'

Tawnie herself was dressed as a zombie nurse, and had done an excellent job with the make-up. Jonah himself hadn't had much time to get ready, as he was too busy dressing Tommy in his spectacular costume.

'Bloody hell, you nearly gave me a heart attack!' Tawnie clutched her chest dramatically as her nephew proudly showed off his outfit.

'You're already dead, remember?' Jonah said, grinning.

'You can talk, Count Dracula!' Tawnie looked with some discomfort at Tommy. 'Honestly, that's scary. You know I'm terrified of spiders.'

'I'm a tarantula!' Tommy announced with glee, waving one of his long, furry legs at his aunt.

Tawnie obligingly screamed and ran away, and a laughing Tommy chased her down the stairs, despite Jonah calling to him to be careful.

They all tumbled into the living room and stopped, seeing Keith sitting in the armchair, having made no attempt to get ready for trick or treating whatsoever.

'What are you dressed as?' Jonah asked.

'A worn-out father of two who's had the life sucked out of him by a nagging wife and demanding kids,' Keith replied. 'Suits me, don't you think?'

'You cheeky sod!' Tawnie rapped him on the arm. 'Go and get dressed. I've got your Beetlejuice costume all laid out.'

'I'm not wearing that,' he protested. 'I've told you. It's too much faff and I'll look daft.'

'You look daft anyway,' she said. 'Surely you're used to it by now?'

Keith sighed. 'Bloody Halloween. I hate it. You know, with all these sarcastic comments you're beginning to sound frighteningly like your mother.'

'Now that *is* frightening,' Jonah said, laughing. 'Go on, get changed and be quick about it.'

Keith lumbered to the hallway door, dropping a quick kiss on Tawnie's cheek. 'You look surprisingly sexy in that costume,' he told her. 'Even if your face is half eaten away by worms.'

'Thanks,' she retorted. 'You've got ten minutes and then we're going without you.'

As Keith ran up the stairs Iris muttered, 'You do know you've just given him a get-out clause? He'll just stay up there now and wait for us to—'

She broke off and they all gazed at each other in dismay as the front door was pushed open and they heard a dreaded voice calling, 'Yoo hoo! It's only me.'

Jonah closed his eyes. Why her? Why now? Instinctively, he pulled Tommy closer to him and kept a hand on his shoulder, as if protecting his son from the wrath of his so-called grandma.

'Well, don't you all look amazing!'

She was actually smiling, and Jonah wondered if that was because tonight was her favourite night. Monsters and evil spirits loved Halloween, didn't they? She'd be in her element.

'We're just going out trick or treating, Mum,' Tawnie said firmly. 'Sorry, but we promised the kids and we can't call it off now. As you can see, we've gone to a lot of trouble.'

'Haven't you just? Well, maybe I could come with you? It's a dry night. Bit cold, but it's not raining, and I'm happy to walk the streets while the children blackmail complete strangers into giving them money and sweets.'

Jonah and Tawnie exchanged glances.

'First dig,' Tawnie whispered. 'Shall we count them?'

'Where's Keith?' Mrs Brewster demanded.

'Gone upstairs to change. He's not so keen on Halloween.'

'Someone with some sense then.'

'Two,' Jonah murmured.

'I'm Bellatrix Lestrange, Grandma,' Lilly informed her.

'I have no idea who you're talking about, dear,' her grandmother said.

'And I'm Wednesday Addams,' Iris added.

'Goodness, is she still a thing? Tawnie that costume you're wearing is disgraceful. Surely you're not walking the streets wearing that?'

'It's all part of the fun,' Tawnie insisted.

'I don't see what's fun about it,' her mother said, curling her lip in distaste.

'I make that five,' Tawnie said, not even bothering to lower her voice.

'Five what? Jonah, you look very handsome. I always think Dracula is the most elegant of all the supernatural creatures, don't you? He may have drunk blood and turned his victims into the undead but he always did it with panache, don't you think?'

'Well,' Tawnie said, sounding as surprised as Jonah felt, 'I'm not sure whether to deduct a point for that. Did I imagine it or was she just nice to you?'

Jonah eyed his mother suspiciously. Just what was she up to, giving him compliments?

'I'm a tarantula,' Tommy announced proudly, and Jonah's heart sank, waiting for the inevitable snub.

Mrs Brewster looked down at the six-year-old and frowned. 'Well, so you are,' she said politely. 'What an impressive costume. Very scary. I'm sure you'll get lots of treats from people when they see you.'

Jonah's mouth fell open and he saw the surprise in Tawnie's

eyes. Coming from his mother, that was practically gushing praise. What was wrong with her?

Keith thudded down the stairs, waved his hands in the air, and yelled, 'Ta-da!' His hands—and his smile—dropped when he saw his mother-in-law standing there.

'Maureen, didn't know you were coming,' he muttered. 'Great costume. Terrifying.'

'Very funny I'm sure.' She looked him up and down in disgust. 'What on earth are you dressed as?'

'Beetlejuice,' he explained, which elicited nothing more than a dismissive wave of the hand from her.

'Honestly, this American nonsense is getting quite out of hand. Trick or treating! I've never heard anything so silly. Still, I'm here now so I'll make the best of it. Shall we?'

Keith gave Tawnie a look of dismay as she explained, 'Mum's coming with us.'

'Right. Great. Ready, kids?'

As they headed out into the night, Jonah wondered what had got into his mother. Okay, she was still bitching a bit and clearly wasn't embracing the Halloween spirit, but she'd been nice to him, and had even been polite to Tommy. He wondered if she was ill. Either that or she'd been visited by three ghosts. Bit early but he couldn't think of a better explanation.

She pulled back, and he realised to his dismay that she intended to walk with him.

'I heard all about it, Jonah,' she said to him, giving him a smug look.

'All about what?'

'About you throwing that woman and her offspring out. She's gone back to Whistlestop Cottage, hasn't she? Good riddance, I say. Let those batty old women take care of her.'

'Who told you about Kat leaving?' he demanded, his throat constricting as he realised that was what had put her in such a good mood.

'Oh, someone at the library mentioned it this afternoon,' she said. 'Mrs Blackstock. Do you remember her? She used to be the lollipop lady but had to give it up because of her veins.'

Jonah knew who she meant. 'Always liked a gossip, didn't she?' he muttered.

'She wasn't gossiping. She was concerned about you. Asked me how you were doing since Katherine Pennyfeather had gone back to her great aunts' place, and if you were managing with the boy on your own.'

'Tommy,' Jonah muttered through gritted teeth. 'His name's Tommy.'

'I said you were managing just fine. After all, you were perfectly okay before she got her claws into you, and you'll be perfectly okay now you've finally seen sense.'

Jonah watched as Iris, Lilly and Tommy knocked on someone's door. Tawnie and Keith waited at the gate, and Tawnie glanced round, giving him a wary look as he stood some feet away with his mother.

'*She* left *me*,' he said coldly.

'I beg your pardon?'

'I didn't see sense, as you put it. It was Kat who left me. I didn't throw her out. I'd never throw her out. I love her.'

His mother seemed nonplussed by his response. 'Well... Either way, whether she left or you threw her out, it's a good thing she's gone. You don't love her, Jonah. You only think you do. You're just trying to recreate what you had with Sofia, because that woman had some kind of power over you, and you thought you could have the same thing with this one. You'll wake up in a few days and realise what a lucky escape you've had, trust me.'

Jonah hardly knew what to say to her. He stared at the ground, knowing he had to keep a lid on his emotions. She fed on human misery. It energised her. He thought dully that she was probably the only real vampire around here, draining the life out of everyone who came into contact with her.

'I know what you're thinking,' she said.

I sincerely doubt it.

'You're thinking that I'm wrong. You're thinking that you and she were meant to be together. One big happy family. You're thinking that this is all some awful mistake and somehow it's all going to be put right and she'll see sense and come back to you. You don't have to tell me, I know you, Jonah. You always did have your head in the clouds, and your head turned by a pretty woman.'

That was so untrue and unfair it was almost laughable, but still he said nothing.

'Don't you remember what she was like with your best friend? How she came between you both? You and Leon went everywhere, did everything together, until she came along. She didn't care about your feelings then either. And where was she when he died, eh? Didn't hang around to comfort you then, did she? Didn't stop to help Jennifer Callaghan, or that poor dying husband of hers. Oh no, she skipped off to Dorset, if you please, to have fun at the beach.'

'She went to see her dad,' Jonah said miserably. 'She was heartbroken.'

'I'm sure she was. And I'm sure all that time in a swanky hotel was just the job to get over it. Pity poor Jennifer didn't have that luxury, isn't it? She was too busy caring for Julian, not to mention a stroppy teenager and a toddler. I'll bet she could have done with seven months at the seaside, don't you? Always was selfish. Just like her father. I remember very clearly how he sold The Black Swan and cleared off, when his poor dead wife was barely cold. Cut from the same cloth, clearly.'

Jonah frowned, as something nagged away at him, barely listening to her as she rambled on.

'And then of course she got shunted off to live with those

doddering old fools, so it's no wonder she's turned out as she has. No doubt that child of hers will grow up to be just the same. I can see it happening. You're well shot of the lot of them. Are you listening to me, Jonah? Jonah?'

Jonah hurried forward, just as the children received their treats from the people at the door and the group was about to move on.

'Tawnie! Can I ask you a favour? Would you mind keeping Tommy with you if I come back for him later? Please.'

She looked annoyed. 'Has she upset you again? If you want me to send her packing—'

He shook his head. 'It's not about her. Actually, I think she's done me a favour. I need to be somewhere, but Tommy...'

She gazed at him, her eyes searching his for any signs that he wasn't being entirely honest with her. Finally she nodded.

'Okay, I'll take care of Tommy, no problem.'

He breathed a sigh of relief. 'Thanks, Tawnie. I owe you one.'

'You owe me several.' She winked at him. 'I hope she listens to you, Jonah. Good luck.'

THIRTY-FIVE

Kat had just finished changing Hattie into her pyjamas when there was a knock on the door.

Birdie clapped her hands in delight. 'Ooh, that will be the trick or treaters! Where's that bowl of sweets, Rita?'

'On the table in the hall,' Rita called from the kitchen. She was making tea, and was in the same high spirits as her sister.

They had it all planned, they'd told Kat. As soon as little Hattie was safely tucked up in her cot, they were all going to settle down together and watch *Hocus Pocus* on the television. It was one of their favourite films, and even though Kat had seen it with them several times, she'd pretended to be just as enthusiastic about watching it again, for their sakes. They were being so lovely to her, the least she could do was join in with their Halloween fun.

She picked Hattie up and kissed her. 'There you go, poppet. All clean and fresh. Don't you look pretty?'

Hattie beamed at her, and Kat held her close, inhaling the scent of baby shampoo and finding comfort in the softness of her daughter's skin. No matter how bad things got, she had Hattie. She would never, ever stop being grateful for that.

'Kat, dear, we have a visitor,' Birdie announced. She sounded excited, and Kat spun round to see who'd turned up.

Her heart leapt as she saw Jonah standing there, looking incredible in a Count Dracula costume. At the same time her stomach plummeted with shock and dismay at having to face him. It was a confusing and disconcerting combination of emotions that left her unable to speak for a moment.

He didn't wait for her to speak, though. He stepped forward and, before she realised what he was doing, he picked Hattie up and hugged her.

'Hello, sweetheart. I've missed you!'

Hattie gurgled in delight, clearly unfazed by his unusual appearance. Evidently, she could see through his cunning disguise and knew immediately that this was Jonah. She rewarded him for his efforts by pulling hard on his nose.

'Ouch!' He laughed and planted a kiss on her forehead. 'Yep, I've really missed you!'

Rita hurried through from the kitchen, having clearly heard his voice. She exchanged gleeful looks with Birdie.

'Jonah, what are you doing here? Ooh, doesn't he look handsome, Birdie?'

'I was just thinking that,' Birdie said with a satisfied nod, a most unsavoury gleam in her eyes. 'A vampire, eh? If you're looking for willing victims, Count...'

Kat covered her eyes in shame. Usually she could laugh at her aunts' cheeky antics, but not tonight. Not after everything that had happened. Why were they all pretending everything was normal? Nothing was normal. This was awful. Why was he here, anyway?

As if reading her mind, Jonah said, 'I need to talk to you, Kat. Urgently.'

'Is it Tommy?' she asked, feeling a sudden anxiety. But then, surely he wouldn't have wasted time with Hattie if something was wrong with his son?

'Tommy's fine. He's out trick or treating with Tawnie and my family,' Jonah said. He gave a sheepish smile. 'That's why I'm dressed like this, obviously.'

'And there's me thinking you were just being kinky,' Birdie said, nudging him playfully. 'What a shame your sister doesn't live in Tuppenny Bridge. We've got lots of treats waiting here.'

'Kat, please,' Jonah said desperately. 'I have to talk to you. It's important.'

Rita and Birdie looked at her. She stared back at them, then up at Jonah who was still holding Hattie.

Rita took the baby from his arms. 'Tell you what,' she said, 'I'll take Hattie upstairs to bed, then Birdie and I were just going to watch *Hocus Pocus*. Why don't you two go and sit in the garden? It's a bit nippy, but it's not raining, and we've got that nice wicker sofa out there. I've made tea, so make an extra one for Jonah, Kat. You can take it outside with you. Keep the cold at bay.'

Jonah gave Kat a pleading look and she shrugged helplessly.

'Fine,' she said, realising that she was outnumbered, and didn't stand a chance even if she protested.

She kissed Hattie goodnight and went into the kitchen to make Jonah's tea, then the two of them carried their mugs out into the garden and sat on the sofa, the only light coming from the kitchen window. There was a patio light, but Kat didn't want Jonah to have a clear view of her face. This was awkward enough as it was.

Her pulse raced as she sat there, all too aware of his presence. He may be dressed as Count Dracula, but like Hattie she could see right through him. His eyes were still Jonah's. His body language was familiar, and she could tell he was as nervous as she was. And there was no mistaking that cologne. She remembered the first time she'd ever noticed it, that day in The Market Café. The day Hattie had thrown up on him and she'd wiped him down. The day their eyes had met and she'd realised how beautiful he really was.

She swallowed down her misery and said, 'So what can I do for you, Jonah?'

He placed his mug on the ground and turned to her. 'Kat, I may have got this wrong, and if I have I'm sorry, but I think I know what it is. What the big secret is that you feel you can't tell me.'

Her eyes widened and she glanced around, as if expecting Rita and Birdie to spring from the shadows, demanding answers.

'I—I don't think you do,' she murmured.

He moved closer to her and took the mug from her hands, placing it next to his.

'Kat,' he said quietly, his eyes full of compassion as he gazed at her. 'I think I do. I worked it out. The way you defended the Corcorans. The guilt you're carrying over Jennifer. How you cried at the anniversary, even after everything that had happened.' He took a deep breath. 'And your trip to Dorset, after Leon died. Seven months with your dad to get over it. But it wasn't about getting over it, was it, Kat?'

She didn't speak as tears rolled down her cheeks.

'I asked you what happened to the baby, and you said, "I couldn't keep it, could I, Jonah?" I assumed—you wanted me to assume—that you'd had a termination. But the truth is, you gave birth, didn't you? You had Leon's baby, and then you gave it up for adoption. I'm right, aren't I?'

She gave a huge, shuddering sob, and his arms went around her as she cried into his chest.

'I'm sorry,' he murmured. 'I'm so sorry.'

'I thought you'd be angry,' she said at last. 'I thought you'd...' She shook her head, not able to say anything else.

'Why would I be angry?' he asked, sounding confused. 'I

just wish you'd felt able to confide in me. This must have been so hard for you. All these years...'

'She'll be thirteen now,' Kat said, wiping her eyes as she sat up. 'I called her Angel, but I have no idea what her real name is.'

'Oh, Kat.' Jonah held her tightly. She didn't mind. She needed his support. She realised she always had; she just hadn't been sure she deserved it. 'Do you want to tell me about it? You don't have to if you're not ready. We can just sit here. I'm just happy to be here with you again. I can't tell you how much I've missed you.'

She gave him a bewildered look. 'How can you say that, Jonah? Don't you understand what I did?'

'The only thing you could do at the time,' he said gently. 'No one can blame you for that.'

'Can't they? Do you think Jennifer would see it that way?' She rubbed her face furiously, picturing Jennifer's expression if she ever discovered the truth. 'She lost Leon. She lost the son she idolised. And she could have had his child as compensation, but I took that chance away from her. Do you honestly think she'd ever forgive me if she knew?' She gazed up at him. 'What sort of person would do that, Jonah? What was I thinking?'

'You were in shock,' he said, stroking her hair. 'Kat, you'd just lost the baby's father in the worst way possible. And before that you'd discovered he was cheating on you and didn't want the baby anyway. What were you expected to feel? It was too much for anyone to cope with. No one could blame you for what you did.'

'I should have offered her to the Callaghans,' she said, shaking with emotion. 'They would have had a part of Leon with them forever then. Maybe Jennifer wouldn't have mourned so long. Maybe Angel would have given her a reason to live again.'

Jonah sighed. 'It would never have worked. You're not thinking straight. Don't you remember what it was like back then? Jennifer was distraught. Ben was in a state of shock and had completely withdrawn into himself. They had a sick and dying man to care for, and Jamie was just a toddler himself. Imagine bringing a baby into that! They couldn't have coped, they really couldn't. It would just have been another pressure, and it would have been the worst sort of environment for a new baby.'

She didn't reply. Wasn't everything he'd just said exactly what she'd told herself hundreds of times over the years? Even so, it didn't stop her feeling sick with guilt every time she looked at Jennifer. Somewhere, Leon's mother had a granddaughter. A living, breathing reminder of her son.

Kat had been so sure that if Jonah discovered the truth he'd be appalled that she'd been so cruel. Yet here he was, reassuring her, comforting her.

'What gave it away?' she asked eventually. 'I mean, how did you guess the truth?'

'It was something my mother said,' he admitted. 'She remembered that you'd gone away after Leon's death. Obviously, I already knew that, but she said you were gone for seven months. I'd forgotten it was that long, and I started to wonder. And then there was the stuff you said about the Corcorans. About grandparents having a right to see their grandchildren, even if they'd been adopted. Something about the way you'd said it came back to me, and suddenly it all fell into place.'

'I'm so sorry,' she said, taking his hand. 'I never wanted to leave you, I really didn't. I wanted to tell you that night, but you were already so upset about Leon, and I couldn't heap any more on you. And I was scared. I was scared you'd look at me with hate for what I'd done. I couldn't bear that.'

'I'd never look at you with hate,' he told her. 'I love you, Kat. Don't you understand that yet?'

'But Leon was your best friend, and I'd already spoiled your memories of him. Knowing I'd given away his child, how could you forgive me so easily?'

'You don't need anyone's forgiveness,' he said fiercely. 'Least of all mine. You did what was right for you and best for your baby. It was your decision to make, no one else's.'

'I can't believe you've taken it so well,' she admitted. 'I'm so lucky to have you in my life. I'm sorry I hurt you. I'm sorry I handled it all so badly.'

He fumbled with his cloak and she sat back, wondering what he was doing.

'I stopped at the forge to pick this up. I made it for you,' he said at last, handing her something heavy wrapped in tissue.

Finally able to face him, Kat stood up and flicked on the patio light, before sitting next to him again.

Carefully, she unwrapped the present and gazed down at the object on her lap.

'It's—it's beautiful,' she said, her eyes filling with tears.

'They're grey wolves,' he explained, holding the artwork up so she could get a proper look at it.

A large, grey wolf was standing on a rock, gazing up at the sky, while next to him a slightly smaller wolf nuzzled against him.

'They mate for life,' Jonah explained. 'The alpha pair, travelling through life with their pack. Together until death. Not many mammals mate for life, but grey wolves—well, they find the one and that's it.'

She smiled up at him. 'Sounds romantic, but I expect it's for practical reasons as much as anything.'

He nudged her. 'Don't spoil the mood. Thing is, you and me, I think we're the type of people who mate for life, too. We've both had false starts, and we've both been hurt. Badly hurt. But now... Well, I think I've found the one. The one I want to be with for the rest of my life. How do you feel, Kat?'

She took the sculpture from his hands and set it down on the sofa, then put her arms around his neck and kissed him.

As he kissed her back, holding her tightly as if he never wanted to let her go, she thought fleetingly of Leon, and of Jennifer, and of Angel. One day, perhaps, her daughter would come looking for her, and then she'd have to explain everything —perhaps not only to Angel, but to Jennifer too. But that day was some time in the future. Or it might never happen at all.

Right now, she was being kissed by a man who genuinely loved her, who was on her side no matter what. Someone who had finally made her believe that she deserved to be loved, and that she deserved to be happy.

Jonah would always make her happy, and Kat knew in that moment that there was nothing more she wanted in life than to make him happy in return.

He pulled away from her and smiled down at her, his eyes bright with tears.

'Come home, Kat,' he murmured. 'Come home where you belong.'

She nodded. 'There's nowhere else I'd rather be.'

THIRTY-SIX

Their first official date had gone beautifully. Jonah had taken her to The Black Swan, and the staff there had done as he asked, seating them in a discreet corner and decorating the table with candles.

They'd eaten a delicious dinner: Jonah had gone for ribeye steak, while Kat had chosen fish pie. They'd both had the Bonfire Night special dessert of cinder toffee ice cream.

'I don't know why we haven't eaten here before,' Jonah admitted, after they'd clinked their glasses in a toast.

'I have really happy memories of this place,' Kat said, gazing round with a smile on her face. 'Thank you for bringing me here.'

'I should have brought you here sooner,' he said. 'I should have taken you out way before now. I can't believe this is our first date. I've been an idiot.'

'No you haven't,' she said. 'We've had a lot going on, remember? Anyway, let's not dwell on the past. It's all about the future from now on.'

'I'll drink to that,' he said.

They sipped their drinks and sat back, feeling contented.

Kat frowned suddenly. 'I did wash Tommy's PE kit for tomorrow, didn't I?'

'I'm sure you did,' Jonah said comfortably.

'Right.' She nodded and drank some more wine. 'I hope Hattie's settled all right with the aunties. It was so good of them to babysit for her again. And wasn't it lovely of Ben and Summer to take Tommy to the firework display on the green? Do you think he's enjoying himself?'

Jonah sighed. 'I'm sure he's having a smashing time of it, love, but what did we say, eh? What did we promise each other before we set off this evening?'

Kat gave him a sheepish look. 'No talking about the kids. Sorry.'

He laughed. 'It's all right. I forgive you. Hey, shall we go outside for a few minutes? Get some fresh air?'

Surprised she nodded. 'If you like.'

He helped her into her coat and nodded at the waiter, who nodded back.

'Won't they think we're doing a runner?' she whispered.

'No. I told him we'd be popping outside for a few minutes, but we'd be coming back.'

'Did you?'

'I did. Well, you want to get a glimpse of those fireworks don't you?'

'I suppose so,' she said. 'Come on then.'

He led her outside and they strolled across the road to the river bank. Jonah put his arm around her, and they walked over the bridge, stopping half way across to gaze down on the river.

In the distance they could hear the bangs and shrieks of fireworks, and Kat imagined the residents of Tuppenny Bridge gathered on the green, watching the bonfire, and tucking into jacket potatoes and hot dogs from The White Hart Inn. She hoped Tommy was enjoying himself.

He'd had a brilliant half term holiday, including another

visit from the Corcorans. Jonah had shared with her what Vince had said, and she'd seen for herself that they were a genuine couple, who just wanted Tommy's happiness.

It was what she wanted too, and she'd been relieved to see how happy the little boy had been to have her back home. His delight at her return had moved her to tears. Hattie had quickly settled back in Forge Cottage, and Kat had felt, almost immediately, as if she'd never left the place.

Rita and Birdie had admitted they'd miss her, but they were over the moon that she and Jonah were going to make a go of it. She'd often wondered how much they'd guessed about the reason for her stay in Dorset after Leon's death, but she'd never told them what had happened, and they'd never asked. Considering how nosy they were, she thought it exceptionally kind of them.

'What are you thinking?' Jonah asked her softly, and she lifted her head to smile at him.

'Just about how perfect everything is,' she said.

He put his arms around her and kissed her gently. 'Would you like me to make it even more perfect?' he asked.

She giggled. 'Here, on this bridge? Certainly not, Mr Brewster!'

He laughed. 'I didn't mean that, although it's a thought.' He reached into his jacket pocket and held out his hand. 'I meant this.'

She stared down at the small, velvet box in his palm and then looked at him, shocked.

'Is that...'

He flipped it open, and she leaned over, gazing in wonder at the diamond solitaire nestling on its velvet bed.

'Jonah...'

'You know how much I love you,' he said. 'It's like I told you, we're alpha wolves, and once we find the right mate we're with them for life. I don't want to be alone any longer, and I don't need to look any further for my soulmate. I've found you. I just want to be with you for the rest of my life, and I hope you feel the same. I know we can be happy. Will you marry me, Kat?'

At that moment, they heard a cacophony of loud bangs and whistles, and a shower of red, blue, and orange lit up the night sky, cascading down over the town as Kat stared up at it, her heart almost bursting with emotion.

This man beside her wanted her, despite everything. He'd been through such a lot with Sofia, but he was willing to put his trust in her. He loved her, and he loved Hattie. She could see it in his face every day. She was so lucky.

For so many years she'd thought Leon was the love of her life. She'd dreamed of a future with him, had so many plans. But that had been taken away from her. Even without the accident, Leon would never have been hers. He'd lied to her and broken her heart. Trampled on her dreams in the cruellest of ways. She'd never thought she could trust anyone again.

'Kat?' Jonah asked, sounding a bit nervous.

She laughed and threw her arms around his neck. 'Yes! Of course I'll marry you, Jonah. I love you so much.'

He hugged her tightly, then slipped the ring on her finger. 'I'm so glad,' he said. 'Not least because the waiter's inside with a bottle of champagne for us, and I'd have felt like a right idiot if I'd had to go back in there and tell them you'd turned me down.'

'I would never have turned you down,' she promised him. 'My future's with you. Just like the wolves. Together forever.'

He wouldn't hurt her, she knew that. He simply wasn't that sort of man. She could think of a hundred different ways to describe him, and all of them would be positive. But she had no need to.

He was just Jonah.

And she loved him.

A LETTER FROM THE AUTHOR

Dear reader,

Huge thanks for reading *Second Chances in Tuppenny Bridge*. I hope you enjoyed Kat and Jonah's journey. If you want to join other readers in hearing all about my new releases and bonus content, you can sign up to my newsletter here:

www.stormpublishing.co/sharon-booth

If you enjoyed this book and could spare a few moments to leave a review I'd really appreciate it. Even a short review can make all the difference in encouraging a reader to discover my books for the first time. Thank you so much!

I've loved writing about Kat and Jonah, even though I had little idea what their story would be when I started the book.

Kat was a character that leapt out at me from the first mention of her name. She first appeared in *How the Other Half Loves* as Sally's best friend, and I knew she had her own story to tell.

As for Jonah—he was a character I'd had planned for a long time. I just didn't know where he fitted in, but as soon as I started working on Kat's story, Jonah made it very clear he was perfect for her!

I've been fascinated by farriers and blacksmiths since I was a little girl and was very excited to discover my own great-great-grandad was a blacksmith. It's been really interesting to find out more about their work, and I've watched so many videos about shoeing horses and creating artwork in a forge you'd never believe it.

One of the many artist blacksmiths that inspired me was Katie Ventress, whose work you can view at https://www. kvblacksmith.com/home. You'll find the little black bat which inspired the one that Jonah made on her site. The horseshoe artwork that Jonah made for his sister and brother-in-law was inspired by Horseshoes, Heart and Home. https://www.horse shoehearts.co.uk/ Both these websites demonstrate the creativity and artistic talent of the artist blacksmiths.

Watching the (many!) videos of farriers at work I was struck by how very talented they are, too. I had no idea there was so much involved with the job, nor how much training farriers must do before they're qualified to work in the UK. Farriers can work as blacksmiths, but blacksmiths can't work as farriers unless they're registered with the Farriers' Registration Council. It's a job that carries a lot of responsibility, and I've got a huge amount of respect for them.

The Tuppenny Bridge Sheep Fair is a big event in the book and was very much inspired by the annual sheep fair held in Masham every September. I stayed in Masham for sheep fair weekend a few years ago and had the best time. It's a really fun event and watching the sheep racing is something to behold! There really are sheepdogs herding ducks and plenty of stalls to visit—some of which sell artwork. Best of all, the market place is full of pens holding just about every breed of sheep you can imagine. The atmosphere is wonderful, and if you'd like to find out more about the event you can do so here. https://www. mashamsheepfair.com/

Thanks again for coming with me to Tuppenny Bridge and I hope you'll return for the next chapter of the story. There are many more stories to tell, and more secrets to reveal, so do keep in touch!

Love, Sharon

linktr.ee/sharonboothwriter

facebook.com/sharonbooth.writer

twitter.com/Sharon_Booth1

instagram.com/sharonboothwriter

ACKNOWLEDGMENTS

I'd like to say a huge thank you to the team at Storm Publishing, who have worked on this book with me. To my editor, Kathryn Taussig, and 'Big Boss' Oliver Rhodes, a big thanks for taking a chance on me. Thanks to Emma Beswetherick for her work on the structural edits, to Shirley Khan for the copy edits, Liz Hurst for the proofreading, Debbie Clement for the fabulous cover design, and everyone else in the team. They're all amazing and I'm so grateful.

Big thanks must also go to my patient husband, who supports me even though I can be a 'proper pain' when I'm lost in writing a book. I think he's got used to me disappearing for the day and has accepted the fact that I can be smiling and nodding at him without listening to a single word he says because my mind is elsewhere. Sometimes it must seem to him that I care more about my fictional characters than I do about him, and the truth is... No, I'm joking. I love him to bits and couldn't do any of this without him, so a big thank you and lots of love to Steve.

Julie Heslington aka Jessica Redland deserves thanks and a hug and cake. She's my sounding board when I'm working on a book and helps me straighten things out in my mind when I'm stuck on a plot point, or just need to figure out who my characters really are. Just talking it through with her—usually, it must be said, over pudding—helps to make it all clear. I hope I do the same for her. Where would we be without friends?

Finally, a massive thank you to you, for reading this book.

None of this would be possible for me if you, and people like you, didn't choose to spend time in my fictional worlds. I appreciate your support so much, and I hope my stories bring you happiness and brighten your day.

Love Sharon xx

Printed in Great Britain
by Amazon

47575003R00229